# ALSO BY JESSICA BRODY

# THE

# Geography

## OF

# LOST
# THINGS

*Jessica Brody*

**SIMON PULSE**
NEW YORK  LONDON  TORONTO  SYDNEY  NEW DELHI

SIMON PULSE

An imprint of Simon & Schuster Children's Publishing Division

1230 Avenue of the Americas, New York, New York 10020

First Simon Pulse hardcover edition October 2018

Text copyright © 2018 by Jessica Brody Entertainment, LLC

Jacket photograph copyright © 2018 by The Adaptive/Shutterstock

Jacket lettering copyright © 2018 by Jess Cruickshank

"Nearly a Saint" song lyrics copyright © 2018 by Len Vlahos

For information about special discounts for bulk purchases, please contact Simon & Schuster Special Sales at 1-866-506-1949 or business@simonandschuster.com.

The Simon & Schuster Speakers Bureau can bring authors to your live event. For more information or to book an event contact the Simon & Schuster Speakers Bureau at 1-866-248-3049 or visit our website at www.simonspeakers.com.

Book designed by Steve Scott

The text of this book was set in Candida

Manufactured in the United States of America

2 4 6 8 10 9 7 5 3 1

This book has been cataloged with the Library of Congress.

ISBN 978-1-4814-9921-7 (hc)

ISBN 978-1-4814-9923-1 (eBook)

FOR MY DAD

A person often meets his destiny on the road he took to avoid it. *—Jean de La Fontaine*


Salvage (verb): to save something valuable from damage, destruction, or loss. *—Cambridge Dictionary*

# THE ENVELOPE

By the time the messenger arrived at our front door, Jackson had already been dead two weeks. I stared at the large yellow envelope in the man's hand, completely blank apart from my name, scrawled crookedly across the center. I recognized the familiar careless handwriting from years of sporadic birthday cards and notes scribbled on Post-its.

*I'm sorry. I have to do this.*

I almost closed the door in the messenger's face. I almost told him to go back to wherever he had come from. He was running a fool's errand.

Because I was so convinced there was nothing Jackson could have left me that would ever matter. That would ever erase what he did to me and my mom. Nothing that could possibly change my life. For better or for worse.

As it turned out, I was wrong.

# THURSDAY

*'Cause in this place,*
*this holy space,*
*solace waits*
*and love negotiates*

—"Sleep," from the album
*Anarchy in a Cup* by Fear Epidemic
Written by Nolan Cook, Slate Miller,
Chris McCaden, and Adam French
Released April 17, 1998

# 4:05 P.M.

# RUSSELLVILLE, CA

## INVENTORY: (0)

I stand on the front porch, watching Mom shove her overnight bag into the cluttered back seat of Rosie's sedan. I suppose I could blame Rosie for getting Mom the job in the first place, but that would be petty and childish. We need the money. I know that. Mom knows that. Even Rosie knows that.

It's why Mom is disappearing to Sacramento for a week to serve fancy appetizers to even fancier people, leaving me to finish packing up the house by myself.

> **Graduation is coming up!**
> **How will *you* be spending Senior Week?**
> A  *Hitting up every party in town.*
> B  *On a beach in Mexico.*
> C  *Trying to fit your entire life into a box.*

Not that I really have anything better to do.

Sure, there'll be parties. My best friend, June, already

told me she was having one tomorrow night. But it's definitely *not* what I had planned for the week between the last day of high school and graduation. Although, to be honest, I'm not sure what I had planned.

I just didn't expect *this*.

I didn't expect Mom to give up so easily.

I didn't expect to be the one still fighting.

Mom comes back to the porch to hug me good-bye. She takes in my crossed arms and the permanent scowl that hasn't left my face since she came home last week with what she called "the keys to our new life."

She really should have worked in advertising instead of food service.

"Don't worry," Mom says. "I'll be back in time for the moving truck."

"I could ask Pam for an advance on my paycheck," I tell her.

*Still fighting.*

Mom sighs. "We've been through this. You know it's not enough."

"Maybe if we sell the car—"

"Ali, give it up. It's over."

"But—" I try to argue.

"But we've been through all the *but*s. A thousand times. There are no more *but*s left."

"There has to be."

Mom brushes a strand of curly brown hair from my face. She's already getting blurry through the tears that are forming in my eyes. I hastily gather up my unruly hair and secure it with the rubber band I always keep around my wrist.

"I think you'll like living in Harvest Grove," Mom says. "They have a pool. And a gym. All the apartments come with new carpeting. No more of that ugly brown shag."

"I like the ugly brown shag."

Mom chuckles. "That's just because you've never seen *nice* carpet before. Plus, you'll have a great place to come home to when you visit me from UC Davis next year."

I swallow down the giant lump that has just formed in my throat.

> **You got a full scholarship to the college of your dreams! What do you do?**
>
> **A**  *Start shopping for dorm room furniture.*
>
> **B**  *Spend the entire summer obsessing over the course catalog.*
>
> **C**  *Hide the letter in your backpack and "accidentally" forget to tell your mother you never accepted the offer.*

"Mom," I say, my voice cracking. "Don't do this. Don't let them take it. We have to fight."

"We've been fighting!" Mom's voice rises and then immediately falls again. "Ali. I'm done. Done fighting. Done trying to get out from under his mistakes. This gives us a fresh start. Please try to understand that I need one."

My gaze falls to the ground. Because I can't look at her when she says stuff like that. Because how do you argue with that? Because she's right.

*I know* she's right.

And yet, everything about this feels wrong.

"I'll see you in a week." Mom kisses me on the forehead before I can come up with any more useless protests. And then, she's gone. By the time I look up again, Rosie's car is already halfway down the driveway.

I turn and head into the house, navigating through the maze of cardboard boxes. I'm surprised there are so many. I didn't think we had that much stuff. Mom and I share a love of decluttering. We're always finding excuses to throw things away, or donate them to Goodwill.

But I guess everyone accumulates things. Even us.

I walk into the kitchen and put on a pot of coffee. As it brews, I head to the desk in the living room where Mom keeps all the paperwork for the house. Bills, bank statements, legal documents. All meticulously organized in hanging file folders in a drawer. I find the folder I'm looking for and flip it open to the first document inside. I skim over all the fake niceties. The "Dear Ms. Collins, we regret to inform you . . ." Like they're simply writing to tell us that the pillow shams we ordered are out of stock.

I scroll down to the bottom. To the giant black box surrounding the words TOTAL AMOUNT OVERDUE and the deadline FRIDAY, MAY 29.

A week from tomorrow.

I sigh and shut my eyes tight.

She's right. It's not enough. Even if we sold the car and the furniture and Pam was able to give me the biggest advance ever offered to an employee in the history of the pet boarding industry, it wouldn't be enough.

I glance around the living room. At the walls that won't be our walls. At the carpet that won't be our carpet. At the boxes that will be emptied somewhere else. Stuff stuffed into new cabinets. New drawers.

No, not stuffed.

Never stuffed.

Neatly stored. Meticulously organized. Maybe even labeled.

I'm sure most people would look at this house and laugh at my desperation. I know it doesn't look like much from the outside. Or the inside. The drywall has cracks in it. The paint is chipping. The bedrooms are tiny. The kitchen is tinier. The microwave hasn't worked in more than two years. The shower stall in the *one* bathroom that Mom and I share leaks.

But it's ours.

Mom's and mine.

No matter what has happened to us in the past eighteen years—no matter how many times he's let us down—this house has been there for us. A rock beneath the trembling ground. It's been our safe haven—our eye of so many storms. Russellville may be saturated with painful memories, but this house is where all the good ones live. The sights and sounds and smells. Mom singing in the bathroom as she gets ready for work. Rain pooling at the base of the front porch, causing us to have to jump off the last step. Pumpkin bread baking in the oven. Not only in the fall, but year-round, because Mom and I both love pumpkin.

Where does all of that go?

How can the bank possibly repossess things like that? How can they just suck it all up into their vaults and lock it away forever?

The coffeepot beeps, interrupting my thoughts. I shut the folder, slip it into place, and close the drawer. I head back into the kitchen and pull one of the two coffee mugs down from the cabinet. We've never kept a lot of stuff in the house. Just the essentials. Two of everything. Two plates, two sets of silverware, two glasses, two coffee mugs. By the end of next week, it will all be in boxes too.

As I pour the coffee, watching the stream of dark brown liquid fill the mug, I think about holes.

Big, gaping holes cut into the ground.

Holes so deep, you can't see the top once you're inside. And the ground keeps sinking beneath your feet. Like quicksand. Pulling you farther and farther down, until your hope of ever climbing out is gone.

And then, of course, I think about Jackson.

Smiling his disarming smile.

Murmuring his empty reassurances.

Holding a shovel.

Neither of us were all that shocked when we learned that Jackson had died. Mom and I both knew it was coming eventually. Jackson's lifestyle wasn't exactly the kind you'd describe as "sustainable." He had always lived by a code of impermanence. It's why we never had a current address for him. Never knew where he was or when or if he would call. Never knew what kind of condition he would be in when he did.

Mom and I didn't even know Jackson had been sick. Which, of course, was typical. He did everything without telling us or soliciting our opinion on the matter. Apparently, that also included dying.

For the next few hours, I blast the bubbliest music I can find on my phone, drink an obscene amount of coffee, and force myself to pack. I start with my bedroom, opening closet doors and dresser drawers and dumping as much as I can into trash bags. The fewer boxes we have to bring with us, the better.

It feels good to throw things away. Like I'm not only making room in the cabinets, but also making room in my head. Clearing space for better and brighter things. Pushing bad, stale memories out the door.

When the coffeepot is empty and the trash bags are full, I collapse onto the couch, take out my phone, and navigate to my favorite personality quiz website. I scroll through all of the new quizzes that have popped up since yesterday, quickly ruling out the ones for which I already know what result I'll get.

**Which Star Wars Episode Best Describes Your Last Relationship?**

*Episode II: Attack of the Clones.*

**How Stubborn Are You?**

*Very.*

**What Do Your Summer Plans Say About Your Life?**

*That I have no life.*

Finally, I find one that looks interesting—**Which Classic Novel Character Would You Most Likely Have as a BFF?**—and start answering the questions.

I've pretty much taken every personality quiz under the sun. I can tell you who I am in relation to every single television show, movie, book, and one-hit-wonder song. I know what my favorite doughnut flavor says about me (simple and non-fussy); what my dream vacation is (Rome); what Disney villain best represents my dark side (Ursula from *The Little Mermaid*); and what my best quality is based on what pizza toppings I like (selfless).

Personality quizzes have always felt comforting to me. They sum people up, distill the complexities of human beings down to a few digestible sentences.

Just as the quiz spits out my result—Jane Eyre—an alarm goes off on my phone, reminding me that I'm due at Chateau Marmutt, the pet hotel where I work, for my overnight shift in thirty minutes. I basically get paid to sleep in a room surrounded by dogs. It's not a bad gig.

I carry the full trash bags out to the bins at the end of the driveway and turn back to the house, bounding up the porch steps. But I freeze when I see the notice pinned to the door.

*Another one?*

How many of those things do they need to send us? We get it. You're serious about it. This is not a joke.

The deadline is stamped onto the page like a searing, red-hot brand.

**Friday, May 29.**

Pay, or else.

*Or else* . . .

Somehow Mom has come to terms with the "or else." She almost seems to have *chosen* it. But I just can't bring myself to choose that.

I can't bring myself to let them win. To let Jackson win. To let the world win.

June would say it's because I'm too competitive. It's the excuse she always gives when she's losing at a board game, which she almost always does.

And maybe I am. Maybe I can't admit defeat. But this feels like more than defeat. This isn't Monopoly. We're not just turning in all of our little green houses to the bank and forfeiting the game. This is real. A real house. A real family. Real memories steeped into the walls.

---

**The bank is foreclosing on your house! How do you react?**

**A** *Keep packing. Can't argue with the almighty bank.*

**B** *Steal all the toilets and fixtures. They can have the walls, but they can't have the towel bars!*

**C** *Refuse to accept the inevitable.*

---

I rip the notice from the door, crumple it up in my hands, and toss it onto the porch. I slam the front door closed behind me and stand with my back pressed against the wall, breathing hard. My eyes squeeze shut, so I don't have to see the boxes. The furniture. The walls. My nine-year-old self standing by the window, her face glued to the glass, wondering when he was coming back.

Back then, it was always *when*. It was never *if*.

The *if* came later.

"Please," I whisper to the quiet house, as though I'm trying to rally its support. As though I'm begging it to fight back too. Don't let yourself be taken. Stand your ground. Lock your doors. Turn your floors into hot lava. Whatever it takes. Haven't you loved us back? Haven't we been just as much a part of you as you have been of us? Do you really want strangers living in your walls?

I don't expect the house to respond. But somehow it does.

Because just then, there's a knock on the door.

Before Jackson died, unexpected knocks on the door usually meant one thing: he was back. The last time he came back, however, he didn't even make it to the front door. Mom and I heard his car pulling into the driveway. We both recognized the familiar roar of that engine. It was my sixteenth birthday. We were doing the dishes after breakfast when the sound stopped us both short. We exchanged a knowing look. It was a look we reserved for moments like this. A silent vow. A reconfirming of the pact that bonded us.

Then, without a word, we both dried our hands and headed outside, intercepting him before he could even make it up to the front porch.

I saw the car first. Jackson's blue 1968 Firebird convertible glinting in the morning sun. That car was one of the only things Jackson took seriously in life. Along with a popular late-nineties post-grunge band called Fear Epidemic. He'd bought the Firebird the day he graduated from high school, approximately eleven months before I was born. It was with him the day he died. I wasn't.

I saw Jackson next. He was drunk—not a surprise—and he had a bleached-blond woman in a leather miniskirt hanging on his arm—also not a surprise. She appeared older than some of the others. More worn, like fruit that had been left in a dehydrator too long.

I remember exactly what the two of them looked like standing in our driveway. They looked like strangers. They looked like washed-out remnants from another time. Artifacts dug up from the dirt.

"Marylou," Jackson slurred to the girl. "I'd like you to meet my daughter."

The woman stared at him, as though this weren't actually her name and she was trying to decide whether or not she cared. Apparently, she didn't. She reached out a bejeweled hand to shake mine. "Hi. You must be the famous—"

"Ali," I interrupted her before she had a chance to utter the name that I'd long since given up. That I could barely stand to hear spoken aloud anymore.

"*Ali*," Jackson repeated with a twinkle in his eye. "That's right. I forgot. She doesn't like the name I picked out for her. She goes by Ali now."

I fought the urge to remind him that I'd actually gone by Ali my whole life. Everyone I knew called me Ali. He was the only one who'd ever called me by that other name.

I'm still not sure why my mom ever agreed to Jackson's ridiculous name choice to begin with. She was probably too hopped-up on labor drugs at the time to disagree. Or maybe she was just too hopped-up on the charm of Jackson. They seemed to have similar effects on a person. They both numbed you until you couldn't feel a thing. Until you believed that you lived in a world where pain was impossible.

"I'm up in Fort Bragg now," Jackson said, even though no one had asked. "Less than an hour up the California coast. Would be nice if you came to visit sometime."

"What are you doing here?" Mom asked, stepping up to stand beside me, creating our usual unified front. Her voice was calm, reasonable. A result of years of practice. You didn't raise your voice at Jackson. Or get too worked up. Because he had this mysterious talent for always making you feel like *you* were the unreasonable one. Like life was one big joke and you just lacked the sense of humor to get it.

"Just thought I'd come see my daughter on her birthday," Jackson responded, winking at me. "It's not every day a girl turns sixteen."

Mom stiffened beside me. I knew why. She was surprised. Surprised that he had not only remembered the date but had also gotten the age right. It was little things like that that poked holes in your anger. That made you second-guess—for even a split second—your silent promises to never let him back in.

Something jangled in Jackson's hand, pulling my gaze downward. It was his key ring with the single silver key dangling off of it. The same nondescript key ring he'd had for as long as I could remember. The same jangling sound that populated my sporadic childhood memories.

He nodded to the Firebird idling behind him in the driveway. The very vehicle that had taken him away seven years ago ironically kept bringing him back. Never on a consistent basis. Never with any warning or phone calls or texts. Always just showing up, the roaring engine audible from the top of the driveway, the polished chrome wheels blinding all passing traffic.

The top of the car was down, and the white leather appeared freshly conditioned. Jackson looked like he hadn't bathed in days, but the car, per usual, was immaculate.

"Want to take her for a spin?" Jackson asked.

Mom answered for me. "She doesn't have her license yet."

"Well, let's go down to the DMV and take care of that right now," Jackson said with the enthusiasm of a father pitching a trip to Disneyland to a small child.

"She's not going anywhere with you, Jack," Mom replied tightly, setting her hands on my shoulders.

Jackson rubbed the dark scruff around his jaw and smiled back at my mother. That same disarming, charismatic smile that she'd fought to break free from since high school.

He tossed the key ring straight up in the air. I imagine he had every intention of catching it. But the alcohol had affected his coordination. I watched the sparkling metal twirl and dance before falling to the asphalt next to his feet with a clank.

It made him laugh so hard, he nearly fell over. Marylou—or whatever her name really was—laughed too.

That's when Mom sent them away. She bent down, scooped up the keys, thrust them into Marylou's hands—the decidedly more sober one—and told them to leave. I didn't argue. I'd stopped being that kid who gave her absent father the benefit of the doubt years ago. I'd stopped blaming my mother for making him leave. I knew exactly why he left.

He left because that's what Jackson did.

The knock comes again. This time, more urgently. My stomach caves in on itself as I push my back further against the door, like I'm trying to literally hold the visitor at bay. Although it feels more like I'm holding back an insurgent army.

*Go away.*

There's no one it could possibly be who I would want to see right now. Ever since that last visit from Jackson two years ago, the only surprise visitors we've been getting around here are the collecting kind. The kind who pin notices with big red dates to your door.

And yet, the knocking doesn't stop. The visitor won't leave.

Finally, I get so fed up, I turn and yank the door open, ready to take out all of my anger and frustration on whoever is standing there. I don't care who it is. A debt collector, the UPS man, the Pope. Whoever is pounding on my door deserves everything that's bubbling to the surface right now, ready to stream out of my mouth like a river of hot lava.

But it's the object in the man's hand that stops me short. That clamps my lips shut. That pushes everything back inside. It's the first thing my gaze lands on. Not the hand holding it. Not the strange man the hand is attached to.

The large yellow envelope with my name scribbled across the center.

The moment I see it, I know that it's from Jackson. Not just from the lazy handwriting—the incomplete *O*s and undotted *I*s that reminded me of burning sauce on the stove and stacks of unopened final payment notices stuffed into boxes. But because Jackson is—*was*—the only person who still uses that name.

The room does a full rotation, causing me to look away and then look back at the envelope just to make sure I'm not imagining it.

"Are you the daughter of Jackson Collins?"

The voice forces me to look up. Up, up, up. Until there's a face. An unfamiliar face I've never seen before, but I immediately distrust. Not because he looks like a distrustful guy, which he doesn't—he's clean-cut, with pressed khakis and a friendly, toothy grin—but because he's now associated. Just saying Jackson's name—just holding an envelope with Jackson's handwriting on it—will forever stain him in my memory.

My head feels heavy, thick with possible reactions to the very simple question of "Are you the daughter of Jackson Collins?"

*Shut the door.*

*Tell him to leave.*

*Play dumb.*

Anything to avoid the real answer. Because the real answer has never served me. Not when Jackson was alive and, I am certain, not now that Jackson is dead.

But somehow, the real answer is what comes out. "Yes."

"I'm Pete. I knew your father before he died. He rented a room from me up in Tacoma."

*Tacoma.*

So that's where he died. We didn't know. When the call came from the hospital, there was no information on the caller ID. Mom didn't ask, and I didn't blame her. But now, I find the name of the city tumbling around in my brain like metal screws in a dryer.

*Tacoma.*

I guess it makes sense. He went back to *them*. To the band he loved. The music that inspired him. Fear Epidemic was formed in Tacoma. All the members were from there. Jackson always liked to say that he *made* that band.

That he discovered them and told all of his friends and that's why they became famous.

"It's just south of Seattle, Washington," Pete explains, clearly interpreting my silence as confusion.

"I know where Tacoma is," I say quickly. Rudely. But I don't care. I don't want to talk geography with this stranger holding an envelope with my real name on it. I want him to get to the point. Tell me what's inside. Because unless he does, I'm not sure I'll actually be able to take it from him. I'm not sure I'll be able to open it on my own. I can't handle any more of Jackson's surprises.

I thought his last surprise was the final one.

Death usually is.

Pete clears his throat. "Right, well, anyway. He wanted you to have this. He made me promise I'd bring it to you."

He smiles and holds out the envelope, looking like a dutiful Labrador retriever delivering a Frisbee, waiting for praise. I stare at the name. Jackson's handwriting, even messier than usual.

*Did he write it when he was sick?*

*While he was dying?*

*Was it the last thing he did?*

"What is it?" I ask, my gaze darting suspiciously between the man and the envelope.

The saying "Don't shoot the messenger" flutters through my mind, but I ignore it.

He looks confused for a moment, as though he were under the impression that I already knew he was coming. He must not have known Jackson very well if that's what he assumed.

He glances behind him and jerks a thumb over his shoulder. *"That."*

I follow his gaze, and that's when I see it. I'm actually not sure why I didn't notice it before. But there it is. Just like I remembered. Jackson's most prized possession.

Why didn't I hear it pull up? Why didn't the sound jolt me to attention like it always did?

Maybe it was never the car that was so deafening, demanding attention. Maybe it was Jackson.

I flounder for words, glancing between Pete and the blue 1968 Firebird convertible parked in the driveway, waiting for him to tell me that this is all a big joke. Haha! What a funny prank. One final rug for Jackson to pull out from under me.

Because the alternative is just too hard to believe. Jackson never left behind anything valuable. Jackson left behind messes. He left behind deep holes that can never be filled.

"A-a-are you sure?" I finally manage to get out.

Pete laughs at my reaction. "She's a beauty, isn't she? Real classic, that car. You're a lucky girl to have a father like that."

*A lucky girl.*

Never in my eighteen years of life have "lucky" and "father" ever been so close together in a sentence.

"Well, I gotta run," Pete says. "A friend is picking me up and driving me to the airport." He thrusts the envelope into my hand. "Paperwork is all in here. Oh, and here's the key."

Pete reaches into his pocket and pulls out a simple silver key ring.

The breath hitches in my chest.

The last time I saw that key ring was more than two years ago. On my sixteenth birthday. It's exactly as I remember.

It's funny how time can weather a man, fade a memory, change a name, but it seems to do nothing to objects. They're like little time capsules buried in your life, digging themselves up all on their own, regardless of whether or not you're ready to see them again.

"Well, enjoy her," Pete says. "She's all gassed up." He tosses me the key. Somehow, despite the numbness that has invaded my entire body like a plague, I manage to catch it.

Pete turns and jogs down the front steps. I stare dazedly at the key ring in one hand, the envelope in the other, and then finally, the car in the driveway. I still can't bring myself to believe that it's mine. That Jackson actually left me something. But then I open the envelope, ripping through the tape that sealed it, and pull out the piece of paper inside. I take in the ornate blue border, the faint "State of California" watermark, the words CERTIFICATE OF TITLE printed in all caps across the top. And my name—my full legal name—typed in a crisp black font.

Jackson's handwriting may have been sloppy, untrustworthy, and barely legible, but this piece of paper is clear enough.

Suddenly, a very different sensation travels through me. An unfamiliar sensation. It's so foreign, I can't even be sure I'm correctly identifying it.

But it feels a lot like hope.

# FRIDAY

*Run away, go away*
*Hide away, sneak away*
*There's got to be*
*An easier way*
*To face each day.*

—"Nearly a Saint," from the album
*Anarchy in a Cup* by Fear Epidemic
Written by Nolan Cook, Slate Miller,
Chris McCaden, and Adam French
Released January 2, 1998

# 7:42 A.M.

# RUSSELLVILLE, CA

## INVENTORY: 1968 FIREBIRD 400 CONVERTIBLE (1)

The next morning the Honda won't start. I can hear it trying, like it really doesn't want to be another item in the
long list of things that have let me down in life. I give it a
few words of encouragement. I find that sometimes helps.
I mean, it's not that I can really blame the car. It's almost
as old as I am.

"Come on, old girl," I say, as though I'm trying to coax
a tired horse that doesn't want to leave its stall. I rack my
brain for every cheesy motivational cliché I can think of.
"You can do it. I know you can! We're in this together! A
chain is only as strong as its weakest link. Don't be the
weakest link! Teamwork makes the dream work!"

For some reason, that one does the trick. The engine
turns, and the car revs with a newfound optimism for life.

"Yeah! That's what I'm talking about!" I shout as I
pump the gas.

The optimism must be contagious.

When I get to school, there's an electrical charge in the air. And it's not just from all the seniors anxiously shuffling their feet on the carpet, counting the seconds (21,600) until we're out of here for good. It's a frenetic energy. A mix of relief and total panic. Most of the people in my class don't know what happens after graduation next week. Including me.

I thought I knew.

I thought I had it all figured out.

Then those hideous notices started appearing on our front door.

The computer lab is jam-packed. Every seat is taken, mostly by underclassmen trying to finish up papers and turn in assignments. They still have a week left of school.

I crane my neck, scanning the three rows of terminals, and notice a freshman girl signing off and gathering her things. She stands, and I immediately start moving in her direction. But I skid to a halt when I see who's sitting at the computer right next to the now-vacant seat.

My throat goes dry and I consider turning around, waiting for another station to open up, or perhaps even waiting until my first free period to come back. But before I can make any sort of decision, he glances up, and our eyes meet.

For a long time, we just stare at each other, a stream of awkwardness passing between us like electricity running down a wire. It feels strangely like a standoff between rival gang members. He looks away first, but only to peer down at the empty seat and then to peer back up at me, his mind putting the pieces together, his eyes judging the distance between his chair and the one I will soon occupy. I notice his body visibly stiffen.

---

**Uh-oh! You've just run into your ex-boyfriend in the computer lab. What do you do?**

**A** *Turn around and run out the door like a pack of Rottweilers is chasing you.*

**B** *Grab the first guy you see and start making out with him.*

**C** *Sit down right next to him. Because you're totally, 100 percent over it.*

---

I blink, coming out of my momentary trance, and approach the chair. As I walk, I mentally calculate how long it will take for me to log in to my e-mail, check my inbox, and get the hell out of this room.

If there's *one* thing to look forward to after today, it's that there will be no more awkward encounters like this one.

I sit down. He clears his throat. I flash a weak smile. He flashes one back. I lunge for the keyboard. He stares hard at his computer screen. Neither of us speaks.

Until . . .

"Hi," he says tightly.

I fight the urge to close my eyes, wishing I could rewind the last sixty seconds, catapult myself back in time, back to the moment I decided to sit in this seat.

"Hi," I say back, keeping my gaze trained on my screen as I log in with my student ID and password.

"How have you been?" he asks.

*No, Nico*, I think as my stomach caves in on itself. *Don't do that. Don't make idle conversation. Don't try to chitchat. Don't acknowledge my existence. Just don't.*

I should have known. I should have known Nico Wright is incapable of just pretending nothing happened. Of just going back to being the comfortable strangers we once were. Isn't that the unspoken rule between people like us? The unspoken pact we made after that dreadful night one month ago?

Erase each other's numbers.

Destroy all the evidence.

Ignore each other in the hallways.

Try to wipe the memories from our minds—the good and the bad. Especially the bad.

*I* did all of those things. I kept *my* end of the silent pact. But Nico is too polite for that. He probably couldn't ignore someone if he tried.

"Fine," I say coolly. "You?"

"Fine," he replies.

I nod. Is that it? Is it over? Pleasantries exchanged? Boxes checked? Obligations fulfilled?

"How's your mom?" he asks.

Apparently not.

Another fleeting smile. "She's great. How are your parents?"

He shrugs. "The same."

I'm not sure if he meant "the same" as in they're also doing great, or "the same" as in they haven't changed since we . . .

Well, since *we* changed.

I decide it doesn't matter. I never knew Nico's parents anyway. We always spent most of our time together at my house while my mother was at work. Or at Chateau Marmutt, surrounded by slobbering dogs. Or taking long drives along Route 128 in his truck. In fact, I never even realized how little I knew about Nico's life until it was all over. And by then, there was no reason to ask any more questions. Besides, I think I already had all the answers I needed.

I turn away from him and focus back on my computer screen.

I can feel Nico's gaze linger on me for a few seconds before he, thankfully, turns away too. I log in to my e-mail account and hold my breath. There are ten new e-mails in my inbox. The subject lines of all of them read:

Re: 1968 Firebird 400 Convertible for Sale

Last night at Chateau Marmutt, as soon as I finished filling water bowls and taking all the dogs out to go to the bathroom, I used the front desk computer to draft a Craigslist post for the Firebird.

I added a few pictures of the car that I'd snapped before leaving for work, and I set the price as "Best offer." As I worked on the description, I could hear Jackson's voice in my head. Like years of listening to the same song on repeat.

*"This baby's not the base model. It's the 400. It's worth much, MUCH more."*

As I stare at the responses in my inbox, I instinctively prepare myself for the disappointment. Maybe it'll be nothing. Maybe the car was only valuable to Jackson. Like a ratty old stuffed animal you've had since you were a kid. It means the world to you, but everyone else looks at it like it's diseased and flea-ridden.

I click on the first one, and my heart lurches in my chest. Actually, I think it might have just skipped several important beats.

> Hi, my name is Tom Lancaster. I own a classic-car restoration shop up in Crescent City, CA. We buy and sell classic cars. Your Firebird is a beauty. I realize Crescent City is a bit of a haul for you, but I can offer you $32,000 if you can drive it up to me. Of course, I'll have to inspect the car, but from the pictures, it looks like it's in immaculate shape. You must have taken good care of it throughout the years. Please respond ASAP and let me know if you're interested.

*Oh my God.*
*Oh my God. Oh my God. Oh my God.*
I immediately feel my lungs fill with air. Beautiful air. I feel like I'm breathing for the first time ever.
*Thirty-two thousand dollars!*
It's enough. Enough to change everything. Enough to fix everything. Enough to tear those atrocious red-ink notices off our front door forever.
Enough to finally erase all of his mistakes.

Because there's no way this car is not in top condition. It was the only thing Jackson ever cared about. The only thing he never neglected. His wife, his daughter, his overdue bills—those were just minor details in his life, easily put off.

The car, however? That was *important*.

And now that same car—the one I've come to loathe, the one that represents everything that's ever been flawed about my life—is being valued at thirty-two thousand dollars. Suddenly the years of neglect, abandonment, lies, lost jobs, missed payments, scribbled Post-it notes stuck to the fridge—*I'm sorry, I have to do this*—it all seems to fade into the background. It all crams together, tighter and tighter, a universe contracting, a lifetime shrinking, until it's nothing more than a tiny black dot. A decimal point.

A decimal point on a check worth $32,000.

I hastily click through the rest of the e-mails. There are a few offers from people in Portland, Oregon; one from someone in Seattle; and two from down south near San Francisco. Each one of them commends me on such a beautiful car, but Tom Lancaster's bid is definitely the highest.

Before I can blink, I'm on Google Maps, calculating how long it will take for me to drive the car up to Crescent City. Google spits out a distance and a time. Two hundred seventy miles. Five and a half hours. I can do that. I can leave right after school. I can get there tonight.

I google "Tom Lancaster, Crescent City" and immediately find his classic-car restoration shop. It looks nice, but most of all, it looks reputable. He has almost all five stars on Yelp, and many of the reviews mention him by name.

This is legit.

This is really happening.

I can drop off the car, find a cheap hotel, and take a bus back tomorrow morning. I'll have thirty-two thousand dollars in my pocket. I think I can afford a hotel room and bus fare. I'll be able to pay the bank before Mom even gets back from Sacramento. I might even have time to unpack all the boxes!

I can only imagine the look on her face when she walks in to see everything as it was, everything as it should be.

I quickly hit reply to Tom Lancaster and start to type. But my fingers halt when I swear I feel Nico's eyes on me. I glance furtively over at him, but he's staring straight ahead, typing something onto his keyboard.

I finish my e-mail to Mr. Lancaster, letting him know that I would very much like to sell him the car and that I can have it to him by nine o'clock tonight. I hover the cursor over the send button.

This is really it. This is the moment I've been waiting for all my life. Waiting for, but never daring to expect would ever happen. This is Jackson finally paying us back. Finally shoveling dirt back *into* the hole instead of out from under our feet.

It's really happening.

Then why in the world can't I bring myself to push send?

My finger shakes over the mouse button.

*Do it, Ali*, I command myself.

*He means nothing to you.*

*This means* everything *to you.*

This is the answer. This is the solution. This is the "but" I've been looking for.

My breathing grows shallow. I close my eyes and force myself to think about every time he left. Every time that car was an accomplice in his getaway scheme. Every notice in the mail that my mother received, alerting her that he had opened another credit card in her name. Every time the phone rang and another cold, emotionless voice informed us that unless payment was received soon, actions would be taken. Every dollar he stashed away, hidden from my mother, so that he wouldn't have to grow up. So that he could continue to live his immature, carefree life without consequences.

But there are always consequences.

Someone always pays.

And it was usually us.

Then, as if on cue, my phone dings with a new text message. I glance at it and my stomach immediately contracts.

> You currently have 10% of your data plan remaining.
>
> We have not yet received payment for . . .

It's another low data warning from our cell phone provider. I've been getting them all week. I angrily delete the message, turn back to the computer, and click send.

"Last-minute assignment?" Nico asks, startling me. When I look over at him, he nods toward my screen, which thankfully is showing my inbox again. The last thing I need right now is Nico asking questions.

"Something like that," I mutter.

I glance at his screen and see that his inbox is open too. And for the first time, this strikes me as odd. I can't remember Nico ever coming to the computer lab before. He has a gorgeous MacBook that he takes everywhere, like an extra appendage. I've never seen him without it. I used to tease him that he probably slept with the thing at night. It even became an inside joke between us. We named it Snuggles.

I gesture ambiguously toward his screen. "What are *you* doing in here? Where's . . ." I fight the urge to call it by its nickname. ". . . your laptop?"

He turns his attention back to his e-mail, and I watch his Adam's apple pulse as he swallows. "It's . . . in the shop. I dropped it."

I can tell instantly that he's lying. When you grow up with a father who's a professional perjurer, you start to pick up on signs. You start to see them on everyone. Mom likes to joke that we should both start playing poker.

I feel the familiar rush of heat flood to my cheeks. The frustration simmering just under my skin. The scream bubbling to the surface.

And then suddenly that's all I can hear.

The screaming. The sobs. The sound of the car door slamming.

*"Don't lie to me, Nico! Stop lying!"*

I shake my head, chasing the memory away, and focus back on the computer, reminding myself that it doesn't matter. Not anymore. Nico can lie to whomever he wants now.

"I'm sorry about your laptop," I mutter politely. "I hope they can fix it."

"Thanks," he murmurs, and that's that. End of conversation. End of obligatory small talk. Maybe now he'll actually stick to the pact.

# 2:32 P.M.

# RUSSELLVILLE, CA

## INVENTORY: 1968 FIREBIRD 400 CONVERTIBLE (1)

The final bell of my high school career rings, and I gather my stuff and head to my locker. Classes today have been a joke. I just left English, but it might as well have been Martian for how much anyone—including the teachers—are taking today seriously.

The whole thing feels like a huge formality. Finals are over. All the assignments have been turned in and graded. We've all been measured for our caps and gowns. I'm honestly not sure why we seniors are even here today. Except maybe to say good-bye to our classmates. Although that feels like a formality too. Hardly anyone ever leaves this town. If our class is anything like Mom's was, we'll all still be here, living the same lives, working the same jobs two decades later.

On my way to my locker, I check my phone to find an e-mail response from Tom Lancaster.

Excellent! I'll stay late at the shop tonight to meet you. Here's the address. And my phone number is below, in case anything happens. I can't wait to see the car in person.

*Well, there's no turning back now.*

With a sigh, I pocket my phone and dial in my locker combination. I open my locker for the last time and stare into it for a good thirty seconds, like I'm trying to memorize something. Take a snapshot of what high school feels like so I can store it away and never look at it again.

I close the locker door and nearly jump out of my skin when I see June standing there. Like she's just been waiting to scare the bejeezus out of me.

"June!" I say, clutching my chest. "Don't do that."

"Sorry," she says with a giggle that tells me she's not at all sorry. "But I have something for you. I've been waiting to give it to you all day!"

She swings her backpack around and unzips the main compartment.

"Voilà!" June says, pulling out some kind of thick booklet made out of multicolored construction paper. She holds it out to me in the palms of her hands, like an ancient offering ceremony.

On the cover is a picture of June and me when we were really young, standing together in front of Russellville Elementary. I recognize the photo. It was taken on our very first day of school. In the picture, June is wearing what can only be described as a collage—a bathing suit, a pink tutu, Converse high-tops, and a bejeweled denim jacket. I, on the other hand, was going for a bit more of the basic look—jeans and a T-shirt. Although June's sense of style has calmed down a bit over the years, mine is pretty much exactly the same.

Right underneath the photo, in silver puffy paint, June has written our names.

"It's a scrapbook!" June announces with a beaming smile. "I've been working on it all week! It's a graduation present!"

"June-bug," I say, my voice cracking. "I can't believe you did this. I didn't get you anything."

She waves this away like it's an annoying fly. "Oh, please, you've been a *tad* bit busy."

June is the only one at school who knows about the foreclosure. It's not exactly the kind of information you want advertised on the school marquee.

Holding back an embarrassing gush of tears, I flip open the scrapbook and literally jump back as a splattering of glitter puffs up like an A-bomb cloud, coating the front of my shirt in a dusting of sparkles. I should have known better than to open the book so close to my clothing. June is obsessed with glitter.

As I flip through the pages, I'm instantly sucked into a vortex of happy memories. June has somehow managed to capture our entire friendship in this one booklet. Everything from ticket stubs for movies we've seen to the board game we made together. She even included the angry letter we wrote (but never had the guts to send) to the author who ruined our favorite book series.

"You're not going to throw it away, are you?" June asks, pulling my attention away from the pages.

I glance up at her in surprise. "What? No! Of course I'm not going to throw it away! Are you crazy?"

"I just know you," she says. "You'll keep it for, like, a few months, and then you'll go through one of your decluttering phases and throw it—"

"June," I interrupt. "I'm not going to throw it away. *Ever.* I love it."

"That's right," June says, giving me a pointed look. "And you don't throw away things that you love."

*Well, I walked right into that one, didn't I?*

I give her an equally pointed look back. "June. Don't start."

June opens her mouth to start, but I cut her off before she can get going. "Please. I don't want to go through this again."

"But maybe if you just let him *explain* . . ."

I sigh. She's going to go through this again. "I *did* let him explain. And he blatantly lied to my face. It's over."

June's mouth puckers up the way it always does when she's mad. She's a classic Staffordshire bull terrier. Loyal, wiggly, playful, but don't piss her off.

"Let's just drop it, okay?"

She seems to relax. "Okay. But you're coming over tonight for the party, right?"

I busy myself with unzipping my backpack and placing the scrapbook inside so I don't have to look her in the eye. "Actually, I just got a text from my mom. She's asking me to come up to Sacramento this weekend to help her with a catering job. I have to leave right now."

June's shoulders sag. "Oh. Well, do you want me to come with you? We could road-trip it."

I shake my head. "No, it's okay. You stay here. Have fun. Celebrate the last day of school. I'll text you when I'm back."

June gives me a hug and tells me to drive safe before disappearing down the hallway to find Tyler, her boyfriend (and ride home).

I swing my backpack onto my shoulder and head toward the parking lot. I know I should probably tell June where I'm really going. Or tell *someone*. I realize driving off to the northern tip of California all by myself to meet a strange man from Craigslist is the stuff that horror movies are made of, but I don't want to have to explain it all. I don't want anyone to argue with me, try to talk me out of it, make me walk through a list of pros and cons. There are no cons. There's just one pro.

We need that money.

And I need that car to be out of my life for good.

I hurry to the third row of the parking lot where I parked the Honda this morning, but I stop abruptly when I notice someone sitting on the hood of my car.

No, not just someone.

Nico.

He has one leg propped up, the other dangling off the side. His backpack is lying on the ground next to the tire.

And for just a split second, I'm not here. I'm *there*. Two months ago. Before it all fell apart. Before I opened the glove box and discovered that everyone keeps secrets. Even him.

This is where I could always find him. Every day after school. Waiting for me on the hood of my car. His favorite Russellville High hoodie zipped halfway up. His dark blond hair mussed from the wind, his blue-gray eyes focused somewhere far away. It's his trademark look. Whenever he's not talking directly to you, he's looking at that indistinct point in the distance.

Back then, I thought it was because he was searching for something. Always searching. Never finding.

Now I know it was because he was hiding something.

When I spot Nico sitting on my hood, my first thought is to wonder if he's hit his head and now has amnesia. Or if perhaps I've time-traveled two months into the past. Because those are the only two explanations for why he's suddenly slipped back into our former routine. Our *abandoned* routine. A routine that now lives in the same box where I packed up every single thing that reminded me of him, including the birdhouse—*especially* the birdhouse— and hand-delivered it to the nearest landfill.

"What are you doing here?" I ask tightly.

He doesn't smile. Not like he used to do whenever he saw me approach. His expression looks hesitant, guarded. And that's when I know that this is not our former routine. This is something new. Something unfamiliar and uncharted.

Which means I don't know what to do with my hands. So I stuff them into the pocket of my sweatshirt, jangling my keys between my fingers.

He doesn't answer my question. Instead, he asks one of his own. "Where are you rushing off to?" I marvel at how much he sounds like a detective catching a wanted criminal who's about to skip town and head for the border.

"Nowhere. June's, maybe." I shrug, averting my gaze.

When I dare to look back at him, he's staring at me, his eyes intense, like he's trying to see right through my skull. Read my thoughts.

"No, you're not."

Anger instantly flares in me. "What do you mean, *no, I'm not*?"

"I mean, I know you're not going to June's."

"What's it to you where I'm going?" I fire back. "What are you even doing here? Do you need a ride or something? Is your *car* in the shop too?"

He flinches. He can hear the sarcasm in my voice. He knows I know about the lie. I have no idea where his laptop is, but I know it's not being repaired. As far as I'm concerned, everything Nico says now is a lie. And who knows? Maybe it always has been. All the way back to the beginning. To the time he told me I was the first face he noticed in the crowd.

Maybe even further than that. How much do we really know about the boy who moved to town? Is he even *from* Reno? It's anyone's guess at this point.

Nico slides his foot down so that both legs are now

dangling off the side of my car. He leans forward, holding my gaze so tightly, I almost feel it again. That flicker, that beautiful uneasiness. But I chase it away with the truth.

"You do realize," Nico says smugly, resting his hands on the hood like he's going to propel himself straight into outer space, "that you're never going to be able to drive that car to Crescent City by yourself?"

Russellville is the type of town that very few people ever move to and even fewer people ever leave. But Nico was an anomaly from the beginning. He moved here three weeks after the start of senior year. A mysterious stranger appearing out of nowhere and with seemingly no past. At least, not one that he openly talked about. We knew he'd moved from Reno with his mom and dad. We knew he lived on Clover Street in a small two-bedroom house with a patchy brown lawn and a gate that didn't always latch. But no one had ever actually been *inside* his house.

I spent the entirety of our three-month relationship trying to figure out what breed of dog Nico was. He was always surprising me. Always jumping right out of every box I tried to put him in. At the beginning, I swore he was a golden retriever—happy-go-lucky, quick with a joke, and eager to please—but by the end, I knew I'd been deceived. He was clearly some kind of terrier. Cute while they're around, but don't turn your back on them for a second or they'll dig up your entire life.

I open the door to the Honda. "I don't know what you're talking about."

Nico slides off the hood and turns to face me. "Yes, you do. You know exactly what I'm talking about. I saw the e-mail. And then I found the Craigslist ad."

I groan. I knew he was looking at my screen. I should have just waited for another computer to open up.

"I know what you're planning," Nico goes on, "and you shouldn't do it alone. It's not safe."

I roll my eyes. Good old protective Nico. Everyone's favorite Boy Scout. Won't even let me stand on the side of the road by myself after I've broken up with him. Too bad the one part of me that *did* end up needing protecting was left wide open.

"I'll be fine."

"Do you know how dangerous this is?" Nico replies angrily. "Driving a strange car to a strange city to meet up with someone from Craigslist. There are weirdos on Craigslist."

"Relax. I googled him. He owns a reputable car shop. It's even on Yelp."

"You could end up getting mugged or kidnapped or raped."

"You watch too many crime shows."

"*Real* crime shows. About real people getting *really* murdered."

"I'm not getting really murdered. I'm just driving the car up to Crescent City and coming right home."

"No, actually, you're not."

I sigh, trying to keep hold of my slipping composure. "Nico. I'm not your girlfriend anymore. You don't need to protect me."

He scoffs. "I didn't say *I* would go with you."

Humiliation warms my cheeks. I get in behind the wheel. "Good. 'Cause I don't need anyone to go with me."

I'm convinced that this is the end of the argument until Nico places a hand on the car door, stopping me from closing it.

"Nico, let go of my car."

"I'm just wondering," he says, feigning curiosity, "how you plan to *get* the car to Crescent City."

I stare blankly up at him. "I just told you, I'm driving it."

An infuriatingly cocky smile makes its way onto his face, like he knows a secret I don't.

"What?" I demand.

His smile doesn't falter. "Did you even look at the pictures you posted?"

I groan. "Didn't anyone teach you that it's rude to spy?"

"Did you?" he repeats.

"Of course I looked at them. Why?"

"I don't think you looked close enough. Otherwise, you'd know that you're not driving that car anywhere."

I ball my fists against the steering wheel. "Yes, I am. And *you* are not going to stop me. You're getting away from my car. Right now." I reach for the handle and try to pull the door closed. But Nico doesn't release his grip.

"Did you get a good look at the gearshift in the center console? Did you happen to notice the lack of letters like

*P* and *D*? That car is *not* an automatic transmission. And if memory serves"—he grins defiantly—"you can't drive stick."

My whole body deflates and I berate myself for not thinking of this on my own. I was so desperate to take the photos and get the Craigslist ad posted, I didn't even notice. Of course the car is a stick shift. I remember Jackson driving it. I remember when he used to let me shift gears for him from the passenger seat. I always fantasized about the day I'd be old enough for him to teach me how to drive the car for real. But he was gone long before my feet could ever reach the pedals.

Nico tried to teach me to drive stick shift in his truck once, during our ill-fated eighty-eight days together. I failed miserably. After countless tries, we ended up just hopping into the bed of the truck and . . .

You know what, it doesn't matter. The point is, I couldn't make it three feet without stalling out. How am I ever going to make it three hundred miles?

Nico's grin widens, as though he's remembering the exact same day. "Well, good luck," he says in an obnoxiously cheery voice. Then he releases the door, hitches his backpack onto his shoulder, and turns to walk away.

Furious, I slam the door shut and fume inside my car.

There has to be someone else.

*Think, Ali. Think! You have to know someone in this town who can drive a stick shift besides him.*

I squeeze the steering wheel until my knuckles turn white, slowly coming to the conclusion that I never wanted to come to again.

No! I can't need him.

Except, I *do* need him. At least for this.

He's the only person I know who can drive a manual transmission. June hates to get behind the wheel. She makes Tyler drive her everywhere.

But five and a half hours?

Trapped in a car?

With *Nico*?

I could barely stand to be in the same computer lab with him for five and a half minutes. There's no way we can survive five and a half *hours* together in car. There's got to be a better way.

But what?

I think about the notice that was pinned to our front door yesterday. The deadline seared into the page. If I don't get that money to the bank by next week, our house will no longer be our house.

I peer through the windshield and watch Nico slowly sauntering down the aisle of the parking lot toward his truck.

---

**You just realized your ex-boyfriend is the only one who can help you solve all of your problems. What do you do?**

**A**  *Swallow your pride and chase after him.*

**B**  *Admit defeat and let the bank take your house.*

**C**  *Stew in this parking lot forever. You'd rather die than ask for his help.*

C. The answer is most definitely C.

And yet, I know that's not an option. I'm out of options. *This* is my only option.

I kick open the car door and get out. "Nico. Wait!"

He turns around and cocks an eyebrow, setting my nerves on fire. It's the same expression he used to get after he thought he'd won one of our fake arguments. An adorable mix of boyish innocence and manly arrogance.

I cross the aisle of the parking lot and stand in front of him, my fists clenching and unclenching at my sides as I work up the strength to do what I know I'm going to regret for the next five and a half hours.

"Look," I begin rigidly. "As you know from reading my computer screen when you were supposed to be minding your own business, I'm selling the car for a lot of money. If you help me drive it to Crescent City, I will pay you five hundred dollars."

He crosses his arms. "Five hundred dollars?"

I sigh. "Fine. A thousand."

"So you're saying you *need* me to help you."

I roll my eyes. "I need someone to help me, yes."

"But you're asking *me*."

"You're . . ." I flounder, roving my eyes over the parking lot. "You're the closest person."

"Uh-huh." The amusement in his voice is making me want to scream.

"Do you want the money or not?" I snap.

Nico shrugs. "Sure. I could use an extra thousand dollars." He brushes past me and starts walking back toward my car. I spin around and watch as he casually opens the passenger-side door and sits down, buckling his seat belt.

I must be insane. I *am* insane. No one in their right mind would knowingly choose to go on a road trip with their ex-boyfriend. But that's just the thing. I'm *not* in my right mind. I'm in a hopeless, desperate state of mind, which is apparently the worst state of mind in which to make decisions.

I blow out a breath and walk unsteadily back to my car. After getting in behind the wheel and buckling my seat belt, I close my eyes.

*Five and a half hours,* I tell myself. *You can do this. One more day and then you'll be free of him forever.*

When I open my eyes, Nico is staring intently at my face, his expression focused, like he's trying to figure something out. Then, before I can react, his hand is reaching toward me. Toward my cheek. I track it like he's moving in slow motion. Like this is one of those stylized fight scenes in movies where the action slows way down, just before someone's face is about to get smashed in.

*What is he doing?*

If this were one month ago, I would close my eyes. I would let his touch send goose bumps over my skin. I would melt into his hand.

But this is not one month ago. This is now. And I feel the sudden urge to swat his hand away.

But I don't. Instead, I freeze, bracing myself for the heat. The contact. It never comes.

"Um, you have . . ." Nico squints. ". . . glitter on your face."

I let out a stutter of a laugh and nervously brush my cheek with my palm, feeling incredibly stupid. "Oh. June made me a . . . thing. There was a lot of glitter involved."

His eyebrows form two question marks. But I'm not about to explain any further. The less we talk to each other throughout this process, the better.

Hastily, I stick the key into the ignition. Nothing happens. The Honda doesn't even *try* to turn over. It's laughing at me. It's laughing at this whole ridiculous situation. I would join in if I weren't so on edge right now.

I let out a loud groan and try again. Still nothing.

"Come on!" I urge the car through gritted teeth. "Don't do this to me right now."

I press on the gas and turn the key with a hard jerk. Nico reaches over and places his hand atop mine. I yank it away like he's just set my fingers on fire. He turns the key back and pulls it from the ignition. "Don't worry. We'll take my truck."

The last time I was in Nico Wright's truck was the night of Fabian's Comet. The night we broke up. Exactly eighty-eight days after we got together. We'd been fighting more and more lately, the glimmering translucent cocoon of our first few months together fading with each argument, each accusation, each lie.

That was the night it disappeared completely, leaving me alone in my cold, damp reality with nothing left to shield me from the elements. The rain had been there the whole time. It drizzled or poured practically the entire three months that Nico and I were together. Some kind of historic California record. But I never felt it until that night. I don't think either of us did.

The night of the comet, the fight was so bad—the ending kind of bad—I made him pull over and let me out of the truck. I told him I'd rather walk home then spend one more second in his car.

I got out. I slammed the door. I started to walk. But I clearly hadn't thought the whole thing through very well because we were in the middle of nowhere, somewhere along Route 128, the only highway that actually passes through Russellville. It's infamously dark in its long, winding stretches of no streetlamps, no houses, nothing but towering trees.

Of course, he didn't just drive away like I wanted him to. He followed after me, inching along the road to keep pace with me. Despite my frustration that he was still there—always there—in that moment, I kind of loved him for it. I didn't really want to be alone. I just didn't want to be with him anymore.

That's when I called June.

"Where are you?" she asked.

I glanced around, seeing only miles of wet road and dense, creepy fog, and Nico's car idling next to me, his wide, worried eyes watching me through the open window.

"I don't know. Somewhere on Route 128. About three miles north of town."

"I'm coming," she said before I could even click over to the map on my phone to check. "Hang tight. I'll be there soon."

I hung up. I stood there on the side of the empty wet road, the engine of Nico's truck the only sound for miles.

"You can leave now," I said without daring to look at him. I knew if I looked at him, I'd cry, and I swore I wouldn't cry until I was safe inside June's car. "June is coming to get me."

There was a long stretch of silence during which I half prayed he would finally leave and half prayed he would stay. "I'll just wait for her to get here," he finally replied. His voice was soft with a rough edge.

I shivered but tried to hide it with a shrug. "Suit yourself."

"Get back inside the truck, Ali," Nico said, sounding annoyed by my shivering. "Where it's warm."

For a moment, I considered it. I could feel the heat from the vents wafting out of the open window, brushing up against my goose-pimpled skin, making the hair on my arms stand straight up. For a moment, I even glanced at the door handle.

But I couldn't.

I knew what would happen if I got inside that truck. I'd lose. I'd cave. I'd get sucked right back in. The way my mother always did whenever Jackson came back. The warmth of the heater would wrap around me, and his kind eyes would hold me, and his pleading words would soften me. And then his lies would fade into the background.

But they couldn't fade into the background. I couldn't let them. I had to keep them right there in front of me where I could see them. Keep tabs on them. Never let them out of my sight again.

And so we both waited.

Him inside the car, fingers drumming on the steering wheel. Me outside, in my muddy shoes and wet hair, fidgeting with my phone, the lingering anger rising off both of us like steam, swirling with the night's mist.

As Nico pulls onto Route 128 and we head west toward my house, I'm grateful that it's not night, it's not raining, and there's no world-famous celestial object streaking through the sky. These are the only consolations I have. The clear blue skies and warm sunlight are what separates me from that night. From our whole relationship. Because the rest of this car—the cracked leather seats, Nico's strong hand expertly maneuvering the tall gearshift from first to second to third, the glove box—they're all like black holes waiting to suck me in, waiting to drag me back to the past. When things were so good, and then so bad.

The downpour finally stopped two days after Nico and I broke up. As though the rain were waiting it out. Waiting for this doomed relationship to end so it could finally stop being such an obvious omen.

As soon as we clear the main drag of town, Nico pushes down on the accelerator and compresses the clutch, maneuvering the shifter into fifth gear and my heart into eleventh.

*Oh God. I shouldn't be here.*

I'm starting to wonder if thirty-two thousand dollars is even worth the agony of being trapped in a car with my ex-boyfriend for five and a half hours. If *any* amount of money is worth that. Is there anything more uncomfortable, more awkward, more unnatural than sitting an armrest away from the boy who used to drive you crazy with just a simple touch? The boy who used to kiss you like you were the only thing that mattered.

Now, it feels like those memories are just hanging between us. Giant elephants in the truck that take up all the space, that leave no room for us. For what we are now.

As Nico drives, I keep my gaze trained out the window, at the passing scenery. But my eyes keep drifting back toward the glove box. It's nearly impossible *not* to see it. It's right there. Inches away from my knees.

*Is it still in there? Does he still have it? Or was that just a temporary hiding place?*

"There's nothing in there," Nico says, crashing into my thoughts, *reading* them as clearly as if they were scrawled across my face. "But you're welcome to look if you don't believe me."

My head whips to him. I can't see his eyes because he's wearing his sunglasses, but his stiff smile lets me know that he's joking. Or at least trying to. Trying to make light of this heaviness that surrounds us like humidity.

*Isn't it too soon?*

What is the acceptable amount of time to wait after a tragedy before you can start making jokes about it?

I guess it depends on the tragedy.

"That's okay," I mutter. Because the truth is, I don't care what is or isn't in that glove box anymore. It's no longer my problem. Or my concern.

As Nico refocuses on the road and turns onto my street, I notice how fast the smile slips from his face. Like it was never that secure to begin with. Held up by cheap, flimsy tape with weak adhesive. "Well, it's empty now," he says, much quieter, the humor in his voice replaced with resentment. "It's all empty now."

I steal a peek at him out of the corner of my eye, wondering if he's still talking about the glove box.

"Whoa! Is that it?" Nico says the moment he pulls into my driveway and his gaze lands on Jackson's open-top Firebird convertible through the windshield.

I roll my eyes. "No, that's the *other* 1968 Firebird convertible I have."

"No freaking way!" Nico says, ignoring my sarcasm. In a blur, he's killed the engine and is out of the truck, bounding up to the Firebird like a kid bounding toward the tree on Christmas morning. He drags his fingertip along the bumper, taking extra care to trace the red 400 emblem affixed to the trunk, just above the right taillight.

*"This baby's not the base model. It's the 400. It's worth much, MUCH more."*

*It better be, for all this trouble I'm going through,* I think.

Then, I watch in amazement as Nico lets out a very unmanly "Whoop!" and runs up the left side of the car, then jumps into the driver's seat, bypassing the door completely. The way Jackson always used to.

"This car is sweet!" he gushes, glancing around the open interior, running his hands appreciatively over the arc of the wooden steering wheel.

I slowly get out of the truck and approach the car. It looks exactly as it does in my memory. The blue exterior is the color of a clear California sky. The white leather seats are as smooth and soft as cotton. The license plate reads FEPDMIC, an homage to Jackson's favorite band.

"Okay, be honest," Nico says. "How good do I look in this thing?" He gives his hair a flip, and bile rises in my stomach.

*They're different,* I tell myself over and over again. *Completely different people.*

Jackson's hair was dark; Nico's is light. Jackson's face had stubble; Nico's is almost always clean-shaven. Jackson liked to break things; Nico likes to build things.

And yet, in this instant, they are the same. Everything is the same. The car. The hair flip. The smile. The arm resting on the open window.

And I just can't. I turn away. I have to turn away. "I'm, um, just going to get some stuff before we leave."

I run toward the house, unlock the door, and dash inside, stopping short when I see the boxes. I almost forgot they were there. They jump out at me from time to time, like ghosts with loud, rattling chains.

I hurry into my bedroom and empty all the things from my backpack, including June's scrapbook, which I store safely in my nightstand. Then I pack a fresh pair of clothes and underwear. I try to ignore the stabbing in my gut reminding me that the reason I'm packing clothes is because Nico and I are not coming home tonight. We're going to have to stay somewhere in Crescent City before we can catch a bus back to Russellville. Which means we're going to have to stay somewhere. Together.

*No*, I tell myself. *Not gonna happen.*

I'll use some of the money I get for the car to rent us *two* separate hotel rooms. There's no way I'm sleeping anywhere near him.

I head to the kitchen and, checking that Nico isn't peeking through the window, I open the freezer, pull out the old box of Lean Cuisine chicken fettuccine, and reach my hand inside. I remove the plastic baggie with my emergency stash of cash in it. A little bit from each paycheck that I've been ferreting away ever since I started working at Chateau Marmutt. A total of seven hundred seventy-two dollars.

This is the money I was going to use to save us. Pay all the bills. Settle all the debt. Salvage this house. Until I realized it would never be enough.

Now I'll have to use it to pay for food and gas to get us to Crescent City.

I grab the key to the Firebird and the envelope with the paperwork from the kitchen table and lock the front door behind me.

Nico is still sitting in the driver's seat, admiring the inside of the car—adjusting the mirror, pushing buttons on the cassette player that Jackson installed himself. I dump my bag into the back seat and toss Nico the key.

With a grin, he sticks it in the ignition, presses one foot on the brake, the other on the clutch, and turns the key. The engine roars instantly to life, and Nico's smile widens. "Now *that* is one of the most beautiful sounds I've ever heard." Then, he lets out a roar of his own and bounces in the seat. "C'mon, c'mon, let's go! I want to see how this baby moves."

"Please, don't call it that," I say as I make my way around the front of the hood to the passenger side.

Nico tilts his head. "What? Baby?"

"Yeah."

"Why not?"

"Because . . . ," I start to say, but I stop myself.

*Because it's what he used to call it.*

*Because it's just a freaking car. It's not a baby. It doesn't breathe. It doesn't cry. It doesn't need taking care of.*

"Just don't," I finally finish. I reach for the door handle but stop just short of making contact. My hands are suddenly shaking.

What happens when I open that door?

What happens when I sit down?

I haven't sat inside this car since I was twelve years old. Since I still believed in the magic of time. That it can change people. That it can bring people home. That it can make people stay.

"What's wrong?" Nico asks, pushing himself up off the seat so he can see the door handle that I've been staring vacantly at for the past five seconds.

I shake my head. "Nothing."

*Nothing.*

*Nothing.*

*Nothing.*

I repeat the word in my mind until it feels true. Until it becomes more than a word, but a motto to live by. Then, before I can second-guess myself, I quickly reach for the handle, yank open the door, and sit down.

I take a deep breath, waiting for the panic to come. Waiting for the memories to flood me like tidal waves. But it doesn't happen. The car feels like a car. The white leather feels unfamiliar beneath me. Like all the memories have been run down, worn off, cast away, with each mile on the odometer.

Maybe my twelve-year-old self was right.

Maybe time really is magic.

# 3:07 P.M.

# RUSSELLVILLE, CA

## INVENTORY: 1968 FIREBIRD 400 CONVERTIBLE (1), CASH ($772.00)

When Nico reaches the end of my street, I expect him to turn right instead of left, toward the other side of town where he lives. But he doesn't. He turns toward the coast.

"Don't you want to swing by your house to pick anything up?" I ask. "We won't be home until—"

"No," he says hurriedly.

I feel somewhat relieved by his response. I'm anxious to get on the road. But I'm also curious about it. Does he, too, not want to be reminded that we're going to have to spend the night somewhere? Or is it something else? Something having to do with the fact that I've never been inside Nico's house and that every time I asked to go there, he'd have a lie ready and waiting to feed me.

*"My mom hasn't cleaned in a while. She'd be embarrassed if you came over."*

"My *dad has the flu. I wouldn't want you to catch any-thing."*

"We have relatives in from out of town—it's a madhouse right now."

At first, I believed them. I had no reason not to. Then, after about the fifth excuse—*"We just had the place fumi-gated. It's not safe."*—I started to notice the signs. The tells. The quick swallows and downcast eyes.

Two weeks later, a comet came barreling through the sky and ended us.

I plug the address of Tom Lancaster's shop into Google Maps and preview our route. Fairly simple. Route 128 west to California 1 north. That turns into the 101 north, which will take us all the way up the coast to the very top of the state. But just as I'm about to hit start on the turn-by-turn directions, a text message appears on my screen.

You currently have 5% of your data plan remaining.

Irritably, I swipe the message away. I guess we'll need to use Nico's phone from now on.

*I really need to get that money.*

As soon as the speed limit changes from forty-five to fifty-five, indicating we're officially out of Russellville, Nico guns the engine and pushes the car up to seventy.

"Wow," Nico says. That boyish smile that took over his face the moment he saw the car is back again. "This car drives like a dream!"

I turn to watch the passing scenery. I admit, the warm

May air feels good on my face, and in my hair. It feels like it's blowing away the past.

If only the past weren't sitting right next to me.

"I can't believe you're selling this!" he calls over the rush of wind. "It's such a classic."

I shrug, keeping my eyes on the road. I kind of hope the shrug will be answer enough, but apparently it's not.

"Why *are* you selling it?"

I want to tell him it's none of his business, butt out. But for some reason I feel like I owe him an explanation, at least a vague one. If for no other reason than because he's the one driving the car to the seller.

"My mom and I need the money."

"What?" he yells. The wind has picked up, making it harder to hear each other with the top down.

"We need the money!" I shout.

He glances at me, confused. "But this car is a classic. It'll appreciate in value. It'll be worth a lot more in ten years than it is now."

I feel the gnawing of agitation in my stomach. Why can't he just be satisfied with my explanation and drop it? Why does he have to pry?

"I can't afford to wait that long," I say quietly, knowing it's inaudible over the wind.

"What?" he yells again.

This time, however, I don't repeat myself. If he can't hear me, that's his problem, not mine. I got the truth out. I said the words. I fulfilled my duty, and now I'm done. But then I feel the car start to slow as Nico pulls it off to the side of the road.

For a moment, I panic, thinking that he's going to demand a real explanation. That he's not going to continue driving until I tell him exactly why I'm selling this car. But instead, he shifts into neutral and pushes a button next to the radio. A second later, I hear a whizzing sound as the convertible soft top starts to rise from the back and sweeps over us like a curtain being drawn, closing us inside this tiny, tiny car.

I never realized how infinitesimally small this car really is until now.

"Um, I kind of liked the top down," I say.

But it's too late; Nico has already locked the latches into place. "I couldn't hear a word you were saying."

*I know*, I think. *That was the whole point.*

He shifts the car into first and pulls back out onto the road. "This is much better."

But I disagree. This is not better at all. This feels like being trapped in a prison cell with the bank job partner who ratted you out. As we drive, the awkward silence is more deafening than the wind. Now it feels like we're *forced* to talk to each other. Forced to pretend we still have something left to say to each other.

Nico must realize his mistake, because a few minutes later, he points to the cassette player in the car and says, "So, uh, do you want to listen to something?"

I breathe out a quiet sigh of relief. Partly because yes, I do want to listen to something. I want to listen to *anything* other than this silence. Nails on chalkboards, feedback from a microphone, a five-year-old playing the violin for the first time. All of those options have got to be better than this.

But mostly I'm relieved because he seems to have forgotten about his previous question.

Before Jackson left for the first time, he could usually be found in the garage. He would spend hours out there, buffing and shining and tinkering. For the three years he was gone, that's how I remembered him: the hood up, Jackson's tall, willowy frame bent over the engine with a tool in his hand.

While everything in his life—his family, his relationships, his appearance—was constantly in need of repair, his car was always in immaculate shape.

Two months before he left, I woke up in the middle of the night from a bad dream. I ran to my parents' room—to Jackson's side of the bed.

I'd always gone to my father with bad dreams. He would carry me back to my bed, tuck me in, and listen as I described the nightmare. Then he would perform an exorcism of sorts, to chase the nightmare back into "Nightmare Land," as he called it, complete with strange chants, ostentatious hand movements, and finally the sprinkling of "hole-y" water (water with invisible holes in it). He'd dip his fingers in my water glass and sprinkle drops across my forehead.

The ceremony was over-the-top ridiculous, but it worked. It kept the bad dreams away.

Until Jackson himself *became* the bad dream.

When I reached Jackson's side of the bed that night, the covers were pushed back, and the pillow was empty. I headed to the garage, where I knew I would find him.

Sure enough, Jackson was sitting in the driver's seat of the Firebird, fiddling with something on the radio.

"Dad?" I said. "What are you doing?"

He glanced at me through the windshield but didn't ask why I was awake. In fact, he barely seemed to register that it was the middle of the night. He simply called me over to him and told me to get in. He had a huge grin on his face.

"Look at this!" he said, after I'd closed the passenger-side door. He held up what looked like a bunch of wires tangled around a small metal box. "Found it at the dump. Do you know what it is?"

I shook my head.

"It's a perfectly good, *working* cassette player. That someone just threw away."

"What's a cassette player?" I asked.

Jackson tossed his head back and laughed. "When I was your age, we didn't have MP3s. We barely even had CDs. We listened to music on these things called cassettes." He held up a black unlabeled tape to show me. "But first, I have to install the player."

For the next few minutes, I sat in the passenger seat and watched as Jackson expertly untangled the wires around the cassette player, connected them to various wires emerging from a giant hole where the car's stereo used to be, and slid the box into place.

"I'll have to retrofit it so it looks more seamless, but let's see if it works." Jackson turned the device on and fiddled with the dials on the front, causing a little white needle to move across a spectrum of numbers.

"That's called a *tuner*," he explained. He turned up the volume, and a newscast in Spanish came over the speakers. Jackson smiled. "Let's try out the tape deck." He inserted the cassette tape into the device, and suddenly a loud, distorted guitar riff blasted through the Firebird's speakers, startling me. Jackson squeezed his eyes shut and began to bang his head violently along with the music. For a moment, he didn't look like my father anymore. He looked like someone throwing a tantrum.

I rested my hand on the door handle, terrified and ready to bolt. But a few seconds later, he opened his eyes and smiled at me, returning to the Jackson I knew and loved.

"What is this?" I yelled over the noise. And that's exactly what it sounded like to me. Like noise. Like a small child had gotten their hands on a guitar and was pretending to know how to play.

The drums kicked in, and Jackson mimed the beats right along with the drummer. As though he'd already heard this song a thousand times and had been rehearsing it for a big concert.

"It's the new Fear Epidemic album!" he shouted back. "It just dropped yesterday. Your mother won't let me play the CD in the house. So I copied it onto this cassette, and now with my new tape deck, I can listen to it in the car! Isn't it amazing?"

I nodded because I didn't know what else to do. It wasn't amazing. It was loud and abrasive, and I felt like the musicians were reaching through the speakers and smacking me over the head with their instruments. But I also hadn't seen my father that happy in a long time.

Actually, come to think of it, I'd *never* seen my father that happy. It was as though something had come alive in him. Someone had plugged him into an amp. He was always charming and upbeat and spirited. But this was something else.

This was Jackson with the volume cranked up.

"I never thought they'd get back together!" Jackson yelled. "This is the best day ever."

He continued to drum against the steering wheel, his whole body convulsing with each strum of the guitar. I watched him with a mix of confusion and fear. I'd come out here because I'd wanted him to chase away my bad dreams with his special nightmare exorcism. But it was as though I'd stumbled upon a very different kind of ceremony. A sacred worship ritual. One that I was clearly not a part of because I suddenly felt as though I were intruding upon something. Something I didn't understand. Would *never* fully understand.

I don't think Jackson even noticed when I opened the passenger door, climbed out of the car, and eased the door shut behind me.

As I lay awake in bed later, thinking about what I'd just witnessed, it was as though, somehow, I just knew that cassette player would change everything. Because as soon as I fell asleep, my dreams were plagued with more nightmares.

As Nico and I pass the sign marking the entrance to Mendocino County, I suck in a breath. We're no longer in our home county of Sonoma. I'm now officially on a road trip with my ex-boyfriend. There's a sentence I never thought I'd say in a million years.

"What do you want to listen to?" I ask, trying to sound diplomatic. If it were just me in the car, I'd put on my favorite playlist and sing along at the top of my lungs. But I know it's an unspoken rule that the driver picks the music.

He glances at the cassette player, and I notice, for the first time, that there's a tape inside. "Let's see what's in here." Nico turns on the radio, and I hear the faint click of the cassette engaging. The sound seems to vibrate through the marrow of my bones, and I brace myself for what comes next.

Then, I hear it.

Those loud, abrasive chords.

That angry voice screaming.

It's different from the album Jackson played for me that night in the garage. That much I can tell immediately. The sound of the guitar is tinnier. The voice of Nolan Cook, the lead singer of Fear Epidemic, has a hollow echo to it. As though the song were recorded in a closet, rather than a professional studio.

But it doesn't matter. It's enough.

I lunge for the cassette player and push eject. The silence that comes next is blissful and soothing. Ice-cold water over burned flesh.

Nico shoots an inquisitive glance at me as he drives, clearly trying to make sense of my over-the-top reaction to something as seemingly harmless as a song.

"Sorry," I mutter as I pull the tape from the cassette player and stash it in the center console. "It was so loud. Let's listen to something else. Something on your phone."

"Okay," Nico says slowly, pulling his phone out of his pocket and handing it to me. Without thinking, I turn it on, type in his password, and start navigating through his playlists. It isn't until I've reached the one titled "iChill" that I realize what we've just done.

We're like play actors who have rehearsed the blocking onstage so many times, it's become second nature. Even after the theater has been dark for more than a month, we can still pick up right where we left off.

How many times have we sat in this same configuration, Nico driving, me working the tech? Scrolling through his playlists, reading questions aloud from my favorite personality quiz website, looking stuff up on Google to settle a fake argument. And now, holding his phone in my hands, my fingers finding the right apps as easily as a pianist finds the right keys, a sourness starts to spread through my gut.

Maybe we should have laid out some ground rules before getting into the car. A code of conduct.

**Ali and Nico's Rules of the Road:**

1.  No mentions of the past.

2.  No references to glove boxes, comets, rain, muddy shoes, or anything else relating to that night.

3.  NO ROUTINES.

Nothing familiar.

"Uh, how about a podcast instead?" I suggest.

"A podcast?" he replies, as though he's never heard the word before.

"Yeah, they're like TV shows but audio only. They have them on practically every topic."

He chuckles. "I know what a podcast is. I'm just not sure why you'd want to listen to one."

I suddenly feel myself getting defensive. "To learn things. To educate myself. To gain a new perspective on the world."

Nico raises one hand up in surrender. "Okay. Okay. Calm down. We can listen to a podcast."

*Calm down.*

Those words. They're like gasoline on a fire. I can hear them echoing in my mind. Two different memories colliding in the middle.

Nico. That night. Telling me to "Calm down. You're overreacting."

And Jackson. Six years ago. The first time he came back. Telling Mom to "Calm down. You're getting worked up over nothing."

*Calm down.*

My fingers are shaking as I search the categories of podcasts. I almost toss the phone right back at him. I almost tell him to forget it. Forget the whole thing.

Just stop here and let me out.

If I got out of the car again, would June come all the way out here to get me? Like she did the last time.

*Calm down, Ali.*

Stop being ridiculous.

I continue to scroll. As much as I hate to admit it, I need Nico right now. I need him to get me and this car to Crescent City by tonight. And with my data plan on the verge of empty and Mom failing to pay the cell phone bill because it was either that or the electricity bill, I need his phone, too.

"Okay," I say, hearing the quiver in my voice. I clear my throat. "So there's an interesting one called 'Dozen,' about a murder that's solved over the course of twelve hour-long episodes."

"No." Nico immediately vetoes that, and I'm relieved. We're only going to be in this car together for five and a half hours. We'd never find out who did it.

I keep scrolling. "How about this one? It's called 'Everything About Everything.'" I click on the description and read it aloud. "'Answers to the most random questions about life, science, humanity, philosophy, and everything in between.'"

Nico shrugs. "Sounds cool. I guess anything is better than dentist music."

He flashes me a tense, hurried smile to let me know he's kidding. A cheap attempt to lighten the mood.

I wince.

"Dentist music" is what Nico likes to call my favorite genre of music, which basically consists of really bubbly pop songs. Nico used to say it's so sugary-sweet, it gave him a toothache, hence the nickname.

I guess that's another thing to add to Ali and Nico's Rules of the Road:

4. No inside jokes.

I click on the first episode of the podcast, entitled "Where do swear words come from?" I punch up the volume on Nico's phone and push play.

A few seconds later, a guy with a chipper, excited voice comes on, introducing himself as Linus McKee and welcoming us to his podcast.

"Why are swear words bad?" he asks. "And where do they even come from? We'll find out in this episode of 'Everything About Everything.'" A catchy music riff plays, and I lean back in my seat, grateful to have someone else talk inside this car so we don't have to.

I turn my gaze out the window and watch the landscape stream by. The trees are already getting taller as the sloping vineyards start to fade into the rearview mirror. Northern California is like a collage of scenery. One minute you're in wine country; the next you're driving through redwood trees as high as cathedrals, and before you can blink, you're cruising alongside the ocean, marveling at the dramatic, rocky coastline. When I was little, I would ask how California got its jagged shape, and Jackson would tell me that a giant cut out the state with a pair of wavy craft scissors.

"When you stub your toe, do you shout out 'Gadzooks!' or 'Gadsbobs!'?" Linus McKee asks us. "Well, if you lived in late-seventeenth-century England, you might have. These are examples of euphemism swear words, words created to avoid using an offensive or taboo word, like the word 'God,' which is why people started using 'Gad' instead."

I steal a peek at Nico to see if he's going to veto the selection, but he looks quiet and focused, his eyes trained on the road. So I let the episode keep playing, thinking if we can do exactly this for four and a half more hours, we might just make it to Crescent City without killing each other.

# 3:49 P.M.

# BOONVILLE, CA

### INVENTORY: 1968 FIREBIRD 400 CONVERTIBLE (1), CASH ($772.00)

By the time we reach Boonville, we've finished the end of the episode and are now well versed in the history (and possible future) of swearing.

Nico pulls into a parking spot in front of the Boonville General Store and answers my questioning look with one word: "Coffee."

I nod. I almost forgot about Nico's addiction. He's a caffeine fiend. He can't go more than a few hours without a fix. "Want anything?"

I reach into the back seat, unzip my backpack, and pull a twenty-dollar bill out of my Ziploc bag of cash. It's still cold from the freezer. "No, but I'll pay."

He guffaws. "You most certainly will *not* pay."

I roll my eyes. There he goes again with the gentleman act. "Nico. You're doing me a favor by driving me. At least let me pay for gas and food."

"I'm not doing you a favor," he reminds me, his voice turning cold. "You're paying me, remember?"

"Yes. I remember. And I'm paying for your coffee, too." Before he can argue again, I walk around him and enter the shop.

The Boonville General Store is cute, with a small-town vintage feel. Outside there are wooden picnic tables shielded from the sun by red umbrellas. Inside, old wooden wagon wheels decorate the yellow-and-blue-striped walls.

Nico orders a plain black coffee, as always. It was something I used to tease him about. He liked to say it was classic. I liked to say it was boring. Then he would turn toward me, brush a strand of hair behind my ear, and whisper, "You're classic, and you're far from boring."

It drove me crazy when he did that. Whisper things into my ear. He did it all the time. Sometimes compliments, sometimes flirtatious comments about what I was wearing, but most of the time it was just mundane, everyday things like, "The vending machine is out of Snickers."

That was one of Nico's skills. To make *me*, the least-sexy person I know, feel sexy, just from a brush of breath against my ear. *His* breath. His words. His scent. His playful smirk as he pulled away, leaving a secret between us that only we knew. Making that secret feel important. Even if it *was* just about the vending machine.

The woman working the counter pumps coffee into a to-go cup, slaps on a lid, and hands it to Nico. He glances at me before taking a sip, as though he's waiting for me to comment on his drink choice like I always used to do.

But I simply hand the twenty-dollar bill to the cashier. As she gives me my change, she cranes her neck to see out the front window of the shop. "Is that a Firebird out there?"

Nico beams, clearly pleased with the attention. "Yes! 1968. 400 convertible. Isn't it killer?"

"Gorgeous!"

I roll my eyes, stuffing the change into my pocket. I had to listen to this exact same encounter for the first nine years of my life. Every time I went anywhere with Jackson, everything was always about the car.

*What year is that?*

*1968.*

*Is that a 400?*

*Sure is!*

*What a beauty!*

*Isn't she, though?*

Whenever that car was around, I may as well have been invisible.

And now, even though Jackson is dead, it's happening all over again. I watch as Nico and the cashier both gaze appreciatively out the window. I push roughly past Nico as I head to the door. "C'mon. We need to get back on the road."

I hear Nico exchanging a few more pleasantries with the cashier before following after me.

When we sit back down in the car, Nico automatically hands me the coffee cup and I automatically take it, realizing a few seconds later that we've just done it again. Fallen back into another routine without thinking.

Nico's truck doesn't have any cup holders. Which means that whoever rides shotgun has to be a human cup holder.

My mind suddenly flashes back to long drives. Winding roads. Blue and red dashboard lights. His hot cup of coffee warming my cold fingers. Nico bringing the cup to his lips, then returning it to my hand, then bringing my hand to his lips . . .

Jackson's car, thankfully, *does* have cup holders. Two of them. Right between us in the wooden console. I set the coffee down in one. Nico notices and flashes me a sheepish grin, before opening his mouth to say, "Oops," but I turn away before he can go there. Before we can share any sort of mutual embarrassment.

5. No sharing of mutual anything.

Nico starts the engine, checks the mirrors, and shifts into reverse, placing his arm over the back of my seat as he turns to glance out the rear window.

I can feel the proximity of his hand to my head. Every follicle of my hair waking up on instinct. Like each one of them has memory.

I instinctively scoot farther away, toward the door. Nico finishes backing up and returns his right hand to the stick shift, putting the car into first gear.

"So," Nico says as we glide along the highway, the blue sky stretching out before us like an open invitation. "I've been thinking."

I feel my body instinctively tense up. "About what?"

A thousand possible answers stream through my mind at once, each one worse than the last.

"About the episode."

This was *not* what I expected him to say. "What episode?"

"The one we just listened to," Nico says, as though it's obvious.

And it's so obvious, I didn't even think of it.

"Oh, right. The episode. What about it?"

"I think we should come up with our own euphemisms." He flashes me a look to make sure I'm following. "For swear words."

"Why?"

"I don't know. Just for *fun*." He says the word tersely, like he's implying I've never experienced it before. "To have something to do. To avoid offending little old ladies in the supermarket."

"Is this a problem of yours?" I challenge. "Offending little old ladies in supermarkets?"

He cocks an eyebrow. "Maybe."

I can't help but chuckle. It comes out before I can stop it. Nico's gaze swivels to me for a second, as if he has to get visual confirmation of my reaction.

"Okay. Whaddya got?"

He scratches his chin, like he's thinking really hard about it. "Hmmm. How about 'fuuuuu . . .'" He draws out the sound, before finally finishing it with, "'. . . ngicide.'"

"Fungicide?"

"Yeah. As in, 'Fungicide! I forgot my lunch!'"

"Well, the ultimate test is whether you can make it into a verb."

Nico shifts into fifth gear. "Stop fungiciding around and get to work!"

"Not bad."

"Your turn."

"Maybe we should just listen to another episode," I suggest, because I don't like where this is going. It feels too much like we're dancing around another Rule of the Road:

6.  No creating fun, new memories.

"What's the matter?" Nico says. "Can't think of anything to top 'fungicide'?"

I know what he's doing. He's appealing to my competitive side. He knows that's the best way to convince me to do something I don't want to do: turn it into a contest.

But it still works.

"Fine. Um. How about 'shiiiiii . . .'" I rack my brain, trying to come up with something clever. "'. . . tzu.'"

"Shih tzu?" Nico repeats skeptically.

"It's a breed of dog."

Nico grabs his coffee and takes a sip. "Use it in a sentence."

I roll my eyes. "The dog was a shih tzu."

Nico slows to steer around a sharp curve. "No. Use it as a swear word."

"Okay, how about, 'If we don't get this figured out, we'll be up shih tzu creek without a paddle'?"

"Will you get your shih tzu together and stop crying?"

"That last curve in the road scared the shih tzu out of me."

Nico laughs. "Okay, that's a pretty good one, but I think I can do better."

I cross my arms. "Go ahead."

"'Shiiiii . . . take mushroom.'"

"No," I say automatically.

"What do you mean, no?"

"It's too long."

"It is not."

"What? Are you going to say, 'You don't know shiitake mushroom about science'?"

"Yes," Nico replies. "That's exactly what I'm going to say. Or even 'This car is the shiitake mushroom.'"

I give him a thumbs-down.

"Fine." Nico admits defeat. "I'll give you that one. But seriously, this car *is* the shiitake mushroom. Are you going to tell me how you came into possession of a 1968 Firebird 400 convertible? Or are you going to leave me to come up with the most far-fetched assumptions in my head?"

I berate myself for not putting the podcast on again the moment we got back into the car. For leaving this opening, this gap for Nico to fill with silly games and probing questions.

Although I honestly didn't think we'd be able to get all the way to Crescent City without this topic coming up.

"That depends," I reply coolly.

He takes another sip of coffee. "On what?"

"On what those far-fetched assumptions are."

"Hmm. Well, let's see. My favorite one is that you conducted a hit for the mafia, the car belonged to the mark, and the mafia let you keep it as a bonus for a job well done." He returns the cup to the holder. "Oh, and the body is still in the trunk."

"Nope."

He nods. "Okay. How about this one? You're best friends with a crazy white-haired scientist who created a time machine out of a 1968 Firebird but then got trapped in the past, leaving the Firebird to you."

"That's the plotline for the Back to the Future trilogy."

"Dang it. I thought maybe you hadn't seen that."

"Who hasn't seen *Back to the Future*?" I ask incredulously.

"People who died in 1984 before the movie came out?"

"Exactly."

He huffs, takes the coffee cup again, sips. "Okay, here's a good one. You challenged someone to a drag race; winner gets the other person's car."

"And I won?"

He nods. "Naturally."

"In my mother's 2001 Honda Civic? The one still sitting in the parking lot of the high school because it wouldn't start?"

"It's possible."

"No, it's not. That car is a piece of shih tzu."

Nico toasts me with his coffee cup. "Dude, good one!"

"Dude?" I repeat incredulously.

He glances at me. "Would you rather I call you what I used to call you?"

And just like that, whatever light breeze we managed to create inside this stuffy, claustrophobic muscle car is suddenly gone. My chest squeezes. I don't say anything.

He peers at me again and scoffs. "I didn't think so."

One month into our doomed three-month relationship, Nico decided that calling me "Ali" was no longer good enough.

"Cuddle Cakes."

"No," I said immediately.

"Georgia Peach?"

"No."

"Cookie Monster?"

I gave Nico the stare of death. "Monster? Really?"

He crossed that one off his list and kept reading. "Frou Frou."

"Nope."

"Honey Bunch."

"Ick. No."

"Honey Bunches *of Oats*."

"Worse."

"Lamb Chop?"

"Seriously?" I tilted my head to try to look at the list, thinking this would go a lot faster if I could just veto everything at once, but Nico slid it away before I could get a peek. We were sitting in the Russellville High cafeteria with our sack lunches spilled out onto the table in front of us, untouched.

"Cupcake?"

"Why are ninety percent of these food-related?" I asked.

Nico shrugged. "Nature of the game, I suppose." He scanned his list. "Oh, here's one that's not food. 'Muggle.'"

"As in non-magical folk?"

He made a face and scratched it off. "You're right. Main Squeeze?"

"No."

"Love Boodle."

I groaned. "Anything but that."

"Okay. Lover Pie?"

"And that."

A tray plopped down next to my untouched container of yogurt, and a second later, June slid onto the bench. "What are you two doing?"

I rolled my eyes. "Nico is insisting that since we've been dating for more than a month, he has to come up with a pet name for me. And I said—"

"Oh cool!" June exclaimed. "Let me see the list!"

Nico slid the piece of paper across the table to her, and she scooped it up and quickly scanned the options.

I shot Nico a look of disbelief. "What? You'll let *her* see the list but not me?"

I leaned in to try to read over June's shoulder, but she leaned back, shielding my view.

"June can help," Nico defended.

"That's right," she agreed. "I can help. Ooh, I like Pancake and Pudding Pop."

"*Pudding Pop?*" I repeated in disgust, and turned to Nico. "Where did you get this list?"

"It's cute," June insisted.

"What's cute?" Tyler said, suddenly appearing behind June and kissing the back of her neck. "You're cute? Yes, I would have to agree." He walked around the table, dropped his tray down, and slid onto the bench next to Nico.

"Nico is choosing a pet name for Ali," June explained.

"Ahhh," Tyler said, his eyebrows shooting up like little arrows. "The pet-name selection. Big step, my man." He slapped Nico on the back. "What are the choices?"

I sighed. "This is not a democratic decision."

June ignored me and passed the list to Tyler. I propped my elbows on the table and buried my face in my hands.

"Dude, why is PB and J crossed off? That one is perfect."

"No," I moaned into my hands. "No, it's not."

"That's why," Nico said, leaning over the table and tapping my head.

"Pookie!" Tyler said, getting way too excited. "I like Pookie."

"Me too!" June chimed in. "Pookie is way cool. I definitely think you should go with Pookie."

I turned to Nico. "I don't know why you have to come up with some stupid, ridiculous nickname for me."

June replied for him. "Because that's just how relationships work, Ali. If you want to stay together forever, you have to come up with the right pet name."

Tyler and June shared a conspiratorial look. I hated when they did that. It was like they had invented their own secret language using only eyebrows and lip curls, and the rest of us were completely left out of the conversation.

"Exactly," Tyler agreed. "Just look at June and me. We have, like, twenty nicknames for each other, and we've been together for almost four years."

"Yeah, but that's different. Yours are all dirty."

Tyler shot June a flirtatious look. "Don't you know it, Miss Sweet—"

I covered my ears with my hands and started singing "La la la!" at the top of my lungs. June rubbed my back, letting me know it was over. I lowered my hands.

"If I were you," Tyler said, handing the list back to Nico, "I would just pick one and go with it. Eventually she'll learn to love it."

"No, I won't."

Nico stood up, walked around the side of the table, and sat down next to me. He turned sideways on the bench, one leg on either side of me, and pulled me in close, kissing my cheek. "Okay," he said a moment later, grabbing the list and holding it between us so I couldn't see the writing on the front. "I'm making an executive decision."

"No, you're not," I said.

He ignored me. "Henceforth, I shall call you . . ." He closed his eyes and ran his finger up and down the page before stopping in a random location. He opened his eyes, and I watched a sly grin snake its way onto his face.

I cringed, waiting for the horror that was about to befall me.

"Monkey Buns!"

June burst into applause. "Yes! I love it."

"No," I screeched. "I hate it."

"Too bad," Nico said. "It is decreed. You are forever known to me as Monkey Buns."

"If you ever call me Monkey Buns, I will never speak to you again."

Nico ignored my protest. "Let's give her a go, shall we?" He leaned into me and, with the grace and precision of a museum curator handling a piece of fine art, pushed a lock of my hair from my ear. As soon as his fingertips flicked again my skin, I knew my protest was all over. I would never survive whatever came next.

Then, he bent close to me, and with his lips barely grazing my earlobe, whispered, "Monkey Buns."

The reaction was immediate. My traitorous body broke out in goose bumps. When Nico pulled back and glanced at my arm, he immediately noticed the hair standing up on end and announced to the entire cafeteria, "It worked!"

Tyler and June cheered. "Mon-key Buns! Mon-key Buns!" they chanted.

I glared at both of them. "I'm not speaking to you two, either."

"Monkey Buns it is," Nico declared.

I crossed my arms over my chest, trying to hide my body's reaction to him. "That's not fair. You could whisper anything in my ear and that would happen."

Nico cocked an inquisitive eyebrow. "Anything? Really?"

He looked pensive for a moment before his face lit up with a bolt of inspiration. He scooted even closer to me, until I was pressed up against him and I could feel his chest slowly rising and falling against my shoulder. He shared a conspiratorial "guy" look with Tyler before cupping his mouth with his hand and leaning in close to me again.

For a moment, all I could feel was his sweet breath on my face as his lips lingered near. I closed my eyes. I waited for the delicious chill. I prepared myself for whatever he was going to say because regardless of what it was, I knew it would show all over my face.

Then, in the sexiest voice I've ever heard, Nico whispered, "The lasagna in the cafeteria looks disgusting."

And I melted right onto the floor.

# 4:51 P.M.

## ROUTE 128

### INVENTORY: 1968 FIREBIRD 400 CONVERTIBLE (1), CASH ($769.35)

Nico rounds a corner and 128 becomes California 1. Through a small patch of trees, I spot the Pacific Ocean in the distance. Blue and sparkling and endless. Like it never left. Like it's just been waiting there for me, wondering when I would ever come back.

Thirty minutes later, we cross the Noyo River and are in Fort Bragg. And just like that, the memories of the last time I was here come flooding back. As though that bridge over the river was actually a bridge back in time. Suddenly all I can see, as we drive down the main thoroughfare of the town, is Jackson stumbling drunk along the street, singing at the top of his lungs, high on music and beer.

"Looks like a nice town," Nico says conversationally.

"Yes," I say, just as conversationally.

"I hear there are some nice beaches here."

"Hmmm," I respond.

This is what we've resorted to over the past hour. Pointless small talk. Meaningless chatter. Safe topics that follow Ali and Nico's Rules of the Road.

"Maybe we should check it out?"

"What?" I ask, before realizing it's too late. He's already pulled over. He's already killed the ignition.

He points just up ahead to a sandy cement road leading to the water. "The beach?" he says, as though it's obvious. "I could use a little change of scenery."

I can't decide whether that comment is meant to be an insult. "Change of scenery" meaning he's tired of looking at the road? Or tired of looking at me? Maybe a little of both.

"Nico, no," I protest. "We don't have time. I promised Tom Lancaster we'd be in Crescent City by nine. It'[s] already almost five and we still have four hours of drivi[ng] ahead of us."

But Nico is already out of the car. "Relax," he[ ... ] clearly annoyed. "We'll just take a few minutes to s[ ... ] our legs."

The car door slams on the argument that's ha[ ... ] my lips. With a sigh, I grab my backpack fron[ ... ] seat, open the passenger door, and get out. I tr[ ... ] Nico down the path to the beach, hoping he'[ ... ] glimpse of the water and then turn around[ ... ]

I don't want to be here.

I want to be *past* here.

I want to keep driving.

I find Nico standing at the edge o[ ... ]

he's afraid to step into it, afraid of sinking straight through to the other side of the world. His gaze is fixed on the water.

"It's been a long time since I've been to the beach," he says absentmindedly.

"Me too."

"My dad used to take me when I was little."

Startled, I turn and look at him. Nico barely ever talked about his parents. And when I asked, he would give me short, impersonal answers that sounded like they were taken straight out of a preapproved script.

I swallow, wondering if I should ask questions, push for more information, but before I can think of anything to say, Nico starts walking, trudging through the sand toward the foamy white surf of the ocean. For a moment, it doesn't look like he has any intention of stopping. As though he plans to walk straight into the sea and disappear.

But he halts just short of the water's edge and sits down, pulling his knees to his chest. His shoulders are stiff. His back is hunched a little.

He looks as restless and agitated as the waves.

I slowly walk toward him, drop my backpack into e sand, and sit down a few inches away, mirroring his sition.

He keeps his gaze trained out to sea. "Sorry. I know re anxious to get back on the road. I just really wanted e the water."

ite my lip, a million questions dancing through my

mind. Questions I know I won't get answers to. Because Nico doesn't answer questions. At least not real ones.

"That's okay," I reply. "It's . . ." I turn and look at the ocean, searching for the right word to describe it. But there is no right word. So I choose the worst word. ". . . nice."

I expect Nico to make fun of me. To flash me that teasing smile and tell me I'm not giving the ocean its due credit. But he doesn't. Actually, he doesn't say anything at all.

"The car was my father's." I finally answer the question he posed way back on Route 128.

I look at him, but he keeps his eyes on the ocean. As though he's giving me space. Privacy. A screen in a church confessional. Obviously Nico knows about Jackson. Well, he knows *some*. I told him just enough for him to recognize that it's not a subject I like to talk about. And after that, he never pressed. He never pushed me to divulge more. He respected my secrets. Now, I wonder if he only did that because he was keeping his own. And if he pried, that would give me the freedom to pry back.

"He left it for me before he died," I continue.

Nico flinches, stealing a glance at me before remembering the invisible privacy screen and quickly turning back to the water. "I . . . didn't know he—"

"No one knew. I mean, I'm sure *he* had people who knew. But Mom and I didn't even know he was sick."

Nico raises his eyebrows, and I answer the question before he has a chance to voice it. "Liver cancer. The hospital called afterward." I unzip my backpack and pull out the envelope, keeping Jackson's handwriting facing away so that Nico can't see my real name scribbled on the front. "This envelope arrived two weeks later. It has the title to the car in it. It was his most prized possession."

I wait for Nico to start asking questions.

*Why are you really selling it?*

*Is this the best idea?*

*What are you hiding from me, Ali?*

But he doesn't ask any of those questions. Because Nico has never done anything I've ever expected. It was always one of the things I loved about him. Until it was the thing I *couldn't* love about him.

Instead he asks in a taut, strangled voice, "Do you want me to say I'm sorry?"

I blink and look at him, but he still won't meet my eye. "What?"

"That's what you do when someone dies. You say, 'I'm sorry for your loss.' But I'm not sure if that applies to you. From the way you talked about him, I figured it might not, so I thought I'd ask."

I stare down at the envelope still clasped in my hands and run my fingertip over the remnants of thick clear tape that once held the whole thing together. That kept the contents locked safely inside. It's funny how you can't unopen an envelope. Can't unopen a glove box. Can't put secrets back in once they're out.

"You can say I'm sorry," I tell him quietly.

Nico pulls his eyes from the ocean long enough to look between me and the envelope. He blinks. Once, twice, three times. As though he's trying to dispel some unwelcome thing from his eyes.

"I'm sorry, Ali."

Then, we both fall silent. We just sit there and watch the violent waves.

Rolling. Crashing. Dragging dead things out to sea.

When I was eight years old, Jackson picked me up from school and told me we were going on a special trip. As I buckled my seat belt in the back seat of the Firebird (my mother never allowed me to ride in the front), I asked excitedly if Mommy was coming on this special trip with us, and Jackson's expression shifted. He said no, Mommy wouldn't like this particular trip. And then he made me promise never to tell Mommy that we had gone.

I remember how those words sunk into my bones, gnawed at them, made me feel nauseous. Jackson had been asking me to keep more and more secrets from my mom, and even though I always agreed, each one seemed to compact upon the growing pile of lies that was already living in our house—lies that I seemed to be a part of. Each one felt heavier than the last. Like another piece balanced precariously on top of a Jenga tower, another likely chance that this could all topple over and bury us.

Jackson wouldn't tell me where we were going or why. For the entire hour-and-forty-five-minute drive, I kept asking him to give me hints. He kept flashing me that mischievous smile in the rearview mirror and saying obscure things that made absolutely no sense, like "Solace waits and love negotiates." Or "Run away, go away, hide away, sneak away."

I told him grumpily that he was terrible at giving hints.

He just winked at me.

I don't know what it was about Jackson's wink, but it always made the world feel like a better place. There was this twinkle in his eye. It was like a lighthouse in a stormy sea. There! There it is! See that? We're safe. Everything is going to be okay.

We arrived in Fort Bragg, at a place called the Black Bear Saloon. After we were seated with menus, he told me this was a special occasion and I could order anything I wanted. At eight years old, I was too young to be suspicious. I was too young to understand what bribery was. Or that the silence of a child could be bought.

Even so, I tested his promise. I ordered french fries and chocolate silk pie for dinner, watching him out of the corner of my eye to see if he balked at this, the way I knew my mother would.

He didn't. He just laughed and said to the waitress, "You heard the boss. French fries and chocolate silk pie."

She nodded and made it official on her little pad of paper.

"And for you?" she asked Jackson.

Jackson caught her eye as he handed her the menu. "What's your name?"

She smiled. "Wendy."

"I'll have a cheeseburger, inside out, with extra pickles and a draft beer." He paused and added in a sweet voice. *"Wendy."* Then he winked, and in a less than a millisecond, that wink lost a tiny drop of its superpower.

By the time we finished our meal, the place was already filled with people. I'd barely noticed them trickle in. But when I looked up from my empty plate of pie, I noticed how crowded the restaurant had gotten. And most people weren't sitting at a table, like us. They were standing around, all facing the same direction as though waiting for something to start.

"What's going on?" I asked Jackson.

He took a sip from his third beer and said, "What's going on is that you're about to experience history in the making."

I frowned at him in confusion, wondering if this was another one of his unhelpful cryptic clues.

He laughed and reached out to ruffle my curls. "The greatest group of people to ever play instruments together is playing here tonight for the first time in nine years!"

He said this like it was supposed to impress me, but I wasn't impressed. I was still confused.

"My favorite band of all time is reuniting tonight," he explained. "And *you* get to witness it. People are going to talk about this day for decades to come. This is going to go down in the music hall of fame."

Then, when he could see my enthusiasm was still not up to the same level as his, he added, "You're named after one of their songs, you know."

My brain scrambled to catch up. To line up all the pieces so that they made sense.

This is what the special trip was?

Jackson had dragged me all the way up to Fort Bragg to see some old band play?

"Why can't Mommy know about it?" I asked.

The smile on Jackson's face instantly vanished, as if I'd just told him that one of the band members had fallen ill backstage and the concert was off. He leaned in close, his eyes boring into mine. "Because your mom doesn't understand how much this band means to me. How much I *need* this right now."

The confusion dug itself deeper into my mind. "Why not?"

Jackson scoffed and downed the last of his beer. "Beats me, kiddo."

I could tell his energy had shifted, and I immediately felt guilty. I'd said the wrong thing. I'd popped a hole in his seemingly impenetrable balloon.

"So, that's what all of these people are here for?" I asked, nodding to the growing crowd that seemed to be closing in on us from all sides.

"That's right," Jackson said, his excitement rebounding. He spread his arms out wide. "These are my people! These people *get* it!" Then he shouted to the entire restaurant, as though they'd all been friends for years, "Fear Epidemic rules!"

This sent the crowd into a tizzy. People cheered and whooped and hollered. Then Jackson stood up in his chair and started singing at the top of his lungs. *"Run away, go away, hide away, sneak away!"*

Everyone in the room started to sing along, not missing a single lyric or beat. *"There's got to be a better way to face each day!"*

Everyone but me, that is.

I was the only one still sitting, the only one not singing. And yet, I didn't feel like the outcast. I felt like the only sane person in the room. And as I glanced up at Jackson, standing on the chair, performing to the crowd like a wolf performing to a full moon, I realized I'd never seen my father look crazier.

I run my fingertips through the rough wet sand beneath my feet, noticing for the first time that it's peppered with tiny colorful pebbles, some of them so small, you can't even distinguish their deep-green and sapphire-blue hues unless you squint.

A wave crashes a few feet out, and the lingering tide creeps up to the toes of my shoes. It comes and goes in less than a few seconds. But this time, instead of taking everything with it, it leaves something behind. Like a gift. An offering.

It's a larger pebble, approximately the diameter of a quarter, and the color is a deep amber, like maple syrup. The real kind. Mom brought home a tiny bottle once from one of her fancy catering jobs.

I reach forward to pick it up, quickly realizing that it's not a stone at all, but a piece of sea glass. All smooth edges and salt-frosted sides.

"Ali," Nico says beside me, oblivious to my find. It's the first time that we've spoken since I told him about Jackson. "I've been thinking about the car."

I scoop the sea glass into my palm. "What about it?"

He leans back on his elbows, like he's sunbathing. "I don't think you should sell it."

I roll my eyes. We're seriously going through *this* again?

"I have to sell it. End of story, okay?"

But it's clearly *not* "end of story." Not for Nico, anyway. "But it's a relic. A piece of history. Even if you had a bad relationship with your dad—"

"No relationship," I correct him. "I had *no* relationship with my dad."

"Even so," Nico goes on, undeterred. "You still shouldn't just throw it away because you don't like what it stands for. It's too valuable."

"It's not valuable to *me*," I snap. I don't like the direction this conversation is heading. It feels too personal.

7.  No psychoanalyzing each other.

"But that's the thing," Nico argues. "It *could* be valuable to you. I just don't think you should make this decision so rashly. I'm afraid you might regret it one day."

"I thank you kindly for your concern," I say bitterly, "but I think maybe you should worry about your *own* regrets."

I know it stings. It's supposed to sting. It's supposed to feel like salt water in a wound because that's how every single second with him for the past two hours has felt for me. A constant reminder of the gash that's been left open. That tries to heal but can't because he's everywhere. In the computer lab, in the parking lot, in the car next to me.

"Ali," he says, an edge to his voice. Like a warning. For a second I think he's actually going to do it. He's going to bring it up. He's going to address head-on the very thing we've been dancing around for the past month.

But he doesn't.

Instead, in a tight voice he says, "I just think maybe you shouldn't be so quick to get rid of it."

I clench my fist around the sea glass in my palm. I wait for it to dig into my skin, to cut my flesh. But it doesn't. The edges are too soft. The ocean has been too merciless against it for too long. It's lost all of its sharpness. All of its bite. Everything that makes broken glass dangerous has been stripped away, until it's just this sad, defenseless little stone.

I open my palm and peer down at it, quietly seething.

---

**Your *ex-boyfriend* won't stop prying into your personal life. What do you do?**

**A** *Stand up and walk away. You're tired of fighting.*

**B** *Scream at him until he finally stops asking questions.*

**C** *Tell him the truth. Maybe that will shut him up.*

"I have to sell the car. Otherwise, the bank is going to take away our house."

I drop the truth like a bomb. It works. Nico visibly flinches, clearly not expecting the situation to be this complicated. I hope that puts an end to this topic, but in case it doesn't, I add, "Besides, some things just aren't worth keeping around."

Nico's surprise instantly flashes to anger. He opens his mouth to say something but is cut off by a tongue. Literally. A long pink tongue whips out and licks him across the cheek.

"What the . . . ?"

We both turn to see a dog panting behind us. He's long, with wiry white-and-brown fur and the cutest, shortest little legs. He glances worriedly between Nico and me, as if to say, *Don't fight. It's stressing me out.*

At the sight of him, all of my previous frustration melts into the sea air. "Well, hello there. Where did you come from?"

I grab on to the green leash that the dog is dragging behind him.

"He's cute," Nico says, patting the dog's head. "Is he a Newfoundland?"

I roll my eyes. "You think every dog is a Newfoundland."

"Only because I've never actually seen one in person. I'm starting to wonder if they really exist."

"This," I say authoritatively, scratching the dog under the chin, "is a Pembroke Welsh corgi."

Nico gives the dog an apologetic look. "Yikes. That's a mouthful. Sorry about that."

The dog licks his face again.

"They're called corgis for short. And they're very affectionate and smart."

The dog dutifully sits, as though to prove my point. Nico and I both laugh. It's the first time we've actually laughed. At the same thing. In more than a month.

We used to laugh all the time. When Nico and I were together, everything was funny to us. Then the comet came and shifted the stars, and after that, nothing was funny anymore.

"We should keep him," Nico says.

I scoff. "We can't keep him. He clearly belongs to someone."

"I'll hide him under my sweatshirt. No one will notice."

I chuckle before realizing I've just broken another Rule of the Road. We both have.

8.   No use of the word "we."

My hand brushes up against a dog tag hidden beneath the corgi's rough, sand-matted fur. "Let's see, what's your name?"

"His name's Gizmo, and thank you so much for finding him." I glance up into the sun to see a middle-aged man approaching us, looking winded. He has a dark, scraggly beard, ripped jeans, and a T-shirt that reads HUG DEALER.

"We didn't find him," Nico tells the man. "He found us."

The man laughs as if this is an inside joke between him and the dog. "Yeah, he's good at that."

I hand the leash over to Gizmo's owner, and as he bends down to take it, his gaze falls to the sand next to me. "Wow. That's a good one. Did you find that?"

"Excuse me?"

The man nods toward the amber-colored sea glass that I'd evidently dropped when Gizmo showed up. "I haven't seen one that big in a while," he says.

"Oh, yeah. It just washed up in front of me."

"Nice. You used to be able to find big ones out here all the time, but then the tourists started coming and picked the place clean. They should change the name, right? Can't really call it Glass Beach anymore, can they?"

"This place is called Glass Beach?" I ask.

He sighs and looks up at a craggy cliff to our left. "Yup. Used to be a dump site. From 1949 to 1967."

"A dump site?" Nico repeats, sounding shocked. "Like, for trash?"

"Oh yeah," the man says emphatically. "Residents of this area had been dumping their trash in the water at various locations up the coast since 1906."

"That's horrible." I peer at the ocean, trying to imagine anyone ever staring out at that beautiful blue water and thinking, *Looks like a good trash can to me.*

"Yeah, pretty horrible, all right," the man says. A seagull lands a few feet away, and I watch the man's hand instinctively tighten around Gizmo's leash. A split second later, Gizmo lunges at the bird with a gleeful bark. "The ocean pounded most of the trash into oblivion, but not the glass. It's been spitting that back out ever since. Smoothed into pretty little pieces like the one you got there. Used to be you couldn't even see the sand underneath with all that glass. Now there's barely any left. People take it home as souvenirs." He nods again at the amber pebble in front of me.

I scoop up the glass from the sand and examine its unusual shape, trying to figure out what it resembles. A teardrop? A giant tooth? A mountain? "So this little thing was once a piece of trash from the fifties?"

Gizmo continues to strain against his leash to get to the seagull. "Fifties or sixties, most likely."

I flip the piece of glass over in my palm, remarking on how beautiful it is now. Smooth and polished. Like a little amber-colored gemstone.

"One man's trash is another man's treasure," Nico says, plucking the thought right out of my mind.

"That's sort of cool," I muse quietly. "Even if it's also sort of awful."

The man guffaws at that. "That's certainly the rub, isn't it?" I peer up at him and notice he's turned slightly away from us and is now gazing into the water. It has that effect on people. It sort of pulls you in. Mesmerizes you. Like a lullaby. "The ocean forgives," he says absently, like he's speaking more to himself than to us. "Even when we can't."

I glance at Nico to find he's already looking at me. For how long, I couldn't say. But something in his eyes tells me it's been a while. We both immediately look away. Him to the water, me to the sea glass in my hand.

I swallow. "Thanks for the history lesson," I tell the man.

He smiles. "Anytime."

"Can I keep this?" I ask him, proffering forward my treasure.

"Of course," he says. "Mark it down as part of the cleanup effort."

I laugh. "Thanks."

The man gives me a salute before turning and taking off down the beach, pulling a reluctant Gizmo behind him.

At eight years old, I didn't know what "too drunk to drive" meant. I just knew that Jackson was acting like a lunatic. Like someone I had never met before and never wanted to meet again.

After the Fear Epidemic show at the Black Bear Saloon was finished, the crowd spilled out onto the sidewalk, still singing and shouting and high on the music that adhered them all together.

"Did you love it?" Jackson asked me. He spoke too loudly for how close I was standing. "Did you love them as much as I love them?"

I nodded because I was afraid if I said no, he would somehow make me go back inside and listen to that angry noise all over again.

"I made those guys, you know?" He was mumbling

now, slurring words together until they barely even sounded like words. "Fear Epidemic is famous because of me. I got them a gig right here in Fort Bragg. Back when they were nobodies. And after that, they skyrocketed." He shot his hand into the air, simulating a rocket ship bound for the stars. Then he fell very quiet, his head bowed like he was either praying or falling asleep. "It's the only thing I've ever really been proud of."

He stood there for a long time, and I studied him, trying to make sense of this strange statement that somehow seemed more cohesive and significant than anything else that had tumbled out of his mouth that night. But before I could dissect its meaning, a voice broke into my thoughts.

"He's too drunk to drive."

I looked up to see the waitress who had brought me my chocolate silk pie earlier. Wendy. She was talking directly to me, a serious expression on her face. I remember thinking it was a grown-up type of expression. And in that moment, I didn't feel eight years old anymore. I felt like I had aged twenty years in the blink of an eye.

"Do you have someone you can call to come get you guys?" she asked.

I nodded, and the woman pulled a cell phone out of her apron and handed it to me. I dialed the number for the house. Mom picked up, and I told her where we were and that Jackson was acting strange. She warned me not to get in the car with him. She would be there soon.

Wendy invited us back inside and fed my father water and coffee for the next few hours until my mom showed up. Rosie dropped her off so that Mom could drive the Firebird home.

She yelled at Jackson the whole way back to Russellville. He was the only person she ever raised her voice to. He just seemed to bring out the worst in her. I sat in the back seat trying to drown out the sound.

"*. . . eight years old, Jackson! EIGHT YEARS OLD!*"

"*. . . a grunge rock concert? Seriously?*"

"*. . . that stupid band again . . .*"

I remember the one-sided conversation in bits and pieces. But what I remember the most is the look Jackson flashed me as he turned around in the passenger seat and our eyes met in the darkened car.

"*Your mom doesn't understand how much this band means to me. How much I need this right now.*"

I offered him a weak smile. Not because I was taking his side. Or because I wasn't mad at him for dragging me into this. I was.

But because I truly did hope that whatever it was he needed from that night, he got.

I stand up and brush sand from the back of my pants. "We should go," I tell Nico. "We need to get back on the road if we're going to get to Crescent City by nine."

Even though this is technically true, mostly I'm just anxious to get out of this town. It feels too much like Jackson's town. I know he lived here at some point before he died. He told us that when he showed up on my sixteenth birthday. But more than that, I can't stop thinking about that night he brought me here.

I hear the soundtrack of his choices echoing off every surface, like too-loud music in a too-small club.

> *Run away, go away*
> *Hide away, sneak away*
> *There's got to be*
> *An easier way*
> *To face each day*

Jackson took that easier way. He always took the easier way. He never stuck around for the hard stuff—the bills, the collection notices, the foreclosure.

And now all that's left of him is that car, and I can't bear for it to be in my life for a second longer than it has to.

Nico stands but doesn't take his eyes off the water. It looks like he's scanning the coastline for something. Something important. And for a moment, I find myself wondering about *his* ghosts. Does Nico have a haunting soundtrack that follows *him* around, reminding him of the past? Does he have a Jackson in his rearview mirror that he's anxious to drive away from?

But when he finally tears his gaze from the water, I don't see someone haunted by the past. I see someone excited about the future. Nico's eyes are all lit up, like he's just had the idea of the century. "What if you didn't *have* to sell the car?"

"Huh?"

*All this time he's still been thinking about the stupid car?*

"What if I could get you the money another way?"

Heat floods my cheeks as splinters of shattered memories flash through my mind.

Glove boxes and unanswered phones and mud caked on the bottom of my shoes.

*Why can't he just let this go?*

"How much do you need?" he presses.

"Twenty-five thousand dollars. By next Friday." I say it like a challenge. Like a trump card. *Let's see you come up with that.*

I hope this is enough to shut him up. I don't know where he is going with this conversation, but I don't like it. It feels slippery and dangerous. Like a water balloon filled with gasoline, being tossed back and forth over an open flame.

But Nico doesn't even flinch. "I think I can get you that."

"What?" I sputter, unable to believe what I'm hearing.

"If I can get you twenty-five thousand dollars by next Friday, would you consider keeping the car?"

For a moment, I'm too flabbergasted to even speak. I just stand there gaping at him. "You're talking nonsense right now. You can't just *get* twenty-five thousand dollars."

"But if I *could*," Nico challenges, "would you think about keeping the car?"

I roll my eyes. "I don't get it. Why do you even care? Why would you even want to help me?"

"I like the car," he says defensively, but there's a flicker in his eyes that tells me he's lying.

*Always lying.*

"Well, forget it. I don't want to get involved in whatever shady illegal money scheme you've got going on."

Nico pauses, looking contemplative. "Wait, is what you think—?" He stops himself, thankfully choosing not to go there. "Trust me, it's nothing shady or illegal. It's perfectly legit."

Trust him?

Is he serious?

I did that already. I fell for that trap. And look where it got me.

I try to walk around him, but he holds out his hand. "Just hear me out. If we do it right, it should take less than a week to get the money."

I sigh. "So, you want me to be your gigolo and hire you out to the Desperate Housewives of Fort Bragg?"

He scoffs. "I'm being dead serious."

I cross my arms. "Okay, Mr. Dead Serious. How do you propose to make twenty-five thousand dollars in a week?" And then I quickly add, *"Legally."*

He smiles. "We trade up."

"Trade up?"

"Yeah," he says, as though it's obvious. "You can take the smallest, cheapest item in the world—like, say, a pen or a Q-tip or a battery—and you can pretty much exchange it for anything you want. A car, a motorcycle, a house. Something worth twenty-five thousand dollars."

I give him another dubious look. "Who is this person stupid enough to trade a Q-tip for a house?"

"Not *one* person," Nico says. "Several people. Several trades. You'd be surprised what people are eager to get rid of. Valuable stuff. But they won't just give it to you for free. They want to feel like they're getting something in exchange."

I squint, trying to make sense of what he's saying. "But if you're just trading a bunch of things of the exact same value, how do you trade up to something worth twenty-five thousand dollars?"

"See, that's the catch. You don't trade things for the same value. At least not the same *monetary* value. You always trade for something bigger and worth more money."

"Again, who would do that? Who would trade a Q-tip for something worth more than a Q-tip?"

"Someone who really needs a Q-tip," Nico says.

I let out a bitter laugh. "You're out of your mind."

"No, I swear it works," Nico insists. "You see, it's all about supply and demand. If you can supply something someone demands, then the monetary value is irrelevant. The item just has to have value to *them*. And you'd be surprised what people value. And what people are willing to throw away."

I shake my head and continue toward the parking lot. But Nico stops me. "Wait. Watch." He glances up and down the beach, his eyes zeroing in on something.

I turn to see he's looking at a woman with thick, wavy hair standing by the edge of the water. Her face is hidden behind a professional-looking camera with the longest lens I've ever seen. It's pointed out to sea, at something beyond the reach of my simple naked eye.

Every few seconds, she lowers the camera to brush away her wild straw-colored hair, which is whipping furiously in the wind, flying into her face and across the lens. Nico turns to me and grins. "Bingo."

And then suddenly his hand is on mine, hovering at the edge of my sweatshirt sleeve, sending a tingle of fireworks up my arm. But Nico seems oblivious to the chemical reaction. He's too busy pushing up my sleeve to reveal the rubber band I always keep secured around my wrist. It's a necessity for anyone with curly hair. You never know when your hair is going to stop behaving and need to be put in ponytail jail.

Nico's fingertips dance around the edge of the rubber band. The hair on my arm stands up, and I pray he doesn't push my sleeve even further up and expose me. "May I?" he asks.

I swallow. I don't even know what he's asking, but I feel my head fall into a nod. The answer has always been yes to Nico.

A one-hundred-percent, nonnegotiable, unambiguous yes.

He gently slips the rubber band from my wrist, and for just a moment, I allow my eyes to close, I allow my skin to feel, I allow my body to yearn. Then the moment is over, and I flutter my eyes open again. I force myself to look at him, to remember, to feel a *different* kind of sensation.

Betrayal.

Regret.

Anger.

Nico starts moving toward the woman. "Come on. I'll show you how this works."

I reluctantly follow after him, sighing at the pointlessness of all this. There's no way he can trade a rubber band for twenty-five thousand dollars. The boy is delusional.

Nico taps the woman on the shoulder, and she lowers the camera to look at him, one hand still vainly attempting to hold back her blowing hair.

Nico holds up the rubber band. "It looks like you might need this."

The woman stares at Nico with a guarded expression, clearly unsure what to make of this random hair-saving boy on the beach. "Um . . ."

"Maybe I can trade you something for it," Nico prompts.

The woman's confusion builds. "Excuse me?"

I sigh and grab Nico by the shirtsleeve. "C'mon. Let's just go." I flash the woman an apologetic look. "I'm so sorry about him. He's trying to prove some inane theory that just because you happen to *need* this rubber band right now, you'll somehow be willing to trade us something of more value for it."

The woman glances between me and Nico, as though trying to figure out if we're a team of con artists she needs to be wary of. Then, suddenly, her expression softens, and her eyes fill with comprehension. "Oh, is this like a social experiment or something?"

Nico nods. "Sort of."

The woman seems to like that answer. "Okay. Cool. Let me see what I have. I *do* need that rubber band."

She digs her hand into the oversize bag hanging from her shoulder and rifles around for a few seconds. "Oh!" she exclaims. "Here. Take this. I found it in a box of junk that my ex-husband left behind at our house. Sorry, correction, as of last week, it's *my* house. I was going to take it to one of those electronic recycling places, but you can have it."

Then I watch as the woman pulls out the oldest cell phone I've ever seen in real life. It's about the size of a deck of cards and has a tiny black-and-white screen, a keypad, and a short, stubby antenna sticking out from the top.

Nico's eyes light up when he sees it. Although I can't imagine why. The thing is a relic. I doubt it even plays music. "Cool! We'll take it!" he exclaims, handing over the rubber band in exchange for the phone. "Thanks."

"Thank *you*," the woman says, lowering her camera so that it hangs from the strap around her neck. She immediately goes to work wrangling her hair into a compact bun and securing it with the rubber band. "Ah. So much better. My hair has been bugging me all day."

With her hair dealt with, the woman picks up her camera again and holds it up to her eye. "Good luck with your social experiment." Then she starts walking down the beach, snapping photos of the sea.

Nico is standing there with the most triumphant smile I've ever seen on his face. He holds up the ancient cell phone. "See?"

I scoff. "That doesn't prove anything! That thing is

**115** →

a piece of junk. You heard her say so yourself. She was going to recycle it. It's worthless."

"It's worthless to *her*," he corrects.

"And to me."

"But not to someone else."

"Who on earth would want a phone that old?"

Nico shrugs. "I don't know. A phone repairman who needs it for spare parts. A museum curator putting together an exhibit on the history of cell phones. A teacher teaching her students about communications. A—"

"Okay, okay," I say, just to shut him up. "One man's trash is another man's treasure. I get it."

His grin widens. "Exactly."

"So, what now?" I ask skeptically. "We comb the beach searching for a museum curator desperately in need of an old cell phone?"

Nico guffaws at this. "Don't be ridiculous."

"*I'm* the one being ridiculous?"

He deposits the antique cell phone in the pocket of his jeans and pulls out his own phone, shaking it tauntingly at me. "Now, we take it to the next level."

"And what exactly is the next level?" I ask, slightly afraid of what his answer will be.

He smiles. "Craigslist."

Sometimes I think that band and that car were the only things Jackson ever really had. That Nolan Cook, Slate Miller, Chris McCaden, and Adam French were his only friends. And that's why, when they got back together, when they announced their nationwide tour a month after that night we went to see them in Fort Bragg, Jackson had no choice but to go with them. He had no choice but to leave.

Which, of course, is a load of crap.

There's always a choice.

And he chose them.

I remember Mom trying to explain it to me. Trying to define what a "roadie" even was. I had a hard time understanding it.

No, he's not actually *in* the band.

No, he doesn't play any instrument or sing any songs.

No, your father is not a rock star.

He helps the band transport equipment and set up for shows.

This sounded infinitely less glamorous and even more of a sting.

He left all of this—Russellville, the Frosty Frog, Mom, and me—to carry around drum sets?

But according to Mom, Jackson had somehow gotten it into his head that *he* had helped in their rise to fame. Just as he had claimed when he was ranting drunk on the sidewalk outside of the Black Bear Saloon.

This gave Jackson a sense of ownership over the band. Like he was an official part of their success. Then, I think he was just so desperate to be a part of *any* success, he clung on to what he could.

Fear Epidemic's debut album was called *Anarchy in a*

*Cup,* but they never released a follow-up. They broke up a little more than two years later, one month before I was born. Jackson named me after his favorite song from the album as some kind of mourning tribute.

Then, nine years later, they magically decided to reunite and release a new album—*Salvage Lot*—and by my ninth birthday, Jackson was gone. He took a single bag of clothes and, of course, his Firebird, and left behind a Post-it note stuck to the fridge:

*I'm sorry. I have to do this.*

Mom didn't cry. It was almost as though, after that night she came to pick us up in Fort Bragg, she knew it was coming. Maybe even expected it, maybe even *hoped* for it.

For the first year Jackson was gone, I kept track of the band. Their new album hovered on the bottom of the Billboard charts for a few weeks and then fell off completely. They played small venues in large cities. They did short interviews on niche radio stations.

*Salvage Lot* clearly didn't do what the title of the album implied they'd hoped it would do. It didn't bring Fear Epidemic back from the dead.

I watched their website diligently to see where they were each day, what they were doing, what new pictures had been posted. I googled the name of each venue and stared at the Google Earth images of the street and surrounding areas, trying to imagine Jackson on that street, in those venues. I would scour fan pictures, searching for signs of him in the background.

I even tried to listen to their music. I wanted to understand what was so special about it. What was so enticing that it would pull a man away from his family. But I could never get through more than two songs. Just like that night in the garage, when Jackson installed the cassette player, and that night in the Black Bear Saloon, it was too loud for me. Too aggressive. Too angry.

I remember lying in bed, trying to listen to "Numb," their latest single. I remember grimacing at its harsh vocals and embittered lyrics. And I remember thinking, *What on earth do you have to be so angry about? You're the one who got my dad.*

# 5:19 P.M.

## FORT BRAGG, CA

INVENTORY: 1968 FIREBIRD 400 CONVERTIBLE (1),
CASH ($769.35), SEA GLASS (1 PIECE),
ANCIENT CELL PHONE (1)

"So how giant *are* the burgers here?" Nico asks the cashier as we step up to the counter of Jenny's Giant Burger, a small burger shack just up California 1 from Glass Beach. It didn't look like much from the road—a dinky little building in the middle of a giant parking lot—and I really didn't want to stop since we're already running late as it is. But Nico convinced me that we need to eat. I'm just grateful he didn't try to stop at the Black Bear Saloon. I definitely wouldn't have agreed to go back there.

"They're pretty big," the cashier assures Nico.

"Okay," Nico says, as though her answer has made his decision, and not our complete starvation. He squints at the menu. "I'll take a Giant double cheeseburger with fries and a Pepsi." He turns to me.

I already know what I want. It's the same thing I

order at every burger place. "Cheeseburger with the bun inside out."

I wait for the cashier to question my request. They always do. And I always have a pre-scripted explanation ready: sesame-seed side down, flat side up, grilled, like a patty melt.

But she doesn't question me. She doesn't even blink. She just taps into her cash register and looks back up at me for the rest.

"And fries and a lemonade, please."

"Nineteen twenty-seven," the cashier announces.

Nico goes to pull out his wallet, but I stop him. "Nuh-uh. Remember? You're driving. I'm paying."

He lowers his hand. "I'm not sure I'm comfortable with this arrangement."

"Too bad," I say, reaching into my backpack and pulling another twenty from the freezer bag. I hand it to the cashier. She gives me my change, and I dump it into the tip cup on the counter.

"Beer money!" the cashier yells to the other restaurant employees, and they all shout "Thank you!" in return.

Cashier Girl gives us a little plastic tent with a number on it, and we find an empty booth.

"So, *why* are you paying for everything again?" Nico asks, sliding into one of the benches.

"Because I can't be sure where *your* money came from," I murmur under my breath.

Nico's gaze cuts to me, and for a long moment, he just studies me, like's he unsure if he heard me correctly.

He heard me.

And he looks like he's going to fire something equally hurtful right back at me, but instead he clears his throat and says, "So, you never told me where your affinity for inside-out burgers comes from."

Back to the safe zone. Back to the meaningless small talk. Although there's a sharp edge to his voice that borders on mockery.

"You never asked," I reply just as sharply.

"I'm asking now."

I shrug. "I don't know. I've just always ordered them that way. For as long as I can remember."

"Were you, like, obsessed with inside-out things as a kid? Like some kind of fight-back against normalcy? Did you wear all of your clothes inside out? Read books backward? Sleep with your feet on the pillow?"

I snort. "No. I just think it makes the burger taste different, that's all."

"Hmm," Nico says, drumming his fingers against the table.

And just like that, we've exhausted this safety topic.

I exhale loudly and glance around the restaurant. That same uncomfortable silence settles back between us. It's like a dark, shadowy pit that follows us around, always right behind us. No matter how many times we seem to take a step forward, if we ever stumble back, even an inch, it's ready and waiting there to swallow us whole.

My fingers itch to pull out my phone and go straight to my favorite personality quiz website. Just so I have something to do. But then I remember I have no data left on my plan. So I guess I'm stuck here in the shadowy pit.

Nico must feel it too, because he reaches into his pocket and pulls out his own phone and the ancient clunker cell phone. He arranges the old phone on the table at a slight angle and snaps a photo of it.

"What are you doing?" I ask.

"Drafting our Craigslist post."

"*Your*," I correct him. "It's your Craigslist post. Not ours. I want nothing to do with this ridiculous plan."

"Just you wait," he says without looking up. "You'll want *everything* to do with it when we start getting into some serious trades."

He taps on his phone screen, narrating his path as he goes. "Craigslist dot com. New posting. Category: Barter. Posting title . . ." He pauses, studying the old phone on the table before resuming his typing. "Nokia cell phone." He hastily jabs at the backspace button. "One *rare antique* cell phone." He looks up at me. "It's all about the way you spin it."

I roll my eyes. I don't like this. It sounds way too much like something Jackson would do. Trying to find too-easy solutions to problems that actually require real work. "You can't be serious about this."

"Oh, I am. I'm going to prove to you that you don't have to sell the car. You can keep it *and* get the money you need."

"There's no way you're going to be able to turn a rubber band into twenty-five thousand dollars!"

"Challenge accepted," he says with a smug grin.

I fight back a groan. I realize I'm being extra cranky right now because of the hunger—I haven't eaten since lunch—but I don't care. Nico is being his typical spontaneous self, and I don't have time for his spontaneous whims right now. I have to get that Firebird to Tom Lancaster in Crescent City by tonight, and we're already way behind schedule.

"But if we don't sell the car, how am I going to pay you the thousand dollars I promised you?"

Nico dismisses this like it's a technicality. "I'll take my cut from whatever we end up making on the trades. Don't worry about me." He stops typing and taps his finger thoughtfully against his chin. "We need an angle. A story."

My head is starting to throb as my blood sugar continues to drop. I press my fingertips into my temples.

"People like a story," Nico explains, even though I *so* didn't ask. "They like to feel like they're *part* of something. We need something to grab people's attention."

I squeeze my head and close my eyes. "Since when are you a Craigslist expert?"

"I'm not," he says so hastily, so decisively, I startle and flutter my eyes back open. For a moment, I swear I see something flash across his face. A reaction of some kind. But it's gone so fast, I can almost convince myself I imagined it.

"But how do you know about all of this trading stuff?" I press. "Where did you even get the idea of being able to trade a rubber band for something worth twenty-five thousand dollars?"

I wait for the reaction again—a flinch, a flash—but he's

prepared this time. Guarded. His expression remains stoically neutral. "Everyone knows you can do that."

"I don't," I insist.

"I think I saw it in a documentary once."

It's a lie, and we both know it. But before I can press him further, a skinny guy in an apron and a name tag that reads SCOTT shows up with our burgers and sets them down in front of us. The smell of cooked meat and melted cheese is so heavenly, I nearly forget my own name. I lunge for the burger and take a huge bite, chewing so fast, I barely even taste it.

"Wow," Nico says, looking impressed. "These really are pretty giant."

Scott smiles. "You're not from around here, are you?"

I'm too busy stuffing my face with burger to answer. Thankfully Nico steps in. "No. Just passing through. We're sort of on a road trip together."

"It's better than it looks, you know?"

Nico glances down at his burger. "I don't know what you're talking about. This looks amazing."

"I mean the town," Scott says. "It's got some great history."

"Like what?" Nico asks, sounding genuinely curious.

"Well, the town itself is a historical landmark. And we've had lots of movies filmed here." He starts listing them out on his fingers. "*The Majestic* starring Jim Carrey, *Racing with the Moon* starring Sean Penn, *Overboard* starring Goldie Hawn and Kurt Russell."

At the name of this movie, I glance up and catch Nico's

eye. Our gazes are locked for only a split second, but it's enough for us to confirm that we both remember.

Lying in the bed of his truck, watching old eighties movies on his phone until the sun came up.

It was one of our favorite things to do. We called them our Epic Eighties Movie Marathons. Nico would bring a blanket and a pillow, and we'd drive out along Route 128 until the lights of the town faded and the night was ours.

With Nico, it was so easy to claim the night.

Like he had it permanently on hold, waiting for him.

"We're also the home to Glass Beach," Scott goes on, bringing me back to the restaurant. The booth. This highly unfavorable situation. "A major tourist attraction."

I smile politely up at Scott, marveling at how desperate he is to impress us with his facts about the town. He reminds me of an eager Border collie who's just herded all the sheep and is waiting for our approval.

"So you see," Scott goes on, "it might not look like much, but we got a lot going on here."

"Sounds like it," Nico says.

Having validated his town, I expect Scott to leave, but he doesn't. He keeps staring at me. "Are you sure you're not from around here?"

"No," I mumble, and take another huge bite.

"You look really familiar," Scott says. "Like I've seen you before." He drums his fingers against the plastic tray in his hands.

His scrutiny is starting to make me uncomfortable. I avert my gaze to the burger in my hand. He couldn't possibly remember me from when I came here at eight years old. Could he?

Suddenly, Scott bangs his hand down on the tray and points to a table in the far opposite corner of the restaurant. "Yes! Over there!"

Nico curiously follows the direction he's pointing and then looks expectantly back at me.

"I've seen your picture!" Scott says. "You're Jackson Collins's daughter!"

Everything inside of me freezes. My heart. My lungs. My blood. Even the chewed piece of giant burger making its way down my throat. I cough and lunge for my lemonade, taking a huge gulp.

Apparently Jackson lived here long enough to make an impression.

Which actually doesn't take very long.

Scott seems oblivious to my reaction. "He used to come in here all the time. He sat at that table." He glances down at my burger and laughs, like the world is one big joke and he's the only one who knows the punch line. "And he ordered his burgers just like that too!"

Nico smiles and sips his soda. "Well, I guess we figured out the mystery of where the inside-out burger comes from."

I shoot him a warning look, and the grin falls right off his face.

"Yeah," Scott goes on. "He showed me your picture a ton of times. Kept telling me how you were going to become a veterinarian."

"She is," Nico says with a pride that surprises me. It

sounds so different from the resentment that has laced all of our interactions up until this point. It sounds like the old Nico. The Proud Boyfriend Nico. "She got a full scholarship to UC Davis for undergrad. They have one of the best vet schools in the country."

"Yeah, well." I'm quick to interrupt. "Nothing is set in stone."

"What do you mean?" Nico asks, and I can feel his eyes drilling holes into my head.

I shrug. "I mean, you just never know what might happen. Plans change."

"But—" Nico starts to say. I give him a swift kick under the table and a look that says *Can we talk about this later?*

"That's awesome," Scott says. "Sounds like your dad had every reason to be proud of you."

I smile up at Scott, trying to figure out the polite way to convince him to leave. I don't want to sit around here reminiscing about Jackson. This is exactly why I wanted to get *out* of this town as quickly as possible. Because of course we'd run into someone who knew him. And of course that person would have fond memories of him. Everyone who ever met Jackson loved him. He was just that kind of guy you instantly fell in love with. His charisma and charm were contagious. He made you feel special. Made you feel funny, important, smart, beautiful, appreciated— whatever you were needing in that moment, Jackson was somehow able to convince you you had.

"It was really nice chatting with you," I say, hoping Scott will get the hint. But he doesn't. He just keeps staring at me in amazement, like he's seeing a celebrity, or the eighth wonder of the world, right here in this booth.

"So you're really Jackson's daughter, huh?"

I raise my eyebrows. "In the flesh."

"What was your name again?"

"Oh, sorry." I offer him my greasy hand to shake. "It's Ali."

But it's almost as though he doesn't even see my outstretched hand. He's too busy thinking hard about something. His eyebrows straining to meet in the center of his forehead. "No," he says absently. "That's not it. I remember Jackson telling me, and I thought, what a crazy name." He snaps his fingers like he's trying to jolt his memory awake.

Nico gaze cuts to me, immediately asking, *Wait, what did I miss?*

"Sorry," I rush to tell Scott, trying to interrupt his thought process. "You must have me confused with someone else. My name is Ali. Nothing crazy about that."

But Scott is still snapping his fingers. "No. I remember it had something to do with that old rock band. What was their name? Not Blind Melon. Not Nine Inch Nails. But you know, same sound."

My stomach clenches. If he gets the band name, he'll get the song. If he gets the song, he'll remember the name. I have to shut it all down.

"Thanks so much for the burgers. I'm sorry we can't chat. We're working on a very important project." I nod to Nico's phone, which is lying on the table, faceup, with the

Craigslist post draft still on the screen. "It's a Craigslist thing. Long story."

I don't care that I'm rambling. Or that I'm being completely rude. I can't let this guy stay here any longer. I'm starting to lose my appetite.

Thankfully, this time, he gets the hint and blinks like he's coming out of a trance. "Oh, right. Of course." He nods to Nico, then to me. "It was nice to meet you. I hope you and your boyfriend enjoy your road trip."

"Thank you," I say as politely as possible. I'm so desperate for him to go, I don't even bother correcting him about the boyfriend part.

Nico, however, clearly doesn't share my desperation. "Oh, we're not together."

I try to shoot Nico another glare, but he's not looking at me.

"I mean, we *used* to be together," Nico goes on. "But we're not anymore."

"That's cool, man," Scott says, sounding impressed. "I think it's great that you can be friends with your ex."

"Oh, we're not friends, either," Nico says, a buoyant quality to his voice. Now I know he's doing this to mess with me. "Ali just needed someone to drive her car. She's paying me a thousand dollars to drive it up the coast for her. Which is a much better way to earn money than being a pimp or a drug dealer, which she evidently *thinks* I am."

My mouth drops open. I can't *believe* what I'm hearing.

"Which, of course, I'm not," Nico continues breezily.

"But there's really no use in trying to convince her of anything once she's made her mind up. *Believe* me."

"Oh," Scott says, suddenly sounding extremely uncomfortable. "Well, I'm sorry about . . . all of that. I hope you guys have fun on your trip." Then he darts back to the kitchen like he's afraid we might start chasing after him.

"What the hell was that?" I whisper-yell as soon as Scott is out of earshot.

Nico stares at me, and for a moment, it feels like a challenge. His gaze is unwavering; his mouth is set in a straight line. As if he's daring me to do something. Although I haven't the slightest clue what it is. "It's true, isn't it? That's what all of those underhanded comments were about, the money? You think I'm involved in something shady?"

"Well, when someone refuses to *tell* you things, you have to make up your own explanation."

"And so you just automatically assume the worst possible explanation?" Nico fires back. The polite, guarded Nico has been banished from the table. And this other Nico, the one who I witnessed for the first time on the night of the comet, he's suddenly back. Unwilling to be caged in any longer. "What does that say about you, Ali?"

I can feel the fight rising in me. In both of us. The familiar anger billows inside of me like smoke. I close my eyes and push it down. Down, down, down.

*You're not together anymore.*

*There's no need to fight.*

*The fight is over.*

When I open my eyes again, Nico is taking angry bites

out of his burger, chewing like a wild beast devouring its recent kill.

"This was a bad idea," I say softly.

"What?" Nico asks, stuffing a fry into his already stuffed mouth.

"This!" I gesture to the restaurant, the booth, us. "You. Me. In a car together for five and a half hours. Thinking we can just talk about stupid nonsense and ignore everything that happened."

Nico takes another bite, this one much less barbaric. He chews pensively, like he's thinking very hard about what I said. And then, just when I think he's going to change his mind about helping me, announce that he's hopping on a bus back to Russellville and I'm entirely on my own, his face lights up with excitement, he grabs his phone, and he says, "That's it! That's the angle!"

**FOR TRADE: One Rare Antique Cell Phone (Ft. Bragg, CA)**

Help! We're two teenagers stuck on the road together, trying to get home. Oh, and we're exes. #Awkward. Help us trade up to something valuable enough to get us home before we kill each other. We're traveling north and are willing to come to you.

Oh, and the phone is pretty awesome too. See picture.

# 5:52 P.M.

## CALIFORNIA ROUTE 1

### INVENTORY: 1968 FIREBIRD 400 CONVERTIBLE (1), CASH ($749.35), SEA GLASS (1 PIECE), ANCIENT CELL PHONE (1)

"No," I say immediately after reading Nico's post. We're back on California 1, heading north, (finally!) out of Fort Bragg. "You have to take it down."

Nico glances at the phone quickly before returning his eyes to the road. The highway has already started to get curvier, hugging the edge of high cliffs as we head up the coast. According to Google Maps, in about thirty miles, California 1 is going to head inland and cut through a forest to hook up with the 101 at Leggett. Then we can take the 101 all the way up through Eureka to Crescent City.

"Why not?" Nico asks with a frown.

"Because it's . . . it's . . . personal."

"Exactly. People like *personal* stories. They want to get involved."

"And it's not true," I point out.

Nico twists his mouth to the side. "It's *semi*-true."

"Semi-true is still a lie."

I see a flash of annoyance pass over Nico's face, and the familiar fire ignites in my gut. It's the same fire that's been turning off and on since the night of the comet.

Apparently nothing has changed in a month. And why should it? People don't change. They're stuck in the same cycle—the same personality—over and over again. They answer mostly As, mostly Bs, or mostly Cs for their entire life. And they're fine with it.

"So what?" I say. "You just expect someone to respond to this Craigslist ad and want to trade some random thing for an old phone that probably doesn't even turn on anymore?"

He shrugs. "Yeah."

I sigh, drop his phone into the cup holder, and turn to stare out the window. I can't talk to Nico anymore. He's infuriating me. And I can tell I'm not doing much for him, either. That's what that whole charade back at the burger joint was all about. Dumping our problems out on poor Scott. Inviting a stranger into our past. That was Nico lashing out. That was Nico getting fed up.

With me.

Well, fine. I'm fed up with him, too.

He can do whatever he wants with that relic. Let him have his little Craigslist project. At least he has something to keep him occupied and out of my hair. I don't care if he's able to trade that old phone in for a castle in Scotland. I'm still selling this stupid car.

The view as the sun starts to set over the Pacific Ocean

lightens my mood a bit. The landscape is rugged yet soothing at the same time. All rocky cliffs and crashing white waves. It makes you feel like no matter how dramatic your life is, it will never be as dramatic as the events that shaped this coast.

As we drive, putting more and more distance between us and Fort Bragg, I can feel my muscles finally start to unclench. The fire inside me starting to simmer. And everything starts to feel normal again.

This temper thing is new to me. New since Nico.

I've never been the kind of person to get worked up, lose my cool, yell. But Nico brings out the worst in me. Just like Jackson used to do with my mother.

Some people are just not meant to be together.

Of course, that's not how it felt at first.

At first, we were magic.

"So," Nico says, crashing into the silence. "About what happened back at the burger place."

For a moment, I think he's going to apologize for what he said to Scott. For completely humiliating—not to mention *insulting*—me. But then he goes on.

"It sounds like your dad really *was* proud of you."

*Oh no. He's not doing this. He's not going* there.

There's nothing he can say to change my mind about Jackson. Whatever he has to say, I guarantee, I've heard it before. I've heard it *all* before.

*People are complicated. You might want to give your father the benefit of the doubt.* (June.)

*Your father had a difficult childhood. His own father left when he was very young. He doesn't always know how to be a parent.* (Mom.)

*Just because your father left doesn't mean he doesn't love you.* (School guidance counselor.)

Actually, that's exactly what it means. When someone walks out on you to go on tour with a bunch of washed-up musicians starving for a comeback, there's no other way to interpret that.

"My dad left us. *Twice.* Once when I was nine, and again when I was twelve. He doesn't get to be proud. He doesn't get to be anything."

Nico opens his mouth to say something, but I cut him off. "I don't want to talk about him," I say as sternly as I can, leaving no room for doubt or misinterpretation.

Because honestly, I will talk about *anything* else.

"Okay," Nico says guardedly. "So what was that whole thing about your name? Is Ali not your real name?"

Anything except that.

My muscles immediately tighten again. So much for unwinding.

"Of course it's my real name," I say dismissively. I stare out the passenger-side window at the jagged cliffs looming next to us. I can feel Nico's gaze darting to me every few seconds.

"That guy back at the burger joint didn't think so."

"Who are you going to believe? Me, or some random guy from a burger joint who's never met me before?"

Nico falls silent, like he's carefully considering the question.

"Seriously? You have to think about that?" I ask.

"Well, you *are* acting kind of shady about it."

"I am *not* acting shady."

Nico skillfully maneuvers the car through a series of tight hairpin turns. We're getting deeper into the mountains now, leaving the ocean behind, making our way inland. I peer out the window and then immediately regret it. There's a five-hundred-foot drop inches away from us. From my view from the passenger seat, it looks like it's literally beneath us. I can't even see the road on my side of the car.

*Hasn't the state of California ever heard of guardrails?*

We finally get to a straightaway, and I release my breath.

"Maybe," Nico goes on, like there was never a gap in the conversation, *"you're* the one involved in some shady moneymaking scheme. And that's why you go by a fake name."

I groan. Why is he doing this? Is he bored? Is he trying to get under my skin again? But when I glance over at him, I see he's smiling. And not in that infuriating, patronizing way. In that fun, playful Nico way. The way I used to love.

And *that* makes it infuriating.

"It's not a fake name."

"What was it that guy said back at Jenny's? Something about you being named after a song?"

I ball my hands into fists, cursing Jackson in my mind.

"If I guess the song, will you tell me?"

"No," I say too quickly.

"So you *are* named after a song!"

*Damn it.*

"So Ali is *not* your real name."

*Damn it. Damn it. Damn it.*

"Which means *you* lied."

Once again, I cut my gaze to Nico. His eyes are intently focused on the road, which is heading into another string of terrifying curves. The playful smile is still on his face, letting me know that he's teasing me. Trying to make light of everything.

I don't know how he does that.

How can he possibly joke about that night?

Unless *he* doesn't feel the sting of the cut like I still do.

Unless *he* never felt the cut to begin with.

"I didn't lie," I say in a measured tone. "I just never told you that my real name wasn't Ali."

"So, omitting the truth is *not* lying."

*You have the right to remain silent. Anything you say can and will be used against you. . . .*

"I'm just trying to get the rules straight," Nico says.

I grab Nico's phone from the cup holder and scroll through the available episodes of "Everything About Everything."

"How about we listen to another podcast?"

Nico ignores me. "So, it's a name of a famous song by some band that sounds like Nine Inch Nails. Who sounds like Nine Inch Nails?"

"How about this one? 'Would a Flashlight Work at Light Speed?'"

"Smashing Pumpkins?"

"'The Five-Second Rule: Fact or Fiction?'"

"Alice in Chains?"

"Oh, this one looks interesting. 'How Does Déjà Vu Work?'"

"You're really not going to tell me your real name."

"I'm really not."

"Wait a minute," Nico says, thinking hard about something. "What did the license plate of this car say? 'Epidemic' or something?"

"Here's a good one!" I say quickly, reading aloud the very next episode on the list before I even have a chance to make sense of the words. "'The Anatomy of Kissing.' Oh wait . . . never mind."

Nico grins. "That one *does* sound interesting."

"No." I veto it and continue scrolling through the list. "Not that one."

"Why not? It sounds *enlightening*."

I feel myself growing flustered. I scroll backward and select an episode at random. "I'm putting on the déjà vu one."

"But I want to learn more about kissing."

*Trust me, Nico. If memory serves, you don't need to* learn anything *about kissing.*

I clear my throat. "Déjà vu it is!" I'm about to push play when a strange sound stops me. A long, deep blast, almost like a foghorn. It's so unfamiliar, it takes me a moment to realize it's coming from Nico's phone. But it doesn't sound like any of the ringtones I remember him using.

Confused, I glance back at the screen to see there's a

notification of a new text message. From a name I don't recognize.

A *girl's* name.

Rachel.

The blood in my veins turns to ice.

*Rachel.*

*Rachel.*

*Rachel.*

I rack my brain, trying to think of a Rachel that goes to Russellville High, but I can't come up with a single one. Which means he met her somewhere else. Outside of town. Far away from boring, lame Russellville and all of us boring, lame people in it.

I think I'm going to be sick.

Then, it comes again.

And again.

And again.

*BOOOOOOMMM*

*BOOOOOOMMM*

*BOOOOOOMMM*

Nico suddenly rips the phone from my hand and starts frantically tapping and swiping at the screen. In fact, he's so desperate to do whatever it is he's doing, he nearly drives us right off the highway.

"Watch the road!" I scream.

Nico looks up and swerves just in time to avoid plunging us off a steep cliff.

"Sorry," he mutters, and drops the phone into his lap. I glance at it, hoping to catch a glimpse of whatever it was that almost got us killed, but the screen is dark.

I tell myself to calm down. *Chill out. Get yourself under control. You're not his girlfriend anymore. You don't get to demand explanations. You don't even get to expect them.*

And yet, I feel like I at least *deserve* one.

But I won't ask. I can't ask. I will never ask.

"Who was that?" I ask, nodding toward the phone.

"No one," Nico says quickly. Too quickly. "A wrong number."

---

**Your ex-boyfriend is dating someone else and lying to you about it.**

**What do you do?**

A   *Let it go. It's none of your business. Remember, you broke up with him.*

B   *Grab the phone and search all of his text messages, e-mails, phone records, and browser history until you catch him in the lie.*

C.  *Silently seethe in your seat. You will not give him the satisfaction of knowing how much this bothers you.*

---

I angle my body toward the door, so I don't have to even see Nico out of the corner of my eye. As we drive, I can feel him stealing glances at me, like he wants to say something, but I don't turn around, and neither of us says a word.

The mountain landscape soon turns into thick forest, darkening the road and hiding the sky. Even though it no longer seems as though we're driving along the edge of the world, the highway is still terrifyingly wind-y, and nausea eventually creeps up on me. I rush to crank open the window.

"Hot?" Nico asks.

"Carsick."

"I didn't know you got carsick," he says, maneuvering around another sharp turn. "We drove around all the time and you never got sick."

*That's because I was properly distracted*, I think but obviously don't say.

"It's just these curves," I mutter, closing my eyes.

"Well, don't close your eyes. That makes it worse. Look out the window."

I open my eyes and turn my gaze to the trees. I hate to admit it, but Nico is right. Of course, he's right. Nico, the Fixer.

"Should only be a few more miles," Nico says after what feels like hours of twisting and turning. The light is almost gone, and the road seems to not only be getting curvier, but also dirtier. There's debris everywhere. At one point, Nico has to swerve into the other lane just to avoid running over a giant fallen tree branch.

"What is all of this stuff?" I ask.

Nico shrugs. "There was probably a storm last night, knocked all of this debris into the road."

"They should really clean it up. It's dangerous."

Nico is silent for a moment. I peer at his face and instantly know that he's thinking hard about something again.

"What?" I ask.

"Have you noticed that we haven't passed a single car in over thirty minutes?"

I hadn't noticed, but now that he mentions it, I realize he's right. We seem to be the only ones on this long, winding, deserted road through the forest. "Why do you think that is?" I ask, starting to feel uneasy.

"I don't know," Nico admits. "But it's kind of freaky, isn't it? This is a state highway. Why wouldn't there be any other cars?"

"Too late at night?"

Nico points to the analog clock on the dash. "It's barely after seven."

As Nico continues to maneuver the car around the turns and the growing piles of debris on the road, I feel my hackles start to go up. I keep waiting to see another car coming from the opposite direction, or pulling up behind us, but the headlights from the Firebird seem to be illuminating nothing but empty dark road ahead of us.

Something is wrong.

I can feel it.

"Do you think maybe—" I begin to ask, but Nico slams on the brakes, causing the car to skid and fishtail. For a split second all I hear is the screeching of tires and my own scream echoing in my ears. An object flashes across my vision, and I realize there's something in the middle of the road. Something Nico had to brake to avoid crashing into.

*What was that? A deer? A bear?*

The car finally comes to a halt, and that's when I realize I've grabbed on to Nico's arm. I quickly release my grip.

"Oh my God. Oh my God," I say. "Did we hit something? What is it? Is it dead?"

"Relax," Nico says with a chuckle. "I think it's a sign."

"A sign of what? That we should turn back?"

He laughs again. "Actually, yes. But it's a *literal* sign." He points at something through the windshield ahead of us, and I squint into the darkness. Nico puts the car in reverse and then backs up, turning the wheel so the headlight beams fall across something white and bright in the center of the highway.

ROAD CLOSED

"What?" I ask, blinking hard. "The road really *is* closed?"

"Looks like it."

"So what do we do?"

Nico looks at me like I'm crazy. "We have to turn back."

"How far?"

He grabs his phone from his lap and checks the map. "Looks like all the way to Fort Bragg. To pick up Highway 20."

"What?" I snatch the phone from him to check. He's right. There's no other way to the 101. We have to go all the way back to Fort Bragg. I glance desperately at the clock again. "But we'll never make it to Crescent City by nine."

"Well, we can't go through here." Nico shifts the car into reverse and does a slow three-point turn until we're facing the direction we came from. The thought of losing all of that time—almost three hours wasted—is sending me into panic mode.

"But what about Tom Lancaster? And the car?"

"You'll just have to call him and tell him we'll be there tomorrow."

"Tomorrow?" I ask, my heart thudding in my chest. "What do you mean tomorrow?"

"Well, by the time we get back to Fort Bragg, it'll be almost nine. I'll get us as far as I can, but I can't drive all night. We're going to have to stop somewhere."

I want to ask why not. Why can't he drive all night? But I soon realize it's not fair of me to ask him to do that. He's already gotten us this far, and asking him to keep going without any sleep feels like some sort of unnecessary torture.

I lean back in my seat with a resigned sigh. I can't believe this. I can't believe we won't make it to Crescent City tonight.

Nico is just about to shift into first gear when his phone chirps. This is a ringtone I actually recognize. It's for new e-mails. He picks up the phone again and glances at the screen. His expression shifts from weariness to elation in a heartbeat. "YES!"

"What?"

He passes me the phone. "Read it and weep!"

I glance at the subject line of the e-mail, and my mouth falls open. I can't freaking believe it.

"Go ahead," Nico prompts as he maneuvers the car back through the debris on the road. "Read it aloud."

I groan and click on the message, reading with about the same amount of enthusiasm as someone reading from a technical manual.

> Hi. I'm Sandy. I just saw your barter post on Craigslist, and I'm VERY interested in the phone. I've been looking for this exact model for weeks, but no one has it. I can trade you my collection of Beatles CDs (4 total).

"Four Beatles CDs! That's amazing!"

"We don't have a CD player in the car," I remind him.

"Well, we're not going to use it ourselves. We're going to trade it up for something even more valuable. See? It's already working. Where is she located?"

I look back at the screen, my annoyance doubling when I read the rest of the e-mail. "Fort Bragg."

"Aha! Now *that* is a sign. Quick! Write her back! Tell her we're on our way to Fort Bragg now and can meet her at . . ." He consults the clock on the dash. "Eight thirty."

How is this possible? Who is bored enough to scour Craigslist for random people wanting to trade random stuff?

I sigh and quickly type out the response. I'm about to drop the phone in the cup holder when my gaze lands on the little green icon on the home screen. The message app. Checking to make sure Nico is properly distracted with the wind-y road, I surreptitiously click on it and scan his list of messages, wilting when I see that the most recent one is from this morning. It seems the mysterious series of texts he just received has been deleted.

"What were you doing?" Nico asks, startling me.

I practically throw the phone into the cup holder. "Nothing."

"You were checking my text messages."

"No, I wasn't."

"You don't believe me. That it was a wrong number."

I stuff my hand in my sweatshirt pocket and feel for the shard of sea glass inside, clasping it tightly between my fingers until my knuckles ache. "Yes, I do."

A smirk breaks out on Nico's face. "No, you don't. You were checking to make sure it wasn't some new girl I was dating."

"I don't care who you're dating."

"I'm not dating anyone." Nico says this so quickly, it makes me flinch.

I cut my gaze to him and study the rigid line of his jaw, searching for signs of the lie.

This time, there are none.

"Well, even if you were," I say with one too many shrugs, "I wouldn't care."

Nico spins the wheel as we pull into another steep bend in the road. I keep my gaze straight ahead. Because I can't bear to look to either side of me. Both have jagged, deadly cliffs that threaten to make my stomach drop.

Nico laughs quietly. It's a different kind of laugh. A gloating kind of laugh. A laugh that leaves a sour taste in my mouth.

"Now who's the liar?"

# 8:20 P.M.

## FORT BRAGG, CA (AGAIN)

### INVENTORY: 1968 FIREBIRD 400 CONVERTIBLE (1), CASH ($749.35), SEA GLASS (1 PIECE), ANCIENT CELL PHONE (1)

We pass a sign welcoming us *back* to Fort Bragg. Like the cosmic board game of life has given us a "Move Back Three Spaces" card, and we've rewound almost the entire day.

When we drive down Main Street again, the town seems to be mocking me.

*Back so soon?* it says with a sneer. As if even the town knows I can't escape Jackson. Both he and this town are like magnets that constantly draw me back in, even when I think I'm well on my way to breaking free.

As soon as we were out of the treacherous forest, I sent a message to Tom Lancaster from Nico's phone, explaining what happened and asking him politely (read: begging) if he'd be willing to meet me tomorrow to purchase the car.

Fortunately, Tom wrote back fairly quickly, saying it's no problem and to just text him when I got close.

*Unfortunately,* Sandy from Craigslist wrote back just as quickly, directing us to meet her at eight thirty in the parking lot of a Denny's, right across the street from the entrance to Glass Beach, reminding me yet again of how much we've had to backtrack tonight.

When we pull into the Denny's parking lot, five minutes before our designated meeting time, Nico is in a jubilant mood. "Isn't this exciting?" he asks, parking the car and compressing the parking brake. He withdraws the small silver flip phone from his pocket and turns it around in his hand. "I can't believe people used to talk on these things." He opens it and pretends to take a call. "Hello? 2001? Yes, I do have your phone. Thanks for calling." He closes it with a self-important snap, then immediately opens it again and punches at random numbers on the numeric keypad. The phone is so old, it doesn't even have a keyboard. "How cool is it that we're about to trade this for four Beatles CDs?"

"Yeah, about that," I say, crossing my arms. "Don't you think it's just a little bit strange? That this woman even wants this worthless piece of junk?"

"You have no idea what she wants it for," Nico says defensively. "It's clearly worth something to *her.*"

"But why?" I ask.

Nico squints at the number keys. "How do you even text on this thing?"

"Exactly!" I say. "What on earth could she want it for?"

Just then, an old minivan pulls into the lot and parks three spaces away. A few seconds later, a middle-aged blond woman gets out and starts slinking around the parking lot, throwing suspicious looks over her shoulder.

"This must be her," Nico says, closing the phone again and slipping it into his pocket.

"Be careful," I mutter. "There are dangerous people on Craigslist, remember?"

"Exactly," Nico says, leaning all the way over me to open my door. "That's why *you're* coming with me."

I groan and step out of the car.

Nico approaches the woman, who seems to startle at the sight of him. "Are you Nico?" she whispers, her wild gray eyes darting around the parking lot.

Nico shoots me a glance. "Yes," he says warily. "Are you Sandy?"

She shakes her head. "Sandy is just an alias. I wouldn't dare give out my real name over the Internet."

"Right," Nico says, even though I can tell he's fighting hard not to laugh.

The woman glances at me. "You must be the ex."

I roll my eyes. I almost forgot Nico told everyone on Craigslist about our failed relationship. "Yes. That would be me."

She glances over my shoulder and her eyes bug out, reminding me of a frightened pug. I turn, fully expecting to see the FBI jumping out of black vans with machine guns and bulletproof vests, given how shady this woman is acting. But all I see is the Firebird.

"Nice car," she says approvingly. "Is that a Mustang?"

"Firebird," Nico corrects with pride.

"So," I say, anxious to move this process along. "You're interested in the cell phone, huh?"

Sandy's face illuminates. "Yes. Do you have it?"

Nico pulls the clunker out of his pocket and hands it over. She takes it and inspects it carefully from all angles.

"You realize it probably doesn't even work," I say, and Nico shoots daggers at me out of his eyes. "I'm just being honest," I tell him.

"It might just need a charge," Nico, the salesman, puts in.

But Sandy waves both of our comments away. "I can get it to work."

Then she reaches into her oversize handbag and pulls out 4 compact disc cases, neatly secured by two criss-crossing rubber bands. She hands them to Nico, who immediately goes to work pulling off the rubber bands and checking each of the cases to make sure there are actually matching discs inside. I don't blame him for double-checking. This woman is giving off a very odd vibe.

"May I ask why you want the phone?" Nico says after he's verified each of the CDs.

Sandy narrows her eyes accusingly at him.

He raises his hands in surrender. "We're just curious."

She beckons us both closer, like she's about to tell us the location of every undercover CIA operative in the country. Nico takes a step in. I stay where I am. I can already smell the beer on her breath. It reminds me way too much of Jackson.

"They can't listen in on these old phones," Sandy whispers, as though this explains everything.

I dart a look at Nico, who looks genuinely interested. "Who can't?" he asks.

Sandy gapes at him in disbelief. "The government! Who else?"

"Ah," Nico says, nodding.

"You know they only sell us those smartphones for one reason: to spy on us. With the cameras and the microphones, it's just like *1984*, except we pay for it. We *want* it. That's the genius part. They made them all flashy and cool. They market them to us with slick ads, and we all line up outside the store to buy the latest model. But really they're using them to watch us." She brandishes the flip phone at us. "These old babies are the only safe way to talk to anyone."

I watch this exchange with a mix of fascination and amusement. Apparently, when Nico came up with his list of possible people who might want to buy an old cell phone, he forgot one: conspiracy theorists.

"They're watching Craigslist, too, you know," she goes on. "That's why I gave you a fake name."

"Right," Nico says, clearly humoring her. "Good call."

"You gotta be careful what you put on the Internet," Sandy says in all seriousness. "They've got eyes everywhere. I was talking to one of my buddies in a chat room about Paul, and suddenly, boom! My friend got hit by a bus the very next day."

Nico cringes. "That's . . . unfortunate. Wait . . . who's Paul?"

Sandy gasps and points to the stack of CDs in Nico's hand. *"Paul.* You know, Paul McCartney."

"The Beatle?" Nico asks.

"Yes," Sandy replies, as though it's obvious.

"What about him?"

"You mean"—Sandy's eyes widen—"you don't *know?*"

Nico shakes his head. "Know what?"

I tug on his hoodie sleeve and whisper, "Maybe we should just go."

He holds up a hand. "One sec." And then he turns back to Sandy. "What about Paul McCartney?"

She glances over both shoulders again before whispering, "He's *dead.*"

"He is?" Nico asks, peering down at the CD on top of the stack. It's the *Let It Be* album, where each of the four Beatles are pictured in four corners of a square. "Why didn't I hear about this? When did he die?"

Sandy looks extremely satisfied to be sharing this news with him. She leans in even closer to Nico. "November 9, 1966."

"WHAT!?!" Nico screeches, and Sandy quickly shushes him.

"It's true. He died in a car crash in 1966. MI5, British intelligence, covered up the death to prevent mass suicides by Beatles fans."

"Then who's this guy?" Nico asks, pointing to the top right corner of the square on the cover of the CD.

"A double," Sandy explains.

"Whoa," Nico says, looking shocked.

"Okay!" I give Nico one final nudge. "Well, we should really get going. Nice doing business with you. Enjoy the phone!"

"Well," Nico says blithely after we're back in the Firebird. "That was certainly interesting."

"That was *scary*," I correct.

"Oh, Sandy was harmless." He flips through the stack of CDs, stopping on the famous *Abbey Road* album, where all four Beatles are walking through a crosswalk. He brings it up to his face and squints at it. "Huh. Have you ever noticed that Paul is the only one in this picture not wearing shoes?"

"Why were you indulging her?"

Nico opens the compartment in the center console and stores the CDs inside. "You have to admit she was *kind of* interesting. And I can't totally disagree about the phone thing."

"Really? You think the government is listening in on all of our conversations and watching us through our phone cameras."

"I think *someone* is listening."

I pull my darkened phone out of my bag. "Hello," I whisper to the camera. "Whoever is listening, I'd just like to say for the record that Nico Wright is officially insane."

Nico grabs the phone and stuffs it facedown under his leg. "Shhh!" he says conspiratorially. "They'll find us."

I burst out laughing.

# 9:32 P.M.

## WILLITS, CA

### INVENTORY: 1968 FIREBIRD 400 CONVERTIBLE (1), CASH ($691.10), SEA GLASS (1 PIECE), BEATLES CDS (4)

"Hello, knowledge seekers! Linus McKee here. Welcome back to another 'Everything About Everything' podcast. In this episode: Where do things go when you delete them?"

The now-familiar opening jingle plays as Nico turns off Highway 20 onto the 101. We have a full tank of gas and a bag full of snacks and are heading north toward Leggett. It feels good to be back on track, traveling in the right direction. But according to Google Maps, we're still four hours from Crescent City.

"Remember that file you deleted three weeks ago from your computer?" Linus kicks off the episode with another series of thought-provoking questions. "Or that blurry picture you swiped off your phone? Or what about those letters you typed into the keyboard but then backspaced because you thought of a better way to say it? Where are all of those things now? Can you really completely *delete* something?"

I steal a glance at Nico.

*No*, I respond silently to Linus. *You can't.*

I lean back in my seat and, for the next thirty minutes, listen to Linus McKee explain about deleted files and memory and data pirates who can resurrect shredded hard drives.

"Can you hand me a candy bar?" Nico asks as the episode comes to an end.

"Sure," I reply, as cordially as I can. I rifle through the bag of snacks Nico picked up at the gas station, finding an impressive variety. "What kind?"

"Dealer's choice," he replies.

"Okay." I find a Milky Way bar, peel the wrapper down like a banana so Nico can eat it while he drives, and hand it to him.

"Thanks."

"You're welcome."

We've now graduated from small talk to nauseatingly excessive politeness.

I reach into the bag again to find myself a snack, pushing around some of the items, until I come across a mysterious cardboard box. I squint to read the label in the darkness.

"What are Sea-Bands?" I ask Nico.

"Oh, right. I forgot I bought those. They're motion sickness bands. I was telling the cashier at the gas station that you got carsick on Highway 1, and he told me to try these.

Apparently, you wear them on your wrists, and they have little balls that push against your pressure points. I don't know. They're supposed to help with car sickness."

Of course he would have a whole conversation with the cashier in the three minutes he was inside the gas station. And of course he would remember I was carsick on Highway 1 and try to help.

Still the Fixer.

Why does he make it *so* hard to stay mad at him?

I blink and glance up at him. I have no idea what kind of expression is on my face right now—gratitude, pain, more confusion—but Nico says, "Look, I don't know if they really work, but they're worth a try. They can't *hurt*, right?"

I swallow. "Right. Thanks."

Nico makes it through another hour of driving before he starts to yawn.

"We might need to stop. I'm having a hard time keeping my eyes open."

I cringe. I knew this moment would come eventually, but I'd sort of been avoiding thinking about it since we turned around. Avoiding thinking about the fact that I don't have the thirty-two thousand dollars that I thought I'd have by tonight. I can't afford to rent us *two* hotel rooms.

Which means . . .

"We should probably find a place to sleep," Nico says.

I stare through the windshield at the darkened sky. The stars are brilliant and white. His statement hangs in the air like a challenge.

My mouth goes dry. "Yes. Sleep."

His gaze darts over to meet mine before quickly returning to the road. We both fall silent. We've reached a stalemate, sinking back into the large, shadowy pit.

Nico is the first to break the silence. "Wanna look for a . . ." He seems to swallow up the next word, like he's trying to bury it. "Hotel?"

I clear my throat as I reach for his phone and unlock the screen. "Yes. Sure. I'll look."

While waiting for the GPS to find us on the map, I glance at Nico again. He has one hand on the wheel, and the other is rubbing anxiously against his jeans.

*Are his palms sweating?*

Google Maps places us about ten miles south of Garberville, where there's a hotel that looks clean and safe.

"Can you make it another ten miles?" I ask.

"Yeah. What did you find?"

"A Best Western. It should be right off the 101. It's nothing special, but it'll get the job done."

"The job?" Nico asks, and I'm grateful for the darkness in this car, because I'm pretty sure I'm blushing.

"I—I mean—" I stammer, but Nico just laughs.

"Don't worry. I know what you meant."

Even though he can't see the pink in my cheeks, I still turn and face out the window again, praying to the almighty god of breakups that this hotel at least has a room with two beds.

The first time I slept next to Nico was the night of the huge January rainstorm. I was working at Chateau Marmutt for the night. All of the dogs were on edge because of the thunder. Normally I spent the few first hours of my shift finishing homework and making rounds to check on the dogs. But not tonight. They were way too riled up for me to get any work done. It was nine o'clock at night, and I'd just finished my third rotation around the kennels, cooing and reassuring everyone that it was okay. I was here. And the thunder couldn't hurt them. But no one seemed reassured. I'd never heard so much crying and whimpering and pawing to get out. It was breaking my heart.

That's when Nico's text came. Syncing up ominously to a giant clap of thunder.

> Nico: This is one hell of a storm. Are you somewhere safe?

I would later come to learn this was a very Nico thing to write. He was always concerned with my safety.

I texted back.

> Me: Yes. I'm safe. I'm at work.

A bolt of lightning lit up the sky, and I silently counted the seconds.

*One Mississippi.*

*Two Mississippi.*

*Three—*

Thunder crashed, shaking the room. The storm was less than three miles away. The dogs were howling. And yet, I couldn't keep the smile from my face.

Nico: Where's work?

Me: Chateau Marmutt in Santa Rosa.

Nico: ???

Me: It's a pet hotel. I get paid to spend the night with the dogs.

Nico: Is that a form of canine prostitution?

I burst out laughing, startling Pixie, a white Malti-poo whose kennel I was standing directly in front of. She yelped and ran to the corner, quivering.

"Oh, Pixie. I'm sorry. Come here." I opened the kennel and scooped Pixie into my arms. "You can help me make my rounds, okay?" She seemed to calm down almost immediately. The problem was, as soon as Chew Barka, Pixie's pug neighbor, saw me holding Pixie, he started to whine and yelp and paw at the latch of his kennel, wanting to be held too.

"Well, I can't hold both of you at the same time," I told Chew Barka. Chew Barka didn't seem to understand this logic. He yapped and yapped, pawing so hard at the latch that I was afraid he might break a nail and start bleeding.

I sighed. "Okay, okay." I took him out of his kennel too.

With a pup under each arm, I couldn't read my phone when it dinged again. So I carried Pixie and Chew Barka into the sleeping suite and sat down on the bed. I pulled my phone out of my pocket to see Nico had texted again.

Nico: Uh-oh. Did I offend you with the canine prostitution comment?

I laughed and immediately sent a reply.

Me: No. Sorry. I couldn't text. Hands were occupied.
Nico: WHAT KIND OF JOB IS THIS?

I grinned, trying to come up with a flirty response, but Pixie and Chew Barka were climbing all over me, begging to be cuddled, and the dogs in the kennels were still howling. My creativity seemed to be left outside in the rain.

Me: I assure you, it's perfectly legit. I'm here for emotional support only. So the dogs don't get scared.

Nico's creativity, on the other hand, was perfectly dry and functional.

Nico: What if I get scared?

I bit my lip as I responded.

Me: ARE you scared?
Nico: Maybe.

My stomach flipped with anticipation.

Nico: I'm more concerned with this so-called "legit"
establishment you're working at. I think I might need
to check it out for myself.

The grin on my face was now the size of the moon. I couldn't stop smiling. I couldn't stop thinking, *This is it, isn't it?* This is the kind of feeling they write poems and songs about. This is what I've been missing out on my whole life.

It wasn't as though I purposefully *avoided* relationships; I had simply known every single boy in our school since we were in kindergarten. I'd had plenty of time to decide whether or not any of them were datable. And I'd decided they weren't.

And then Nico moved to town.

He was different.

He was exciting.

He was *new*.

And there was something about his newness that made me bold. That made me throw all my fears about high school relationships out the window, into the storm. There was something about his natural confidence that turned my natural caution into a chaotic pile of mush.

It's the only explanation for what I texted next:

Me: 7787 Pacific Ave.

By the time Nico arrived at Chateau Marmutt, the storm (and the dogs) had gotten worse. He must have thought he'd arrived at a canine insane asylum with all that whining and whimpering. The ones who weren't pacing anxiously in their kennels were curled up in the corners shaking.

But if he was at all put off by it, he didn't let on. In fact, he barely even flinched when I let him in the back door with Pixie and Chew Barka in my arms. He just glanced around the kennel room with an interested expression and said, "So this is where you work?"

I laughed. "It's not always like this. It's the storm."

He nodded like he understood.

"Do you have a dog?"

"No," he said, so quickly it startled me. Then, upon seeing my reaction, he went on, "I mean, yes. Once. A long time ago. But it didn't work out."

I frowned. "Oh, did you have to put him down?"

He seemed to fall into a daydream for a moment before shaking his head and saying, "No, we had to give him away."

I waited for him to elaborate, but he didn't. Already I could feel the energy between us turning awkward. I shifted Pixie and Chew Barka in my arms. They were getting heavy. Another clap of thunder struck a moment later, and the dogs started howling again, effectively ending the awkward silence. Nico walked over to the nearest kennel and peered inside at Charlie, the Cavalier King

Charles spaniel, with pity in his eyes. "Poor little guy."

Charlie was standing next to the latch, panting wildly.

"I've been doing my best to calm them," I explained. "Walking around, talking to them. But they don't like being locked up during the storm."

"Then why don't we let them out?" he suggested.

I bit my lip. I'd thought about it. But the problem was, I had no idea where they'd all go. During the day, they play outside, but I knew that putting them out there would only freak them out more.

"I'm not really supposed to let them out at night. Except the ones who have sleeping-suite status."

Nico blinked like he'd misheard me. "Excuse me? What status?"

I chuckled. "Sleeping suite. Some of the owners pay extra for their dogs to stay overnight in the sleeping suite with me."

"This sounds like a very elitist system."

I laughed. "It is! I always feel so bad for the others."

"The peasant dogs, you mean?"

"Yeah. They clearly want to sleep with me but—"

"Naturally," Nico interrupted. "I mean, who wouldn't?"

I tried to slug him, but my arms were full of dog and I nearly dropped Pixie. She whined and clawed at my shirt.

"Here," Nico said, taking her from me and tucking her adeptly under one arm, like he'd done this a million times. Then he turned the other arm toward me. "Now you can hit me."

I smirked. "Never mind. The moment is gone."

At first Pixie looked a little freaked out to be held by a stranger, but I guess she figured it was better than being put back in her kennel, so she settled into Nico's arms and seemed to relax.

The sight of him with a Maltipoo tucked under his arm like a fluffy white purse made me laugh.

"What?" Nico asked, feigning confusion.

I shook my head. "Nothing. It's just, I don't know. You don't seem like a Maltipoo type of guy."

"And what kind of guy do I seem like?"

I paused, seizing this rare opportunity to outwardly study him. I took in his soft cheeks and strong jaw, his longish dark blond hair that swooped over his forehead and tickled the tops of his ears. I ran my gaze over his thick eyebrows, the sprinkling of freckles over his nose and under his eyes. I wanted to stare at him forever. And in that moment, I felt like I *could* stare at him forever.

But then he said, "Well?" and I knew my free pass was expired.

"A Newfoundland," I decided confidently.

"A what?"

"A Newfoundland. Sometimes called a 'Newfie.'"

"I've never heard of that dog."

"Oh, they're great. Really friendly. And optimistic. They make great family dogs. Although they do drool a lot."

Nico stared at me as though he wasn't quite sure how to respond to that. He started walking up the aisle of kennels. "Okay, I gotta see one of these Newfer-wafer things for myself."

"*Newfoundlands,*" I corrected with a laugh.

"Is that one?" he asked, pointing to Howie, who looked up expectantly at him, hoping to be let out.

"That's a beagle," I said.

"What about that one?" He pointed to the kennel next to Howie.

"And that's a labradoodle."

Just then, lightning streaked across the sky, momentarily lighting up the darkened kennel room. I started to count.

*One Mississippi.*

*Two Mississi—*

The thunder crashed less than two miles away. Howie let out a pitiful howl of fear. Pixie nearly crawled down the neckline of Nico's shirt.

"It's getting closer," I said, glancing anxiously around at the dogs who had all started to pace and whine again.

"That's it," Nico said. "We're bringing down this elitist system once and for all. Everyone is coming into the sleeping suite."

"Uh—" I stammered. "There's twenty-five dogs here. The sleeping suite was designed to fit five . . . plus *one* person."

Nico pointed to Howie, who was now staring at us through the bars of his kennel, his wide eyes pleading. "Are you really going to say no to *that?*"

Twenty minutes later, we'd somehow managed to cram every single dog—plus the two of us—into the sleeping suite. The twelve-by-twelve-foot room smelled like fish breath and farts. But the dogs seemed happy. They were all still panting from the stress of the storm, but the howling and pacing had stopped. Probably because there was nowhere *to* pace. We had squeezed in as many dog beds as we could, and still the dogs were practically on top of each other. Nico and I lay on the single bed with Pixie, Chew Barka, Charlie, and one giant Great Pyrenees named Marshmallow, who was pretty much the size of a polar bear.

"Tell me more about these Newfandangos," Nico said, his eyes locked on mine. His nose was inches away. We were sharing the same pillow, and our bodies were crammed so close together I was practically on top of him.

I snorted out a laugh. "Repeat after me," I said. "New . . ."

"New . . . ," he said diligently.

"Fin . . ."

"Fin . . ."

"Land . . ."

"Land . . ."

"Newfoundland."

"Newfarklehead," Nico said.

"You're doing that on purpose."

His smile grew. "I just like watching you say it."

"What? Newfoundland?"

He closed his eyes, and for a brief moment I was able to stare at his long eyelashes. "Mmm. So sexy."

And even though I laughed, I couldn't help but think, *Yes. So sexy.*

*So dangerous.*

I swallowed hard, trying to remember every fact I knew about Newfoundlands.

"They're very friendly and loyal. Great with kids. But they need lots of exercise," I began, and Nico's eyes fluttered open. He remained quiet, listening intently. "They're excellent swimmers. Very strong."

"Strong," Nico repeated, in an overly macho voice. "That's obviously why you thought of me."

"No," I corrected. "I thought of you because they're giant goofballs."

"Like me?" Nico confirmed.

I shrugged. "Maybe. I don't really know you all that well yet."

Nico smiled, but he didn't respond right away. He just continued to look at me, those small blue-gray eyes staring intensely into mine. "I think you should," he finally said.

"Should what?"

"Know me."

There was a gravity to his words. A heaviness that made me feel like something was cracking open. To this day, I couldn't tell you if it was me or if it was him. Maybe we both broke open a little bit that night. Maybe we both had every intention of staying open. Of continuing to crack wider and wider until there was nothing left of our protective shells but dust.

"Maybe I should," I replied softly.

Out of the corner of my eye, I saw a flash of lightning. My back was to the window, but I silently started counting.

*One Missi—*

*BOOM!*

The storm was right over us now. We were trapped beneath it. All twenty-seven bodies stuck in this room. Pixie whimpered and climbed over my hip, burrowing herself between us, pushing us a few more inches apart. Like a chaperone at a middle school dance, making sure we didn't get too close.

But it was too late for that. We were already too close.

My heart was already too open.

And Nico had already climbed inside and made himself at home.

That night was the start of so much. We crashed together like the charged particles of air crashing outside in the storm. We collided fast and so furiously, there was nothing to stop us. We were helpless. We were useless. We were just along for the ride.

Nico didn't go home that night. He stayed with me— with *us*—until morning. Until light streamed in through the windows and the rain slowed to a gentle drizzle.

I made sure to kick him out before Pam, the owner of the pet hotel, arrived. I didn't know what the policy was about overnight visitors in the sleeping suite, but I didn't exactly want to find out the hard way.

After putting all the dogs back in their kennels— except Pixie, who cried when I tried to put her down—I walked Nico out to his truck. He opened the door and then turned back to me with an urgency in his eyes, like he wanted to say something. Like he wanted to tell me all of his secrets.

**169 →**

But instead, he put one hand behind my head, pulled me toward him, and kissed me.

Right there in the parking lot of Chateau Marmutt, with raindrops falling quietly between us, and Pixie still tucked in my arm. He kissed me like a conversation. A heated dialogue. Every spark that had passed between us with words was intensified by a thousand without those words.

It was the first of many kisses. Seemingly endless kisses. More than I could ever count. But it was the one that counted.

"Can I see you later?" he asked as he pulled away and reached out to give Pixie a quick scratch under the chin.

"Who? Me? Or Pixie?"

Nico laughed. "Whichever of you wants to see me more."

It was a challenge; I knew that. It was a request for validation. Nico never struck me as the kind of person who needed assurance. He always seemed so confident. So incapable of vulnerability.

And yet, there he was.

Standing in front of me.

Vulnerable.

"That would be me," I said. "And yes, you can see me later."

He kissed me again and then left. As I watched his truck drive down the driveway, the buoyant smile returned to my face. The one my mother would later ask me about. The one I would study in the mirror for days to come, trying to figure out where it had been all this time.

# 11:02 P.M.

## GARBERVILLE, CA

### INVENTORY: 1968 FIREBIRD 400 CONVERTIBLE (1), CASH ($570.89), SEA GLASS (1 PIECE), BEATLES CDS (4)

Nico and I stand in the middle of the small rustic-themed hotel room and stare at the single king bed in front of us, like we're two lone rangers starting down the incoming cavalry.

The god of breakups—if he even exists—sure has a warped sense of humor.

When we arrived at the front desk, there was only one room left. And, of course, it only had one bed. I considered walking right back to the car and telling Nico he'd simply have to stay awake. I'd pump him with as much coffee as it took to get to the next town. But he was already looking worse for the wear, yawning every few seconds and blinking rapidly to keep from falling asleep at the wheel.

"You can take the bed," Nico finally says. "I'll sleep on the floor."

I know common decency and politeness tell me that I should reject the offer. *No, Nico. Don't be silly. We'll share the bed.*

But I'm no longer living by the rules of common decency. I'm living by Ali and Nico's Rules of the Road, which clearly state:

9.  YOU MAY ABSOLUTELY NOT, UNDER ANY
    CIRCUMSTANCES, SHARE A BED!

"Okay," I say quietly, and drop my backpack on the comforter. "Thanks."

Nico and I don't utter a single word as we get ready for bed. It's almost as though we've turned into an old married couple, moving silently around each other, anticipating each other's movements, giving each other space.

When I emerge from the bathroom, Nico has already pulled the spare blanket and pillow from the closet and made himself a makeshift bed on the floor. He's lying on his side, the covers pulled up to his chin.

Guilt twists my stomach. Can I really let him sleep on the floor? After all, he's the one who has to do all the driving. Should I let him sleep in the bed with me?

But then I notice his long-sleeve T-shirt, hoodie, and jeans hanging over the wooden chair in the corner, and by process of elimination I deduce that he's only wearing his boxers under that blanket. And that's when my heart practically shouts the answer back at me.

*No, you should NOT.*

I quickly climb into the bed and switch off the bedside lamp, plunging the entire room into an uncomfortable darkness.

There's no storm tonight. Not like that night at Chateau Marmutt. But the wind is harsh and relentless. Beating ferociously against the sliding glass door, demanding to be let in. I can't help but wonder if it's an omen. Like a neighbor wildly banging at your door to warn you about an incoming tornado. *Quick! Get to safety!*

Under any other circumstances this would be romantic: a cozy little hotel room in the middle of nowhere, the wind howling, our breaths practically synchronized.

But we're not under any other circumstance.

We're under *this* circumstance.

So it's torture.

There's just something about Nico's presence. I'm acutely aware of it. Like he's messing with gravity and the entire room is tilted toward him.

I reach up to adjust the four pillows behind my head, and the guilt immediately returns, this time hitting me like a truck.

"Here," I say, pulling two of the pillows out. "You should take these." I climb to the side of the bed and peer over the edge at Nico. He blinks up at me in the darkness.

"Thanks." He sits up to grab the pillows, and that's when I realize my mistake. The blanket falls to his waist, revealing his bare chest and stomach. I suddenly feel like the bed has dropped out from under me.

There's absolutely no reason to believe that Nico's body

would have changed in the one month since we broke up, but the sight of his lean, toned muscles still startles me. There was a time I used to get lost in those curves, running my fingertips around their smooth edges.

He catches my eye, and I swallow and force myself to look away. There can be no eye contact right now. This room is already too small. This situation is already too intimate. Adding eye contact would be like striking a match near a puddle of spilled gasoline.

Dangerous and stupid.

Because we both know what a little eye contact in the dark can do. We were both there that night. Crammed onto the single bed in the sleeping suite at Chateau Marmutt, staring into each other's eyes while lightning veined through the sky and thunder crashed.

I hastily scramble back up and settle under the covers. I lie in the darkness and listen to Nico's soft breaths, the hum of the air-conditioning, the squeak of the bed every time I so much as twitch.

There's no getting comfortable in this room.

It's too dark.

The sound of Nico's breathing is too loud.

The air feels too hot and stuffy.

I gather my hair atop my head and go to secure it with the rubber band around my wrist, before remembering that it's gone. Nico traded it with that woman on the beach for the old cell phone.

And then suddenly, all I can think about is the way Nico's hand felt on my wrist as he pushed up my sleeve.

# SATURDAY

*She keeps her distance
She knows this world's not safe
It's full of minefields
She won't go down that way*

—"Numb," from the album
*Salvage Lot* by Fear Epidemic
Written by Nolan Cook, Slate Miller,
Chris McCaden, and Adam French
Released February 20, 2009

# 8:32 A.M.

## REDWOOD HIGHWAY

### INVENTORY: 1968 FIREBIRD 400 CONVERTIBLE (1), CASH ($570.89), SEA GLASS (1 PIECE), BEATLES CDS (4)

Miraculously, Nico wakes up to a response to his updated Craigslist post. Someone in Fortuna, about fifty miles north of here, wants to trade the Beatles CDs for a fifty-dollar gift card to Tomato and Vine, one of the most popular Italian restaurant chains in the country. This puts Nico in an insufferably good mood.

All I wake up to is a text from my mother, asking how the packing is going. I text her back and tell her I'm "almost there." It's only *partially* a lie. We *are* almost there. Just not to where she thinks.

Nico and I grab some muffins, fruit, and coffee from the breakfast buffet at the hotel and check out. We're both anxious to hit the road, although admittedly for very different reasons. I'm eager to finally get up to Crescent City and ditch this car, while Nico is eager make his next trade.

As soon as we're back in the Firebird, I slide on my Sea-Bands—which, it turns out, are pretty magical—and cue up another episode of the podcast. "I think this one is about fonts," I say, trying to sound upbeat. Today is a new day. We only have a few more hours left together before we're on a bus home to Russellville. I'm determined *not* to let Nico get to me today.

Nico straightens up in his seat, giving the steering wheel a firm pat. "Bring it, Linus. Tell me everything there is to know about Times New Roman."

"You know, I've always been more of an Arial type of girl."

Nico scoffs. "Arial is the dullest font there is."

"It is not! And I'm not dull."

"I didn't say *you* were dull. I said your choice of font was dull."

"So what's your favorite font?" I challenge.

"Comic Sans," he says proudly. "Because I'm *hi-larious*."

I grunt. "Yeah. Right. If anything, you're Edwardian Script. Cheesy and over-the-top."

Nico feigns offense. "Fine. Then you're Pristina. Overly pretentious."

"I am so not pretentious," I argue.

Nico sighs. "Yeah, I know. I just couldn't think of any other fonts."

I laugh. "Maybe I should just play the episode."

As Nico and I listen to the history of fonts—which is actually more interesting than it sounds—I stare out the window at the passing scenery. We head into the

Humboldt Redwoods State Park, and the road becomes heavily wooded, the massive trees rising on either side of us like fortress walls. According to a sign we pass, we're officially on the Redwood Highway.

"I've never seen redwoods," I say to Nico as the episode comes to a close.

Nico's face scrunches up. "Is that a font?"

"No. They're really huge trees."

"I know what redwoods are."

I shrug. "I don't know. You looked really confused there for a moment."

"Only because you suck at making segues."

I roll my eyes. "Sorry. Let me try again." I clear my throat theatrically. "So, Nico. What a lovely episode about fonts that was. I particularly enjoyed the part about the history of Bookman Old Style, and how it's meant to look like fonts used in old books. Speaking of things made from trees, I've never seen the redwoods. Have you?"

He laughs and plays along. "What a fantastic conversationalist you are. In fact, I have seen the redwoods. Once."

"Oh really?" I ask, sounding overly interested. "When was that?"

The playful expression falls right off Nico's face. He tries to resurrect it a moment later, covering the transition with a sip of water from his bottle, but I see the gap. "When we drove out from Reno."

My stomach tightens. It's the first time he's really even mentioned Reno since we started dating. I used to notice that he never brought it up. And the one time I casually mentioned it, he quickly changed the subject. I just assumed he had a girlfriend back there that he wanted to forget, and I certainly wasn't going to be the one to remind him of *that*. So I never mentioned it again. But here he is, openly mentioning his past life. I want so badly to ask questions, find out more about why they'd move from a big, exciting city like Reno to a sleepy little town like Russellville. But for some reason, his brief mention of his past life doesn't feel like an open invitation to ask questions. It doesn't feel like a welcome mat. *Come inside! Make yourself at home, Ali!*

So I click another podcast at random and press play.

Thirty minutes later we arrive at a thrift shop in Fortuna called Second Chances. It's owned by Vick Leeman, who wants to trade the Beatles CD for the gift card because apparently his new girlfriend is obsessed with the Beatles and he's trying to educate himself.

"Also," Vick says as he hands over the Tomato and Vine gift card, "she can't stand corporate restaurants. So this doesn't do me much good."

As Nico takes the card, my gaze falls on the familiar logo on the front—a bright red tomato with a grapevine tangled around it—and I have to shut my eyes against the incoming tidal wave of memories from the last time I ever went to a Tomato and Vine. One week before Jackson left to join the band on tour.

Nico thanks Vick for the exchange and immediately updates his Craigslist post with the new item. We walk back out to the parking lot, and I wait for Nico to unlock the car, but something seems to have caught his eye. "How about a quick pit stop?"

I turn to see a small coffee hut across the street called the Jitter Bean, and my shoulders slouch. "You're stalling."

Nico grins. "No, I'm not. I just want some coffee."

"You had coffee back at the hotel."

"You can never have too much coffee."

He takes off toward the crosswalk, and I run to catch up to him. "Fine, but let's make it quick."

"What's the rush?" Nico asks. "I thought Tom Lancaster said you could basically show up whenever you wanted."

"Yes, he did. But I'd still like to get there as soon as possible, which means there's still no time for dawdling."

Nico guffaws. "Dawdling? Really?"

"Yeah, really," I snap. So much for not letting Nico get to me this morning. That lasted a whole hour.

"Who, under the age of sixty, says 'dawdling'?" Nico asks.

"I do. Now let's get the coffee and get back on the road."

"Okay," Nico says, raising his hands in a defensive gesture. He lines up behind the four other people waiting to place their orders at the outdoor counter. We've been waiting for less than a minute when Nico's phone lets out a chirp. He raises his sunglasses to peer at the screen. "Wow. That was fast."

Dread sweeps over me. "What was fast?"

"Looks like we'll have to make a quick stop in Eureka on our way up to Crescent City."

"Why? What's in Eureka?"

Nico's eyes continue to scan the screen. "Some kid named Mack Polonsky." He sucks in a breath. "Yikes. Rough name."

I blink, confused. "Who the hell is Mack Polonsky?"

"He wants to trade our Tomato and Vine gift card."

"Already?" I ask, shocked.

"Yeah. I know, right? It's almost as though he was sitting in front of his computer screen, waiting for this post." The man in the front of the line gets his coffee, and we move up.

"Okay," I say, trying to sound supportive. "I get it. You proved your point. You turned a rubber band into a fifty-dollar gift card. Can we stop with the whole Craigslist thing now?"

Nico looks scandalized. "What? No! Why would we stop now? It's working. So let's go all the way, baby!"

"We're meeting Tom Lancaster *today*."

"So?"

"So, that's it. Crescent City is only two hours from here. And then it's all over. If you think you're going to make enough money in two hours to convince me not to sell the car, you're delusional."

"Goonies never say die," Nico says triumphantly, raising a fist in the air.

He needs to stop with the old eighties movies. Yes, it was one of the things we bonded over at the beginning. But we don't need to bond now. In fact . . .

10. The less bonding, the better.

I roll my eyes and turn my attention to the board hanging outside the counter window, scanning the list of drinks for something that looks good.

"You know you know the reference," Nico taunts.

"Of course I know the reference. I just don't agree with the sentiment."

The woman at the front of the line pays, grabs her coffee in a to-go cup, and leaves. Nico and I take a step forward.

"You don't agree with the sentiment?" Nico repeats mockingly as the couple in front of us places their order.

"No. I don't think you have any hope of trading a fifty-dollar gift card up to something worth twenty-five thousand dollars . . . in two hours."

He points at his phone. "Mack Polonsky did say we could have anything in his room. Well, except his Battle Royale. He was very clear about that. I think he even bolded it in the e-mail."

"What's a Battle Royale?"

Nico shrugs. "I assume it's some sort of video game I've never heard of. Anyway, he sounds pretty desperate. I feel sorry for the kid. Listen to this." He flips his sunglasses onto his forehead and reads aloud from the screen.

"'DUDE! I NEED THAT GIFT CARD!'" Nico looks up at me to add, "That part is in all caps." He goes back to the e-mail. "'Jasmine Ramirez just agreed to go out with me. Me! Jasmine Ramirez! I know you don't know who that is, but just trust me, she's *hot*. Like, superhot. And I never in a million years thought she'd ever be into me.'" Nico glances at me again to add his commentary. "She does sound hot." He continues reading. "'I really didn't expect her to say yes. In fact, I wasn't even going to ask. I sort of did it on a dare from my friend Brett, because he didn't think I would ever do it. But I proved him wrong. And now I think he's really depressed because he's had a crush on Jasmine Ramirez since elementary school, but he's too much of a wuss to do anything about it. But that's a whole other story.'" Nico looks up at me. "Don't worry. He doesn't go into that story. After that, he just says, 'So anyway, Brett's out and I'm in. But here's the problem. I am broke. Dead broke. I spent the very last cent of my allowance losing a wager to stupid Brett on White Tower Blitz.'" Nico lowers his phone to add, "Another video game, I guess?"

I sigh impatiently, glancing at the couple ahead of us in line who seems to be taking a really long time making a decision about something as simple as coffee.

He continues reading. "'So now I have absolutely *no* money to spend on my date with Jasmine Ramirez. Did I mention she's hot?'" Nico looks up. "I think he did mention that, actually."

The couple finally decides on what they're having, pays, and steps aside. I anxiously approach the counter.

"Hi," I say to the girl behind the register, trying to keep the previous irritation out of my voice. "I'd like a white chocolate mocha, please."

The cashier inputs my order and turns to Nico. "Will this be together?"

"Yes," I say, and nudge Nico, who thankfully lowers his phone and glances at the menu board.

"Black coffee, please."

I snort. "Of course." I turn to the cashier. "He means he'll have the most boring possible item there is on your menu."

"Excuse me?" Nico says, pretending to be offended.

"Do you have anything more boring than a black coffee? Because if you do, he wants that instead."

"Someone got up on the wrong side of the bed today," Nico says.

"Yes, that's right. I had to squeeze between the bed and the wall to avoid stepping on you."

The cashier glances uneasily between us, not quite sure what to make of this situation.

"We're exes," Nico explains. "And she's cranky because we just had to spend the night together. It's a long story."

I huff. "That's *not* why I'm cranky."

"See, even she admits she's cranky."

"And will you stop telling every stranger we meet our entire life story?"

"Hey! She looks interested." Nico turns to the cashier. "Aren't you interested . . ." He bends down to read her name tag. "Laurie?"

"Um . . . ," Laurie says, looking panicked.

"See?" I tell Nico. "You've completely freaked her out. Aren't you freaked out, Laurie?"

"Um . . . ," Laurie repeats.

"So," Nico says imperiously to me. "What would *you* have me order? Since you clearly have life all figured out?"

"Something more interesting than black coffee!" I say, throwing my hands in the air.

"Fine," Nico says. "You order for me. I'll drink *whatever* you choose."

I scoff like this is the stupidest idea I've ever heard. "Don't be ridiculous."

"I'm serious," Nico says. "Order for me. Lady's choice."

Laurie is still glancing uneasily between us. "So, um, should I cancel the black coffee?"

"Yes," Nico says at the same time that I say, "No."

"Yes," Nico repeats. "Ali here—which isn't her real name, by the way, but don't bother asking her what it is because she won't tell you—is going to order for me." He turns to me and practically bows like he's greeting the queen. "Go ahead."

I roll my eyes. Why is he being so annoying?

But fine. If he wants to play this ridiculous game, I can play that game. I scan the menu, looking for the sweetest, most undrinkable coffee drink I can find. "Okay," I say, flashing an innocent smile to Laurie. "He'll have the Nutella S'mores Latte Explosion with extra whipped cream and extra syrup."

Nico grimaces for a brief moment but catches himself

and turns it into a wide grin. "Sounds delicious. In fact, make it a large."

Laurie hesitantly enters the order and rings up the total. I pay, and we step aside while we wait for our drinks.

"Okay," Nico says, whipping out his phone again. "Back to the Mack Polonsky saga."

I let out a soft groan. Nico ignores it and keeps reading the e-mail, which I'm now convinced is more like a novel than an e-mail.

"Where was I?" Nico scans the screen. "Oh, right. Here. 'So now I have absolutely *no* money to spend on my date with Jasmine Ramirez. Did I mention she's hot? Well, she is. And so you can see why I desperately *need* that gift card, bro. If I roll up to Tomato and Vine with Jasmine Ramirez and am able to say, "Order anything you like, babe. It's on me," I will look like such a playa pimp!'"

I bark out a laugh. "Somehow I doubt that."

"Right?" Nico says, and continues reading. "'Please, please, please trade it with me. I'll give you *anything* in my room. Anything. Well, except my Battle Royale. **Definitely not my Battle Royale! So don't even think about it, bro!**'"

Nico turns the phone around. "See, that last part is in all bold."

I nod. "I see."

"'Please write back ASAP and let me know. I'm in Eureka. If you knew how hot Jasmine was and how freakishly improbable it is that she actually said yes to me, you wouldn't hesitate for a second.'" Nico takes a breath and returns his phone to his pocket. "So you see, we have to go save this kid."

"Mmm," I say noncommittally.

"Otherwise, who knows what Jasmine Ramirez will do? She'll probably start dating someone else. Maybe even Brett!"

"You sound like a soap opera right now."

"His life is a soap opera!"

I impatiently tap my foot, peering at the counter to see if our drinks have appeared. Maybe I shouldn't have ordered Nico that Nutella S'mores Latte Explosion. It sounds really complicated. It probably takes two hours and a small army of people to prepare. "Every teenager's life is a soap opera," I point out. "Mack Padansky better get used to it."

"It's *Polonsky*," Nico says, like he's offended on Mack's behalf.

"Sorry," I mutter.

"Have some heart, Ali," Nico says earnestly. "The future of this nerd boy's life depends on us right now."

"How do you know he's a nerd boy?" I challenge.

Nico raises his eyebrows. "Seriously? Do you want me to read the e-mail again?"

I shrug. "I'm just saying that's a little judgmental."

"I guess you would know," Nico says, and when I cut my eyes to him, I see there's absolutely nothing playful about the jab.

"What's that supposed to mean?" I ask.

Nico scoffs. "I think you know."

"Well, I don't."

"You're the one who likes to pass snap judgments on people."

I feel my fists balling at my sides. I tell myself to relax. *Don't play into this. He's trying to bait you.*

"So, tell me," Nico goes on, "how would *you* judge Mack Polonsky?"

I resume my air of annoyance. "I won't. I don't give a crap about Mack Polonsky. Because we're not driving to Eureka."

"It's not that far," Nico insists. "It's right off the 101. We're going to drive through it anyway. The whole stop will take ten minutes at the most. We can't let him down."

"And I can't let Tom Lancaster down. Again. We don't have time for random stops at random losers' houses."

Nico smirks. "Ah, so you *have* passed judgment on him."

I close my eyes and try to take in a calming breath.

"Anyway," Nico goes on. "Mack Polonsky is *not* a random loser."

I shoot him a look.

"He happens to be a very *specific* loser who I now consider a friend."

"You consider everyone a friend," I point out. "You probably think Laurie is your friend."

"Laurie *is* my friend!" Nico says, loud enough for Laurie to glance apprehensively over at us from the cash register. I think she's legit afraid of us right now.

"The best part about a road trip is making friends," Nico goes on, undeterred by the look of panic on Laurie's face. "You get to meet new people, get involved in their lives—"

"Force yourself into their lives is more like it."

"Well, whatever," Nico goes on. "I already told Mack we were coming."

"What? When?"

Nico swipes on the screen, types in a few words, and presses send. "Right now."

I glare at him. He glares back. It's a bona fide standoff. And it probably would have lasted forever if Laurie hadn't announced that our order was ready.

I stalk back up to the counter, grab my coffee, and take a long gulp. It's scalding hot and burns the crap out of my tongue. "Argh!"

Nico picks up his large Nutella S'mores Latte Explosion with extra whipped cream and extra syrup and takes a reluctant sip. I watch his face carefully, waiting for him to cringe or gag or even spit it out onto the sidewalk because I *know* he hates it. He already told me when we were together that he hates fussy coffee drinks.

But he just closes his eyes and smiles, like a food critic on TV, tasting an especially exquisite appetizer. "Mmm. That's amazing."

"Shut up. You despise it and you know it."

"I'm serious!" he insists as we head back across the street to the car. "It's really, really good. You should try it. I'm letting you pick out my coffee drinks from now on."

I reach the passenger-side door and pause. "I'm holding you to that."

He flashes me a lighthearted grin over the top of the Firebird. "I would expect nothing less from you, Ali." Then he opens the door just before adding, "Or whatever the hell your name is."

The last time I went to a Tomato and Vine was the week before my ninth birthday, two months after Fear Epidemic released their comeback album, *Salvage Lot*, and announced they were going back on tour. Although, technically, we never got to the restaurant.

Tomato and Vine was one of my favorite places to eat as a kid. There was a location nearby in Santa Rosa—a thirty-minute drive from Russellville. Jackson had been promising me for two weeks that we would go for a pre-birthday dinner. Just the two of us. I remember counting down the days on a puppy calendar that hung by my bed. I remember getting all dressed up, putting on my favorite yellow dress, brushing out my hair, braiding it myself, and tying a ribbon at the end. I wanted to look perfect for my date with Jackson. That's how I thought about it for those two whole weeks. A date with my dad. The thought always made me giggle.

It was rare that Jackson and I did anything together, just the two of us. My mother usually didn't like him taking me anywhere alone. Especially after what had happened in Fort Bragg.

I remember sitting by the window that looked out at

the driveway and waiting for him. My mother was working the night shift, and Jackson and I were supposed to leave at five.

Five came and went. Six came and went.

Jackson didn't show.

Eventually I moved from the window to the couch. I turned on the TV. I kept one ear trained on the Animal Planet show I was watching and the other trained on the driveway, waiting for the sound of the Firebird on the asphalt.

I watched seven, eight, and nine pass by on the clock. And still no sign of Jackson.

Sometime after nine o'clock I must have fallen asleep because the next thing I knew, Jackson was shaking me.

"Hey, hey," he whispered, his voice hoarse as though he'd been screaming all night. "Wake up, sleepyhead. It's time to go."

"Go?" I asked groggily, wiping the sleep from my eyes. "Where?"

"To Tomato and Vine, silly. I didn't forget!"

I knew, in the way he said it, that he *had* forgotten.

I shook my head and let it fall back onto the throw pillow. "I'm too tired now."

"No!" Jackson said, a spark of desperation in his voice. His breath was sour and rancid. "I promised I would take you for your birthday. We're going to Tomato and Vine. You're getting your unlimited pasta and breadsticks."

"I'm not hungry anymore," I muttered, tucking my knees into my chest. "Let's go tomorrow."

But Jackson clearly wasn't having it. He slid his arms under me and lifted me off the couch. "No way, kiddo. We're going now."

I chuckled sleepily. "Daddy," I said. "It's late."

"The restaurant is open until eleven. I already checked."

He held me close to him, and I snuggled against his chest as he carried me out to the Firebird and deposited me into the back seat. After he buckled my seat belt, I immediately lay down and went back to sleep, hearing the familiar sound of the engine roaring as my eyes sank closed.

The next time I opened them, we were stopped. The motor was running, the interior of the car was dark, and Jackson was sitting behind the wheel, staring vacantly out the windshield, his fingers gripped around the steering wheel.

I sat up and glanced out the window, expecting to see the familiar parking lot of the restaurant, but outside of the car was dark too. I could make out what looked like miles of emptiness. Through the windshield, illuminated by the headlights, I saw a small, rusty swing set with two swings missing and a warped slide.

"Where are we?" I asked.

Jackson jumped as though he had sat on a nail. "Ali, you're awake." There was something about his voice that sent a shiver through me. It sounded hollow and robotic. Like every ounce of Jackson's usual charm and gravitas had been sucked out the window.

"Where are we?" I repeated.

"The park," Jackson replied. He turned toward me, and even in the low light, I could see his face was pale.

"But," I began uneasily, "I thought we were going to Tomato and Vine."

Jackson smiled at me. A slow, vacant smile. "Change of plans!" He seemed to be trying to force energy into his limp voice, but the end result sounded strained. "We're going to the park!"

I glanced at the decrepit swing set in front of us. "But I've never been to this park. I don't like the way it looks. Can't we just go to the restaurant?"

Jackson shook his head. "Sorry, kiddo. Tomato and Vine is closed. The park it is."

I bit my lip and looked at the clock on the dashboard. It was a little after ten. "But I thought you said it closed at eleven."

Jackson turned his gaze back out the windshield, falling silent for a long time. Finally, he spoke, and the cold timbre of his voice sent another chill through me. "I was wrong, kiddo. I'm sorry."

In that moment, I was suddenly overcome by a deep sadness. And I knew it was originating from Jackson. Emanating off of him like steam from a heated pool on a cold night.

I leaned forward and placed a hand on his shoulder. He startled again. "It's okay, Daddy," I told him. "We can just go home."

He covered my hand with his. "Good idea, kiddo," he replied, but once again, his voice was empty.

We didn't just go home, though. Jackson told me we had to stay there and wait. He took out his cell phone and called someone. I heard a man's voice on the other end. Twenty minutes later, that same man arrived in an SUV. I'd never seen him before in my life, but Jackson introduced him as a friend and told me he was going to drive us home.

I remember watching in confusion as the Firebird vanished outside the window of the strange man's car. I remember thinking how odd it looked just sitting there, abandoned, left behind. Jackson had never left his Firebird anywhere.

When I asked him why we were leaving his car in the middle of that creepy park, he didn't have an answer for me. And I never asked him again.

Because a week later, he was gone.

# 10:15 A.M.

## EUREKA, CA

### INVENTORY: 1968 FIREBIRD 400 CONVERTIBLE (1), CASH ($564.72), SEA GLASS (1 PIECE), TOMATO AND VINE GIFT CARD ($50 VALUE)

The girl who answers the door of the one-story ranch-style house on Humboldt Hill Road is tall and lanky. She's wearing faded ripped jeans and a gray T-shirt, and her blond hair is cut in a sleek and stylish A-line bob with pink streaks. She looks to be about fifteen years old.

"Hi," Nico says, straightening up into his prim and proper Boy Scout stance. "We're looking for Mack Polonsky."

The girl doesn't blink. "Yup. What do you want?"

Confusion flashes across Nico's face as he attempts to look over the girl's shoulder. "Is he here?"

The girl eyes me as if to say, *Is he stupid or something?* and then turns back to Nico. "Yes. *She* is."

It takes me about two seconds to put the pieces together, and Nico about a second longer. "Oh," Nico says, his whole body shifting slightly as though he's trying to figure out what to do with this new information.

"You're . . . ," Nico begins, then stops himself and raises an eyebrow. "So . . . Jasmine Ramirez, huh?"

The girl's face blooms red at the mention of the name, and I immediately know we're in the right place. She looks between the two of us. "Oh my God! It's you! You're the famous ex-couple from Craigslist."

"I wouldn't call us famous," I say uneasily.

"Well, you're famous among my crew," Mack explains, which doesn't exactly make me feel any better. "I showed all of my friends your Craigslist ad after I responded this morning. And they were all dying to know what you looked like."

I flinch when I realize she's staring straight at me as she says this.

"Me?" I ask incredulously.

"Yeah," Mack says, as though it's obvious. "Brett thought you'd be hot. I swore you wouldn't be. We made a bet."

"Excuse me?" I say, looking from Mack to Nico, as if to ask, *Did you have anything to do with this?*

But Nico just shakes his head.

"No offense," Mack is quick to add. "I just got a—I don't know—*not* hot vibe from the Craigslist post."

"You're kind of obsessed with hotness," I point out.

"So?" she asks, immediately assuming a defensive stance.

"I . . ." I struggle for something to say. "Nothing. I just . . ."

"You just thought a teenage lesbian from Eureka would be less superficial than that?"

"What?! No! I . . ." But once again, I can't find the words. My tongue is completely tied.

Nico smirks at me. "She kind of got you there."

"Shut up."

Mack looks between us. "So, who broke up with who?"

"I broke up with him," I say quickly, although why I feel the need to clarify this to a perfect stranger, I'm not sure. Nico snickers next to me, and I make a mental note to murder him later.

"It's true," Nico says. "She did break up with me. And I'm sorry to say you lost that bet."

I cut my eyes to Nico, but he doesn't look back at me. He's too busy sharing a consolatory look with Mack.

"Yeah," Mack says with a laugh. "I guess I did. Which sucks because that means I have to let him borrow my Knights versus Zombies for a whole month."

"Sorry about that." Nico puts out his fist to her, and she bumps it.

I can't believe this is happening right now. Is there a person out there who *doesn't* end up liking Nico? Is the boy simply incapable of offending anyone?

"So, are we doing this or not?" Mack says, glancing between us again. "Do you have the gift card?"

Nico pulls the plastic card from his jeans pocket and holds it up, like he's doing a commercial for a new low-interest, high-perks credit card. "Your date with Jasmine Ramirez is secure."

Mack's face brightens with a smile so big, it makes my chest ache a little. Because it reminds me of the smile I wore for most of my relationship with Nico.

"You guys have no idea how much you've saved me

right now!" Mack says, reaching out and touching the gift card as though it were a magic pony. "I've never met anyone like Jasmine before. She lights up rooms. And, well . . ." Her voice trails off, like she's not sure if she wants to continue. "I mean, I know all teenagers deal with the torment of not knowing if someone you like is going to like you back. But it's different for . . . people like me. It's almost like you've got two hurdles to jump over."

When I look at the lightness in Mack's face, I'm hit by another pang of longing. To feel that way again. To bask in that glow again. There's really no better feeling in the world than knowing that someone you like feels the same way. And for a moment, I wonder if Nico was right to insist that we come. This girl is going to go on a date with the girl of her dreams because of us.

Then, a second later, the voice of reason hits me. The one that tells me it won't work out. Jasmine will break her heart. Or vice versa. Because they're in high school, and that's how high school relationships end. With broken hearts. With shattered dreams. With awkward silences in computer labs.

People like June and Tyler are the exception, not the rule. They'll probably be together forever. I have no doubt I'll be a maid of honor at their wedding within the next five years.

People like my mom and Jackson, and me and Nico? We're the rule. We're the norm. I'm not one of those teenagers who is naive enough to believe that people who fall in love in high school will ever end up together.

"C'mon!" Mack says, opening the door wider. "Come

in! I'll show you my room. Like I said in my e-mail, you can have anything in it except—"

"Your Battle Royale, we know," I interrupt, now eager to get this over with.

Mack gives me a *What's your problem?* look that I promptly ignore, and follow her into the house. She leads us down a long, narrow hallway and into a room that literally makes me blink in disbelief. I'm not sure what I was expecting, but it certainly wasn't *this*.

The room looks like a museum. More specifically, a *chess* museum. There are at least twenty different chessboards set up on every available surface. Three on the desk, one on each nightstand, two on the dresser.

I shiver at the sight of all of them. Memories flicker through my mind like a phone call with a bad signal, fading in and out, swallowing giant chunks of the full picture.

*"Of course I know how to play chess. Don't you?"*

"Holy crap," Nico says, stepping in behind me. "Let me guess. You like chess?"

Mack guffaws. "Very funny. You couldn't tell from my e-mail?"

Nico and I exchange a baffled look. "No," Nico says.

"Battle Royale?" Mack prompts.

"We thought it was a video game," Nico replies.

Mack's face scrunches up. "Ew."

She walks around the foot of the bed and stops in front of a chess set stored inside a glass case with a spotlight pointed at it, like it's the crown jewels of a small country or something. Mack gestures to it with a grandiose flourish. "This is Battle Royale."

I take a step toward the box, careful not to touch it in case I trigger some kind of sensor alarm. I bend down and peer through the glass at one of the most exquisite chessboards I've ever seen in my life. The pieces are hand-carved out of stone—the kings in the shape of fat Henry the Eighths, the queens in the shape of Anne Boleyns, and the rooks in the shape of little Towers of London.

"Wow," I say, smiling. "This is amazing. Are you a fan of Tudor history?"

Mack shrugs. "I could take it or leave it, really. It's more that my dad left me this set when he died. He was a world-champion chess player. He was the one who taught me how to play. Although I don't dare play on this one." She taps the glass with a fingernail. "Nope, this baby stays locked up tight." She gestures to the rest of the room. "But seriously, any other set, you're welcome to have! Well, except Wizards versus Zombies, obviously, because now Brett gets that one for a month." She points to a chess set on her dresser with an army of various robed men and women, staged and ready to take on an army of the undead.

I return my gaze to the Battle Royale set walled off behind the protective glass, and it makes me think of the blue Firebird parked outside. The thing my own dad left me when he died. Mack won't even touch her inheritance, and how long did it take me to list that car on Craigslist? A few hours?

A rush of guilt clobbers me, but I quickly push it away. Our situations are completely different. Mack's dad was a world-champion chess player who actually stuck around long enough to teach her how to play the game. The only thing Jackson taught me was how fast people can disappoint you.

"Are these made out of wood?" Nico asks.

I glance over to see he's bent down, studying an adorable *Alice in Wonderland*–themed set on Mack's desk. The pieces on one side are painted in blues with Alice as the queen, the Mad Hatters as bishops, and eight little White Rabbits as pawns, while the pieces on the other side are painted in red hues with the Queen of Hearts leading a court of playing cards.

Mack beams. "Yes. Hand-carved. Pretty cool, huh?"

"Astonishing," Nico replies.

Of course he would gravitate toward the set made out of wood. Watching him examine the piece suddenly brings me back to the night of my birthday. When we spent the evening alone in the woodshop at Russellville High, his hands guiding mine over the sanding block, turning rough into smooth, splintery into soft. Skin on fire, lips searching . . .

"But trust me, you don't want that one," Mack says, thankfully interrupting my thoughts.

"Why not?" Nico asks.

"It's . . . um . . ." She looks around. "One of the pieces went through my dog."

I cough. "Excuse me?"

"Yeah," she says quickly. "The Tweedledee rook. Dog ate it, and we had to wait two days to get it back, if you know what I mean."

Nico slowly backs away from the board. "I think I do."

Despite how horrified I am, I kind of like how each of her chess sets has a story of some kind. They feel like pieces in her life.

"Are you sure you want to trade one of these sets?" I ask. "Aren't they all kind of special to you? Plus, they look like they're all worth more than fifty bucks."

"Oh, they are," Mack says proudly. "Most of them are worth at least two hundred."

"Two hundred?!" I repeat, baffled. I'm really not understanding the logic of this trading-up thing. "Why would you trade something for a lesser value?"

"Trust me," Mack assures me. "Jasmine Ramirez is *not* a lesser value. She's worth all of these chess sets combined."

"But," I argue, "if the chess sets are worth that much, why not just sell one on Craigslist and use the money to take Jasmine on a date?"

"I tried that," Mack laments. "I've had a few of them listed all week, but the only takers were too far away. No one wanted to come out to Eureka. Which is why I'm so desperate." She gives me a pleading look. "Seriously, you can have *any* other set. Just pick one."

I glance around the room, feeling strange about this whole arrangement. My eyes land on Mack's sliding closet door, which hasn't been closed all the way. Through the small gap I can see the corner of another chess set. One that's been banished to the closet for some reason.

"I like that one," I say, walking over to it and pushing

open the closet door a smidge so I can see the rest. It's an exquisite set. Pirates vs. the British Royal Navy. And as soon as I see Mack's face brighten, I know I've made the right choice.

"Yes!" she exclaims. "That's an amazing set. You should totally pick that one!" She glances back at Nico for a moment and gives a shrug that I suppose is meant to look casual. "Or whichever. Honestly, I don't care."

"Why is this one in the closet?" I ask.

"It's a long story," she says dismissively, refusing to meet my eye. "There was this other girl . . . at chess camp last summer . . ." She trails off for a moment. "Let's just say she didn't make it over both hurdles."

I flash her a warm smile. Because I get it. Mack and I are suddenly more alike than I realized. That chess set is her equivalent of everything I threw away that reminded me of Nico. Every item I packed up in a box and drove to the dump.

I suddenly picture this girl at camp, falling in love over that chessboard, stealing furtive glances across the table at her opponent, hoping and praying that she'll look back.

And she didn't.

You keep the things that give you good memories. You throw away the rest.

"We'll take it," I say.

"Awesome!" Mack claps her hands. "It's a deal, then?"

Nico offers her the gift card, which she takes with the delicacy of a white-gloved archivist. "It's a deal."

# 12:22 P.M.

## CRESCENT CITY, CA

### INVENTORY: 1968 FIREBIRD 400 CONVERTIBLE (1), CASH ($564.72), SEA GLASS (1 PIECE), PIRATES VS. BRITISH ROYAL NAVY CHESS SET (1)

Tom Lancaster is not what I expected. I'm not sure why, but I pictured him as a large, burly brute with a beard and maybe a hook for a hand. I realize how ridiculous that seems now as I watch the lean, middle-aged, clean-faced man tinkering around under the hood of the Firebird.

We're standing inside the spacious, well-lit professional garage in his classic-car shop. There are about ten other old cars surrounding us, in various stages of restoration. One car has been stripped so far down, it looks like a metal skeleton. Another is in the process of being repainted from white to orange.

Nico stands next to Tom, pointing at stuff and asking questions. Tom seems to like the attention and the opportunity to spread his obviously extensive knowledge about Firebird engines. For a minute, you could almost believe the two were father and son, sharing a mutual passion.

I don't know why, but watching Tom poke around in there, I suddenly feel nervous. Like I'm waiting for a doctor's diagnosis.

Tom closes the hood with a bang and wipes his hands on a red rag that's hanging from the pocket of his jeans. "Beautiful car," he says, smiling a wolfish smile.

I feel my tightly wound stomach start to slowly unclench. "Thank you. My dad took good care of it," I say.

"I can tell. She's really well kept up." He pauses, pressing his lips into an unsettlingly straight line. "Unfortunately, she's a clone."

"Excuse me?" I say, not understanding.

Tom points to the small 400 emblem on the hood of the car. "This was not put on in the factory. This was added years later. And according to the VIN—" He catches my confused expression and explains, "That's the vehicle identification number." Tom walks around the side of the hood and taps his finger against the corner of the windshield.

I walk over and squint at the series of twelve numbers etched into the metal.

"It's like a code," Tom explains. "It tells you about the car. Like these two digits—twenty-two—mean it's a Pontiac. Obviously. Then this number—eight—tells you it was made in 1968—okay. Good. But here's where we get into some trouble."

That word—"trouble"—causes my gut to clamp up again.

"If it's truly a Firebird 400, it would have an eight-cylinder engine. This number right here—six—indicates it's a six-cylinder engine."

Tom looks at me, as though I'm supposed to be following.

I'm not following.

"So?" I ask.

"So, according to the VIN, this car was never a 400. It's a base model. The car *does* have an eight-cylinder engine installed—a good engine—but I'm afraid it's not an original Firebird engine. Someone installed it more recently." He walks to the back of the car and gestures to the other red 400 symbol, affixed to the trunk. "Whoever owned this car last—your father, I guess—obviously slapped on a few of these emblems to make it seem like it was actually a 400. It happens a lot. You can buy the emblems online pretty easily."

The space around me starts to hum, louder and louder until I feel like I'm trapped inside a speaker with the bass turned all the way up.

"W-w-what?" I manage to stammer. "Are you saying the car is a fake?"

Tom clucks his tongue. "Not really. The word we use is 'clone.'"

I press my fingertips into my eyes. "I don't understand."

"I think what he's saying . . ." Nico steps in, his voice gentle, like he's afraid his words might break me. ". . . is that your father made changes to this car to make it seem like it was worth more than it is."

I shoot Nico a glare.

"He's right," Tom agrees, and then, as if it's supposed to make me feel better, he quickly adds, "Most laypeople can't tell. You need a trained eye, like mine, to spot the differences."

My hackles immediately go up. Is he trying to con me? Take advantage of me because he knows I don't know anything about cars? How on earth do I know that he's telling me the truth right now?

I swallow hard, trying to keep the shakiness from my voice. "Are you saying you don't want to buy it?"

Tom winces, like he was dreading this very question. "If I did buy it, I'm afraid I'd only be able to pay you three thousand for it."

"Three thousand!?" I repeat, in shock. For a second I'm certain I misunderstood.

Tom gives me a sad nod. "Afraid so."

Suddenly everything comes crashing down around me. The foreclosure notices. The boxes of stuff packed away in our living room. My mom's face telling me it's time to let go. Give it up. Surrender to the evil bank.

Three thousand won't be nearly enough. It won't hold them off. We need at least twenty-five. It's the reason I came all the way out here—endured hours of awkward silence and terse, emotionally loaded conversations with Nico, spent the night in a hotel room with him, surrounded by a dark, shadowy pit. For a minimum of twenty-five thousand dollars. For our escape. For our house.

Not so I could get all the way here and have Tom Lancaster take it all away!

"But," I argue, my voice weak, pitiful. "You said you would pay thirty-two."

He blows out a breath. "Yeah, that's when I thought it was a 400. And it's definitely not."

He's lying. He's conning me.

Suddenly, all of my panic and desperation evaporates, replaced with only white-hot rage. How dare he take advantage of me! How dare he make me drive all the way up here just to try to pull one over on me. He probably had this planned from the very beginning. He probably could tell from my Craigslist post and my e-mails that I was completely ignorant about cars. He probably scours the postings, looking for people he can swindle.

Nico was right. Craigslist is full of dangerous people. I was just focused on the wrong kind of danger.

I straighten up. I speak loudly and clearly. "Well, that's too bad," I say. "I guess I'll have to sell it to someone else. I've received a *lot* of other offers, you know?"

I expect Tom Lancaster to back down. To cave. To backpedal by saying something like, "Well, let me take another look around and we can talk." But he doesn't. He just gives me a pathetic little nod and says, "I understand. Although, I'll be honest with you. You're not going to be able to get more than four or five grand for a clone."

*Stop calling it that!* I want to scream.

Jackson would never own a fake car. He would never slap an emblem on the hood just to make it *seem* more valuable.

But as soon as the thought flashes through my mind, I know, without a shadow of a doubt, that it's *exactly* the kind of thing Jackson would do.

I feel like I could slink onto the floor right now. I want to scream. I want to fight. I want to shout that they're all in it together. Tom, Nico, the whole freaking universe. They're all conning me. It's one giant scam to see just how far I can fall.

And at the center of it all is Jackson. The ultimate con man. The ultimate swindler. Making you love. Making you trust. Making you feel safe. And then pulling it right out from under you. Like a magician with a nifty card trick. You thought you had the ace of spades? Look again, it's actually the two of clubs.

It's actually worthless.

I thought this car was his final act of redemption. A gift to me to say, *I'm sorry for all the "I'm sorrys."*

But no, it was just another con. Another sleight of hand. Jackson letting me down, even from beyond the grave.

*"This baby's not the base model. It's the 400. It's worth much, MUCH more."*

I feel cheated. Out of everything.

A car.

A dad.

A house.

A life.

*You're too trusting, Ali. That's your problem.*

"Ali." Nico's voice comes from the end of a long tunnel. "Are you okay?"

"No, I'm not okay!" I snap. "Why on earth do you think I would be okay?"

Nico shoots Tom an apologetic glance.

*Yes, Nico. Go ahead. Apologize for your ranting ex-girlfriend. Fix the situation. Smooth everything over. Make friends with Tom, and Scott the waiter, and Laurie the barista. Make everyone love you.*

"I'm sorr—" Nico begins to say, but I don't let him finish. I don't even know *who* he's apologizing to. Maybe to Tom. Maybe to me.

But I can't take one more apology. "Stop!" I tell him. "Just stop."

"Ali," Nico tries again, but again, I don't let him finish. In fact, I don't even wait around for him to try. I run right out of the shop.

One day, when I was twelve years old, a dining room table arrived at our front door. We'd never had a proper one before. We'd always used our dining room for storage.

To this day, I have no idea where that table came from. It just showed up on a random delivery truck. And tumbling in after it came Jackson.

It was two years after Fear Epidemic had broken up for the second and final time, their *Salvage Lot* album failing to re-rocket the band into stardom.

Jackson made a big fuss about the table. He went on

and on about how he was finally providing for his family. Making amends for lost time.

The surface was cracked. The legs were wobbly. And it smelled. Bad. Like Jackson had picked it up on the side of the road. And who knows? Maybe he had.

"Now we have something to play board games on," he told me, giving me that same irresistible wink that I remembered from my childhood.

But I was wary. Two years of living without him, of hearing my mother complain about his irresponsibility, had built a hard shell around me. A shell that was quickly cracking with each day that he was back.

"Do you still like board games? I remember you being obsessed with them."

That one sentence was all it took for my smile to break free. Jackson remembered. He remembered something about *me*. Suddenly I felt special all over again. I felt like maybe all of this time he'd been gone, he'd been thinking about me, keeping a mental log of the things he remembered, maybe even writing them down.

"Yes. I still like them."

"Good!" Jackson exclaimed. "Me too! We can play."

"What kind do you like to play?" I asked, feeling uncannily like I was talking to a stranger.

"Any kind. Clue. Risk. Monopoly. Chess."

"Chess?" My eyes lit up. I'd been wanting to learn chess for a while, but I didn't know anyone who could play. I'd tried to read the directions online, but I ended up just getting confused. "Do you know how to play?"

Jackson guffawed. "Of course I know how to play chess. You don't?"

I shook my head.

Jackson reached out and ruffled my hair. I admit, at twelve, I was too old for hair ruffling, but I didn't care. "Well, we have to do something about that, don't we?"

The next day when I came home from school, there was a chess set on the table. Once again, I have no idea where he got the chess set. He didn't seem to have any money. But it didn't really matter to me.

I dropped my backpack in the hall and ran to the table. Jackson came in a moment later, beaming. "Pretty nice, huh?"

"Are you going to teach me?" I asked.

"Absolutely. Sit down."

I slid into the chair and scanned the board in wonderment. All of the pieces were placed on their squares, like little soldiers ready to go into battle. It wasn't a fancy set. The pieces weren't carved from stone or wood or marble. They were plastic and chipped. But that didn't matter. They were mine. And Jackson was going to teach me how to play.

"Okay," he said, rolling up his sleeves. "First things first." He picked up the white piece in the corner. It looked like a little castle. "This is called the Fortress. It never moves. It stays in one place. Other pieces are protected if they're standing next to it."

I nodded, eagerly gobbling up the information.

"And this," he said, picking up one of the little stout

pieces in the front row, "is a scout. It goes out on missions to infiltrate the other player's Fortress. You have to have at least three scouts per mission. But you can't take too many scouts, otherwise you leave your Fortresses unprotected, and then this piece"—he picked up the little white horse—"the Cavalary can attack the Fortress and bring it down."

"What's the point of the game?" I asked. "How do you win?"

Jackson chuckled affectionately. "By getting all of your pieces to the other side of the board before I do."

I bit my lip. "But how can you do that if the Fortresses don't move?"

Jackson reached across the board and tapped my nose. "Good question." He paused, like he was trying to remember, and I wondered how long it had been since he'd played. "Oh, right. You *can* move the Fortresses if you free them with a spell."

My eyes widened. "A spell?"

Jackson nodded, looking serious. "This piece right here"—he picked up the white piece that sat next to the queen—"is the sorceress. She can cast spells to protect your pieces."

"Cool," I marveled.

"But be careful. She can *also* cast spells on the other person's pieces to freeze them in place or send them backward." Jackson studied my confused expression. "You know what? Let's just play. You'll pick it up as you go."

He was right. I did pick it up as I went. And it quickly

became my favorite board game ever. Jackson and I would have long, drawn-out battles, throwing curses and spells at each other's pieces. We would play until it got so late, my mom had to interrupt the game and send me to bed.

It wasn't until two years later, when I decided to join the chess club on my first day of high school, that I realized—with utter mortification—that Jackson's version of chess had been made up. In fact, he probably made it up right there on the spot. The way he made up everything.

"Of course I know how to play chess" was just another lie he told.

But for the next month, that dining room table made us feel like a family for the first time. We ate at it for breakfast and dinner. Mom cooked. Jackson did dishes. And after dinner, each night, Jackson and I played "chess."

One month later, Jackson was gone again.

We found the exact same Post-it note pinned to the exact same fridge. Like an echo through time. A reminder of just how stupid we had been to believe him.

*I'm sorry. I have to do this.*

Two months after that, one of the legs on Jackson's table broke, and we threw the whole thing away.

## 2:12 P.M.

## CRESCENT CITY, CA

INVENTORY: 1968 FIREBIRD ~~400~~ CONVERTIBLE (1),
CASH ($564.72), SEA GLASS (1 PIECE),
PIRATES VS. BRITISH ROYAL NAVY CHESS SET (1)

I had to run ten blocks to get here, but finally I reach the water. I stop at the end of the empty road, my shins pressed up against the metal guardrail. I stare out into the rocky tide pools below me, watching the waves fill up the giant craters cut into the ground before stealing the water right back out again.

I can hear the voice of that man from the beach in Fort Bragg echoing in my head.

*"The ocean forgives."*

And I want to scream, *No, it doesn't!* It doesn't forgive. It just gives and takes, gives and takes. Like the ultimate thief, the ultimate con man: promising fulfillment, then leaving you empty.

I pull the amber-colored sea glass out of my pocket and run my fingertips over the smooth edges. Maybe it's not smooth because the ocean is patient and forgiving and kind. Maybe it's smooth because the ocean is neglectful. Taking things in and then spitting them back out again.

Jackson used to try to smooth things over. He'd use soft words and empty promises. *I'll be better. I'll stick around. I'll help with the bills. I'll stop hoarding money and using it to fund my unsustainable lifestyle.*

For a while, it worked. On both of us. For a while, we believed him. Because we wanted to. Then we simply stopped wanting to.

We learned the natural rhythm of his movements. Like ancient people studying this very tide.

He came, he left.

He came, he left.

And we were the ones who had to learn how to forgive. Or at the very least, forget.

I hear the sound of an engine behind me. It's so familiar, I don't even have to turn around to confirm that it's the Firebird.

The worthless, piece of crap, *cloned* Firebird.

The sound of that engine is engrained in my memory. The sound of those tires crackling on the asphalt is like a permanent piece of my soul. Jackson's ghost haunting me from beyond the grave.

But when I turn around, I don't see Jackson behind the wheel.

I see Nico.

And the sight of him unnerves me. But to be fair, everything about him on this trip has unnerved me. The way he looks. The way he talks. The way he walks. The way he jumps in and out of the car, flips his hair, runs his hands along the steering wheel.

Because everything about him is Jackson.

They've merged into one person. One bad memory. One lying, deceiving disappointment.

It was something I fought throughout our entire relationship. The comparison. The hardwired inclination to distrust everything he said. And for eighty-eight days I managed to keep it at bay. I managed to tell myself every day that they weren't the same person. That Nico was nothing like Jackson. That I would never let myself fall for the same person that my mother had. That Nico would never lie to me.

Until he did.

And then it was like glass breaking.

The beautiful, shimmering dome of our relationship came shattering down around us. And I was left with the cold, harsh reality that I'd somehow managed to ignore for eighty-eight days.

They are exactly the same.

They both lied and broke my heart. They both let me down.

Because apparently that's what people do.

They make you trust them, and then they bolt.

*Except Nico is still here*, a small voice reminds me.

But I ignore it.

Nico isn't here for me. He's here for the thousand dollars I promised him. He's here for the money. Nothing else.

Nico kills the engine of the Firebird, and my gaze falls on the car. Jackson's perfect, immaculate car, with its shiny blue paint and soft white leather seats and the license plate that reads FEPDMIC.

> **You find out your irresponsible, flighty, unreliable, reckless, lying father has let you down, yet again! What do you do?**
>
> **A** *Snap.*
> **B** *Snap.*
> **C** *Snap!*

With a roar that sounds like some kind of ancient clan battle cry, I run full speed at the car. I kick the tires repeatedly and pound the hood with my fist. I've never been in a fight before, and I never imagined my first time would be with a 1968 Firebird convertible. But it doesn't last long.

"Hey! Hey! Hey! Hey!" Without opening the door, Nico jumps out of the car and grabs me, wrapping his strong arms around my waist and pulling me back, out of striking distance. I struggle against him, turning my rage against Jackson onto him. Kicking and twisting and jerking. "Ali!" Nico says in a tender but firm voice. "Stop. *Stop.*"

His arms tighten around me, holding me close. So close I can smell him. The scent is familiar. Comforting. Even though I don't want it to be. I want it to be repulsive. I want to hate it. I want to hate *him.*

I do.

I hate him.

I hate Jackson.

I hate this stupid, stupid car and that stupid, stupid band.

Again I try to twist out of Nico's grasp, but all I manage to do is twist into him, until I'm facing him. Until his gaze latches on to mine. Until his mouth is inches away. Until I can feel his heart beating under his shirt, through his skin.

Until I melt.

And collapse.

And he catches me.

Always catching me. Always fixing me. Always there.

Stupid, stupid Nico.

"We're stuck." The words choke out of me. The realization overwhelms me. Will my mom and I ever get out from underneath his mistakes? Will I ever escape Jackson Collins? My mother divorced him. I changed my name. We kicked him out. He *died*.

And yet he's still there. Digging the dirt out from under us with each step that we take. So that we're always sinking.

"We're stuck," I say again. I no longer know if I'm talking about Jackson or the road trip or something else entirely. But it doesn't really matter. It seems to be a catch-all phrase right now. It seems to be the sentence that perfectly encapsulates my life.

"Nothing he had was ever as valuable as he made you believe it was," I tell Nico.

For a long time, he doesn't reply. He doesn't ask who

I'm talking about. It's obvious. He doesn't ask how I'm feeling. That's obvious too. But eventually, he asks, "Why are you so desperate to save this house, Ali?"

I gently lower myself down so that I'm sitting on the hood of the car. "Because it's my house. It's my home." I'm surprised by the sound of my own voice. The words come out flat and empty. Like the voice of that bank manager on the day my mother and I went to try to fight the first foreclosure notice.

I remembered thinking the manager didn't sound like a person. He sounded like a robot. An ATM machine with a preprogrammed script.

*"I'm sorry, Ms. Collins. There's nothing we can do."*

*"I'm afraid it's too late for an extension."*

*"Yes, Russellville Bank is very sympathetic to your situation."*

Nico sits down next to me, but again he doesn't say anything. I think he's waiting for me to continue.

Waves crash. Water comes in. Water goes out.

And I'm still here.

"Is it . . . ," Nico begins, but then seems to be searching for the courage to finish. "Will you be homeless if you lose the house?"

I shake my head. "No. It's not like that. My mom already rented us an apartment in Harvest Grove."

"Harvest Grove is nice."

"But it's not *ours*. It's not home." I run my fingers through my hair. "It's all Jackson's fault. When he was still married to my mother, he would open credit cards in her name, max them out, and then not pay them off. By the time she filed for divorce, she was so far in debt, it was impossible to climb out. Everything we earned went toward paying off his mistakes. There was nothing left over for the mortgage. And when that car appeared Thursday afternoon, I thought . . ."

That's when my voice finally cracks. That's when *I* finally crack. Like a tide pool that's suffered too much abuse from the reckless ocean and is now breaking open, spilling over, unable to take the pressure any longer. Tears stream down my face in long rivers, pooling under my chin.

"You thought, for once, he could *help*," Nico finishes the sentence for me. "Instead of destroy."

His words are so spot-on, his comprehension so profound, I flinch and look at him.

"I get it," he says to my questioning gaze. Then he laughs darkly and drops his head into his hands. "Trust me, I get it."

I feel a tingle shoot up my spine. I'm suddenly certain he's going to come clean too. He's going to break open that locked vault of a mind and tell me everything. Everything he refused to tell me in our eighty-eight days together.

I brace myself for it.

I promise myself that whatever it is, I will not judge. I will not condemn. I will just listen. I will understand the way he seems to understand me right now.

But the truth never comes.

The vault remains locked.

Instead of revealing his own mess, Nico, true to form, tries to clean up mine. He lifts his head and says, "I know you don't want to hear this, but you don't need to sell that car to get twenty-five thousand dollars."

I hide my crushing disappointment with a scoff. "Right, the stupid trades."

"Are they, Ali?" Nico fires back, that tenseness returning to his voice, as though he, too, has reached the end of his rope. "Are they stupid? Because if I recall, we started out with a rubber band and now we have a chess set in the back seat that's probably worth more than two hundred dollars."

"Did you not hear me? I need the money by next week!"

"Or what?" Nico challenges. "What happens if you don't get the money by next week?"

I throw my hands up in the air. "I lose everything."

"No," Nico corrects. "You lose a house. That's not everything."

"It may as well be! It's everything to me."

"Okay," Nico allows, although he still doesn't look convinced. "So, what are you going to do about it? Now that the car is no longer in play?"

"I . . . ," I rush to say before realizing I have no idea how to finish that sentence. I don't know what I'm going to do. I haven't thought much further than my plan to run out here and wallow at the sea. My shoulders sag with defeat. "I don't know. Go home and start packing, I guess."

Nico stands and faces me. "Exactly."

I look up at him, shielding my eyes from the bright sun overhead. "Exactly what?"

"You have nothing to lose by giving this a try."

"That's not true," I argue. "I could call Tom Lancaster back right now and sell him the car for three thousand. At least it'll be something."

"We can sell the car to anyone at any time for three thousand dollars."

I huff out a breath and continue to stare up at him. He looks so confident right now. So sure of himself. I wish, for one second, I could share that confidence. I could live in Nico's skin and feel what it's like to be so dang optimistic all the time.

"Why are you really doing this, Nico? Why do you even care?"

He lowers his gaze, and I see his confidence waver for just a flicker of a second. "I need the money too." But he won't look at me as he says it.

"And you really think you can trade up to something worth twenty-five thousand dollars by next week?"

"I really do." He finally lifts his eyes and looks at me. "But I can't do it alone. Or rather, I don't want to. Will you do this with me? Will you take a chance on me?"

Despite the humid sea air, my throat goes bone-dry. For some unfathomable reason, I want to say yes. To whatever he's asking. That's the power of Nico's eyes, Nico's words. They have the ability to entrance. To form spells.

But the problem is, I've already taken a chance on him. And it failed.

And he can never fix that.

Which means, he's right. What do I have left to lose?

## [DRAFT] FOR TRADE: Hand-carved wooden chess set (Crescent City, CA)

Help! I'm stuck on the road with my ex-boyfriend and he's driving me crazy. Literally. (He's the one driving.) I need your help. The faster I can trade up, the faster I can get out of this car and go home. We currently have a gorgeous wood-carved chess set with a Pirates vs. British Royal Navy theme. What will you trade for it? We'll pretty much take anything at this point, and we'll pretty much travel anywhere. Can you tell I'm desperate? Pictures below. The pieces are really exquisite.

# 3:02 P.M.

## CRESCENT CITY, CA

### INVENTORY: 1968 FIREBIRD CONVERTIBLE (1), CASH ($564.72), SEA GLASS (1 PIECE), PIRATES VS. BRITISH ROYAL NAVY CHESS SET (1)

Nico and I are both starving, and we need a place to stop so we can set up the chessboard and take photographs for the Craigslist post. We find a restaurant right on the water called the Chart Room and order grilled crab sandwiches, which apparently are a special around here.

Nico removes the chessboard from the box that Mack gave us to carry it in and starts pulling red pirate pieces out and assembling them on his side of the board. I reach into the box and grab blue naval officers and soldiers and position them on the opposite side.

With each piece that I place, I can't help thinking about Jackson and that chessboard he came home with when I was twelve. How his made-up rules caused me to completely humiliate myself at that first chess club meeting.

"The craftsmanship on these pieces really is exquisite, isn't it?" I ask Nico.

"Yes," Nico says, and I can hear the reverence in his voice. He's impressed.

I pick up one of the pieces—a soldier in a blue coat and white pants, holding a tiny telescope. "Which do you think this one is?"

Nico leans across the table and squints at it. "The knight, I think."

An involuntary smile dances on my lips as I think about the looks on the faces of those kids at the chess club meeting, when I moved my knight—or the "Cavalary," as I called it—to the far corner of the board, next to my "Fortress."

"What are you doing?" my assigned opponent asked.

"It's the most vulnerable piece to the Sorceress's spells," I explained as though it were obvious. "I'm protecting it behind the Fortress."

The laughter followed me out the door of the library and all the way home. After I finished crying from the humiliation, I went online and spent hours watching chess matches on YouTube, studying the *real* rules of the game and cursing Jackson's name the entire time. But even though I was angry at him for lying to me—for causing me such mortification on my first day of high school—I remember thinking that Jackson's version was *way* better than the real version. It felt more fun. Less stuffy. More creative. Less rigid.

Regardless, I never went back to the chess club.

"What?" Nico asks, breaking into my thoughts. And that's when I realize that I'm still smiling.

I shake my head. "Nothing." I place the knight on its proper square. "Have you ever made a chess set? Out of wood, I mean?"

Nico shakes his head. "No, but I've always wanted to."

I pluck the next blue piece from the box. This one is a foot solider with a musket; I assume it's one of the pawns and position it in front of the knight. "What theme would you pick?"

Nico smiles. I think he likes this question. "Hmm. Maybe I'd start with a classic set. Just to see if I could do it."

"You could do it," I say confidently. Nico lifts his head and meets my eye. I flash him a kind smile and reach into the box for another piece.

"What makes you so sure?" he asks, clearly trying to milk the compliment.

I play along, shaping my voice into something professional and serious, like an art critic. "I've seen your work, Mr. Wright. You have a strong future."

"Princeton could use a guy like me?" he asks, quoting *Risky Business*, another installment from one of our Epic Eighties Movie Marathons.

I laugh. "Yes. Exactly."

I assume Nico is going to drop it now. We've made the joke. We've followed the topic to its conclusion. What more is there to say? But then, after an extended silence, he asks, "What's your favorite piece I've ever built?"

I flinch and look up at him. This time, he won't meet

my eye. He's busy arranging the little pirate pawns with their black-and-white-striped shirts and red belts.

The real answer to his question is easy. It comes to me instantly. But I can't say that. I can't give him the real answer. And I can't mention any of the other things he made for me because they're all sitting in a landfill somewhere.

I rack my brain for something safe. But I come up with nothing.

Everything Nico ever made—everything Nico ever touched—is too sacred. Too many memories are seeped into the wood.

So I just grab another piece from the box—an eighteenth century British warship, which serves as the rook—and place it on the board. "I don't know," I mutter, refusing to look him in the eye. "I guess there are just too many good ones to choose from."

Thankfully, our grilled crab sandwiches arrive a moment later, and I have something to stuff into my mouth.

I'd always known Nico liked to build things out of wood. Even before we became a couple, I would occasionally see him leaving school with some kind of handmade object he'd crafted in woodshop. Stools, boxes, clocks, bookends.

After we started dating, those were the kinds of gifts he would give me. Other boys might bring flowers or write poetry or take girls on fancy dates to fancy restaurants. Not Nico. Nico carved little dogs out of wood (inspired by the regular clients at Chateau Marmutt). He sanded down splices of tree trunk to make beautiful ringed coasters. He even made me a checkerboard once, after he found out how much I love board games. And two nights later, he showed up with hand-carved wooden pieces to match.

Every time he picked me up, every time he showed up at my door, he would have something in his hand. An offering of sorts. *Sorry I can't take you somewhere nice*, his eyes would say.

*Nice places are overrated*, mine would say back.

On the night of my eighteenth birthday, two months into our relationship, Nico picked me up at my house in his truck.

I asked where we were going. He said it was a surprise.

It certainly was. When we pulled up in front of our high school at eight o'clock at night, I thought he had to be joking.

"You're taking me to school?" I asked. "For my birthday."

"Not exactly," Nico said, and killed the engine. When we hopped out of the truck, he took me by the hand and guided me past the main entrance, around the side, near the gym. He paused at one of the back doors, and I yanked on the handle.

Just as I suspected. It was locked.

"How do you expect us to get in?" I asked.

Nico fished a key out of his pocket and held it up triumphantly. "With this."

My mouth fell open. "How do you have a key to the school?"

He inserted the key into the lock and turned. "Mr. Canter."

"The woodshop teacher gave you a key?"

He held the door open for me. "I come here a lot. He trusts me."

I had to laugh at that. Of course he did. Everyone at school loved Nico.

As soon as we were inside the darkened hallway, Nico reached for my hand again and led me up the back stairs and down the hall. I'd never actually been inside the Russellville High woodshop before, and as soon as I entered, I wondered why.

It seemed like such a wonderful place. Such a place of possibility. With its mysterious-looking tools and machines and large sheets of wood.

A magical place.

Or maybe that was just because I was there with him.

Nico looked so sexy standing there among the musty scent of oak, I could barely form words.

"W-w-what are we doing here?" I stammered.

"What do you think we're doing?" he asked. "We're going to build something amazing." He led me over to a table where a blueprint had been spread out. I tilted my head to try to decipher the shape of the design.

"A birdhouse?" I asked.

He ran his hands across the paper, smoothing it down. "Yes. A birdhouse."

For the next two hours, Nico taught me how to saw, sand, nail, and finish. By the end, we had done exactly what he said we would do. We had built something amazing.

Nico held up the tiny wooden house for my inspection. "Do you like it?"

"I love it."

"And I love you."

It was the first time either of us had said those words. I went completely numb. I couldn't speak. But Nico didn't seem to mind. He gently set the birdhouse down on the table, gathered me in his arms, and kissed me.

When we finally pulled apart, he looked deep into my eyes. He gave me silent permission to say it back. He waited for me to say it back.

I didn't say it back.

Instead, I crushed my lips against his once more. He responded immediately, pulling me into another intense, all-consuming, debilitating kiss. His arms wrapped around me, his fingers found their way up under my hoodie, pressing into my skin, leaving little white Nico-was-here indents that would soon fade.

There was an urgency in his kiss that told me exactly what he was asking for. But somehow, I couldn't bring myself to give it.

I told myself it didn't matter. Words weren't everything. After all, Jackson had said I love you a thousand times to me and my mom, and he was the one who kept leaving.

I didn't need to say the words. My actions would speak for me. And it would be enough.

But as Nico drove me home later that night and I held our beautiful creation in my hands, the birdhouse no longer felt like it was constructed out of solid wood.

It felt like it was made out of thin, flimsy paper.

It felt like one gust of wind might blow the whole thing down.

After we've finished eating and paid the bill, and the chess set has been fully assembled, Nico barely has time to get out his phone, let alone take a picture, before we hear a voice call out, "Oh, how *darling*! Howie, look at that chess set!"

We both look up to see a gray-haired woman waddling over to our table. She picks up the royal commander of the British Navy—the king piece—and studies it through the bottom half of her enormous bifocals. "Just look at that craftsmanship. Howie! Get over here!"

A moment later, a man with matching gray hair and bifocals comes scuttling over.

"Will you look at this?" she says. "This is exactly what we need for room seven!"

I glance between them. "Room seven?"

The woman laughs. "Sorry. We own a bed-and-breakfast up in Seaside, Oregon. Have you ever been?"

I shake my head. "I've never left California."

"Really?" Nico and the woman say at the same time.

Heat fills my cheeks. "Really."

"Oh, you must come visit!" the woman crows. "It's simply beautiful. Our little inn is right on the coast. Gorgeous views. I run the front of house—decorating the guest rooms and designing the breakfast menus—and Howie here runs the business."

Howie gives a weak little wave, like this whole conversation is making him uncomfortable.

I smile politely. "Sounds nice."

"Oh, it's just delightful. Ten guest rooms, all with their own elegant charm. We're currently in the process of remodeling room seven. According to that Rip Advisory, we need more family-friendly rooms."

"Rip Advisory?" Nico repeats.

"She means TripAdvisor," the old man says.

"Thirty years we've run that B and B," the woman goes on, like her husband isn't even there. "Thirty years! And we were doing just fine. Wonderful comments in the guest book. We even got a write-up in one of the big travel guidebooks! They gave us four stars. And then that awful Rip Advisory comes along, and suddenly people got mean, you know? Someone actually had the audacity to write a scathing reviewing about *my* blueberry pancakes. Saying they had *too* many blueberries. Too many! That recipe has been in my family for generations. No one has ever had a single bad thing to say about those pancakes until Rip Advisory came along. It's that Internet business. People feel safer hiding behind their computer screens and fancy snaps."

"Apps," her husband corrects.

She waves this away. "It's almost as though human

courtesy went right out the window, along with those travel guidebooks everyone used to use. We were written up in one, you know? They gave us four stars."

"You said that already," Howie reminds her.

"Now it's all about the Rip Advisory. People can say anything they want about your business, and no one can argue." She returns the chess piece to the board. "So, anyway, we're trying to make room seven more family-friendly. Our grandson suggested we decorate it with a pirate theme. He's seven. Don't know how we got to the place where we're taking business advice from a seven-year-old, but here we are."

Nico shoots me a look across the table, then turns to the couple. "Pirates *are* pretty cool."

The woman stares at him through her thick glasses. "Really?"

"Oh yeah. And this chess set would make an *excellent* edition to a pirate-themed room."

She sighs wistfully down at the set. "Yes, it would. Maybe if you tell me where you got yours, I can go on the eBits and find one."

"She means eBay," Howie chimes in.

"Well, actually," Nico says beaming up at her, "today must be your lucky day, because we were about to post this on Craigslist."

The woman frowns, confused.

"It's where people sell stuff," Nico quickly explains.

The woman looks like she just won the lottery. "Did you hear that, Howie?"

"I'm standing right here, Blanche."

Blanche reaches into her purse and pulls out her wallet. "Well, tell me, how much do you want for it?"

"Oh, we're not selling it," Nico says.

"But you just said—"

"We're *trading* it."

Blanche looks to Howie, but Howie seems just as confused. "Is this what the kids are doing these days?"

Nico chuckles. "Sort of, I guess."

"Oh!" Blanche says excitedly. "We just cleaned out the attic of the house and found a bunch of old stuff from when my son was a kid. We drove it down to him this morning, but he doesn't want any of it. We were going to bring it to the Goodwill. Do you want to have a look and see if there's anything in there you want to trade?"

"Sure!" Nico says. He quickly packs up the rest of the chess set and hops out of the booth. He follows the old couple out of the restaurant, and I follow reluctantly behind.

"What are you doing?" I whisper to him. "What makes you think we're going to find anything of value in that car?"

"Haven't you ever seen *Antiques Roadshow*?" he asks. "People find junk in their attic worth thousands of dollars all the time."

We reach the parking lot of the restaurant, and Blanche opens the trunk of their hatchback, gesturing ceremoniously to the collection of open boxes.

I cringe as it immediately reminds me of the house full of boxes waiting for me back in Russellville. At least *our* boxes are neatly packed. This stuff looks like it's just been tossed in haphazardly. I catch sight of old ratty sweatshirts and useless trophies with cracked gold paint.

"Wow," Nico says, and I can hear the disappointment hiding under his fake enthusiasm. "This looks great."

Well, what did he honestly expect to find?

He sets the box with the chess set down on the ground and picks through a few of the boxes, but I can tell he's just going through the motions. There's no way he's trading our Pirates vs. British Royal Navy chess set for any of this junk.

Nico flips through a dusty blue photo album, revealing old, blurry pictures of a bunch of kids in baseball uniforms. Half of them are out of focus.

"Dennis took those with his first camera," Blanche explains.

"Cute," Nico says, closing the album and setting it down. He pushes a few children's books aside, and that's when my gaze falls on something familiar. Painfully familiar.

I know, even before I can see the whole thing, that it's a Gibson Les Paul electric guitar. I recognize the black wooden surface and silver strings.

"That," I say quietly, pointing toward the object partially hidden in the back of the trunk. "Trade the chess set for that."

Nico follows the direction of my finger, and when he sees what I see, his head falls into a nod. "Good eye, Collins."

He reaches deep into the trunk and pulls out the guitar.

"It's worth at least four hundred," I whisper to Nico as he holds the guitar by the neck and admires its design.

"Are you sure?"

I nod, unable to look directly at the instrument. "I'm sure."

Nico turns to Blanche. "We'll take this."

"Oh, splendid!" says Blanche. "Dennis just had to have that guitar. He swore he would take lessons and practice every day. He played it for about a month before giving up. I'm happy you spotted it."

Nico picks up the box with the chess set in it and hands it over. "I hope everyone who stays in room seven will enjoy this."

Blanche beams. "Thank you! I'm sure they will. And hey, if you ever want to stop by the inn, we'd love to have you! No charge. On the house!"

"Wow," Nico says. "That's very generous. Thank you."

After Blanche and Howie get into their car and pull out of the parking lot, Nico and I head back to the Firebird. He rests the guitar against the side of the car and snaps a few pictures for Craigslist before storing the instrument in the back seat.

"How did you know how much this guitar was worth?" Nico asks as he gets in behind the wheel.

I shrug. *"Antiques Roadshow."*

Nico gapes at me as he starts the engine. "Really?"

I turn and look out the window. "No. Not really."

I was seven years old when I found Jackson's secret stash. Hundreds of hundred-dollar bills rolled up and rubber-banded, hidden beneath the spare tire in the trunk of the Firebird.

The day I found it, Jackson was in the garage, his head and torso hidden beneath the front of the car, only his legs visible. I was looking for a stuffed rabbit that I'd sworn I left in the trunk after Jackson picked me up from a sleepover at June's. The rabbit was nowhere to be seen. But the stash seemed to jump out and bite me.

"What is this?" I asked Jackson, standing next to his legs.

Jackson rolled out from underneath the car, a wrench dangling in his grease-stained hand. He looked at the wad of cash, and a chuckle of sorts trickled from his mouth. He sat up and patted the ground next to him, asking me to sit down. I happily obliged. Back then, I coveted any and all attention I could snag from Jackson. Maybe some part of me just knew that it wasn't going to last forever. That I should store it up.

The truth was, I was enamored with Jackson. Everyone was. Including Jackson. *Especially* Jackson.

He took the wad of cash from me and ran it under his

nose, closing his eyes as he inhaled. "This," he said, his eyes popping open, "is my escape fund."

"What's that?"

He laughed and pressed his forehead against mine. His face was so close, his piercing blue eyes so full of mischief. "It's what we use to buy ice cream when your mom's at work."

"Mommy's at work now," I pointed out.

He tweaked my nose, making it feel like the most important nose in the world. "Exactly. So let's go."

We went to the Frosty Frog, and Jackson bought me a triple scoop. I couldn't even finish a third of it. He finished the rest.

As he chomped on the last bit of cone and tossed his napkin into the trash, he explained that whenever we took money out of the escape fund, we had to put money back in. So we wouldn't ever run out. When I asked how we do that, Jackson drove me to the other end of town, to a shop I'd never seen before. They seemed to sell all manners of used and old things.

Jackson had clearly been a regular at this place because the man behind the counter smiled and greeted him by name when we walked in.

"Got anything new for me?" Jackson asked.

"Right over there." The man pointed to a beat-up-looking black electric guitar sitting in the corner of the shop, crammed between an old video game console and a dusty toolbox, and said, "Sounds like crap but—"

"I'll fix it," Jackson said before the man could finish. "How much?"

The man seemed to balk, afraid to commit to a number. Jackson arched his eyebrow. "Don't try anything, Rick."

Rick sighed. "Fine. Two hundred."

Jackson seemed satisfied with this, and I watched him lick his fingers before counting out two hundred-dollar bills from the wad of cash in his pocket and handing them over in exchange for the guitar.

"I don't understand," I told Jackson as we left the shop. "I thought you said we were going to put money back *in* the escape fund."

He winked at me. "We are."

Jackson spent the rest of the day in the garage. He took that guitar apart and pieced it back together as easily as if he'd made the thing himself. I sat on the hood of the Firebird and watched, marveling at how I never knew Jackson could fix a guitar. Car engines, yes. But not musical instruments.

When he was done, he gave it a good polish and played a few chords. "See? Now it's worth double."

"How?" I asked.

"You can't take anything for face value, kiddo. Everything's got the potential to be worth more if you're creative enough."

Jackson snapped a few photos of the guitar and created a listing on eBay, and for the next few days, we watched the bids go up and up, until the instrument finally sold for nearly five hundred dollars.

"And that's how it's done," Jackson said in the parking lot of the bank, as he added the five new, crisp hundred-dollar bills to his stack, rolled it up, and secured it with the rubber band. "Pretty cool, huh?"

I nodded. Because it *was* pretty cool. Jackson made it look so easy. I immediately wanted to go back to that shop and do it all over again. But Jackson laughed and guided me back to the Firebird. "Maybe next week, kiddo. You gotta be patient. The big finds don't come along every day."

On the way home, Jackson made me promise never to tell my mom about the escape fund. When I asked why, he told me it was because she would get mad. She would make him give her all the money he'd made so she could spend it on boring things like mortgage payments and insurance. I didn't know what either of those things were, but they certainly sounded boring to me.

"I'd much rather spend it on ice cream, wouldn't you?" he asked.

I nodded, because this sounded perfectly rational to my seven-year-old brain. And I was a rational person. Of course, that was before Post-it Notes and broken dining room tables and made-up chess rules and Jackson walking out on us not once, but *twice*. That was back when I thought I had a dad who would be around forever.

So I kept my promise. I never told my mom. And Jackson continued to buy me secret ice cream when she was at work, making the escape fund pretty much my favorite thing ever.

It wasn't until my ninth birthday that I first learned what an escape fund really was.

# 5:20 P.M.

# HIGHWAY 101

### INVENTORY: 1968 FIREBIRD CONVERTIBLE (1), CASH ($529.10), SEA GLASS (1 PIECE), GIBSON ELECTRIC GUITAR (1)

According to the map on Nico's phone, we'll be in Oregon in only thirty-three minutes.

We received a trade request for the guitar quickly. A man up in Brookings, just across the state line, wants to trade it for a vintage typewriter that he swears is worth more than five hundred dollars. Nico searched the model number online to confirm this, and that was that.

We're heading to Oregon.

I feel a small rush of excitement at the thought of leaving the state for the first time in my life. But I also feel uneasy about the direction we're so obviously heading. Oregon is only one state away from Washington. Technically we're supposed to be going where the trades take us, but there's no doubt we're on a clear path north. If we keep going the way we're going, eventually we'll end up . . .

*There.*

Tacoma, Washington.

The last place Jackson ever ate. The last place Jackson ever ordered a drink. The last place Jackson ever stumbled out of a bar, ranting about Fear Epidemic and how important he was to their success. And did you know that they were formed right here? In Tacoma?

Poetically, like a bizarre circle of life, Tacoma, Washington, was where Fear Epidemic began and Jackson ended.

"Do you want to listen to something?" Nico asks, interrupting my thoughts. The top is back down, so the car is quiet again.

"Sure," I say, swiping away from the map on his phone and opening the podcast app. "I think I downloaded an episode about emojis."

"Actually," Nico says, gently removing the phone from my hand. "I created a playlist last night. Can we listen to it?"

I shrug. "Sure."

Nico cranks up the volume on his phone, presses play, and drops the device into the compartment in the driver's-side door. Like he's purposefully trying to hide it from me.

"What is this new playlist?" I ask, but a second later the familiar hard-hitting guitar riff of the first song comes on, and the blood freezes in my veins.

I know this song.

I *hate* this song.

The lead singer launches into the first verse in his annoyingly scratchy voice. *"Phone ring. Voices meander like waves. Beating up the air."*

This is "Nearly a Saint" by Fear Epidemic. Their first big single. And the first song on their debut album.

"The playlist is called 'What's Her Name?'" Nico explains.

I grit my teeth. "Turn it off."

"Can't," Nico says innocently. "Gotta keep my hands on the wheel."

I click off my seat belt and lean over him, reaching for the phone in the driver's-side door. He pushes me back. "Hey! Hey! Do you want to run us off the road? Sit down. Put your seat belt on."

I plop back in my seat and fasten my belt with a groan.

"Since you *still* won't tell me which song you're named after—and I'll admit it wasn't entirely obvious when I scanned the list of their titles—I figured I'd just download them all and we'd make it a little road trip project!"

"Shut it off, Nico."

"Well, technically, I only downloaded the first album. I figured you probably weren't named after a song that was released in 2009. Did you know Fear Epidemic went on a reunion tour? When we were nine."

"Shut. It. Off."

He grins at me. "Fine. Tell me your real name and we won't have to listen to it."

I fall silent and look out the window.

The song reaches the end of the first verse.

*She's nearly a saint*
*And no one notices*
*When she scrapes the ground*
*She never has the time*
*To hear pleasant sounds*

"Your name is Saint!" Nico says with sudden inspiration.

"No," I mutter.

"Your name is Pleasant Sounds."

"No."

Nolan Cook launches into the chorus.

*Run away, go away*
*Hide away, sneak away*
*There's got to be*
*An easier way*
*To face each day*

"Your name is Hideaway?" Nico scrunches up his nose.

"This is ridiculous."

"Will you at least tell me when I guess it?"

"No."

"Hmm," Nico muses. "That does make it a bit more difficult. I'll have to read it on your face."

"You can't read it on my face."

"I can read a *lot* on your face. After all, I've spent *many* hours studying that face." His eyebrows lift. "Among other features."

11. No comments about my face . . . or any other body parts.

Nico laughs at my expression, which I'm sure is beet red, and reaches into the door compartment to switch to the next song. I immediately recognize the opening guitar riff as "Sleep," and I breathe out a sigh of relief. He's playing the songs in album order. Which means I'm safe for a while. But I also know Nico won't give this up. He won't stop until he finds *the* song. *The* title. *The* name.

And now it's only a matter of time.

"I was doing some research about this band last night," Nico says. "They're kind of fascinating."

"No, they're not."

Nico ignores this. "They only recorded one album before they broke up, but it was a pretty big success. Four of their singles went gold. Their first single, 'Nearly a Saint,' was released in 1998, only four years after Kurt Cobain of Nirvana killed himself, putting an end to what music buffs call 'real' grunge rock. Fear Epidemic was labeled as 'post-grunge.'"

I close my eyes, trying to drone out the sound of his voice. But with the music blasting and Nolan Cook screaming in my ear, it's too much. I can't block out everything. I have to listen to *something*.

"Then, get this," Nico goes on. "They break up, and *nine* years later, they get back together. They record a second album, they go on tour, and then they break up *again*."

I fight the urge to put my hands over my ears and sing one of my favorite bubbly pop songs at the top of my lungs.

Nico keeps talking. Like an oblivious tour guide who doesn't realize his entire tour group has deserted him in the middle of the museum. "Also, did you know that Fear Epidemic was writing a third album when they were on their reunion tour? But they broke up before they got a chance to go back into the studio to record it. Apparently all the fans were *livid*. And I also read that—"

"Track nine!" I finally explode, unable to take it anymore.

"What?"

I sigh, resigning myself to my fate. "Track nine," I repeat, keeping my gaze out the window. If this is what will shut him up and make him turn off this stupid album, then so be it.

With one hand on the wheel, Nico scrambles for the phone, and a moment later, the one and only ballad on *Anarchy in a Cup* begins to play.

Nico steals peeks at me out of the corner of his eye. Like he's not sure whether he can believe me. Maybe I'm purposefully trying to deceive him. Maybe I'm leading him *away* from the song, instead of toward it.

But I'm not.

This is the one. The song I've avoided since I was nine years old. My plan was to legally change my name the minute I turned eighteen. But in that minute I was too distracted with foreclosure notices and building birdhouses in Russellville High's woodshop with a cute boy.

I never got around to it.

Which means legally I'm still named after this song.

The ethereal wind track of the opening instrumental

fades out, and the first verse fades in. Nolan's voice sounds even raspier as he tries to infuse emotion into the lyrics.

> In this city by the sea
> The roads take us back to you and me
> The time beats like rain against the drums
> The ocean can't remember where it started from

Nico's gaze is on the road, but I can tell every ounce of his concentration is on the song. Waiting. Listening. Processing every word.

> There's a man who's lost his sanity
> He's waiting for the sky to sing

I researched the meaning of the song once. Apparently Nolan Cook wrote it about Los Angeles, where Fear Epidemic signed their first record deal. It was also where Nolan Cook met a girl that he fell in love with. The relationship didn't last. But the song continued to be their tribute to the great big state that Nico and I have been driving through for the past two days.

> He shouts into the void, "I tried to warn ya!"
> But I'd still do anything, anything, anything
> for California

Nico jabs at the screen of his phone, pausing the song. He doesn't have to listen any longer. He knows.

He *knows*.

"Anything for California," he repeats the lyric, which is also the name of the song.

I shiver. Somehow it sounds sweeter coming from his mouth. More earnest. Less of a pain in my side. Less of this ugly shadow that's been following me around for the past nine years, reminding me of how untrue it is. How much of a lie it turned out to be. A thing that I couldn't wait to legally expunge from my record.

"*Cali*fornia," he says quietly. "Ali."

I glance out the window just in time to see the WELCOME TO OREGON sign as we officially leave my namesake behind.

When Jackson left to tour with the band, he would only call me when he knew my mom would be at work. For the first few weeks after he left, I would come home from school, grab the cordless phone, and sit with it in my ldap, waiting to hear what exotic new location he would be calling from next.

*I'm in Bakersfield!*

*I'm in San Jose!*

*I'm in Sacramento!*

Then, after every call, I would race to the computer, open Google Maps, and search for the city, calculating just how far away he was and just how long it would take for him to come home from there.

He would always tell me one fun fact about the place

he was in, like he was reading them off a brochure for the city.

*Did you know that Bakersfield has the two largest carrot farms in the world?*

*Did you know there's a thirty-foot statue of Chuck E. Cheese in San Jose?*

*Did you know that parts of the city of Sacramento are haunted?*

Then he would gush about life with the band. How amazing it was to be traveling. About what a good roadie he was. "They really appreciate me around here. I'm a big part of this tour. Today, I actually fixed Nolan Cook's guitar!"

Back then, I believed him. I wanted to think that my dad was important. That he was needed somewhere. It was the only way I could cope with the fact that he left us for them. Maybe they really did need him more than we did.

A month after my ninth birthday, he called later than usual. Mom was already home from her late lunch shift at the restaurant. I tried to hide the call from her, knowing it would only upset her. When the phone rang, I took it into my room and hid in my closet as Jackson announced, "I'm in Eugene, Oregon!"

Before he even had a chance to tell me a fun fact about Eugene, Oregon, my mother was in the closet, ripping the phone from my hand.

"You cannot keep doing this, Jackson," she bellowed as she stormed out of the room, taking my one remaining connection with my father with her. "You don't get to walk out on us and still have some secret relationship with her."

I followed after my mom, wanting so badly to plead with her, "Don't take him away from me. Please! Don't tell him not to call. The phone calls are all I have left."

The words bubbled up inside of me. They were right on the tip of my tongue. And then I heard my mom say, "I don't understand! You're broke! Where are you getting the money to support yourself? Because I *know* those supposed *friends* of yours from the band aren't paying you for this."

*Money.*

The word bounced around in my mind for a few seconds before finally settling with a thud. I ran to the garage and flipped on the light. I stared at the empty spot on the cement where Jackson's Firebird used to be. My mind struggled to put pieces together. Pieces I didn't understand. Until now. Until the memories drifted back to me.

The trunk.

The spare tire.

The roll of cash.

The pawn shop.

eBay.

The secret trips to the ice-cream store.

*Jackson's Escape Fund.*

I'd promised I would never tell her about it. It was my secret. *Our* secret. Jackson's and mine.

Then everything fell into place.

Late electric bills. Calls from debt collectors. Mom swearing to some disembodied voice on the phone that she'd have money in another week.

As I stood in the center of the garage, breathing in the fading scent of motor oil and car wax and leather conditioner, the guilt crawled into my bones and curled up to stay.

I switched off the light. I closed the garage door. I sat down on the couch and waited for the conversation to be over. I waited for my mom's angry, trembling voice to quiet. I waited until her tears stopped. Then I walked into her bedroom. She was sitting on her bed with the phone clutched in her hands. Tears streaked down her face.

I saw the bravery in her eyes.

I saw the strength she was struggling to hold on to.

I saw the way her face was fighting a battle between being stoic and being real.

And then I made another promise. This time to myself.

I swore I would never lie to my mother again.

Despite my mother's warnings, Jackson continued to call me when she was at work. But I stopped picking up. I would see the number on the caller ID. I would watch the names of the cities flash on the small screen of the phone.

*Portland, Oregon.*

*Boise, Idaho.*

*Salt Lake City, Utah.*

I would feel him getting farther and farther away each day.

Until finally, he stopped calling altogether.

# 5:55 P.M.

# BROOKINGS, OR

## INVENTORY: 1968 FIREBIRD CONVERTIBLE (1), CASH ($529.10), SEA GLASS (1 PIECE), GIBSON ELECTRIC GUITAR (1)

"What can I get for you guys?"

We've found a coffee hut called Dutch Bros—which features a blue windmill on the menu—and are standing at the outdoor counter.

Nico looks at me. "She's ordering for me."

"You're serious about this?"

"Dead serious," he says.

"Okay. You asked for it." I scan the menu, once again searching for the most ridiculous-sounding drink they have. My eyes light up when I land on something called the Banana Cream Pie Freeze.

I point to it. "He'll have one of those."

I turn to Nico, watching his face pale as he sees what I'm pointing to. "Does that even have coffee in it?"

The barista shakes her head. "The freeze doesn't, but the Banana Cream Pie Latte does."

Nico looks positively horrified.

"Yeah," I say excitedly. "He'll have that one."

He covers his reaction with a totally fake smile. "YUM! Another winner!"

"You're so full of shi—"

"Shih tzu!" Nico interrupts loudly, glancing at everyone in line behind us to make sure they heard his PG version of the word that almost slipped from my mouth. "She was going to say 'shih tzu'! The dog breed."

"Actually, I wasn't."

"You know," Nico says diplomatically, "if you're going to be choosing my beverage, I think it's only fair that I get to pick *your* drinks from here on out too."

"That wasn't part of the deal," I say.

He shrugs. "I'm changing the deal."

"You can't change the deal."

"And you still can't drive stick. Life's a Bitcoin sometimes." He grins at me, waiting for my praise of his new euphemism.

"Did you just come up with that on the spot?"

"Actually, no. I thought of it a while back. I've just been waiting for the right time to use it."

I sigh. "Fine. Whatever. Pick my drink." I glance up to see the woman behind the counter staring at us like we just crawled out of a hole in the ground.

Nico rubs his hands together as he studies the colorful

blue-and-white menu with stylized pictures of giant red slushies, frozen espresso drinks drenched in chocolate syrup, and steaming hot cups of coffee nestled among a bed of artfully scattered coffee beans.

"Alrighty. Today, Ali is going to be enjoying a . . ." He pauses for effect, stretching out his finger and running it up and down the board like he's trying to build suspense. He stops and announces his pick. "A Cotton Candy Mocha!"

My stomach rolls at the very sound of it, but I attempt to duplicate his nonchalance, painting on a smile and saying, "That's exactly what I was going to order anyway."

Nico sees right through my charade. "That's because I know you so well."

The barista makes our drinks, and we bring them back to the Firebird parked nearby.

"Where are we meeting this guy with the typewriter?" I ask, taking a tentative sip of my mocha. It tastes like someone melted flavored sugar right into the cup and then poured a drop of coffee on it. I have to force myself to swallow.

Nico sets his drink in the cup holder and swipes on his phone to check the e-mail again. "The Chetco Community Public Library. I think it's only a five-minute drive from here."

"Even so," I say, reaching out and plucking the phone right from his hand, "I think I better choose what we listen to next."

"Excuse me?" Nico feigns insult.

"After that little stunt you pulled with the Fear Epidemic playlist, I don't trust you with the listening selection anymore."

He chuckles. "Fair enough. What are you going to put on? Another podcast?"

I scroll through one of his music apps, flashing him a smile that's about as sugary as the mocha in my cup. "Maaaaaybe."

Realization dawns on his face. "Oh God! You're going to put on the dentist music, aren't you?"

"Maaaaaybe."

He tries to snatch the phone back, but I pull it out of his reach. I press play on the song I was looking for and blast the volume.

The next moment, a bubbly, synthesized melody filters through the phone speaker, sounding like the start of a bouncy workout video. It's so loud, some of the customers still standing in line at Dutch Bros turn to look for the source of it.

Nico covers his ears. "Gah! Make it stop!"

"This is your punishment!" I scream over the music.

The first verse kicks in, and the lead singer of my favorite British pop band starts singing excessively upbeat lyrics about being yourself and never giving up.

Nico lets out another cry of agony. "I think my teeth are falling out! Shut it off!"

"Nope."

He lunges for the phone again, but I keep it safely in my right hand, tucked between the seat and the door.

Nico sprawls across the console, leaning right into my lap, his hands grappling for the device. When his fingers fail to reach the phone, they find my waist instead. He starts to tickle me. I squirm and giggle and thrash, nearly dropping the phone.

"Stop!" I squeal.

"Give me the phone!" He tickles me harder.

"No!"

I twist in my seat until my back is to him and try to jab him away with my elbow, but he leans even farther over the center console, his chest pressing against my back, his arms reaching around me.

"Give it up!" I tell him. "You're not getting the phone! You're going to listen to this song and you're going to like it!"

He tickles me harder. Through my fits of giggles, I somehow manage to turn the volume up even higher just as the chorus revs up and all seven members of the band start singing.

"No!" Nico cries. "There go my molars!"

I turn around to flash him a self-satisfied smirk before realizing what a colossal mistake that was. Because suddenly his face is only inches away from mine. His lips are only inches from mine. His scent pushes its way into my nostrils. His gaze latches on to me. And for a brief moment, it's as though we're suspended in midair. Not crushed together on the passenger side of the car.

If the gravity in the hotel room last night was an issue, it's nothing compared to the gravity I'm experiencing right now.

I try to block it out by pushing my thoughts back to the night of the comet. Back to the lies. The glove box. The heated words shouted at each other.

But it's no use.

The memories won't come.

It's like I suddenly can't remember what we were fighting about. Ever. All I can remember is what was good about us. The shimmering cocoon. The playful banter. Nico's eyes sparkling in the dashboard lights.

Suddenly the music stops, and at first I think Nico somehow got hold of the phone. But then I realize it's still clutched in my hand.

*BOOOOOOMMM*

The deafening sound of that foghorn ringtone blasts through the car.

The one that caused Nico to freak out after we left Fort Bragg.

The one signifying a text from *Rachel*.

Nico's eyes fill with panic, and he makes one last attempt to reach the phone. This time, however, it's not a playful attempt. It's a desperate attempt. It's a *real* attempt.

His hand dives into the crevice between the seat and the door and rips the device right out of my hand. He pushes himself back to his side of the car. His side of the world.

And just like that, the spell is broken. My body stops thrumming. My heart stops pounding.

*BOOOOOOMMM*

*BOOOOOOMMM*

*BOOOOOOMMM*

Three more messages blare onto Nico's phone. With the volume turned all the way up, they seem to vibrate the entire car. Like little bombs dropping onto the console between us.

And just as he did before, Nico works frantically to delete them.

The phone falls silent. And the shadowy pit descends around us once again. Making itself comfortable. Filling in all the empty spaces between us.

"Another wrong number?" I ask, stealing furtive glances at Nico.

For a long time, he doesn't answer. He just stares blankly at the phone in his hand. His body is all hunched, his shoulders up to his ears, his head low. It's a protective posture. He's readying himself for another attack.

When it doesn't come, he tosses the phone into the compartment in the driver's-side door and starts the engine. "Something like that," he mutters.

There was nothing official to mark the day Nico and I got together. No questions asked, no tiptoeing around labels, no hours spent agonizing with my best friend. *Are we or aren't we? Is he or isn't he?*

It just happened.

One moment we were virtual strangers; the next we were a couple. And we both knew it. I walked away from that night at June's party knowing, without any doubt or hesitation or common early-relationship insecurities, that I had a boyfriend.

That's all there was to it.

I'll always remember that day because it was the day the first foreclosure notice was pinned to our front door. I saw it before Mom did. She was still at work when I got home from school.

I stood on the front porch and stared at that notice for what felt like centuries. I swore suns set and seasons changed behind my back, but that piece of paper refused to go away. I knew things had gotten bad. Mom never hid our declining financial situation from me. But I didn't realize they had gotten this bad. Notice-on-the-front-door kind of bad. And I don't think Mom did either. Because when she got home and I showed her the toxic piece of paper, she started to cry. Then, once she'd collected herself, dried her tears, put on her reading glasses, and read the fine print carefully, she assured me that there was nothing to worry about. This was just a warning. We still had plenty of time to set things right.

That was back when she still had hope. Back when she was still convinced something miraculous would happen and we wouldn't be kicked out of our house like squatters from a condemned building.

That was before she gave up completely.

June's parents were out of town, and she was throwing a party that night in her junkyard. June lives on five acres, just outside of Russellville, and you can barely see the ground anywhere. Her family has lived there for three generations, and I don't think any of them has thrown anything away in all of that time. So it's basically like a hundred years' worth of junk.

But June's junkyard parties were everyone's favorites. There was always something new to discover—a new surface to dance on, a new centerpiece to talk about.

I didn't want to go. I called June to tell her what had happened and that I wasn't feeling up to a party, but June refused to let me back out. She said this would make me feel better. It would get my mind off of things. It would give me something else to think about.

She had no idea, at the time, how right she was.

I went to the party. I faked a smile. I chatted. I laughed. I lasted a whole forty-five minutes before my facade started to slip and I could feel my melancholy creeping back in, like water being held back by a faulty dam.

*Drip . . . drip . . . drip . . .*

I needed to get away from everyone. Before the dam came crumbling down and flooded the whole party. I wanted to leave, but I knew I'd never hear the end of it from June, so instead I slipped into the darkness of the junkyard, away from the loud voices and tinny music being blasted from a busted speaker. Using my phone as my flashlight, I found a hiding spot in a stripped-out frame of an old VW Beetle that had probably been parked on June's parents' lot since the sixties. There was no steering wheel, no windshield, and no back seat. Just two bucket seats in the front with cracked leather, and a giant, cavernous hole where the stereo used to be.

I plopped down in the driver's seat and tried to quell the storm of panic that was growing inside of me.

*Deep breaths. Calming thoughts. Close your eyes.*

It wasn't working.

I swiped on my phone and immediately navigated to my favorite personality quiz website and scrolled through the list of newly published quizzes, ruling out "What's Your Harry Potter Fashion Style?," "Which Fictional Vampire Are You Most Destined to Date?," and "What Horror Movie Best Represents Your Life?" My eyes stopped on the fourth down from the top. It said:

> **Everyone in the World Can Be Broken Down into 16 Personalities. Which One Are You?**

I immediately clicked the button to take the quiz. As I started answering the questions, I could tell this quiz was different from any other one I'd taken on the site. More serious and grounded in reality. And the questions—*Do you often find yourself getting overwhelmed in social situations and seeking solace by yourself?*—made me feel like the result was going to magically fix everything that was wrong with my life. Every unanswered question, unsolved dilemma, unwanted quality about myself was going to disappear that moment I clicked submit and the algorithm calculated me and placed me in a safe, contained little box.

This quiz felt less like a distraction and more like a lifeline.

I clicked submit.

And that was the moment I heard his voice. Emerging from the darkness as clear and bright as a light source. Jumping into my thoughts, breaking through my bubble, infiltrating my space.

"Hey. Nice ride."

I looked up to see Nico standing outside the driver's side of the VW Beetle, leaning in through the large gap where the door used to be.

"What are you doing?" he asked, nodding toward the illuminated phone in my hand.

"Oh," I said clumsily, lowering my phone before I even had a chance to look at my results. "Nothing. Just taking a stupid personality quiz."

There was a split second where my life could have gone two different ways, traveled down two different roads. On one road, Nico smiled, wished me luck with my quiz, and disappeared back into the darkness. On this road, we never dated. We never kissed. We never shared eighty-eight amazing days together. He never tried to teach me how to drive stick shift. He never lied to me. I never opened that glove box. I never stood in the mud on the side of Route 128 while a three-thousand-year-old comet lit up the entire sky.

On the other road, however, Nico sat down in the passenger seat, smiled that adorable roguish smile of his, and asked to see the results of my quiz. On this road, we date, we kiss (a lot), we share eighty-eight amazing days together. He tries (and fails) to teach me how to drive stick. He lies to me. I open the glove box. I stand in the mud on the side of Route 128 while Fabian's Comet streaks through the sky, wishing we had taken the other path. Wishing he had simply walked away. Wishing I had ended that night the way I had started it: alone.

"Well, let's see it. What did you get?" Nico asked.

"Huh?" I had forgotten momentarily about the quiz on my phone. Because right then, all I could think about was Nico sitting next to me. Nico in this car with me. Even with no doors, no windows, no windshield, it felt crowded. The car felt crammed with his energy, his scent, his tall, slender form, the messy mop of dark blond hair that was constantly falling into his eyes.

And then all I could think about was that I didn't mind it.

I should mind it. I knew that. I was convinced that when I turned my phone screen around and read my quiz results, it would say I was the kind of person who minded. The kind of person who was protective of their space, didn't like surprises, preferred being alone when feeling anxious or stressed. The kind of person who didn't like to be interrupted when doing personality quizzes, even when the interrupter was as cute as Nico Wright.

But I didn't mind.

My energy seemed to miraculously scoot over, make room for him, welcome him in. The involuntary reaction came as such a surprise, it took me a moment to catch up.

"The personality quiz," Nico reminded me, nudging his chin toward the phone still clutched in my hand, the screen facedown in my lap.

I blinked and glanced down at my phone, the rest of

the evening suddenly coming back to me in a flash. Me running away from the party. Me hiding in this car. Me losing myself in a stupid quiz that was supposed to give me all the answers.

It all seemed so silly and foolish now.

It all seemed so pointless. Especially because it somehow felt as though the real answer had just plopped itself down onto the seat next to me.

"Oh," I said, peeking at the screen of my phone. "It's no big deal. It's just a stupid quiz that's supposed to tell you everything there is to know about you." I let out a snort, to hopefully convince him that I don't put any stock in this kind of thing. That I wasn't lame enough to define myself by something as trivial and simplistic as an online quiz.

"Well then I definitely want to see it now," Nico said, grinning again.

"What?" I asked, confused. "Why?"

"Obviously because I want to know everything there is to know about you."

We arrive early to the Chetco Community Public Library. While Nico sits down at one of the public computers to check his e-mail, I go off exploring.

I've always loved libraries, but this one has a cozy, old-fashioned feel that makes me want to curl up with a book somewhere and forget about everything that's happened over the past few days.

I wander through the stacks, running my fingers across the book spines, loving the way the protective plastic feels on my skin. When I emerge from the nonfiction section, I notice a large display case on the far wall, near the entrance. I make my way toward it, trying to figure out what's behind the glass. It almost looks like a . . .

A samurai sword?

As I get closer, I realize that it is, in fact, a samurai sword, which seems like such an odd thing to have on display in a library. I approach the case and see that the sword is accompanied by a sheath, a tiny model of an old military plane, and a model submarine. I lean forward to read the engraved wooden plaque behind the glass.

THIS FOUR-HUNDRED-YEAR-OLD SAMURAI SWORD WAS PRESENTED TO THE COMMUNITY OF BROOKINGS BY NOBUO FUJITA OF TSUCHIURA, JAPAN, ON THE TWENTIETH ANNIVERSARY OF HIS HISTORIC INCENDIARY BOMBING OF THE FOREST NEAR BROOKINGS ON SEPTEMBER 9, 1942.

NOBUO FUJITA WAS THE ONLY ENEMY TO BOMB THE U.S. FROM THE AIR. HE PRESENTED THIS SWORD DURING THE 1962 AZALEA FESTIVAL, WHICH HE AND HIS FAMILY ATTENDED AS GUESTS OF THE BROOKINGS HARBOR JUNIOR CHAMBER OF COMMERCE.

THIS SYMBOLIC SWORD WAS PRESENTED IN THE INTEREST OF PEACE AND FRIENDSHIP BETWEEN THE NATIONS OF JAPAN AND THE UNITED STATES OF AMERICA.

THE PERSONAL VALUE OF THE ANCESTRAL SWORD TO MR. FUJITA ATTESTS TO THE SINCERITY OF HIS GESTURE.

Fascinated, I place my palms flat on the glass and stare at the ancient weapon. He bombed the United States and then came back with a gift? That takes some guts. How come I've never heard of this guy?

I glance around to see if anyone else is as interested in this display as I am, but all I see is a lone librarian stocking shelves nearby. I hurry over to her.

"Do you know anything about that sword?" I ask, jabbing my thumb over my shoulder.

She looks up from her book cart and flashes me a kind smile. "Of course. Mr. Fujita returned to the United States after World War Two and offered the sword to the city of Brookings as an apology."

"An apology?"

"That's right. Mr. Fujita fought for the Japanese navy during the war. He was the only person to ever successfully launch an air attack on the American mainland."

My eyes widen. "Really? Where did he drop the bomb?"

"Just inland from Brookings. In the forest. It was an incendiary strike with the intention of igniting the redwoods."

My heart cramps at the thought of all those beautiful trees burning. "Did it ignite?"

"Fortunately no. It had been a very rainy season, and the woods were too damp. But Mr. Fujita was still considered a hero in his country."

"But then he apologized?" I ask, confused.

She nods. "That's right. Shortly after the war, Mr. Fujita became a pacifist, and in 1962, the town of Brookings held a ceremony marking the twenty-year anniversary of the attack. They invited Mr. Fujita to the ceremony. As a pledge of peace and friendship, Mr. Fujita offered the city his samurai sword, which he'd had in the plane with him when he dropped the bomb. It's one of the most valuable gifts a samurai can give to a former enemy. He also apologized to the forest by planting a redwood at the bomb site in 1992."

"And the city forgave him?"

She smiled and gestured back toward the display case. "Yes, we did. In fact, we even made him an honorary citizen of Brookings. After Mr. Fujita died in 1997, his ashes were scattered among the redwoods and—" The librarian stopped abruptly and studied me with a concerned expression. "Are you all right?"

It's only then that I realize tears have formed in my eyes and are starting to leak out. I chuckle, feeling silly, and wipe at my cheeks. "Yes. Sorry. It's just so . . ." I can't find the words.

Thankfully, she seems to understand. "I know."

She pats me affectionately on the shoulder. "You're not the first one to become emotional over Mr. Fujita's gift. It's definitely a true testament to the forgiving nature of the human spirit, isn't it?

I nod, unable to respond.

"Well," she says, gesturing to her cart full of books. "I have some more work to do. Let me know if you have any other questions."

The librarian walks away, and I return to the glass

case. I must fall into a trance because a moment later, Nico is tapping me on the shoulder.

"He's here." He glances momentarily at the display and says, "Cool sword," before turning toward the entrance to the parking lot where our next Craigslist "customer" is waiting.

I follow behind him, letting my gaze fall one last time on the sword and the wooden plaque beside it.

*This symbolic sword was presented in the interest of peace and friendship . . .*

He dropped a bomb right near the city.

He tried to ignite one of the most famous forests in America.

He committed an atrocious act of war.

And yet they forgave him.

I push my hand into the pocket of my hoodie and run my fingertips around the piece of sea glass I picked up in Fort Bragg, trying to find inspiration in its smooth edges, trying to extract some ounce of its ancient wisdom.

But all I feel is emptiness.

If the entire city of Brookings can forgive—if the whole damn *ocean* can forgive—then why is it so hard for me?

# 6:34 P.M.

# BROOKINGS, OR

## INVENTORY: 1968 FIREBIRD CONVERTIBLE (1), CASH ($522.86), SEA GLASS (1 PIECE), VINTAGE TYPEWRITER (1)

After Nico has updated the Craigslist post, we stash our newly acquired vintage typewriter in the back seat of the car and walk down the street to a pizza place I found online that had decent reviews.

We order a medium pineapple and jalapeño—the only pizza toppings we could ever agree on during our three-month relationship—and find a booth in the back.

"So, what are we supposed to do now?" I ask as Nico scrapes the last piece of cheese from the metal tray.

He dangles it over his mouth and lets it drop in. "We wait for someone to respond."

"I know, but . . ." I glance around the restaurant, which is slowly filling with locals. "Do we just stay here?"

"Not in this restaurant, no."

I roll my eyes. "You know what I meant."

"I think it would be a good idea to stay in Brookings, yes. Since we have no idea where the next trade will come from. North, south, east, west." Nico flashes me a smirk. "Those are pretty much the only options."

I feel my stomach clench. I don't like the idea of just wandering around with no direction. No plan. "But what are we supposed to *do*? What if we don't get a response for days?"

"It won't take days."

The server brings our check, and I pull a twenty-dollar bill out of the plastic bag in my backpack and toss it down. "I honestly don't know if this is going to work, Nico."

Nico shoots me a look. "Really? This again?"

"I just . . . I mean, yes, we traded a rubber band up to a vintage typewriter, and that's great. But I can't see us getting up to twenty-five thousand dollars."

"I can."

"Yeah, maybe in a *year*. But the foreclosure deadline is this coming Friday," I remind him.

Nico balls his napkin and tosses it on the table, clearly done with this conversation. He scoots out of the booth. "C'mon. Let's go check out the town."

With a sigh, I stand up and swing my backpack over my shoulder, completely forgetting that the zipper is still open until the contents of the compartment spill out all over the restaurant floor.

Nico bends down to help me scoop everything up.

"It's fine," I mutter. "I've got it."

But, of course, he doesn't let it go. Once a Fixer, always

a Fixer, I guess. As I pick up the large yellow envelope with the car's title inside, Nico unwittingly goes for the *other* envelope that fell out of my backpack.

The one I'd nearly forgotten about until this very moment.

Until I see it clutched in Nico's hands.

He tilts his head, curiously reading the delivery address on the front, his mouth falling into a scowl. "What's this?" he asks.

"None of your business," I say, snatching it out of his hand and stuffing it back into the bag. I zip the compartment and stand up.

"Ali." There's shock and disbelief in his voice. "Was that your acceptance letter to UC Davis?"

"I said, it's none of your business."

He rises to his feet, shaking his head. "Why do you still have it? The deadline to send that in was a week ago."

"I—I—" I stammer. "I just haven't gotten around to it."

"But they're going to give away your scholarship and they're not going to let you—"

"Can we just drop it?" I snap, pushing my way through the restaurant toward the front door. I'm hoping the tone of my voice is enough to shut him up.

Obviously it's not.

"But what about your dream to become a veterinarian?" he says as soon as we're outside on the sidewalk.

"People can have more than one dream."

"Ali, that scholarship was your future."

"That's right. My future. Not yours. Not anymore. So just let it go, okay?"

He scratches at his eyebrow, seemingly debating whether to push the issue. But I don't give him the chance to decide. I turn my back on him and start walking down the street.

"Where are you going?" he calls after me.

"Checking out the town!" I call back. "Remember?"

According to the quiz I took in the hollowed-out VW Beetle in June's backyard the night of her party, my personality type is "the Commissioner." I am defined as being honest, patient, loyal, reliable, and strong-willed but with a stubborn streak and an obsession with creating and enforcing order.

"Uh-oh," Nico said as we read the results together. "Sounds like I need to watch out for you."

"What?" I joked back. "No you don't. It says right here I'm an excellent organizer. And people look to me to lead things."

"It also says that you can be inflexible and judgmental." He pointed to a section of text at the bottom of the screen.

"Keep reading. It says only when I feel like the high standards of society are not being withheld. That's admirable."

Nico chuckled. "It does say Commissioners make excellent politicians and community leaders. Maybe you should run for mayor of Russellville after you graduate."

I laughed at the thought. "Yeah right."

"Okay, so if you don't want to run the world—or Russellville—what do you want to do?"

I shrugged. "Something where I get to work with animals."

"Like a vet?" he asked, and I immediately felt the squeeze of anxiety in my chest.

"I actually applied to UC Davis for undergraduate, hoping to stay on for their vet school. It's one of the best in the country."

"That's awesome! Do you think you'll get in?"

I bit my lip. "It's not a matter of just getting in. I need a full scholarship, or I'll never be able to afford to go."

"So?" he said, like the world's largest stumbling block was nothing more than a pebble.

"So," I replied as though it were obvious, "they don't give out a lot of those. They're very competitive. I'm not sure I have a shot."

For a long time, Nico didn't reply, and when I looked over at him, I noticed he was studying me, like he could see right through me. Read every thought. Dissect every feeling. Then, he did the first unexpected thing of so many unexpected things in our eighty-eight days together. He reached toward me, grabbed the phone right out of my hand, and started diligently scrolling through my personality description, his brow furrowed in deep concentration. "Sorry," he said with a tone of someone giving bad news. "It doesn't say anything in here about Commissioners having self-doubt. Actually, it says the opposite. They're very confident in their abilities. Looks like you're going to have start expecting that scholarship."

I scoffed. "Okay, smarty-pants. Your turn. You take the quiz."

Nico cocked an eyebrow at me, and right then and there, I felt my whole body melt into the seat. There was so much wrapped up in that single gesture. So many silent phrases. And I heard them all at once.

*I like you.*

*I like hanging out with you.*

*You're not like any other girl I've met.*

Maybe it was all wishful thinking. Maybe his eyebrow raise was just an eyebrow raise. But I didn't think so. And just like the personality quiz said, when I made my mind up about a person, the opinion tended to stick.

"Gladly," Nico said, and clicked the back button to start the quiz over. "But it's a pointless exercise. I already know what I'm going to get."

I smirked. "And what is that?"

"'The Champion,'" he said confidently.

"I don't think that's an option."

"Okay, what about 'The Best at Everything'?"

"And I suppose your strengths would be listed as 'humble, modest, and realistic.'"

"See?" Nico said with a grin. "I told you I don't have to take it."

But he took it. And for the next few minutes, I leaned in and watched over his shoulder as he answered the twenty questions that would eventually tell me everything there was to know about Nico Wright.

I tried to pretend like I wasn't committing every response he clicked to memory. I tried to pretend that I wasn't fascinated by this rare inside peek into the mind of one of the most enigmatic boys in school.

Nico hit submit, and we both waited for the results to calculate.

"'The Fixer,'" Nico read aloud, smiling. "I like the sound of that."

I rolled my eyes. "Just read what it says."

"Optimistic?" Nico read. "Check. Energetic. Check. Creative yet practical. Check, check. Great in a crisis?" He shot me a look. "Oh, I am *amazing* in a crisis."

I chuckled. "I bet."

"Relaxed?" Nico made a show of stretching out his legs and getting more comfortable in the incredibly uncomfortable ripped-up seats. "Check."

"'Spontaneous.'" I pointed to the screen. "What does that mean?"

"Well," Nico said, clearing his throat importantly, "according to Webster's dictionary, 'spontaneous' means . . ."

I slapped his arm. "I know what the definition is. I'm asking, is it true? Are you spontaneous?"

"Oh, you mean, like, do I just do things without warning?"

I nodded. "Yeah."

"Like do I just decide I want to, I don't know, kiss someone and then just do it?"

Nico turned toward me and latched onto my gaze. The night was dark. The only light between us was the screen of my phone, lighting up Nico's face from below. Like a precious work of art on display in a museum. I suddenly found it difficult to breathe. I swallowed hard and commanded myself not to look away. "Yeah," I whispered.

But Nico did look away. And for a moment, I felt the sensation of falling. He cleared his throat again. "I guess I can be spontaneous." He glanced back down at the phone, using his thumb to scroll through the page. He stopped, his brow furrowing again. "Uh-oh."

"What?" I asked, leaning in to see what had stolen his attention away from me.

"It says here that Commissioners and Fixers don't make very good matches."

I tilted my head to read the screen and let out a dramatic sigh. "Well, I guess that does it," I say with an air of finality.

"Yup," Nico said, matching my tone flawlessly. He held out his hand for me to shake. "Nice knowing you?"

I shook it. "Nice knowing you, too."

I turned to go. I knew it was a charade. But I wasn't sure how far he was willing to take it. Or if he would really let me leave. I started to stand up.

"Although . . ." Nico's voice stopped me, and I smiled into the darkness.

"Yes?" I asked, presuming innocence.

"How accurate *are* these personality quizzes?"

I lowered back into the seat and turned to him. "In my experience, they're never foolproof."

"It could be wrong about this."

"It could," I admitted.

"Should we chance it?" Nico asked, cocking his eyebrow once again.

If I could go back to that night—if I could hover like a ghost in the air—I would shout at myself. I would scream until I could be heard.

*Don't!*

*Don't chance it!*

*It's not worth it!*

I would tell myself that the personality quiz was right about us. About Nico and me. About Commissioners and Fixers. They don't mix. They don't match. They only cause each other pain.

But even now, I know that I wouldn't have listened.

Half an hour with Nico, and I was already too far gone to listen to reason. I was already smitten. Which explains why I went home later that night and reread the list of Fixer strengths over and over again, committing them to memory like the properties of a chemical compound. Like I would later be tested on the subject.

Optimistic.

Creative.

Spontaneous.

Great in a crisis.

So many things that I lacked. So many skills that, at the time, seemed to complement my own. I felt like his optimism was already rubbing off on me because I'd never felt more hopeful than on that night.

Too bad I didn't keep reading. I would have gotten to the section about the Fixer's weaknesses:

Insensitive.

Easily bored.

Secretive.

But I never even read those. I didn't care about his weaknesses. In that moment, sitting in that VW Beetle, he didn't have any. Neither of us did. We were just two personalities fitting perfectly together. We were two balls of pure possibility, colliding to create one perfect, infinite horizon.

Which is probably why I said, without any hesitation, "Maybe we *should* chance it."

As Nico and I wander the streets of downtown Brookings, we're both silent. Neither one of us wants to speak first in fear of triggering the fight that we left hanging back in the restaurant.

Eventually, we stumble upon a small section of town that holds a collection of art galleries. One shop in particular grabs my attention. It's called Mottainai: Treasures of the Lost and Found.

The storefront window is relatively bare, apart from something hanging from the ceiling by a long chain. When I step closer, I see that it's actually a wind chime. And it's made entirely of sea glass. A small shiver runs through me as I reach into my pocket and touch my own piece of sea glass, feeling its soft edges. I make a split-second decision and duck inside the shop.

Nico follows me, and we both freeze the moment we step through the door and take in the awe-inspiring sight in front of us.

We seem to be the only people here, but we are definitely *not* alone. Everywhere I turn, there's a quirky-looking sculpture staring back at me. And, upon closer inspection, I soon realize that all the sculptures are made of the most unusual, seemingly random things. There's a tiny duck whose face is constructed out of a light bulb and whose body is nothing more than a rusty old metal funnel with ornate keys attached to the sides as tucked-in wings.

Next to that is a robot with a metal olive oil tin box for a body, an upside-down paintbrush for a neck and head, and antique hot and cold faucet handles for arms. Beside him is an adorable kitten who sits on bent-fork legs, gazing at us through button-eyes attached to a face fashioned from an old alarm clock.

"What is this place?" I whisper, afraid to speak too loudly, in case the peculiar objects in here have ears.

"I don't know," Nico admits, gazing around the gallery in wonder.

And that's really the only way to feel in here.

Wonderment.

"Look at this one," Nico says, pointing to a table where a two-foot-tall figurine stands erect and proud. Its face is made out of a stripped tuna can, and its body looks like one of those old-fashioned sugar bowls that come with tea sets—two ornate curving handles protruding from the sides, making it look like the figure is standing with its hands on its hips. We both lean in to study the craftsmanship.

"Cute little guy," Nico says, grinning.

"Um, that's definitely a girl."

"How can you tell?"

I point to the upside-down mini–Bundt cake pan fastened to the bottom of the sugar bowl, creating a billowing skirt to cover the sculpture's candlestick legs. "It's wearing a skirt."

"It's actually gender-fluid," a voice says, causing both of us to startle and jerk upright. A man has suddenly emerged from a back room. His long white hair has been tied in a ponytail with little wisps flying out around the ears, reminding me of a West Highland white terrier after an open-window car ride. He wears a pair of shop goggles on his head.

"All of my sculptures are genderless."

"Oh!" I smile at the man. "Hi. Is this your shop?"

"Yes, it is. I'm Wes Kapoor. Welcome to Mottainai."

"Thank you," I say. "We were just admiring your . . ." I search for the right word. "Art."

Wes laughs a buoyant, infectious kind of laugh. "Thank you for calling it that. Most people don't know what to make of it."

"It *is* art, right?" I ask.

"It's whatever you need it to be," Wes says with a twinkle in his eye.

Nico points to a mouse whose face is constructed from a hollowed-out bell and whose ears are measuring spoons. "I think this one is my favorite."

Wes smiles and approaches the creature. "Ah, yes. That's Ziggy. Ziggy likes to watch over the shop. Every time I come out here, Ziggy is always facing a different direction." Wes affectionately pats the mouse on the head, tweaking its electrical wire whiskers. "Sneaky little thing, Ziggy is."

"So, you make all of this stuff out of . . ." Nico also seems to be struggling to find the right word.

Wes steps in to help. "Found objects. That's what I call them, anyway. Most people call them trash. Junk. Garbage. Take your pick."

I peer around the shop once again. "Everything in here is made from something someone threw away?" I ask in disbelief.

Wes flashes me a warm smile. "Exactly. I named the shop Mottainai, which is a Japanese term meaning 'the sacredness of a material entity' because everything, even this old pepper grinder"—he taps the long wooden body of a nearby dachshund sculpture—"has a story to tell."

I bend down to examine the sculpture of a sad-looking turtle made almost entirely out of jewelry.

"The Buddhists believe that every object—regardless of whether it's 'alive' or not"—Wes makes air quotes around the word "alive"—"has a soul. And I agree. So I take things that have been discarded, and I turn them into these creatures. That way, nice folks such as yourself can come into the shop and see the objects the way I see them."

I turn and study another robot. This one has a face made from an old pair of opera glasses, a coffee-can body dressed in a pair of measuring-tape suspenders, and wrenches for arms.

It's uncanny. You can't really help but see something when you look into his eyes. Something almost human.

"Well, it's pretty spectacular," Nico says.

"Yes," I echo dazedly, grateful that Nico has come up with the right word, because I'm not sure I could have. "Spectacular."

Wes bows his head. "Thank you. That's very kind."

"Do you sell these sculptures?" Nico asks.

Wes shrugs. "Not really, no. I'm not in the business of selling. I own this building and rent out the stores to other shop owners. That brings me all the income I need. I create these just for the joy of bringing them to life."

I smile at that. "So, where do you find all of this lost stuff?"

Wes shrugs. "Everywhere and anywhere, really. Sidewalks, trash dumps, junkyards. Junkyards make me the saddest. So much waste. So many discarded souls, waiting for a second chance. I always wish I could adopt them all."

"I love that." I don't even realize I've said that aloud until Nico turns to look at me, an inscrutable expression on his face. I clear my throat and refocus on Wes. "How do you know what to make out of each object?"

Wes flashes me another one of those twinkly smiles. "I don't. The objects tell me what they want to be, and I listen."

I can't help the giddy grin that spreads over my face. The guy might be bonkers, but he also might be a genius. Maybe there's a fine line.

I take another glance around the small shop, marveling at the way the eyes of Wes's sculptures seem to be watching me. Each of them speaking a different language, sending a different message through the air-waves.

Then, as though someone turned on a giant spotlight, my eyes gravitate toward a tiny creature hidden behind one of the robots. All I can see are his beady little eyes poking out between the robot's legs.

Without a word, I make my way toward the hidden sculpture. The invisible force pulling me toward it is so strong, I can't fight it or even understand it. I just know I have to see what's hiding back there.

I gently scoot the robot aside, revealing a beautiful steel butterfly that looks to be made entirely out of . . .

"Are those keys?" I ask no one in particular.

But somehow Wes is already there, as though he's been watching me, waiting for me to find this very thing. "Yes. This is Kunjee. He's made of lost keys."

"*Lost* keys?" I repeat.

Wes nods. "They're everywhere. You just have to keep your eyes out for them. When I find them, I like to hold them in my hand and imagine what secrets they might unlock."

I turn back to the butterfly—Kunjee—and run my fingertips over its outstretched metal wings. The keys are all different sizes, shapes, and colors. Some look brand-new, maybe even freshly cut, while others are stained crimson with rust.

"It's beautiful," I say.

Wes slowly reaches toward the butterfly and picks it up. I like watching how reverently he handles it. As though it were a real butterfly with wings as delicate as paper. He brings the sculpture up to his face and looks it in the eye, exchanging inaudible words, then he nods and extends his hands to me.

Confused, I look from the sculpture up to him. "What?"

"She belongs to you now."

"No," I say, waving my hands. "I'm sorry. I don't have enough money for—"

"Like I said," Wes interrupts, "I'm not in the business of selling things, but I can tell when someone is meant to have something."

"I-I-I couldn't possibly take that."

"You have to take him now," Wes says. "He's already found you."

"Found me?"

"I hid Kunjee way back here so that only the right person would be led to her."

I struggle to find words. "No. That's not what . . . I mean, I was just curious."

"Please," Wes says, pushing the butterfly toward me again. "Take him."

"But—" I begin to argue.

Wes cuts me off. "One of these keys will unlock what you're looking for."

I glance around the shop for help. This conversation is starting to make me uneasy. Nico is on the far other side of the room, bending down to examine the face of a Roman warrior made entirely from mismatched silverware.

I turn back to Wes. "I'm not looking for anything." But the words come out cracked and broken.

Once again, Wes flashes that twinkly smile of his. "Well, I know that can't be true."

I give him a blank look, afraid to speak again for fear that my voice will fail me.

"You must be looking for something," he explains. "Or you wouldn't be here."

For the next thirty minutes, Nico and I drive around town, looking for somewhere to sleep for the night. Kunjee, the butterfly, is sitting on my lap. I can't stop staring at all of those lost keys, wondering what they might have once unlocked. Wondering what Wes could have possibly meant by what he said.

*Looking for something.*

He said it with such authority. Such certainty. As though he'd known me my entire life.

"Look," Nico says, pointing to a motel off the main road. "That place has a VACANCY sign."

I yawn, the mention of a place to sleep already triggering my fatigue. "Great. Let's pull over."

Nico parks the Firebird in the front of the motel and

kills the engine. I glance around the interior of the car for a safe place to store the statue, finally deciding on the center console. I lift the lid and am about to place the butterfly inside, when my gaze falls on the black cassette tape that I stashed in there at the beginning of our trip. I remember that loud, angry guitar. Nolan's voice screaming from the speakers.

It's only now, however, as I stare into the console that I notice the cassette tape has a white label on it. And on the label, someone has scribbled:

FE UNTITLED #3 7/17/10

I tilt my head, trying to make sense of the writing. "FE" obviously stands for Fear Epidemic, and that date—July 17, 2010—was during the period of time when Jackson was on tour with the band, but what does "Untitled #3" refer to?

"Are you coming?" Nico asks, and I glance up to see he's already out of the car and is leaning back through the open door to talk to me.

You know what? It doesn't matter. I don't care. That band means nothing to me.

I return the tape to the console, gently set the butterfly statue on top of it, and close the lid.

Nico locks the car, and we walk toward the front entrance of the hotel. But for some reason, my attention is pulled back to the Firebird. There's a question still gnawing at my mind. An itch I have to scratch.

*You must be looking for something . . . or you wouldn't be here.*

"Can I have the key?" I ask Nico.

"What? Why?"

"I just need to . . ." I pause, trying to explain it to myself so I can explain it to Nico. But I can't manage to do either of those things. ". . . check something."

He fumbles to get the silver key ring out of his pocket and hands it to me. Without thinking, I sprint back to the Firebird, drop my backpack on the ground, and jam the silver key into the lock of the trunk, popping it open.

I stare into the open cavity, momentarily paralyzed. It's the first time I've actually looked inside the trunk since that Pete guy dropped off the car at my house.

My gaze zeroes in on the spare tire, tucked into the far left corner, and suddenly I'm seven years old again, searching the car for my stuffed rabbit, discovering Jackson's secret stash instead. His "escape fund."

Before I can think or even explain what's happening, I'm suddenly moving. I practically climb inside the trunk, pushing the spare tire aside and running my hands up and down the metal compartment.

But there's nothing.

*Nothing.*

And yet, I need there to be something. I need to know that my father didn't leave me with nothing but a fake car, a cassette tape full of angry noise, and a mountain of debt. I need to find some tiny, infinitesimal proof that he wasn't the man I always thought he was. That he wasn't someone who just left. That maybe, just maybe, he cared enough to leave something valuable behind.

So I keep searching. My hands running everywhere. All over the inside of the trunk. I search every inch, every pocket, every recess, every corner.

But there's still nothing.

Of course, there's nothing.

Because this is Jackson we're talking about.

"Ali?" Nico asks from somewhere behind me. "Are you okay? What are you looking for?"

"I'm looking for something that doesn't exist!" I shout as I shove the tire back into place. I'm just about to slam the trunk lid shut when I see it. Tucked under the corner of the cargo mat. As though it had been jostled around over too many miles, too many curves in the road, until finally getting stuck there.

A white letter-size envelope.

Not unlike the one Nico found hidden in my backpack tonight.

It seems Jackson and I were both keeping secrets stashed away.

My heart catches in my chest as I think about what could possibly be inside. Was Jackson planning another escape before death took him first? Could he have possibly left me more than just a worthless clone of a car?

I can sense Nico watching me. I don't think he's spotted the envelope yet. I think he's too busy waiting to see what I'm going to do next.

There's only one thing to do next.

I reach out and pull the envelope free from the mat. But my shoulders wilt when I feel it in my hands. It's too thin. Whatever's inside is definitely *not* the thick wad of hundred-dollar bills that I found at seven years old.

There's writing on the front of the envelope. An address scribbled in black pen. But I don't even bother to read it. I turn the envelope over and open the flap, holding my breath as I pull out a faded old photograph. It looks like it was taken outside of one of those fancy, luxurious buses.

*A tour bus*, I instantly realize.

Because standing in front of it, right next to Jackson, is Nolan Cook, the lead singer of Fear Epidemic. I recognize him from the countless photos I found of the band online after Jackson first left. And from that night Jackson took me to see them at the Black Bear Saloon in Fort Bragg. Nolan's ratty dark hair looks like it hasn't been brushed in days. He still has that signature smudge of dark eyeliner ringing his eyes and that tangle of silver chains hanging from his neck.

In the photograph, Jackson and Nolan are both striking ridiculous matching poses, strumming powerfully on invisible air guitars, as though the photographer shouted out at the last second, "Give me your best rock star!"

Nolan is taking the direction very seriously. His mouth stretched wide—mid-scream—his eyes wild. Jackson, on the other hand, is laughing. His eyes are crinkled at the corners; his teeth are showing.

He looks . . .

I feel nauseous.

*Happy*.

On the back of the photograph, in the same handwriting

that appears on the envelope, someone has written, "Good times."

My gaze drifts back to the empty trunk that stands in front of me like a giant, gaping cavern. And suddenly I feel my own emptiness thrumming inside of me. It's cold and bitter and dark. It's an emptiness that I don't think any amount of trades or money or things will ever fill. It's an emptiness that feels like the deepest hole Jackson ever left behind.

And then, I just feel stupid. Stupid for looking. Stupid for hoping.

Of course there would be nothing of value in here. *This* is what Jackson valued. This photograph represents everything that was meaningful to him. Nolan Cook. The band. Being on the road. Being free.

Of us.

*Good times.*

I quickly stuff the photograph back inside the envelope, toss it into the trunk, and slam the lid closed.

"You okay?" Nico asks. He's still standing beside me, his mind processing, analyzing. He's struggling to put pieces together. Well, he might as well give up on that effort, because apparently some things can never be pieced back together once they've been broken.

"Yes. Fine. Let's go." I scoop up my backpack and stalk toward the motel. Maybe Wes was right. Maybe I *am* looking for something. Maybe I've been looking for something my whole life.

But I'm now more certain than ever that it's not something that can be found.

# SUNDAY

*I don't want to fight with you tonight*
*Shouldn't be this hard to keep alive*
*Everything you do is all stained red*
*Can you ever really raise the dead?*

—"Salvage Lot," from the album
*Salvage Lot* by Fear Epidemic
Written by Nolan Cook, Slate Miller,
Chris McCaden, and Adam French
Released April 18, 2009

# 8:05 A.M.

## BROOKINGS, OR

INVENTORY: 1968 FIREBIRD CONVERTIBLE (1),
CASH ($390.20), SEA GLASS (1 PIECE),
VINTAGE TYPEWRITER (1),
LOST-KEY BUTTERFLY SCULPTURE (1),
USELESS PHOTOGRAPH (1)

The next morning I wake up to Nico's phone chirping. The sun is streaming in through the window of our hotel room. Thankfully, last night we were able to get a room with two beds, and when I look over, Nico is lying propped up on the pillows, holding his phone above his head.

I yawn. "What's that?"

"Response to the Craigslist post."

I'm suddenly wide-awake. "Really? Who? Where? What do they want to trade?"

Nico chuckles. "Whoa. Slow down. I'm still reading it."

Relief floods through me. After getting so many lightning-fast responses for the last few items and then *none* last night, I was beginning to worry that trading the electric guitar for the old typewriter was a bad idea.

Nico continues skimming the e-mail. It seems to take forever. I wonder if it's another Mack Polonsky, sharing her life story. Finally Nico relays the news. "A woman named Emily Sweeney wants the typewriter. She's in Bandon, Oregon. It's about eighty miles north of here up the coast."

"Emily Sweeney," I repeat. "Why does that sound so familiar?"

Nico shrugs. "Doesn't sound familiar to me."

"What is she willing to trade?"

He squints at the screen. "That can't be right."

"What?"

"She says she wants to trade a brand-new Microsoft Surface Pro. Those things are worth, like, two grand."

I jump to my feet. "Two grand?! That's amazing!"

"But why?" Nico asks, still scowling at the screen. "Why would *anyone* want to trade an old typewriter for a brand-new tablet?"

"Who cares! It's just like you said, we have no idea why the typewriter is valuable to *her*. It just is. We don't question. We go where the trades take us, remember?"

I rush into the bathroom, brush my teeth, comb out my hair, and stuff my toiletries into my backpack. When I'm finished, Nico still hasn't even gotten out of bed. He's just lying there, watching me with an amused expression. "What are you doing?" I ask.

He props himself farther up on the pillows. "I'm just enjoying this moment."

I glance down at my flimsy nightshirt and shorts and quickly cross my arms over my chest. "Ew! Stop! Are you checking me out?"

12. No lustful leering of any kind.

Nico chuckles. "No. I was basking in my victory."

I lower my arms. "What victory?"

He smirks. "You suddenly realizing that I was right all along. About trading up. It's a nice feeling. Being right."

I groan, pick his jeans up off the floor, and throw them at his face. "Yeah, well, don't get used to it."

# 10:10 A.M.

## BANDON, OR

INVENTORY: 1968 FIREBIRD CONVERTIBLE (1),
CASH ($390.20), SEA GLASS (1 PIECE),
VINTAGE TYPEWRITER (1),
LOST-KEY BUTTERFLY SCULPTURE (1),
USELESS PHOTOGRAPH (1)

By the time we reach Bandon, the temperature outside has already risen to ninety degrees. It's turning out to be a very hot day. We park in front of the Arcade Tavern, where Emily Sweeney has asked us to meet her, and Nico lugs the extremely heavy typewriter out of the back seat.

"This can't be right," I say as we approach the front door of the single-story wood building. "It says it doesn't open until eleven. What time did she say to meet her?"

Nico tries to shrug with the typewriter in his arms, but his shoulders barely twitch. "I don't remember. Check the e-mail." He juts his hip toward me, and my cheeks flush as I realize he wants me to reach into the front pocket of his jeans to retrieve his phone.

"Um," I falter, staring blankly at his pants.

"Ali, this is kind of heavy."

"Sorry!" Trying my best to avoid any contact with any body parts, I quickly dip my hand into Nico's jeans and pull out the phone. I swipe to the last e-mail from Emily and scan the text. "Huh. She just says, 'Come whenever. I'll be here.'"

"Try the door," Nico says.

I do. Surprisingly, it's unlocked. I push it open, and Nico follows behind me into the building. The Arcade Tavern is clearly a dive bar of sorts. It has several pool tables, TV screens mounted to the walls, and even an old jukebox in the corner. But the place is completely empty and dark.

"Hello?" Nico calls out, shifting the weight of the typewriter in his arms.

"I don't think this is the right—"

But I'm cut off when someone shouts, "Oh, thank God, you're here! I was afraid you wouldn't come."

I glance up to see a woman rushing toward us. She's very thin, with a knot of messy brown hair atop her head, reminding me of a greyhound in a wig. Her clothes—sweatpants and a T-shirt—are all wrinkled, like she hasn't changed them in days, and she has an unidentifiable brown stain on the front of her shirt.

"Is that it?" she asks, her gaze darting anxiously to the typewriter that Nico is struggling to keep hold of. There's something about this woman's eyes that isn't quite right. Like she's on something. Or needs to be.

"Yes," Nico says, sounding a little uncertain about this whole exchange.

"It's gorgeous. It's perfect. It's exactly what I need. You two have *saved* my life."

I peer between her and the typewriter.

*Is this a prank?*

Nico clearly is asking himself the same question because he says, "So, you really want to trade this for a Surface Pro?"

The woman scowls as though just the name of the device makes her ill. "Yes. I need to get rid of that thing. It's ruining my life."

A typewriter is going to save her life, and a Surface Pro is ruining it?

"Great," Nico says uneasily. "Uh, can we see it?"

The woman gets a far-off look in her eyes for a moment, as though she's lost the train of this conversation and is trying to remember where she put it. Then her gaze suddenly snaps back to Nico. "Oh, right. Of course. It's over here."

Emily beckons for us to follow her as she leads us through the bar, weaving around the pool tables to the very back of the room.

"Still think you know her?" Nico whispers to me.

"I was sitting near the door," Emily explains over her shoulder. "But it was too much of a distraction. People coming and going, coming and going. So I moved back here." We reach a small table in the corner, and my eyes widen as I take in the state of it.

Yup. Emily Sweeney is definitely missing a few (very important) screws.

The table is littered with what can be best described as debris. Empty paper coffee cups, used tissues, stacks of books, and countless pieces of paper with random scribblings on them. I tilt my head to try to read one of them, but all I can make out is:

*Broken tire swing in backyard?*

*Maple?*

*Oak?*

*Something bonsai-ish. But not.*

Do the owners of this establishment know she's here? Did she break in?

Emily sifts through several random items on the table before finally locating a sleek silver tablet hiding under a yellow legal pad filled with more nonsense scribblings. She pushes it into my hands as though it were plague-ridden. "Here. Take it. Please. Get it out of my sight."

I flip the device over until I have it right side up and lift the cover. To my surprise, it actually turns on. I tap on the screen and test out a few apps. Nico watches over my shoulder, clearly just as flabbergasted as I am to see that it works.

"What's wrong with it?" Nico asks, but Emily doesn't answer, and when we look down, she's leaning over the table, writing furiously on one of the pieces of paper. She has to write infinitesimally small to fit it into the two inches of space left on the page.

"Locked in a supermarket?" she mutters as she writes.

"No. How would they get past the cameras?" She then proceeds to violently scratch out what she just wrote before glancing up at us again. "What did you say?"

"What's wrong with the Surface Pro?" Nico repeats.

"It connects to the Internet," Emily says, as though this explains everything and she fully expects us to nod like we get it.

We both nod, but certainly *not* because we get it.

"Charlotte Brontë couldn't get on the Internet and look how well that turned out. Jane Austen couldn't get on the Internet and we got Mr. Darcy because of it. I was trying to find inspiration on Craigslist when I ran across your post and I thought, *that's* what I need! I need to go old-school or go home on this one. I need to channel the greats!"

Comprehension suddenly filters through me. "Wait. You're a *writer*?"

Emily casts her eyes around the table, gesturing to the mess. "Well, yeah."

"Emily Sweeney!" I repeat the name, all of the pieces falling into place. "I knew I'd heard that name before. You write those romance novels."

She looks offended. "*Those* romance novels?"

I clear my throat, embarrassed. "I mean, those *famous*, amazing romance novels. I see them everywhere."

"Well, this one is not going to be *anywhere* unless I can get my act together."

I glance at the pages of scribbles and watch them morph before my eyes. They're not the aimless rants of a madwoman; they're brainstorms!

I feel a flutter of excitement. I want to ask her all sorts of questions about her process, her inspirations, what it feels like to see something you wrote on a bookstore shelf.

"So you're writing a book right now?"

She scoffs. "I wouldn't say *that*."

"What do you mean?"

"First I need an idea."

My gaze drifts back to the pages of scattered notes. "So, you haven't started yet?"

Emily sighs. "Nope. But don't tell my agent that. He's expecting the full manuscript in two weeks."

"Two weeks?"

"Yes. Two weeks. So I really need to get a move on. Do we have a deal?"

Emily stares expectantly at Nico, who seems to just now remember that he's holding the insanely heavy typewriter. "Oh, right. Yes!"

Emily's eyes light up as she clears a space for Nico to set the machine down on the table. Once he does, Emily sits in front of it and runs her fingers reverently over the keys. "Yes. This is what I need. No distractions. No e-mail notifications. No Internet. I'll be able to finish the novel in no time with this thing." She glances around her cluttered table. "Oh, crap. I need to go out and buy some paper first."

She leaps to her feet and starts to stuff seemingly random items into the bag hanging from the back of her chair.

"Do you need help carrying the typewriter to your car?" Nico asks.

Emily waves her hand. "Nah. I'll leave it here with the

rest of my stuff. The owner of the bar and I have a special arrangement. She lets me sit here all day, even after closing. I have a key to the front door."

"Do you think she'd mind if I use the bathroom?" Nico asks, glancing around for a men's room.

"Sure. Go ahead. It's over by the bar."

"Cool. Thanks." Nico turns to me. "I'll meet you out front?"

I nod and watch in fascination as Emily continues to throw items into her bag, mumbling to herself. "Okay, wallet, phone, notebook. Keys!" She searches the debris on the table. "Keys, keys, keys."

"So," I say conversationally, "how long have you been trying to come up with a new idea? I mean, how long does it normally take?"

"Depends on the idea," Emily replies absently, still hunting for her car keys.

"What do you mean?"

Emily grabs a half-full coffee mug from the table and downs the rest of it in one gulp. "Writing a novel is a two-way street. You have to like the idea that you're writing, but the idea has to like you, too. It doesn't matter if you are in love with a story idea; if it wants out, there's nothing you can do to stop it. Now, where are those keys?" She sets her coffee cup down and then lifts it up again, checking underneath it.

"Like a relationship," I say quietly, causing Emily to stop her search and peer over at me.

"Yes, exactly." She glances in the direction of the bathroom. "What's the story there? The Craigslist post said something about the two of you being exes."

I nod. "Yeah. We broke up a little over a month ago."

"So what the hell are you doing on a road trip with him?"

I laugh. "I ask myself the same question every five minutes. I'm trying to earn enough money to save my house. The bank is foreclosing on it."

She winces. "I'm sorry."

I'm actually surprised at how easy it was to tell her that. I haven't told anyone about the foreclosure except June and Nico, and this woman is a perfect stranger. Somehow, though, I just feel comfortable talking to her. Maybe *because* she's a perfect stranger.

"Thanks," I say. "I thought I was going to be able to sell this old car my dad left me when he died, but it turned out not to be worth as much as I thought. So Nico is helping me trade up to something worth enough money to get the bank off our backs."

Emily frowns. "Why is he doing that?"

"What do you mean?"

"Does he want to get back together?"

I shake my head, thinking of all the glares and underhanded jabs Nico has thrown at me since the start of this trip. "No. I really don't think so."

"Then why would he go through all that trouble?"

"I'm paying him."

Emily stares at me for a long moment and then bursts out laughing. It's a deep belly laugh that suddenly makes me sorry I did open up to her.

"What?" I ask.

"No, that's *definitely* not the reason."

I gape at her. "How do you know?"

But she doesn't answer that question. "Why did you two break up?"

I sigh. "It's a long story."

She tilts her head, studying me, and for a moment I think she's going to ask me to rehash the whole story—the night of the comet, the text messages, the glove box—but instead she asks, "You know what the biggest complaint is that I get from readers of my romance novels?"

I shrug. "Um, too much sex?"

She shakes her head.

"Not enough sex?"

She laughs again. "Definitely not that."

"I give up."

"Unrealistic heroes."

I squint, confused. "What do you mean?"

"People claim that guys like the ones I write about in my books don't really exist. There's no such man. No one would ever do the kind of things my characters do, go to the kind of lengths they go to. My response to those comments is always the same." Emily scoops up a pile of used tissues, frowning when she still can't locate her keys.

"What's that?" I prompt.

"I tell them that men like that *do* exist. They're just rare. That's why I write about them." She nods in the direction of the bathroom again. "If he's still around after all of this, if he's really willing to go the lengths he's gone to help you, it's not for *money*."

I snort. "What else could it be for?"

Emily stuffs her hands into the pocket of her sweatpants and pulls out a key chain. "Aha!" She grabs her bag and starts for the front of the bar.

"What else could it be for?" I call after her, this time more insistently.

She stops and turns around, looking bewildered, like she forgot what we were talking about just a second ago. Then she blinks and focuses on me. "I'm just saying, maybe you should take a second look at that 'long story' you mentioned. It might be due for a revision."

After a dockside brunch with some *very* chatty sea lions (who reminded Nico of some of the girls who used to sit next to our table in the cafeteria), we walk back to the Firebird.

It didn't take us long to find a taker for the tablet. In fact, it's proven to be our most popular item yet. Within twenty minutes of updating our post during brunch, Nico had five offers in his inbox. We chose to accept the one from a travel blogger named Kamil who lives 190 miles north of Bandon in Tillamook, Oregon, where the famous cheese is made. According to Kamil's e-mail, he's leaving on a yearlong trip around the world and needs a nice compact computer to take with him. He's offering to trade us his entire season of Seattle Seahawk tickets (two seats!), since he won't be around for this year's football season.

"It should only be another ninety minutes to Tillamook," I tell Nico as we reach the car. I wipe a bead of sweat from my forehead. The day has continued to heat up, and now it feels like it's almost a hundred degrees outside.

When Nico doesn't respond to my comment, I look up to see he's not even focused on me. Something behind me has caught his attention.

"What?" I ask.

His face breaks into a wide grin. "Is that a Newfoundland?"

I roll my eyes as I turn around. "For the last time, not *every* single dog we come across is a—" But I'm cut off when I see what Nico is looking at. Sure enough, farther down the street, tied up outside a candy store, is a very large, very black, very fluffy, and very *hot* Newfoundland.

The dog's tongue is hanging out the side of his mouth, and he looks like he might pass out at any moment.

"He's cute!" Nico exclaims at the same time that I yell out, "He's overheated!"

"What?" Nico asks, but I'm already dashing down the street toward the dog.

I hold out my hand cautiously toward the dog's nose. When I'm certain he's not going to bite me, I reach for his mouth and pull up his lip to reveal his gums. Sure enough, they're dry and blue.

"What are you doing?" someone asks, and I look up to

see a young woman walking out of the candy shop, her gaze darting between me and the dog.

"Your dog is dehydrated," I tell her.

Her eyes widen. "What? How do you know that?"

I show her the gums. "See that color? That's not a good sign."

The woman gives me a concerned once-over. "Are you a vet or something?"

"Not y*et*," Nico chimes in, giving me a pointed look.

I shoo him away. "I work with dogs. You need to get him home right away and soak his paws in cold water. It's the fastest way to cool him down."

The woman glances anxiously up the street. "My car is parked a few blocks away. Would you mind waiting with him?"

I nod. "Sure."

The woman hurries away, and I turn to Nico. "Can you go inside and see if they have some water for him to drink?"

"On it," Nico says, disappearing inside the candy shop and reappearing less than a minute later with two over-flowing paper cups. We tip one toward the dog, and he eagerly laps up the water, finishing it off quickly before turning toward the second cup.

"So," Nico says, jutting his chin toward the water-guzzling dog. "This is the famous Newfoundland. You really think I look like that?"

As if sensing that we're talking about him, the dog stops drinking and looks up at us, his tongue still hanging clumsily out of his mouth.

I give him a scratch under the chin. "Yup. You're definitely a Newfie."

Nico studies the dog, a look of mock disapproval on his face. Just then, a huge pile of drool drips from the dog's mouth, making a large splash on the pavement by Nico's feet. I stifle a laugh.

"That's cool," Nico says with a nonchalant shrug. "I bet these dogs are really good kissers."

# 12:07 P.M.

## HIGHWAY 101

INVENTORY: 1968 FIREBIRD CONVERTIBLE (1), CASH ($345.12), SEA GLASS (1 PIECE), LOST-KEY BUTTERFLY SCULPTURE (1), USELESS PHOTOGRAPH (1), SURFACE PRO TABLET (1)

It's a four-hour drive from Bandon to Tillamook, but the day is way too hot to put the top down. So Nico blasts the Firebird's air-conditioning, I slip on my Sea-Bands, and, with a full tank of gas, we set off again, filling the drive with more episodes of *Everything About Everything*.

Our route takes us through countless more trees, the Oregon sand dunes, and several state parks. The scenery out the window is breathtaking. Towering, rocky cliffs plunging toward the sea on one side of the car and thick green forest on the other. As though this part of the planet was having an identity crisis when the earth was being formed and couldn't decide whether it wanted to become an ocean or a forest.

"Keep your eyes open," Nico says after another episode comes to a close. "We're officially in the Pacific Northwest now. This is prime Bigfoot country."

I roll my eyes. "I can't believe there are people out there who actually believe in Bigfoot."

Nico scoffs. "You don't *believe* in Bigfoot. That's like saying you don't believe in oxygen."

"You *don't* believe in oxygen. It's just there."

"Exactly," Nico says.

I stare at him, agape. "Wait, you're kidding, right?"

"About what?"

"*You* believe in Bigfoot?"

He steers the car around a sharp turn. "Like you said, you don't *believe* in Bigfoot. He's just there."

I scoff. "Stop messing with me."

"I'm not messing with you. Why would I joke about a giant, hairy half-man-half-beast?"

"Um, maybe because he's not real," I say.

Nico pretends like he's choking on something. "Not. Real? Of course he's real!"

"Have you ever seen him?"

"Have you ever seen *oxygen*?"

I throw my hands up. "That's completely different."

"How?"

"Well, for starters, you can see oxygen molecules under a microscope."

"So? People have seen Bigfoot in the woods."

"You're starting to sound a lot like our friend Sandy back in Fort Bragg."

"There are photographs."

"That are clearly Photoshopped. People haven't *seen* Bigfoot in the woods. People have *claimed* to have seen Bigfoot in the woods."

Nico seems undeterred by my logic. "Maybe those scientists are only *claiming* to see oxygen molecules under a microscope."

"That's the most ridiculous thing I've ever heard!" I'm still unable to believe where this conversation is going. I keep waiting for Nico to flash that infamous smirk of his to let me know that he's kidding. But he doesn't. He's being perfectly serious. How, after dating him for three months, are there still things about him that I don't know? For our entire relationship all we seemed to do was talk and drive and kiss. And yet, somehow, out of all those hours of talking, we never made it to the topic of Bigfoot? I thought we'd covered *all* topics under the sun. But apparently not.

The sun, as it turns out, is huge. And there are infinite topics hiding underneath it. Things you'd never even thought to ask.

"I'm just saying," Nico goes on, "no one believed that the giant squid was real until one washed up onto shore. One of these days a giant Sasquatch is going to be found dead in someone's backyard, and then all of you skeptics are going to be like, 'Ooh, um, yeah, sorry about that, I guess we were wrong. Derp. Derp. Derp.'"

I laugh aloud at his impersonation. "Is that what skeptics sound like? Like the bumbling Swedish chef from the Muppets?"

"Yes," Nico maintains.

"So, you're saying that after all of these years, even though every inch of this planet has been explored and no one has ever come up with undeniable proof that Bigfoot exists, you still think he does?"

"You really think we've explored every inch of this planet?"

I balk. "Well, no. Not *every* inch. I just think if he's out there, we would have seen him by now. Someone would have captured him in a picture that doesn't look like a grainy, Photoshopped tabloid magazine photo."

Nico shakes his head, making a *tsk* sound with his tongue.

"What?"

"I just think it's sad."

I cross my arms. "What is?"

"That you're so unwilling to trust in something you've never seen."

The comment stings, and I can feel an argument sneaking up on us. "Let's just listen to another podcast," I suggest, scrolling through Nico's phone. "Here's an interesting one. We can learn about how Stockholm syndrome works."

Nico hesitates. "I think I'm learned out for the moment."

"Oh, okay. Do you want me to find another podcast?"

"How about a personality quiz? Do you still do those?"

I feel my muscles involuntarily seize up.

"Sometimes," I say. It's the understatement of the century. The truth is, I don't just *do* personality quizzes. I live for them.

"Got any good ones?"

I force out a laugh. "Feeling the need to define yourself?"

"Always."

I click off the podcast app and navigate to my favorite quiz website. Seeing all the new quizzes that have been added brings me an instant wave of comfort. With my phone data hovering between low and nonexistent, I haven't had a chance to visit the site since we left.

"Okay," I say, scanning the list. "How about 'Which Disney Prince Are You?'"

"Sounds good."

I click the quiz and read the first question. "What is your best physical trait?"

"That's easy. Hair."

I groan. "I haven't even read the answers yet."

*And the answer is your eyes*, I add silently in my head.

"Fine," Nico allows. "Go ahead."

"Eyes, chin, hair—"

"Hair!"

I chuckle and tick the box. "Okay. What is your idea of a perfect day? Hiking in nature, combing the seven seas hunting down pirates, riding your horse looking for damsels in distress, running cons on royalty—"

"That one," Nico decides.

I snort. "Why am I not surprised?"

After eight more questions, I hit submit, and the site spits out Nico's result.

"You got Flynn Rider."

"Which one's he?"

"From *Tangled*."

"Which one's that?"

"The Rapunzel story."

"Which one's Rapunzel?"

I sigh. "The one with the long hair."

"How long is the hair?"

I glance at him to confirm that he's messing with me. "Let's find you another quiz." I swipe through the list. "How about 'Which Summer Crush Song Are You?' Or maybe 'Which *Crusade of Kings* Character Are You?' Or how about—"

"Do you remember that first quiz we took?" he interrupts me.

I swallow. "Which one?"

Even though I know which one. Of course I know.

"The sixteen personalities one," he clarifies. "Remember, we took it the night of . . ." His voice trails off.

But we both know what he was going to say.

*The night of June's party.*

*The night all of this began.*

*The night we crashed into each other like two helpless stars colliding, leaving behind a black hole.*

I fight to keep the pain from flashing across my face. I fight to keep my voice calm. Neutral. Professional. Like the Commissioner that I am. "Right. Yeah. Why?"

"That one was fun. Let's do that one again."

I peer at him in the darkness, confused. "Why would you want to do that one again? You already took that one." I continue to scroll through the list on the screen. "How about 'Find Out Which *Sesame Street* Character You Are Based on Your Choice of Salad Toppings.'"

"Ali?" Nico says pensively.

"Mmm?"

He suddenly sounds nervous as he navigates around another steep curve in the road. "I never told you this, but I sort of fibbed my answers."

I freeze. "What? You mean on the Disney prince quiz?'

"No, on the personality type quiz."

"But—" I stammer, my stomach curdling. So much for the magic Sea-Bands. I suddenly feel like I'm going to throw up. "*Why?* Why would you do that?"

"You were looking over my shoulder the whole time. I couldn't exactly answer honestly. I was trying to impress you."

My head is reeling. This is his idea of lighthearted road trip conversation? A confession that our entire relationship was based on a lie? That's like saying, "Oh, since we seem to have nothing else to do, let's drop bombs on people and watch as they explode."

"But . . . ," I begin again, struggling to stay calm. But the calm is slowly slipping away. I'm running out of it. "That whole time we were together, we made jokes about you being the Fixer and me being the Commissioner."

He shrugs. "Yeah, exactly. *Jokes.* Wasn't that all they were?"

I think back to the nights I spent reading and rereading his personality profile, committing it to memory, planning my whole life around it. "Right. Yeah. Jokes."

"Are you mad?" he asks. Like he can just tell. Like he's always right there, inside my brain. Is "Mind Reader" the name of his *real* personality type?

I swallow, trying to keep my voice steady. But I can hear the waver in it. "No."

Nico glances at me out of the corner of his eye. "You're mad."

"I'm not." I assure him. "I'm just..." I pause. "...wondering why you didn't tell me earlier."

He shrugs. "I didn't think it was a big deal. And you seemed to be having so much fun with our two personality types. Plus, I kind of liked you calling me the Fixer."

"But it was a lie," I blurt out before I can stop myself.

He grows quiet for few seconds. "I shouldn't have told you."

"You shouldn't have lied on the test."

"Relax, Ali," he says, the easiness in his voice gone. "It's just a stupid test."

"It's not a stupid test!" I fire back. "It's . . . it's . . ."

"It's what?" he challenges. "What is it?"

*It's everything*, I think, but I know it sounds ridiculous. Even in my head.

"You can't judge someone based on a single personality quiz," Nico says.

"I don't do that," I shoot back, but I can tell he doesn't believe me.

I barely believe myself.

I glance down at the phone still clutched in my hand.

At the countless personality quiz options stretching for miles and miles, just waiting to tell me some random, useless fact about myself. Just waiting to define who I am. Who everyone is.

Just waiting to put the world in a safe little box.

> **You just discovered your entire relationship with your ex was based on a lie! What do you do?**
>
> **A** *Force him to pull over and take the quiz again . . . truthfully this time!*
>
> **B** *Admit to yourself it doesn't matter. His true identity was sealed the moment you opened that glove box.*
>
> **C** *. . .*

"Ali." Nico's voice breaks into my thoughts before I can come up with an option C.

"Yeah," I reply, bracing myself for the lecture I'm sure is coming. He's going to tell me I put too much stock in stupid things like personality quizzes. He's going to tell me to just let it go. It's not important. It doesn't matter.

But he doesn't. Instead he says, "Can we stop? We're almost out of water."

Because the truth is, Nico has never done anything that I've ever expected him to do. He's never behaved solely like a Fixer or a Commissioner or any of the other fourteen personality types on that quiz.

He's never fit into a box.

And I suddenly know what option C is.

It's the option I've been avoiding for the past five hundred miles.

> **C** *Start over, forget the past, and let the real*
> *Nico reveal himself to you.*

# 4:15 P.M.

## TILLAMOOK, OR

**INVENTORY: 1968 FIREBIRD CONVERTIBLE (1),
CASH ($345.12), SEA GLASS (1 PIECE),
LOST-KEY BUTTERFLY SCULPTURE (1),
USELESS PHOTOGRAPH (1),
SURFACE PRO TABLET (1)**

Less than an hour later, we walk into a used camera shop in Tillamook, Oregon, with a Surface Pro tablet and walk out again five minutes later with an envelope of Seattle Seahawks tickets that Nico estimates is worth more than five thousand dollars, based on their face value.

Just like that.

*Five thousand dollars.*

That, combined with the car, will take us up to eight thousand.

I still can't believe we've made it this far. From a rubber band, no less! It boggles my mind that this even works. That Nico *knew* it would work.

He makes it look so easy. To dig your way out of life's problems.

I think about how he first proposed this crazy plan to me on the beach. *"We trade up!"*

He said it like we were seven and he was pitching me the idea of starting a lemonade stand.

*Easy. We make the lemonade. We sell the lemonade. Life's problems, solved.*

Nico quickly updates our Craigslist post and suggests we keep heading north up the coast while we wait for responses.

"If they're Seattle Seahawks tickets, we should have better luck trading them if we're closer to Seattle."

So, I guess we're heading north . . . *again.*

As we continue to drive up the coast, I steal glimpses at the map on Nico's phone. We don't have much of the state of Oregon left. Pretty soon, we'll have no choice but to cross over the border to Washington. Pretty soon, I'll be forced to be in the same state where Jackson died.

"Whoa!" Nico shouts, jerking my attention back to the car, which is now decelerating at a breakneck rate as Nico swerves off the highway. He yanks the steering wheel and pulls into one of those scenic overlook parking areas. But he's still going so fast, I'm terrified he's going to drive straight over the guardrail and send us plummeting off the cliff to the beach below.

I grab hold of the seat as Nico slams on the brakes and we stop just short of the edge. "What the hell!?" I scream.

But Nico ignores me, leaping out of the car without opening the door.

I really wish he would stop doing that.

He runs to the edge of the lookout point and shields his eyes from the sun. "Yes!" he shouts, pointing at something in the distance. "That's it! That's totally it!"

"What are you doing?" I call out from the passenger seat.

"Come look at this!" is all he says in response.

I get out of the car—utilizing the door like a normal person—and tentatively walk over to where Nico is still gaping at the ocean. I'm starting to worry that after three days in the car with his ex, he might have actually cracked.

But then I see what he sees, and a shiver of exhilaration travels through me. "Oh my God! Is that for real?"

"It has to be, right? It looks just like it!"

I squint at the giant rock formation in the distance: one large cone-shaped boulder flanked by two smaller, pointier ones on either side.

We watched the movie at least five times in the three months we dated. It was one of our go-to favorites for our Epic Eighties Movie Marathons.

"Totally," I agree. "This *has* to be the rock formation from *The Goonies*."

Nico fishes his phone out of his pocket and types something into a web browser. A few moments later he confirms it. "Yup. Haystack Rock. Featured in the movie *The Goonies*, which was filmed nearby in Astoria, Oregon." He pockets his phone and taps his chin contemplatively. "How did that movie end again? It's so weird. For some reason, I can't remember the ending." He flashes me that mischievous look of his. "I wonder why."

I roll my eyes. "You know exactly why."

"Oh, that's right. We never quite made it to the end. Of *several* of those films."

I go to jab him in the arm, but he catches my hand before I make contact. At first I think he's just trying to stop me from hitting him. And maybe that *was* his original intention. But then, he doesn't let go. And for a long, tense moment, he's just standing there, holding my hand. His warm fingers tangled up with mine.

And for some reason, I don't pull away.

But I can't look at him. I turn back toward the rock. I let the silence fall between us. It feels lighter somehow now. Less a shadowy pit and more a warm summer breeze.

"That was really amazing what you did back there." I can tell from the hesitant tone of his voice that it's a subject he's been trying to broach for a while. "With the dog. How did you know what to do?"

I glance down at our entwined fingers. "Chateau Marmutt. Last summer we had a massive heat wave, and I watched Pam save one of the Saint Bernards from the same fate. Those cold-weather breeds are just not cut out for the heat."

"You're going to make a really great veterinarian one day."

I rip my hand away. So that's where he's going with this. "Nico—"

"I just don't understand. Why would you give up a full

scholarship to your dream? Why is that acceptance letter still sitting in your backpack?"

"I told you I don't want to talk about it."

"Ali, you're meant to be a vet. You should go to school to become a vet."

"Vet school will be there next year."

"Yeah, but that scholarship might not be!"

"Stop," I say so sternly it causes Nico to flinch. "Please, just stop."

Nico falls silent. But he looks too contemplative. I worry he's not going to just let this go. He's going to keep pushing and pushing and—

"I couldn't send it, okay?" I explode.

Nico's eyes flicker to me, but he doesn't speak.

"I tried," I go on. "I had it all stamped and ready. I walked it right down to the mailbox. But my hands were trembling so badly, I couldn't drop it in."

"Why?"

I close my eyes, letting the question wash over me. It's a good question.

*Why?*

I shrug. "I don't know."

Nico presses. "I think you do."

I sigh. He's right. I do know. I've known since the moment the envelope first arrived. Since the first fore-closure notice appeared on our front door. Maybe since the day Jackson first left.

"Because if I leave my mom now," I say quietly, "then I'm no better than him."

Nico looks like he's going to respond to this, but I don't let him. I turn my back to him and stare out at the ocean. Even from way up here, high on this cliff, I can still hear the waves crashing far below.

We stand there for a long time, neither of us saying anything. Finally, without a word, I turn and walk back to the car.

"Any responses to the season tickets?" I ask as Nico sits down in the driver's seat, hoping the change of topic will keep him from trying to continue our previous conversation.

It works. He fishes his phone out of his pocket. "Yes. Wow. Five."

"Five?" I repeat, flabbergasted. "Already? What are people willing to trade?"

"Let's see." Nico scrolls his thumb up the screen. "The first response is from someone in Vancouver, Canada. Nope. We don't have passports. Next. There's also a response from someone in Portland. That's not far too from here."

"What are they offering?"

Nico peers at the screen and frowns. "Whoa. A bedroom furniture set. Nope, too big."

As he continues to scroll through his e-mails, vetoing trade options, I think about the question Emily Sweeney asked me this morning.

Why is he really doing this?

If I asked him, would he tell me the truth? Or would he just lie to me again?

The way he lied to me about his laptop being in the shop. The way he lied to me about never having traded up on Craigslist before. Which is clearly not true. The way he lied on his personality quiz.

And, of course, the way he lied about where he was that night of the comet.

Yet, I'm starting to wonder if all the lies are somehow connected. Like threads branching out from a complex spiderweb that I can't see. All I can feel are the wispy spindles of cobwebs tangling around me.

But what if they all lead back to something? What if I could follow each individual strand all the way back to the center? To the piece that ties everything together.

The missing laptop.

The Craigslist trades.

The night of the comet.

The glove box.

Would it revise the story? Just like Emily Sweeney told me to do?

Would it rewrite our history?

Could it change everything?

"Okay, here's a promising-sounding one," Nico says. "Someone wants to trade their old RV camper!"

I frown. "An RV camper sounds promising?"

"Yeah, those things are worth some big bucks!"

"I can't drive an RV camper around."

Nico looks undeterred. "I would drive it."

"And who would drive the Firebird?"

"Oh, right." He takes a deep breath and lets it out slowly, like air hissing out of a slashed tire. Then, with some kind of newfound determination, Nico straightens up in his seat and says, "Okay, enough is enough. No more excuses. You're going to learn how to drive this car once and for all."

Nico wasn't technically the first person to ever try to teach me how to drive stick shift. Jackson started to teach me when I was twelve years old, after he came back from touring with the band.

Of course, I never actually got in behind the wheel. I was still too young (and too short) for that. First, he taught me how to shift gears.

We sat at the end of our driveway in Russellville with the car idling in neutral. Jackson was in the driver's seat and I was in the passenger seat, my left hand placed tentatively on the stick shift.

"Okay, do we need to go through it again?" he asked me.

Jackson had his faults. But impatience was never one of them.

I shook my head. "Nope. I got it."

He smiled that dazzling smile at me. "Good. Then let's take this baby on a ride."

He compressed the clutch and gave me my first directive. "First gear."

I easily maneuvered the shifter to the left and up into first. Jackson slowly eased off the clutch and onto the gas. The car rolled forward. "Well done. Let's try second gear."

Jackson engaged the clutch, and I pulled the shifter straight down.

"You're a natural!" he called out as we picked up speed, inching up to twenty miles per hour.

I grinned, feeling the wind on my face and the summer breeze in my hair.

"Okay, let's move her up to third gear."

This one was trickier. I bit my lip and concentrated on the little diagram etched into the top of the shifter. I maneuvered up and slightly to the right. But I didn't quite get there. The gears screeched and whined. I looked to Jackson in a panic, certain I had ruined his most prized possession. But he just laughed. "It's okay, kiddo. Third is the hardest to find. Here. I'll help."

His hand landed atop mine. It was warm and comforting as he helped guide me and the shifter into the slot between first and fifth gear.

"Okay," Jackson said, giving the engine a playful rev. "Are you ready to bring her up to fourth?"

"Yes!" I shouted over the rush of the wind.

"Get ready . . . steady . . ."

Jackson poised his foot on the clutch.

I gripped the shifter.

Jackson lifted his hand from mine.

And for a split second, I felt like I was free-falling.

"Now!"

I yanked the stick shift down into fourth. The car zoomed forward. Jackson let out a "Woo-hoo!" and I squealed with laughter.

For the next few hours, Jackson and I drove all around town. Up Route 128 and back again. Past the Frosty Frog, the library, the high school, and Brewed Awakenings (the local coffee shop). When we slowed at intersections, we waved and catcalled to people. When we streamed down open roads, we made animal noises into the wind. And the whole time, Jackson worked the pedals while I shifted. Up and down. From first to fifth and back again. Until I really did feel like a natural. Until the last three years felt like just a bad dream, and now I'd woken up to find that Jackson had never left on my ninth birthday. Had never written that Post-it Note. Had never forgotten to take me to Tomato and Vine for an early birthday dinner and then driven me to that creepy abandoned park. Had never chosen Fear Epidemic over us.

To this day, those few hours in the Firebird remain one of my favorite memories of Jackson. If I close my eyes tightly enough now, I can still feel the breeze on my face. If I listen closely enough, I can still hear him shouting into the wind beside me. If I try hard enough, I can still feel his hand atop mine, helping me maneuver into those tricky gears. And in that moment, I can almost glimpse the life I would have had if he'd stayed for good. If that large, reassuring hand had always been there. Forever. If it had waved to me as I took off on my first day of high school. If it had shaken Nico's hand the day I first brought him home. If it had embraced me when I found out I was accepted to UC Davis with a full scholarship.

If it had never let go.

If it had stayed around, worked hard for a decent wage, signed mortgage checks.

If it had never scribbled that second Post-it Note.

*I'm sorry. I have to do this.*

What would have become of us if he'd stayed?

Would Mom and I still be losing the house?

Would I be going to the college of my dreams in the fall?

Would Jackson still be alive?

Later, after our hair was windblown beyond repair and our voices were hoarse from all the screaming, Jackson took me to the Frosty Frog and bought me a triple scoop. For old times' sake, he said. I tried to ignore the gnawing of guilt in my stomach as I remembered the last time we'd come here. Back when Jackson was hiding money from my mom in his trunk and I was his unwitting accomplice.

The weather was perfect. We sat outside on a park bench, licking our cones in silence, until Jackson nudged me with his elbow and said, "Hey, I want to ask you something."

"Hmmm?" I responded, chocolate fudge brownie melting between my fingers.

"Do you remember your ninth birthday?"

My fingers (and tongue) froze. I nearly dropped my cone on the sidewalk. Never in the past three years had Jackson ever spoken directly about the day he left. Never had he admitted to what he'd done. How badly he'd let us down.

Every conversation I'd had with him since that day was always some veiled attempt to justify or excuse or redeem.

I swallowed down the lump of ice cream in my mouth. "Yes."

The word felt like it was balancing in the air between us. A fragile thing that, if not caught, could crash to the ground and shatter.

Jackson stretched his legs out in front of him on the

bench and took a large bite of his cone, chewing pensively. "I think about that night all the time."

There was something different about his voice. It wasn't the same charming voice he used on Mom when she was yelling at him or on strangers to instantly gain their trust. It was raw and hesitant.

"Really?" I asked. I didn't know what was happening right now, but I knew I wanted more of it.

He placed that same reassuring hand on my arm but didn't look at me. "Yes, kiddo. Every single day, for a year, on that tour bus, I thought about it. About how badly I screwed up. About what a mess I was. About how much I regretted what I'd done." His voice started to crack.

I gaped at him in disbelief. Was Jackson Collins actually going to cry? I'd never seen my father cry. My mother cried all the time. Mostly in secret when she thought I couldn't hear or didn't know. But I'd always assumed Jackson was incapable of any emotion but frivolity.

In the end, though, he didn't cry. He simply took another bite of his cone and swallowed hard, like he was swallowing down much more than just sugar and flour. He continued to stare at the ground in front of him. "Well, anyway, I just wanted you to know I will never do that to you again. I promise."

I sat there in silence for a good minute. I didn't know what to do with what he had just given me. I wanted to wrap it up, protect it, store it on the highest shelf of my closet so it would never break. I wanted to let it sink deep into me and fill all the holes he'd left behind.

I wanted to believe it.

Wholeheartedly.

Without reservations.

The way daughters are supposed to believe their fathers.

And maybe, just a small part of me did.

"Okay," I finally said.

But, as it turned out, I was right to be wary. Because two weeks later, he was gone again. This time there was no reunited band to steal him away. There were no more excuses for him to hide behind. No brushes with success for him to cling to.

This time, he left without a reason.

And the hole felt so much deeper than the last one.

The note he left was an echo of the past. Like someone had rewound the tape of our history and played it over again.

*I'm sorry. I have to do this.*

The only difference was me. I was older. I was wiser. I was harder. At twelve years old, I didn't feel sadness or abandonment or confusion. This time, I felt only anger.

I stared at the note for a long time, the rage building inside of me, the bitterness solidifying, before I finally ripped it from the fridge, crumpled it in my hands, and whispered aloud to the empty kitchen, "You lied."

# 6:52 P.M.

## SEASIDE, OR

INVENTORY: 1968 FIREBIRD CONVERTIBLE (1),
CASH ($323.38), SEA GLASS (1 PIECE),
LOST-KEY BUTTERFLY SCULPTURE (1),
USELESS PHOTOGRAPH (1),
SEAHAWKS TICKETS (12)

With a lurch and a horrible grinding sound that I *know* does not sound good, I manage to successfully inch the Firebird across the deserted parking lot of the Pacifica, a drive-in movie theater just north of Haystack Rock in the town of Seaside. Nico thought it would make the perfect place to teach me how to drive stick shift.

"Good," Nico praises. "You're almost there. Just a few more feet. Now press down gently on the accelerator."

I push my foot against the gas pedal, and the Firebird engine roars like it's on fire and is about to explode.

"And now shift into second," Nico instructs.

I lift my foot off the gas, press down on the clutch, maneuver the gearshift into second, and return my foot to the gas. But I must not do it right because the car lets out another dramatic screech.

"Easy," Nico says patiently. "You've got to release the clutch and compress the gas at the *exact* same controlled pace."

I let out a groan. "This is impossible."

"No! You're doing better," Nico tells me. "Much better than the last time I tried to teach you."

I turn to flash him a dirty look, but in the process, both feet come off the pedals and the car sputters and stalls, sending us both slamming against our seat belts. I cringe. "Whoops. Sorry."

"Don't apologize to me. Apologize to the car."

"I will not do that."

Nico laughs and pats the console. "Don't worry. Deep down, she's really sorry."

I swat his hand away. "Stop it! No, I'm not. I hate this car, remember?"

Nico flashes me a knowing look. "No, you don't. You *love* this car."

I catch his gaze and hold it tightly. "No. I hate this car. It's a clone. It *lied* about who it was."

Nico's eyes narrow slightly. "Maybe"—he lets the word hang tauntingly in the air—"the car had good reason to lie."

"What would be a *good* reason to lie?"

Nico shrugs. "I don't know. There are plenty of good reasons to lie."

"Like what?"

"Maybe the car only lied because it was trying to seem cooler than it was. Maybe it was just trying to impress you."

"Impress me?" I repeat carefully, knowing we're treading on uneven ground that could drop out from under us at any moment. "Why would it need to do that? Why couldn't it just be confident in who it was?"

Nico rakes his teeth across his bottom lip, and I feel myself involuntarily holding my breath. "Well," he begins haltingly, "maybe it didn't want you to know the truth about who it really was—that it isn't the car you thought it was—because . . ." Just then, I see something flash in Nico's eyes, but I can't tell if it's anger or regret or some combination of the two. He runs a hand through his hair and glances down at his lap. "Because it was afraid you'd get rid of it."

I let my eyes close for a moment as his words rush over me like violent waves, pulling me into their rough, wild current. "Why would I get rid of it?" My voice comes out as a shattered whisper. Barely audible. But it doesn't matter. I already know the answer:

Because that's what I do.

I get rid of things.

I throw things away.

Just like I did with every single piece Nico painstakingly made for me out of wood.

Just like I planned to do with this car.

Just like June said I would do when she gave me that beautiful scrapbook.

*"I just know you. You'll keep it for, like, a few months, and then you'll go through one of your decluttering phases . . ."*

Just like I did with Nico.

But that was different. He let me down that night. He lied about where he was. He was going to leave anyway. Just like Jackson did. I felt it. I *knew* it.

I . . .

*I could have been wrong.*

A lump forms in my throat. I open my mouth to say something, but no words come out. Because there are none left.

Thankfully, someone else speaks instead.

"You know you're going to have to pay if you want to stay for the movie."

I look up to see a man has approached the side of the car. He's wearing a blue Pacifica Theater uniform with matching cap.

I fumble to start the stalled car again. "Oh, sorry. We'll leave."

"Wait." Nico puts a hand on mine, stopping me from turning the key in the ignition. "We're going to stay for the movie." He reaches into his pocket and produces a twenty-dollar bill, handing it over to the employee.

I look at him in confusion. "We don't even know what's playing."

The employee hands Nico two tickets in return for his money and flashes me a smile. "Tonight, we're showing *The Goonies.*"

My mouth falls open, and I turn to Nico. "Seriously? That's, like, a major coincidence."

"Actually," Nico says with a guilty grimace, "it's not, really."

My mind puts the pieces together. "Wait, you knew about this?"

He shrugs sheepishly. "I saw the movie was playing here when I was looking up Goonies stuff back at Haystack Rock. I thought it would be fun to see it on the big screen."

"Enjoy the show." The employee turns and takes off toward the snack stand.

As soon as he's out of earshot, I turn back to Nico. "What about the Craigslist trades? Do we have time to stop and watch a movie?"

"C'mon." Nico gives me a friendly nudge. "We've just hit the five-K milestone. That's a big deal! We need to celebrate! The trades can wait for one more night."

I laugh at his enthusiasm. "Okay, fine. We need to wait for another response anyway because there's no way we're trading the Seahawk tickets for that RV camper. I'm not ready to drive this thing by myself."

"What are you talking about? You were doing great! In fact, you should drive us the rest of the trip."

I scoff. "Yeah, right. Do you actually *want* to die?"

Nico shoves his fist in the air. "Goonies never say die!"

"Well, technically," I remind him, pointing at the drive-in screen, "we've never seen the end. So maybe they *do* eventually say die."

Nico deflates like a popped balloon. "You think they all die in the end?"

I shrug. "I'm just saying it's a possibility. Maybe they find that pirate ship with all the gold in it, and then it blows up and they all drown."

Nico gives me a frustrated look as he slinks back in his seat. "Well, fungicide, Ali. You've just ruined a perfectly good movie."

# 8:04 P.M.

## SEASIDE, OR

INVENTORY: 1968 FIREBIRD CONVERTIBLE (1),
CASH ($323.38), SEA GLASS (1 PIECE),
LOST-KEY BUTTERFLY SCULPTURE (1),
USELESS PHOTOGRAPH (1),
SEAHAWKS TICKETS (12)

"This car was *made* for drive-ins," Nico says as we settle in for another trailer.

I'm still sitting behind the wheel, and Nico is reclined in the passenger seat. The giant parking lot is already packed with cars. Almost every spot is filled, and the snack stand looks more hopping than a nightclub. I didn't realize drive-ins were so popular these days.

"Just think about how many teenagers in the sixties got it on in this very car while sitting in a drive-in," Nico marvels.

"Ewww!" I screech, dramatically leaning away from the back of my seat.

Nico laughs and reclines his seat back even farther, wiggling to get comfortable.

I point to one of the tiny rusty speakers that stands atop a metal pole on the side of the car. "Are we really supposed to hear the movie out of that thing?" I lean my ear out the open window, just barely able to make out the background music from the current trailer.

"No, watch this!" Nico turns on the Firebird's old stereo and starts fiddling with the radio knobs, causing a little needle in the center of the console to glide across a spectrum of lit-up numbers.

Suddenly a deep, booming voice blasts out of the car speakers. "When you live in my city, you either fight for me . . . or you die."

I stare in disbelief at the stereo, which is now completely synced up to the preview showing on the screen. "How did you do that?"

"The theater broadcasts the soundtrack over a radio frequency. You just have to tune in to the right station to pick it up. Now it's like surround sound right in your car." Nico flashes me a flirtatious smirk. "Much better than watching it on my tiny phone in the back of my truck, right?"

I bite my lip to hold back the smile that threatens to give me away. "Yes, *so* much better."

Nico opens the car door and hops out. "I'm gonna grab some snacks before the movie starts. You hungry?"

"Sure, I'll have some—"

"I know," he interrupts. "Milk Duds and buttered popcorn. Mixed together. I remember."

I feel myself blush. "Right. Thanks."

Nico disappears, and I lean back in the driver's seat, trying to focus on the images playing on the big screen. But my gaze keeps drifting back to the stereo. To the little illuminated numbers behind the glass.

*"That's called a tuner,"* I can hear Jackson's voice say as he proudly showed me the new cassette player he'd found at the dump. Trash turned into treasure. I shiver as the memory comes back to me. Jackson sitting in the driver's seat, banging his head violently along with the new Fear Epidemic album. My father, the wannabe rock star. My father, the roadie.

I run my fingertips over the empty tape slot, remembering the cassette that Nico and I found inside when we first got into the car. The cassette that I stashed in the center console. And then, without thinking, my hands find their way to the latch. I lift the lid and pull out the tape, turning it around so I can study the handwritten label once again.

FE UNTITLED #3 7/17/10

Was this tape in the cassette player when Jackson died? Was this the last thing he ever listened to? Some random recording from the final days of the Fear Epidemic tour?

I sigh and am about to return the tape to the console when I remember something Nico said yesterday right as we crossed the California-Oregon state border. Something about how the band was writing a third album while they were on that tour. An album they never got to record in the studio because they broke up for the second and final time.

I turn the tape around again and read the label with new eyes.

UNTITLED #3.

Could this tape have something to do with that lost album that never got recorded?

I gnaw the inside of my cheek, staring at the tape in my hand. Then, before I can stop myself, I shove the tape into the player and listen to it click into place. The sound of the trailer playing on the movie screen cuts off as the cassette engages.

A second later, a loud, angry noise attacks me through the speakers. I quickly reach out and turn down the volume. The song sounds a lot like the noise on their other two albums, except less polished. More raw. It's clearly not being recorded in a studio. There's a loud, whooshing noise in the background. I recognize it as the now all-too-familiar sound of a highway whizzing by outside the window.

They must have recorded this while literally *on* the road. Perhaps in the tour bus.

Nolan belts out the final scratchy note, and the song blissfully comes to an end. But the noise is far from over. After that, someone on the recording says, "Well, that royally blew."

To which Nolan Cook bitterly replies, "Thanks, Adam. Way to be constructive. How about when you start contributing lyrics, you get to have a say?"

Adam (who I assume to be Adam French) fires back with a stinging remark. "If I recall, my face is still on the album covers, and my name is still on the copyright."

"Well, you know what they say," Nolan retorts. "Change a word, get a credit."

"You know what, Nolan?" Adam says, clearly pissed off. "Why don't you go fu—"

"Guys! Guys!" someone interrupts. They sound far away, like they've just stepped into the room and are lingering in the doorway. I assume it must be the band's manager or agent or something, but then the voice speaks again, this time closer to the recording device. "Calm down. You're getting worked up over nothing."

My whole body freezes.

*Calm down.*

I stare in awe at the tape player. Is that Jackson?

It has to be. I haven't heard his voice in more than two years, and yet I'd recognize it anywhere. The sound of it—that soothing, amiable way of his—sends shivers up my arms. I can almost see the easy smile that accompanies what he's saying.

I reach for the stereo to turn up the volume, but before anyone on the recording can say another word, I hear Nico approaching. "All they had was the small box of Milk Duds."

I jab at the stereo to eject the cassette and glance up to see him standing next to the passenger-side door, giving the popcorn bag a shake. "Not sure if the ratio will be right." He thrusts the bag at me. "You try it. You're the expert."

I try to read his expression to gauge how much of the recording he heard. But he doesn't even seem to notice there's a tape in the player.

"Thanks." I give the bag another shake and reach in, taking out exactly two pieces of popcorn and one Milk Dud and popping the combination into my mouth.

They say scent is one of the most powerful memories humans have. But I disagree. I say it's taste. The taste of a kiss. The taste of rain on your tongue. The taste of popcorn and Milk Duds—an unlikely match made in heaven. The moment the salty chocolate-caramel mixture hits my tongue, I'm no longer at this snack stand.

I'm back in the bed of Nico's truck. Our legs tangled together. Our heads close. Our eyes devouring *Footloose* or *Overboard* or *Ferris Bueller's Day Off* or *The Goonies.* Our fingers brushing against each other as we both scoured the bag of popcorn and chocolate for the last remaining kernels.

"So?" he asks, crashing into my thoughts and nodding toward the bag. "Good?"

I swallow the half-chewed lump of Milk Dud and popcorn, coughing slightly as it wedges its way down my throat. "Yes. Perfect."

Nico smiles, content with my answer, and reaches for the door handle to get into the car. But a squeaky, high-pitched voice stops him short, causing us both to look behind him.

"Oh my gosh! Look! It's happening! Just like I always said it would. *The Goonies* is reaching the next genera-tion!"

Suddenly, a woman appears next to Nico. She looks to be in her early forties, but she's dressed like a teenager in a short white tennis skirt and a bright yellow letterman's sweater. She also appears to be wearing a red wig. At least, I hope it's a wig. Otherwise, that is some very waxy hair. She pops her head over Nico's shoulder to study me. "How old are you?" she asks eagerly, like I'm a game show contestant and she's the host.

"Uh—" I stammer, glancing at Nico for help. He just shrugs. "Eighteen."

"Eighteen!" she calls back to some unseen person behind her. "Honey! They're eighteen!"

"Excellent," says a man who appears next to her. His outfit is even more outrageous. He's wearing gray sweatpants with very small blue gym shorts *over* the pants, a gray sweatshirt that has been cut at the shoulders, and a red sweatband over his floppy brown hair.

It takes me a moment, but once I see them standing side by side, I realize that they're dressed as two of the Goonies: Brand, the fitness-obsessed older brother of Mikey, and Andy, the cheerleader he has a crush on.

Were we supposed to come to this thing in costume?

The woman—Andy—leans over the top of the door. "So, tell me. I have to know. How did you hear about the movie tonight?"

"From the Internet," Nico replies.

"Excellent," the man says again.

Nico takes a step away from the couple and sizes them up. "You must be, like, *really* big *Goonies* fans."

"The biggest," the man says, putting his arm around his wife and flashing a toothy grin. "We went to see it in theaters on our first date. It sort of, you know, brought us together. We live in Maryland, but we're here on the Oregon coast for our twentieth anniversary. We're visiting every filming location from the movie. Today we went to Haystack Rock, and tomorrow we're going to visit the Goonies house in Astoria."

"There's a Goonies house?" I ask. "Like a museum?"

"Not *technically*," the woman replies. "It's just the house where Mikey and Brand lived in the movie. We're going to get some pictures and maybe some video of us doing the truffle shuffle outside the gate. Then we're going to head over to the Oregon Film Museum in downtown Astoria where there's apparently some cool stuff from the movie."

"Wow," I say, slightly speechless. "That sounds . . . fun."

"It's going to be *amazing*," the woman says. "You and your boyfriend should totally check it out."

Nico catches my eye, and in an instant, I understand exactly what he's asking, without either of us having to exchange a word.

*Are you going to correct them? Or should I?*

Dread trickles through me as I think about telling yet *another* person the whole story of our past. The breakup, the road trip, the house foreclosure, the Craigslist trades, the agony of being on the road with your ex-boyfriend. It seems like everyone we've met so far has heard at least some part of the saga: Scott, the waiter at Jenny's Giant Burger; Laurie, the barista; Mack Polonsky; Emily Sweeney; every single person who read our Craigslist post.

I'm so tired of hearing the same story.

I'm so tired of *living* the same story.

For three days on this road trip, I feel like I've been trapped inside of it, unable to escape. And now I just wish we could unwind it all. Go back to the beginning. The *very* beginning. To the moment Nico first stepped up to the passenger-side door of that old VW Beetle parked in June's junkyard, commenting on my "nice ride." Before it all began. Before we became Nico and Ali. The Fixer and the Commissioner. The couple doomed by rain and an impending comet.

Before trust was built and broken.

Before Nico lied and I ran away.

Before it was good. And before it was bad.

Back when it was all just . . . endless possibility.

And then, as I sit there in the driver's seat, staring up at Nico standing next to the passenger door of the Firebird, I think, *Why can't we?*

Here we are, in almost identical positions. The location is different. The car has more walls. The sky has more stars.

But couldn't we still have endless possibilities?

At least for one night?

At least for one movie?

I tear my gaze away from Nico and smile at the costumed couple. "Oh, we're not together."

Andy looks from her husband to Nico to me. "You're not?"

"No," I say quickly, before Nico can interject. "Actually, we just met. A few minutes ago."

"You did?" Andy's face lights up as she turns to Nico for confirmation.

Nico looks at me and cocks his eyebrow. This clearly wasn't what he was expecting me to say. The question is whether he understands what I want him to do. What I suddenly, desperately *need* him to do.

His eyes sparkle with mischief, and in that instant, I know.

He does.

"That's right," Nico says, nodding to the couple. "I just saw her sitting in this *awesome* car and thought she was cute. So I came over to ask if she wanted to share my popcorn and Milk Duds."

Andy practically melts. "Awww. That is so romantic! Another love match brought to you by *The Goonies*!" She gently slaps Brand with the back of her hand. "Isn't that romantic?"

"Almost as romantic as when Brand and Andy kiss in the water after she walks the plank," the man says, bowing down to kiss his wife.

"I don't remember that part," Nico says. "Was that at the end?"

"Don't spoil it, honey!" the woman chastises. She then leans in to Nico and whispers, "Don't worry, you're in good hands. This is the *perfect* first date movie."

"Good," he whispers back, giving the woman a thumbs-up. "Although, we sort of haven't gotten to that part yet." He nudges his chin meaningfully toward the car.

"Oh!" the woman says with sudden understanding.

"Right. Of course." She grabs her husband by the elbow and pulls him away. I expect them to scurry off somewhere and give us some space, but they only take a few steps back, and the woman keeps her gaze trained on us, as though *we're* the movie she came to see tonight.

Nico peers at them and fights hard to keep a straight face. "Hi," he says to me, and I'm surprised to hear he sounds genuinely nervous. Like he really is meeting me for the first time. "I'm Nico."

"Hi," I say, smiling. "I'm Ali."

"Come here often, Ali?"

I snort out a laugh. "Nope. First time. You?"

"Same."

He tilts his head and scrunches up his eyebrows, like something is bothering him. "Ali," he repeats. "Is that short for something?"

I flash him a beatific smile. "Yes. Actually, it is. It's short for California. I'm named after a Fear Epidemic song."

He nods. "Great band. It's a shame they broke up."

"*Twice*," I add.

"I think it's going well," I hear Andy say to Brand in a quiet voice.

Nico stifles a laugh as he leans over the passenger-side door. "Is she right?" he whispers to me. "Is it going well?"

"It better be," I whisper back. "I think Andy has staked her life on it."

"Well, then, you better invite me to sit down."

I cross my arms and scrutinize him. "Hmm. I don't know. Are you trustworthy?"

Nico grins. "Oh, I'm definitely trustworthy. And very friendly. Plus, I'm an excellent swimmer. I'm basically a Newfoundland in human form."

I burst out laughing. "Well, I can always trust a Newfoundland." I nod to the big screen, which is currently showing the Warner Bros. logo, indicating that the movie is about to begin. "Would you care to watch this classic eighties film with me, Nico?"

Remarkably, Nico somehow manages to keep a straight face as he says, "Why, yes, I would, *California*."

He opens the passenger-side door, but just before lowering himself inside, he catches my eye, winks, and says, "By the way, nice ride."

This time, we manage to watch the movie all the way through to the end. We don't miss a single scene or a single line.

Unfortunately, I can't say the same for Andy and Brand, who seem to be more focused on us than the movie. As if the future of their own relationship is somehow dependent on this "first date" going well. They're sitting in the car parked right next to the Firebird, and every so often, during an especially funny or suspenseful part, I catch Andy stealing peeks at us to make sure we're reacting properly.

"So, what did you think?" Andy asks as the closing credits start to roll. She's leaning out the window of their sedan to speak to us.

Nico gives her another thumbs-up.

"And you?" She turns her gaze on me.

"Excellent movie. Loved the ending."

"And . . . ?" she prompts, motioning ambiguously between us. When we return her question with blank expressions, she clarifies. "Did you two, you know, hit it off?"

I bite back another fit of giggles as Nico responds, "Well, there wasn't a lot of time to talk. Because of, you know, the movie."

Andy chuckles. "Of course. Carry on." She gives us a dismissive wave and ducks back into the window of her car.

Nico and I can't even look at each other for fear of cracking up.

"So this is what it feels like to be a lab rat," Nico says. "I've always wondered."

"I think she's a sociologist running an experiment on the effects *The Goonies* has on modern youth."

"Seriously, right?"

"Is she still watching us?"

Nico pretends to yawn and stretch so he can glance over at the next car. "Yup."

I laugh into my hand. "What the hell?"

"Maybe we should just get out of here."

"No way!" I practically screech. "We can't just leave."

Nico looks confused. "Why not?"

"Because she'll think we're leaving, you know, *together*."

"So?"

"So! We're supposed to have just met," I remind him. "Plus, I can't drive this car. I won't make it three feet."

"Hmm. That does leave us in a bit of a lurch." Nico screws his mouth to the side. "Although, if I drive the car out of here with you in it, I will look like *quite* the player."

"No. Not gonna happen. We just have to say good-bye. End the date and wait for *them* to leave."

"Ah," Nico says, like he's caught me out. "So you think this is a date?"

I roll my eyes. "Don't start."

"Which means technically it should end with a kiss."

I feel my cheeks grow hot. I pray that Nico can't see them in this darkness. I cross my arms to hide the goose bumps forming on my skin. "For your information, I don't kiss on first dates."

"No, you just invite guys into the sleeping suite."

I slap him. "That was *not* our first date!"

"Don't hit me," Nico warns playfully, jutting his head toward Andy and Brand's car. "What will our audience think?"

"That you're being a jerk! I should just yell at you and kick you out of my car. Let's see how much of a player you look like then."

"Fine," Nico gives in. "We'll just have a nice, civil good-bye. Like friends. Then I'll go hide out in the snack stand until they leave."

"Fine."

I open the door and get out of the car. Nico does the

same. I can feel both Andy and Brand's eyes on us as we meet in front of the hood.

Nico dramatically straightens his posture. A stage actor about to put on a finale performance. "Well, Ali. It was lovely to meet you. I hope we can watch a movie in a car again sometime."

I fight to keep my composure. "Yes, Nico. Lovely to meet you, too. Good luck."

I extend my hand toward him. But he doesn't shake it. He just stares at it, as though he's a foreigner, unfamiliar with our customs. The seconds pass, and my hand continues to hang there.

I clear my throat, causing Nico to look at me.

*Come on*, I urge him with my eyes. *Move it along.*

Slowly, Nico reaches for my hand, his fingers barely brushing my skin.

The reaction is instantaneous. An electrical charge running down a wire. My body remembers. Tiny flames ignite all over my skin. As though the fire that constantly lived inside of me for those eighty-eight days had never been fully extinguished. It had just been reduced to embers. Still glowing. Still smoldering.

Still waiting.

Nico slides his hand further into mine until our palms are touching. But he may as well be touching everything. Because, in that moment, I feel everything. Just as I did from the very beginning. Just as I did until the very end.

Just as I've continued to do on almost every second of this road trip, despite my attempts to fight it.

Nico's eyes lock into mine, and I instantly know that there's no turning back now.

There's no way this moment can end in anything else but disaster.

He wraps his strong fingers around my hand, and I feel the slightest tug. The slightest ounce of pressure pulling me toward him. It's a question. It's an invitation.

All I have to do is say yes.

Take one step.

Make one move to close the gap.

And I know Nico will be waiting for me on the other side.

My heart hammers in my chest like a war drum. And that's exactly how this feels. Like a war. Like a battle neither of us can win.

Nico blinks and drops my gaze. "Well," he says, his voice sounding unusually thick. "Good night, Ali."

I swallow, suddenly overcome with the sensation that I'm too late. "Good night."

He gives my hand two firm pumps and then slowly withdraws, letting his fingers and all their warmth fall away.

My breathing slowly returns to normal.

Nico flashes me a smile. It's the kind of smile that closes open questions. That concludes things.

Then he turns and starts walking toward the snack stand, leaving me frozen and speechless in front of the Firebird. I don't dare look over at Andy and Brand for fear of seeing the disappointment etched into their faces. For some reason, I don't think I can handle it.

I'm suddenly anxious to get back into the car and close the door and lower the convertible top down, cocooning myself away from this place. Away from this night.

With a shaky breath, I turn and walk toward the driver's-side door. I reach for the handle, but something catches my arm, spinning me back around. Before I can even make sense of Nico standing there, his hands are cupping the sides of my face. Before I can utter a single word, he's steering my mouth to his.

And before I can even contemplate what it means, I'm kissing him back.

# 10:22 P.M.

## SEASIDE, OR

**INVENTORY: 1968 FIREBIRD CONVERTIBLE (1), CASH ($323.38), SEA GLASS (1 PIECE), LOST-KEY BUTTERFLY SCULPTURE (1), USELESS PHOTOGRAPH (1), SEAHAWKS TICKETS (12)**

"Are you sure you don't remember the name of it?" I ask Nico for the third time as we drive up and down the streets of Seaside.

"I don't think she ever told us. I just remember her saying it was right on the beach."

I scan the map on Nico's phone and shake my head. "Well, there are, like, ten hotels right on the beach in this town. It could be any of them."

For the past twenty minutes, we've been searching for the bed-and-breakfast owned by Blanche and Howie, the couple we met back in Crescent City who traded Mack's chess set for the Gibson guitar. It's proving more difficult than expected, but at least it's giving us something to do and, more important, something to talk about.

It's like we've made a silent pact *not* to mention what just happened at that drive-in. Neither of us have said a word about it. Not one word. We're both just pretending it didn't happen.

Because it's not like it meant anything. It was a *fake* kiss. A performance. A make-believe ending to a make-believe first date. Nico was just playing a part. And so was I. It doesn't matter how good the kiss was. It doesn't matter how easily we fell back into each other, how adeptly our mouths came together. Now we're back in the car, back on our quest, and the moment is over. End of story.

Except why doesn't it *feel* like the moment is over?

Why does it feel like the moment has been following us ever since we left? It's shoved the shadowy pit aside and has taken its place. And now the silence between us feels more awkward than ever. And that's saying a *lot* given the awkward silences we've had on this trip.

Nico sighs as he turns right on Avenue G, starting our third tour around the tiny town. "Who offers someone a free night's stay at their bed-and-breakfast and then doesn't tell them the name of the bed-and-breakfast?"

I laugh. "Someone who doesn't *really* want you to stay there. Maybe we should just pick one of these others hotels and rent a room." I click on the nearest one, glance at the rate, and wince. "Ouch. Never mind."

We're almostdown to our last three hundred dollars,

and I really don't know what we're going to do for food and lodging for the rest of this trip.

"Rip Advisory!" Nico exclaims.

"Excuse me?"

"What did she say about that review on Rip Advisory?"

"You mean TripAdvisor?"

He waves his hand. "Yeah, whatever. Wasn't she going on and on about something with pancakes?"

"Yes!" I say, suddenly understanding where he's going with this. I open the web browser and navigate to Trip-Advisor. "She said they were complaining about the blueberry pancakes having too many blueberries. I'm on it." I type "Seaside, Oregon" into the destination box and click enter. Then I do a search for "blueberry pancakes" in all of the hotel reviews.

A huge grin spreads across my face as the results are narrowed down to one.

"Nice work, detective." I put my hand up, and Nico high-fives it. "It's called the Cascade Country Inn."

"Oh! I saw that place back a ways." Nico yanks on the wheel and turns the Firebird into a sharp U-turn. A few minutes later, we're standing in front of a beautiful colonial-style cream-colored house with red roses lining the front walkway and a white picket fence surrounding the property.

"I hope we're not too late," I say. "Should we just ring the bell?"

Nico shrugs. "I guess. I've never stayed at a bed-and-breakfast before."

"Me neither."

I tentatively reach out and press the buzzer. A moment later a young woman dressed in striped pajamas answers the door. "Hi. Can I help you?"

"Um," I say awkwardly. "Hi. We're looking for Blanche or Howie."

"Sorry. They're already asleep. They go to bed pretty early. I'm the night manager."

I deflate. So much for that plan. "Oh, okay. Never mind. Thanks."

I turn around because it's not like I can just claim that the owners promised us a free room. How shady would that look?

"You aren't, by chance, the Craigslist couple, are you?" the woman says.

I spin back. "Yes, we are. Why?"

"Awesome! Blanche said you might come by the inn. And she told me I should wake her immediately if you showed up."

I share a look of disbelief with Nico. "She did?"

The woman nods. "Apparently you made quite an impression. She said, and I quote, 'If that sweet young couple from Greg's List comes by, be sure to wake me up, no matter the hour." She chuckles and opens the door wider. "So, right this way."

The woman leads us into a gorgeous living room decorated with ornate wooden furniture, gold damask wallpaper, and a red-and-white floral rug. The room looks like it was transported right out of the early 1900s.

"I'll go wake up Blanche," she tells us before disappearing up a creaky wooden staircase.

Then, Nico and I are alone.

And, now that we've located the inn, we no longer have anything to occupy our minds. Or fill the silence with. The moment that followed us here from the drive-in seems to grow and expand until it's taken over the entire room, shoving us to opposite corners.

I explore my little section of the living room, admiring the furnishings and framed sepia-toned photographs hanging on the wall. When I glance over at Nico, he appears to be doing the same, running his hands obsessively over a Victorian-style tablecloth, as though checking each individual strand for defects.

It's ridiculous. We've been alone together this entire trip. For three whole days, there have barely been more than a few hours combined when we were *not* alone. We've shared *two* hotel rooms. How could a single *pretend* kiss change so much?

And yet, suddenly, the idea of sharing another hotel room with Nico seems impossible. Insurmountable. Insane.

"You're here!" comes a bright, bubbly voice. I breathe out a sigh of relief, grateful to have a third person between us.

Blanche waddles into the living room in a fluffy pink bathrobe, matching slippers, and pink curlers in her hair.

"We're so sorry to wake you," I say quickly.

"Oh, don't be." Blanche flashes me a beaming smile. "I'm thrilled you stopped by. I was just telling Howie how nice it would be if you came to visit, and here you are. How is your little quest going?"

I brave a glance at Nico. His eyes meet mine, and we both quickly look away.

He clears his throat. "Good. Great. It's been . . ." His eyes dart toward me again. ". . . interesting."

Blanche claps her hands. "Wonderful. I just love that young people are still going out there and having real old-fashioned adventures. It feels like all your generation does these days is sit around and play games on those MegaPads."

I bite my lip to stifle a laugh.

"Yes," Nico says, and I can hear from his voice that he's also fighting to keep a straight face. "We teenagers do love our MegaPads."

"Well, I won't keep you," Blanche says. "I'm sure you must be tired from the drive. I'll show you to your room." She starts to turn but then stops, as though remembering something, and narrows her eyes accusingly at us. "Wait a minute, did you just say *teenagers*?"

Nico and I share another brief look.

"Yeah," I reply hesitantly. "We just graduated high school. Is that a problem? We're eighteen. Legal age to rent a hotel room."

"And you're newlyweds?"

I choke on empty air, barely able to stutter out a response. "What?"

*How did we go from a fake first date to suddenly being married?*

Thankfully Nico steps in. "No. We're not . . . um, married."

My face feels like it's on fire.

Blanche glances between us, her tongue poking the inside of her cheek. "Well, legal or not, I can't allow two unmarried teenagers to sleep in the same room together. Call me old-fashioned, but I just don't feel comfortable with that at all."

"That's okay," Nico and I both say at the exact same moment.

I glance over at him, and our eyes meet. His gaze is hot and intense and all-knowing. Like we're sharing one thought. One memory. One nagging, constant temptation.

I clear my throat and look straight down at the floor. "Two rooms would be great. Thanks."

The old wooden staircase creaks as Nico and I make our way to the third (and top) floor of the inn, brass keys in hand. The ceiling up here is low, and Nico has to incline his head slightly as we walk down the hall to our respective rooms.

"I'm here," I say, stopping in front of the door marked with a gold number 10.

"And I'm here," Nico says, nodding to the door just across the hall.

"Great."

"Great," he repeats.

Then, we both just stand there, staring at each other.

There's nothing but an empty, quiet hallway between us, and yet it feels like an uncrossable chasm.

Nico is wearing an inscrutable expression. It feels like we're trapped in some kind of standoff. Each one waiting for the other to say something. Do something. Move somewhere.

As soon as we disappear behind those doors, it'll be the first time we've been apart for more than a few minutes since this whole journey began.

And yet, somehow *that* seems more impossible now than being together.

Nico flashes me a smile. It looks forced. "Sleep well."

I return the exact same smile. "You too."

He spins around, inserts his key into the lock, and opens the door to his room. I do the same. But just as I'm about to push the door open, somewhere behind me, I hear Nico say, "Ali?"

"Yeah?" I reply, turning around so fast, I get dizzy.

As I stare at Nico standing there across the hall, for the shortest flicker of a moment, I find myself fantasizing about all the things I want him to say to me right now.

"Don't go."

"Don't close that door."

"Can we talk?"

"Can I kiss you again?"

"Can we really, truly start over?"

*Can we?*

*Can we?*

*Can we?*

And in that same flicker of a moment, I somehow think

we can. It all jumps out of the realm of impossibility and right into that other realm.

The one where impossible things can happen.

Where fights are resolved.

Where mistakes are forgiven.

Where Nico doesn't lie and I don't judge.

Where I'm not a Commissioner and he's not a Fixer.

Where shadowy pits disappear.

Where Nico wraps his arms around me and we sleep tangled up in each other all night. Just like we used to.

"Despite what you might think of it," Nico says, crashing into my thoughts, "I think you're really lucky to have that car."

I deflate just a little. "Why is that?"

"I think it's a sign that your dad is looking out for you. Maybe even making amends for his mistakes."

"You think people can make amends for their mistakes?" I ask, my voice tight.

Then I count the seconds. One, two—

I thought I'd get to at least infinity. I thought we'd both disappear into our rooms, fall asleep, and wake up and I'd still be waiting. But Nico already has the perfect answer right on the tip of his tongue.

"I do."

He flashes me a smile. It's unlike any I've seen on the road over the past three days. It's an old smile. A vintage Nico smile. A lost smile.

A found smile.

Then, he slips into his room and closes the door.

# MONDAY

*The fog is setting in*
*And we can't see yesterday*
*The rules for this arrangement*
*Are starting to lose shape*

—"Done," from the album
*Anarchy in a Cup* by Fear Epidemic
Written by Nolan Cook, Slate Miller,
Chris McCaden, and Adam French
Released November 10, 1998

# 2:00 P.M.

## ASTORIA, OR

INVENTORY: 1968 FIREBIRD CONVERTIBLE (1),
CASH ($323.38), SEA GLASS (1 PIECE),
LOST-KEY BUTTERFLY SCULPTURE (1),
USELESS PHOTOGRAPH (1),
SEAHAWKS TICKETS (12)

Gabe from Craigslist told us that he'd be wearing light jeans and a Seattle Seahawks jersey. We arrive at the Safeway parking lot—where he told us to meet him—right on time, but so far, there's no one fitting that description.

The neighborhood is nice. The shopping center has a Starbucks and an orthodontist's office. There's even a Tomato and Vine restaurant across the street, reminding me of how far we've come since that fifty-dollar gift card. This morning, after emerging from our separate rooms and enjoying a delicious homemade breakfast prepared by Blanche, Nico received the e-mail from Gabe, wanting to trade the Seahawks tickets for a Rolex watch that he claims is worth around sixty-five hundred dollars.

"How will we be able to tell that the Rolex is real?" I ask, sipping from my paper coffee cup. Today, Nico ordered me a Butterfinger Mocha, and I ordered him an English Toffee Latte.

Nico pushes the button to lower the top of the Firebird. It's thankfully much cooler than yesterday, and the warm air feels good on my skin.

"I know a little bit about Rolexes," Nico says, averting his gaze. "I'll be able to tell."

Once again, I want to ask him *how*. How does he know about Rolexes? How does he know about *any* of this stuff? But I keep my mouth shut. Because it's just not worth the frustration when he gives me a bogus answer.

So instead, I lean back in my seat and take a deep breath. I can't seem to stop fidgeting.

"What if—" I start to ask, but I'm not able to finish because just then Nico points to something out the windshield.

"Is that him?"

I sit up taller in my seat, but all I see is what appears to be a young boy—no older than thirteen—walking toward us.

"No, that can't be him," I say confidently. "What would a kid that young be doing with a six-thousand-dollar Rolex?"

Nico shrugs. "He's wearing the Seahawks jersey."

The kid catches our eye through the windshield and his face lights up. He waves a jerky little wave and literally runs toward us, his brown bowl-cut floppy against his forehead.

"Do you think he *stole* the Rolex?" I ask Nico.

Nico scoffs. "That kid doesn't look like he could steal candy from a baby, let alone a Rolex."

I watch as the boy continues to bound toward us. Nico's right. He does look pretty harmless. But something is setting me on edge. I bite my lip, trying to pinpoint what about this situation is making me so apprehensive. Apart from the fact, of course, that we're about to trade thousands of dollars' worth of merchandise with someone who looks like they haven't hit puberty yet.

"Are you the couple from Craigslist?" Gabe asks, his voice cracking with every syllable.

*Or* just hitting puberty now.

Nico gets out of the car to greet him. "Hi. You must be Gabe. I'm Nico."

"Oh my God. This is so cool! I can't believe you came! You're really here!" He's practically exploding with energy. "You have no idea how much this means to me. I'm such a huge Seahawks fan. Like, the hugest. And they're supposed to have an amazing season this year. And now I can go to all the games. Every single one of them!"

I get out of the car and stand beside Nico. "Hi, I'm Ali," I say.

The boy beams up at me. "Hi, Ali! Nice to meet you!" He shakes my hand like a perfect little gentleman.

"How exactly do you plan to *get* to the games?" I ask, looking him up and down. He definitely doesn't look old enough to drive. "Isn't Seattle three hours from here?"

"Oh, don't you worry about me," he says confidently.

"I'll take the bus if I have to. But I am getting to *every* single one of those games." He glances between us, his eyes wide and expectant. He almost reminds me of a cartoon character. "So, do you have the tickets?"

"Yes," Nico says, pulling the envelope out of his back pocket. "They're right here. Do you have the watch?"

"Duh," Gabe says with a nerdy little laugh. He flips his backpack around, unzips the small pocket, and pulls out a beautiful hunter-green box with the word *Rolex* inscribed across the top in gold letters. Gabe pops open the lid like a suave hero in a romantic comedy proposing to his girlfriend. Except instead of a shiny diamond ring inside, there is the most beautiful watch I've ever seen. It has a sparkling gold band with a flawless black face. The glass surface glints in the afternoon sun.

"May I look at it?" Nico asks.

"Of course!" Gabe says, pushing the box into Nico's hand. Nico is gentle and diligent as he removes the watch and inspects it from all angles, checking the weight in his palm, giving the winder a few turns.

He looks like a professional watch dealer.

Honestly, *where* on earth did he learn to do that?

"It's real," Nico confirms.

I look to Gabe, whose jubilant expression has suddenly turned crestfallen. "It was my grandfather's. He used to love to collect watches." He points to the timepiece in Nico's hand. "Watching you do that just . . ." He sniffles. "Reminded me of him. He died a few months ago and left me this."

I feel a pang in my chest as I watch the boy's eyes well

up with tears. I reach out to touch his shoulder. "Gabe. Are you sure you want to get rid of it? It's a beautiful watch. I think your grandfather would want you to keep it."

Nico looks at me, and I know immediately what he's thinking.

*How ironic. Ali Collins advising someone to keep what was willed to them.*

Gabe wipes his nose. "My grandfather knew how much I love the Seahawks. He would have wanted me to have those tickets even more."

"Are you positive?" Nico asks. "I wouldn't want you to do anything you might regret." When he says this last part, I notice he's not looking at Gabe. He's looking right at me. He's talking about the car.

"This is different," I say in a hoarse whisper.

"I'm sure," Gabe says, completely missing our exchange.

Nico nods and hands him the envelope with the tickets. "Okay. Have fun, then."

When Gabe opens the envelope and peers inside, it's as though someone has turned a light on from within him. It makes all of my uneasiness vanish, leaving nothing behind but a smile on my face.

I have to say, there is something magical about these trades. It's not only that we're working toward something, trading *up*. There's just something about watching these people get what they want. Watching the way it illuminates them. The way, I suppose, that Firebird and that band once illuminated Jackson. Even though it was at the expense of his family.

Gabe leaps forward and wraps his arms around me. "Thank you so, *so* much!"

Startled, I awkwardly hug him back. "You're welcome. Enjoy the games. I hope the Seahawks win."

"I will! And they *definitely* will." Gabe turns and walks away.

Nico returns the watch to the box and snaps the lid closed. "Well, that was sort of adorable."

"Yes, it was," I agree as we head back toward the Firebird.

But I'm barely able to get the passenger-side door open when I hear the sound of tires squealing on the pavement and the deafening roar of an engine behind us. I spin around to see a very angry-looking woman getting out of an SUV and slamming the door.

"GABRIEL!" she screams loud enough for all of Astoria to hear. "What have you done?"

The boy skipping through the parking lot freezes, immediately gripping tighter around the white envelope in his hands.

Nico and I watch in shocked silence as the woman stalks toward Gabe, grabs him by the arm, and practically drags him to the car. She pushes him into the passenger seat and closes the door. Through the back window of the SUV, I can see Gabe sulking in the front seat.

Then the woman turns her sights on us and her expression softens. *Somewhat.*

She tucks some loose strands of hair back into a messy

ponytail as she approaches. "I'm so sorry," she says. "My son, he's . . ." She stops, takes a breath, like she's trying to find the strength to continue. "He wasn't supposed to take that watch. It was my father's. And it's all we have left of him. It's a very special piece."

I panic as I look back and forth between Gabe and his mother. "I'm s-s-so sorry," I stutter. "He said his grandfather gifted it to him. We didn't realize—"

The woman holds up her hand to stop me. "I know. I *know*. He can be very persuasive when he wants to be, but he had *no* right to trade that watch. What did he get for it? Comic books? Baseball cards?" She spits out the options like they're cursed.

Nico bows his head, looking ashamed. "Season tickets to the Seahawks."

The woman scoffs. "Of course. *Of course.* Those damn Seahawks." I watch, tormented, as tears start to form in her eyes. She presses her fingertips into them, as if to try to hold the tears back. "I'm sorry. We're all having a rough time with his death. Maybe me most of all. Would you mind if we—if I—traded them back to you?"

"Of course!" Nico and I both say at once.

"No problem at all," Nico assures her.

She struggles for a moment, covering her mouth with her hand. "Thank you. Thank you so much." Then, like a light switch, her anger flips back on. She stomps back to the SUV and reaches into the open passenger-side window. "Hand 'em over," she commands Gabe. *"Now."*

I can't see Gabe's face. I hope he at least looks apologetic. I can't believe what he just did. I can't believe he managed to scam us like that.

I watch Gabe's arm extend reluctantly from the window, the envelope clutched between his fingers. Gabe's mother snatches the tickets and returns to us, her demeanor shifting once more.

"Again, I'm so sorry about this. Believe me, he's about to lose *all* of his computer privileges for a year."

"I heard that!" Gabe shouts from the car.

"Good!" his mother shouts back. She smiles at Nico. "Here you go."

Nico takes the envelope and hands her the Rolex watch. She gets teary-eyed again as she brings it to her lips and kisses it. "Thank you." She tilts her head back and looks up at the sky. "Sorry, Daddy. I won't let it happen again." Then she turns back to us. "Good luck to you guys."

"You too," I say, getting a little emotional myself.

I watch as she gets in behind the wheel and slams the door shut. The car peels away, tires screeching and dirt spraying. It isn't until right then, as the SUV zooms out of the parking lot—at an unusually fast pace—that I notice something peculiar about the car. It takes a moment to put my finger on what it is, but as soon as the car turns the corner and disappears onto the street, I realize it doesn't have a license plate.

I turn back to Nico and flinch when I notice all of the color seems to have drained from his face. He looks deathly pale. Like he might throw up or collapse or both.

"What?" I ask, that uneasy feeling instantly back. "What is it?"

But he doesn't have to respond. Because when I look down, I see it too. Nico is holding the white envelope in his hands. He's lifted the flap and opened it. But there are no Seahawks tickets valued at five thousand dollars inside.

Instead, someone has stuffed the envelope with twelve playing cards, all of them jokers.

"Oh my God!" I screech, my head jerking up to see if I can still spot the SUV. But it's long gone. "That kid scammed us *again*!"

"No," Nico says, burying his face in his hands. "They both did."

# 2:33 P.M.

# ASTORIA, OR

## INVENTORY: FEELS LIKE (0)

The chasm opens up beneath my feet.

The gaping hole swallows me, and I'm sinking.

Sinking.

Sinking.

Sinking.

Into the dark, vast nothing.

*Nothing.*

We have nothing.

We are broke. We are broken. We are done.

The ground keeps disappearing beneath me. The hole that Jackson dug so relentlessly during his life seems to cover this entire parking lot, this entire city, this entire planet. It hasn't stopped growing since he died. It's only grown faster. The rate of deterioration has only accelerated.

And now I'm trapped inside of it.

The walls are too high to climb out.

The dirt is too soft to stand on.

I will continue to sink deeper and deeper until I disintegrate into the earth's core.

They conned us. They took those Seahawks tickets right out from under us. They planned the entire thing. The fight, the sulking, the tears. That woman put on a whole performance about her dead father, while Gabe was in the SUV making the switch. I wonder how many times they've used that same Rolex to do exactly what they just did to us.

How could we let this happen? How could *he* let this happen?

The blood boils in my veins.

The simmering fire inside of me bursts into wild, destructive flames.

I glance over at Nico, his head still buried in his hands.

"This is all your fault!" I scream.

Nico looks up at me, completely taken aback. "Excuse me?"

"You heard me!"

"Um, how is us getting scammed by a mother-son con-artist team *my* fault?"

"You're the one who convinced me to go on this stupid journey to begin with. You're the one who said we could make money on Craigslist. Craigslist will fix all of our problems. All we have to do is trade up. You made it sound so easy. But I told you. I told you Craigslist was full of dangerous, shady people!"

"Actually I think *I* said that part." He tries for humor.

I ignore the attempt. "And now we're stuck here with no

money, nothing to trade, a car that's practically worthless, and they're going to take my house away! They're going to take my house away, and Jackson is going to win!"

I lean against the side of the Firebird and sob into my hands. Nico doesn't say anything for a very long time. And for a moment, I'm pretty convinced he's left. Walked away. Just like I always knew he would. Just like Jackson always did.

But when I lift my head and brush the tears away from my cheeks, I'm surprised to see he's still standing there.

He hasn't left.

Throughout this entire trip, he hasn't left.

*Why hasn't he left? Why is he still here? Why is he helping me?*

"Ali," Nico says carefully, and I know from the tone of his voice that whatever he says next, I'm not going to like. "Is this about the house? Or is this about Jackson?"

And I was right. I don't like it. Because it's a stupid question to ask.

"What are you talking about? It's about both!"

Nico's gaze softens as he comes to stand next to me. "I don't think it's about both. I think this is *all* about him."

I roll my eyes and sniffle. "Of course it's *all* about him. Everything is all about him. Jackson *is* the house! He's tied up in everything! There's nothing in my life that's *not* about Jackson."

"So why not make a fresh start? Leave him and the house behind?"

"Because . . . because . . ." I hiccup. "Because . . ."

No matter how many times I start that sentence, I can't seem to finish it. I no longer know what comes next. Why *not* leave the house behind, with its cracked paint and ugly shag carpeting and leaky shower and broken first step? Why not just let it go?

"Maybe because somewhere deep inside, you don't actually want to leave him behind?" Nico guesses.

Something sharp stabs me in the chest. "Are you crazy? Of course I want to leave him behind. What do you think I've been doing this entire time? I've been trying to leave him behind. I've been trying to get out from under his mistakes. Why else do you think I've been on this road trip with you? It's certainly not for my health."

Pain flashes across Nico's face, and I suddenly feel horrible. I open my mouth to apologize, but he doesn't let me get there. "I think you've been on this road trip because you're trying to find something."

I scoff. "Yeah, I'm trying to find twenty-five thousand dollars."

"No," Nico says gravely. "I think you're looking for a reason to forgive your father."

I push myself off the Firebird like a rocket coming off a launchpad. "You're wrong. You're so wrong, it's funny. I don't give a crap about my father. My father was a lying, cheating deserter who never stopped disappointing us. He never did *anything* for me. I don't need to forgive him because I don't care enough about him to even bother."

"He left you the car," Nico points out.

"Which was worth *nothing*."

"It was worth something to him."

"And nothing to me."

Nico smiles as though he knows a secret. "I don't think that's true."

"Why are *you* here?" I shoot back, turning the tables. Let's put Nico under the microscope and see how he feels about all the pushing and prodding.

He flinches at the tone of my voice. "What do you mean?"

"I mean, what are *you* doing on this trip?"

"You needed someone who could drive stick shift. And you promised me a thousand dollars," Nico replies, as though it's the obvious answer. And it may be the obvious answer, but it's certainly not the truth.

I scoff and cross my arms. "That's a load of crap and you know it. What are *you* looking for, Nico? Why are you really helping me? I know now it's not because you're a Fixer. So, why, Nico?"

He runs his fingers through his hair and speaks haltingly. "I don't know, I guess because I . . . wanted to try to make things right between us."

Of all the things I thought he would say, that was not one of them.

I take a step back, unable to speak.

But Nico closes the space between us, and suddenly his hand is wrapped around mine. It's warm. It's comforting. It's unexpected. A chill starts in my toes and travels all the way up through the top of my head, leaving me feeling . . . not cold, yet not warm, either. Almost numb.

I turn away because I can't look at him anymore. I can't

make sense of him. But mostly because I can't hold on to my anger when he says stuff like that. It's like a slippery eel that keeps wiggling out of my fingers.

But I *have* to hold on to it.

Because that anger is all I have left to protect myself against him. It's the barrier that sits between us, dividing the world in half.

Nico's side.

Ali's side.

It's the only thing that keeps me safe.

And yet now, with Nico's hand still wrapped around mine, it's as though he's reached across that barrier, broken through it. Trespassed right over to my side of the universe. My side of this breakup. He's bridged a gap that suddenly seems impossibly smaller than it once did.

But I can't. Because I've seen how this goes. I've heard those words before.

*"I can make it right."*

It was Jackson who said them, but the outcome is the same. It will always be the same.

I pull my hand away from his. "You can't. You can't make it right."

*Neither of you can.*

Nico suddenly lets out an animalistic growl. "Why not, Ali? Why can't I make it right? Because I'll leave again? Because eventually I'll walk out on you, just like Jackson did?" He starts pacing in front of me. "You know, when we were together, sometimes I felt like you were just waiting for me to screw up. Every day, I felt like I was on trial, but I didn't know what the crime was. And then when I did screw up—when I let you down *once*—that was it. You jumped ship. You walked out on us. You left me out there in the rain. And I could never figure out why. But now I know. It was never because of me. It was because of *him*."

"Are you kidding!?" I scream back at him, causing a few people in the parking lot to glance anxiously over at us. "You left *me*! You disappeared that night. With no explanation. Only lies."

Nico stops pacing; he closes his eyes like he's trying to control some wild beast that's been living inside of him this whole time, begging to be let out.

When he speaks again, his voice is fierce but controlled. Soft but raw. "I might have disappeared, but I came back. Don't forget, *you're* the one who left that night. You're the one who threw us away. Just like you throw everything away. Because nothing is sacred to you. As soon as something lets you down, you simply write it off and toss it in the trash."

My voice is tight, my throat stinging with another influx of tears. "I don't throw *everything* away."

"No," he agrees. "Just the things that matter. Just the things that could possibly love you back."

I feel like I've been punched in the gut. Tears are streaking down my face. "That's not true, Nico. It's not true."

"What happened to the birdhouse we made on your birthday?" he challenges, like he just knows. Like he was at the dump that day. "Do you still have it?"

I ball my hands into fists. I dig my fingernails into my flesh. But I don't say anything.

"You know what I think?" Nico says. All of the kindness has been stripped from his voice. The only thing left is resentment. "I think you wanted me to be Jackson. I think I got that label from the very start. And then, you were just waiting for me to prove you right. You were just waiting for me to become him so you didn't *have* to love me back." He scoffs. "You wanna know the truth? You wanna know why I *really* came on this trip? It was never because of the money. It was always to prove you wrong."

"Prove me wrong?" I repeat in bitter disbelief.

"Yes. I had to prove I'm not the guy you thought I was. I'm not the guy you were so quick to label and cast aside. I am not him! How can I make you understand that, Ali? I AM NOT JACKSON!"

Suddenly I can't be here anymore.

I can't stand to look at him for another second.

I turn, yank open the driver's-side door of the Firebird, and get behind the wheel. I jam my foot down hard on the clutch as I start the engine and peel out of the parking space. The car doesn't judder or shake or halt; it just drives. As though it knows exactly what to do. As though it's practically driving itself.

And I guess that makes sense.

It has done a lot of leaving in its lifetime.

For a moment, I swear I hear Nico's voice calling out to me, but the engine is too loud and I'm already too far away. Still, I don't turn around. I don't look back. I just drive.

Because apparently escaping in a 1968 Firebird convertible is in my DNA.

**387** →

## 2:45 P.M.

## ASTORIA, OR

### INVENTORY: LESS THAN (0)

I don't get very far.

The car keeps stalling.

I keep stalling. In life. In love. In everything.

And now I'm stuck.

Stuck in the middle of this massive parking lot with the memory I've been avoiding for the past month.

On the night of Fabian's Comet—eighty-eight days after Nico and I got together—the rain didn't clear up as everyone hoped it would. The clouds still hovered ominously above our little town, blocking everyone's view of this supposedly spectacular cosmic event.

Maybe I was just being overly cynical, but I couldn't help thinking that it was all our fault. That if Nico and I hadn't been together, hadn't been so doomed from the start, that maybe the town of Russellville would have been able to get its unobstructed view at this rare object in the sky.

Maybe the rain had been a sign from the very beginning.

A sign we just failed to see until it was too late.

That night, Nico was supposed to pick me up so we could drive somewhere to watch the comet. Somewhere far away from the lights of our little town and the lingering clouds. Somewhere where hopefully the rain couldn't find us.

But Nico never showed up.

He didn't text.

He didn't call.

He just sort of vanished.

I left him seven messages. I sent him as many texts as there were unseen stars in the sky. He didn't answer them.

As darkness fell and the entire town was staring up, trying to catch glimpses of the bright bullet of light streaking across the sky, I was the only one looking down. Looking at my phone. Waiting for my own streak of light to come.

But worry clouded my vision until I couldn't even see the screen anymore. I convinced myself that something had happened to him. His truck had gone off the road and was lying in a ditch somewhere. He'd run out of gas and was stranded in a place with no cell phone service. A meteor, jealous of the comet's worldwide attention, had plunged down to earth and destroyed him.

Or maybe it was much simpler than that. Maybe his phone had just run out of battery and he'd forgotten his charger.

Night settled around Russellville, and I braved my first glance up at the sky. I expected to see some wondrous light show, worthy of a big-budget Hollywood movie. I expected to feel changed somehow, the way people claim to feel after witnessing something of cosmic proportions. I expected to feel less significant in the grand scheme of things, my little domestic problem eclipsed by the massive celestial object hurtling through space.

But all I felt was more hopeless.

The comet, from what was visible through the gaps in the clouds, was small. Nothing more than a passing blur, dwarfed even by our measly little moon.

I got in my car and headed into town. I drove from one end of Russellville to the other, looking for him. I drove past his house, but his truck wasn't in the driveway. I considered knocking on the front door and breaking through the barrier that Nico seemed intent on building between me and his home life, but the lights in the house were all off.

I drove downtown and ducked into the Frosty Frog. It was empty. I walked over to the library and checked every stack and every cubicle. No Nico. I went by his favorite coffee shop—Brewed Awakenings—but it was closed. A big handmade sign had been posted in the window that said: GONE TO CHASE FABIAN—SEE YOU TOMORROW!

The town felt deserted. As though Nico wasn't the only one who'd abandoned me that night. I checked my phone a thousand times, until my battery started to die.

But there was no denying it. Nico was gone.

I thought about going to June's—she was having some friends over to watch the comet—but the idea of seeing all those people and talking to anyone made me want to stick my head in one of those rusted cast-iron ovens sitting in June's yard. So I went home instead.

When I turned down the driveway, I saw two bright red taillights cutting through the darkness. I slammed on the brakes, coming to a jarring halt.

My first thought was Jackson.

He was back. This strange celestial event had guided him home once again. A surprising sting of hope filled me. But then I noticed the taillights were too high off the ground to be the Firebird. And they were the wrong shape.

Jackson's taillights were two thin, rounded rectangles, stacked on top of each other.

These lights were tall and stout, with sharp edges.

A truck.

My stomach swooped. It was part relief, part dread.

The motor was running, exhaust from the tailpipe visible in the crisp night air. I wasn't sure how long he had been waiting for me. I wasn't sure why he didn't text me to tell me he was here. A small, foolish part of me wanted to believe he'd actually been here the whole time. And, like a lost shoe hidden under the bed, I'd simply overlooked him.

I pulled up alongside him and killed the engine of the Honda. For a few seconds, I sat perfectly still behind the wheel, telling myself to take deep breaths. Don't overreact.

I opened the door and stepped out. I half expected Nico to leap from the truck as soon as he saw me, wrap his arms tightly around me, and whisper sweet apologies into my hair, but his door remained closed. As though he'd fallen asleep inside. I walked to the passenger-side door and opened it.

Nico was looking straight out the windshield, his face gaunt, his expression stony.

"Hi," I said, keeping my voice steady. "Where have you been? I texted you, like—" The words got caught in my mouth when my gaze fell on the phone plugged into the charger, perfectly functional. The screen was alight with a notification of my latest attempt to get ahold of him.

Disregarded.

Ignored.

I expected an explanation, right then and there. I prayed it would be a short, simple one that would somehow magically erase the last few hours and return us back to where we started eighty-eight days ago.

One that would finally prove once and for all that Commissioners and Fixers could last.

But I didn't get one.

I *never* got one.

At least not a real one.

Nico simply turned toward me with deadened eyes and a somber expression and said, "Will you take a drive with me?"

My heart told me not to do it.

My brain told me not to do it.

Even my feet were screaming at me not to do it.

*Do NOT get in that truck with him!*

I got in the truck.

Nico and I drove in silence until we were out of Russellville, until we were twisting and turning around the tight bends of Route 128. As though we were afraid the town had ears.

I stole furtive glances at him. I saw him struggling. His mouth twitching, his hand returning to his jaw over and over, rubbing at the stubble, as though he were trying to wear it clean off.

I saw him fight.

What he was fighting against, I still don't know.

The truth?

The lie?

Some space in between, where all breakups live?

"I'm sorry," he finally said, and I blew out a breath I'd been holding since I got into that truck.

He paused.

I waited.

He sighed.

I waited.

He peered at me out of the corner of his eye.

I still waited.

Because it wasn't enough. Because I needed more. Because I *deserved* more.

He let out a chuckle. To my astonishment, it sounded light and airy. Like the kind of laugh that follows an awkward misunderstanding. A "You're not going to believe what just happened to me tonight" kind of laugh.

"I was studying at Brewed Awakenings, and I completely lost track of time."

The blood in my veins turned from ice to fire and back to ice again. Every gauzy layer that had surrounded us over the past eighty-eight days was suddenly gone.

Nico hadn't thrown a stone into our beautiful glass wall.

He'd admitted that the glass wall was never there to begin with. That it was made of nothing but air and illusions.

I felt nauseous. I felt cold. I felt cheated. I felt betrayed. I felt . . .

*Stupid.*

Every day since my ninth birthday, I promised myself I would never fall for the kind of guy my mom fell for. I would never end up like her: single with a child and a lying, leaving husband.

I never blamed my mother for loving Jackson. For believing Jackson. For letting Jackson back into our lives so many times. But I'd managed to convince myself that it would never happen to me. That it *could* never happen to me. Because I wouldn't let it. Because I grew up with it. I could read the signs. I could spot a charming charlatan from a mile away.

But it turns out I couldn't.

I didn't.

Because there was one sitting right next to me.

And the lies were still coming. "I know, I know," he said. "I should have had my ringer on. I'm sorry I made you worry. It's that stupid history final next week. I was trying to cram a hundred years' worth of European drama into two hours. This is what I get for spending all my time with you and not enough time reading. Not that I have any regrets on that part."

He reached for me. He rested his hand on my leg. As though it belonged there. As though it would always belong there.

I felt his touch everywhere. Like my body was purposefully betraying my mind and my heart.

"Pull over," I told him, keeping my voice as steady as possible.

Nico looked to me, his eyebrows pinched with worry. "What's wrong?"

"Just pull over."

"Ali, are you—"

"PULL OVER RIGHT NOW!" The dam broke. The emotions flowed. The tears followed.

Nico slammed on the brakes. The force of the deceleration was so strong, his glove box door popped open. I saw a small green-and-white object come flying out of the compartment and land on my lap. I looked down at my jeans, and that's when I saw it.

Rolled up and secured with a rubber band.

A wad of hundred-dollar bills.

With shaky hands, I reached for it, but Nico was too quick. He grabbed the bundle, stuffed it back into the glove box, and slammed the door shut. His movement was so fast, it was almost as though he were hoping I didn't see it.

But I saw it.

I kicked open the passenger-side door and hopped out of the truck. I heard Nico swear, and then I heard the screech of the parking brake engaging. A second later he was in front of me, his hands on my shoulders, his head dipped so he could look into my eyes.

"Ali, talk to me. What's wrong?"

"You're a liar!" I shouted into his face.

The confusion contorted his features. He stammered. Like he had any right to stammer. Like he had any right to act surprised. "W-w-what? I'm not lying."

"Where were you tonight?" I demanded.

"I told you. I was at Brewed Awak—"

But I couldn't stand to hear it again. It was too painful. I pushed his hands from my shoulders. "You know, you should probably check your facts before you blatantly lie. Brewed Awakenings was closed for the comet tonight. *I* know that because I circled the entire town looking for you."

I pushed past him and kept walking. Nico didn't follow me at first. I think he was too stunned. But then his brain caught up to the conversation, and he was suddenly in front of me again.

"Ali, stop!"

"Leave me alone!"

"Please. Don't jump to conclusions."

"I'm not jumping to anything. You lied, and that's that."

"I didn't lie."

I scoffed. "Excuse me. You're going to lie about lying now? What are you doing? Trying to trick me? Let's go round and round in circles until Ali gets so confused, she doesn't know what to think."

"I mean—" Nico tried again, but I didn't let him finish.

"Are you saying you were studying in a closed coffee shop with all the lights off? What, did you break a window? Pick the lock? Or is there another Brewed Awakenings in Russellville that I'm not familiar with?"

"Ali, please. Just let me explain."

"Why? So you can lie to me again? How am I supposed to believe anything you say now? How am I supposed to know what the truth is?"

Nico's jaw tightened, his lips forming a solid line. "I don't know, Ali. Maybe trust. Maybe *faith*."

His tone had turned bitter. Sharp. The kind Fixer Nico was gone, sucked into that glove box where nice boys go to die.

"Faith?!" I repeated in disgust. "Trust?! You act like those are simply given out for free! Those things are earned, Nico. And you just lost both."

I continued walking, my breath ragged, my heart pounding. I heard the gravel on the side of the road crunch behind me. "Don't follow me!" I yelled.

The crunching stopped. "So, what?" he called out a moment later. "That's it? We're done? Three months thrown away, just like that?"

"Yes!" I called over my shoulder. "Just like that." I swallowed, feeling the weight of what I had just said. It crushed me and sucked all the air out of my lungs. But it was too late to take it back now.

And if I did, I would be an even bigger fool than I already was.

As I glanced upward, I could just see the tail of Fabian's Comet through the break in the clouds. So bright. So promising. But I knew that in another few hours, it, too, would be lost in the sky.

*BOOOOOOMMM*

The sound of a foghorn brings me back to the car. The parking lot. Astoria. I glance at the clock on the dashboard. I've been sitting in this stalled Firebird for more than an hour.

Then, it comes again.

*BOOOOOOMMM*

I recognize the sound as that strange text message alert on Nico's phone.

*BOOOOOOMMM*

*BOOOOOOMMM*

*BOOOOOOMMM*

I didn't even realize his phone was still in the car.

*BOOOOOOMMM*

*BOOOOOOMMM*

I search the cup holders and the console below the radio, but the phone isn't there.

*BOOOOOOMMM*

*BOOOOOOMMM*

This Rachel person, whoever she is, is apparently *really* desperate to get ahold of him.

*BOOOOOOMMM*

The sound is coming from below me. I lean over the passenger seat and finally locate the phone on the floor. It must have slid down there during all my stopping and starting, trying to get away from Nico.

I reach down and grab it. I hold it tightly in my hands, staring at the screen.

And then, all at once, everything changes.

> Rachel: Baby, I need your help. Can I borrow two hundred dollars?
>
> Rachel: I got a really hot tip on a horse that's running tomorrow. It's a no-lose situation.
>
> Rachel: I promise, after this, I won't ever have to ask to borrow money again. And I can pay back everything else I owe you.
>
> Rachel: I would just use my own money but those bastards at Mountain Rock Casino threw me out again last night. I was on a big winning streak too. I was about to win it all back but they told me I had to leave.
>
> Rachel: They clearly didn't like that I was winning.☺
>
> Rachel: Please, baby. I'd ask your dad but he's on another trip.
>
> Rachel: Just tell me where you keep your extra cash and I can get it myself.
>
> Rachel: You don't have to come home. I promise it'll all be returned tomorrow.
>
> Rachel: I love you.

The numbness continues to spread through me as I stare down at Nico's phone. At the messages I clearly wasn't supposed to see. But now that I've seen them, the pieces are falling into place like they're falling from the sky.

Like debris from a passing comet.

It's the spiderweb I've been walking through. I somehow managed to stumble my way to the center.

And just like Jackson is at the heart of all my problems, my secrets, my dysfunctions, Nico's mom is at the heart of his.

Rachel.

I never knew her name. I never met his parents. I never saw the inside of his house.

*"Please, just let me explain . . ."*

But I didn't. I didn't let him that night. Maybe if I had, he would have eventually told me the truth. Maybe if I hadn't walked away, left him standing there alone on the side of the road, we wouldn't be here right now.

Maybe we don't *need* to be here right now.

I slam one foot against the clutch and the other against the brake. I turn the key, and the Firebird roars to life. I suddenly remember all the steps, all the movements, the way everything is supposed to feel.

I ease my foot halfway off the clutch until I feel the engine drop into a low, patient rumble. Then, I remove my foot from the brake. The car, miraculously, doesn't stall. It actually starts to inch forward. I gently press down on the gas, releasing the clutch with the same amount of reverse pressure. The car rolls forward.

I move far enough to pull into a nearby parking spot (so I'm not parked at a strange angle in the middle of the lot) and kill the engine. I jump out of the Firebird and dash back through the parking lot. To the scene of our Craigslist scam. To the place I abandoned Nico.

But he's not there.

I glance anxiously around, searching for a sign of him, but all I see is the Safeway, the Starbucks, the orthodontist, and the . . .

*Tomato and Vine.*

I take off at a run. I don't even bother using the crosswalk or waiting for the light. I dart around cars like I'm in one of those high-octane action flicks with no plot.

When I reach the restaurant, it doesn't take me long to spot him. He's sitting in a booth in the back with empty plates of pasta and breadsticks spread out around him like fallen soldiers on a battlefield.

"Waiter!" I hear him call out, sounding grouchy and irritable. "Bring me another round!"

A waiter approaches and stares disapprovingly down at the table. "Haven't you had enough?"

"Another round," Nico spits, sounding very *un*-Nico.

"That's it," the waiter says, gathering up the empty plates. "I'm cutting you off."

"You can't cut me off. It's *unlimited* pasta and breadsticks. Now bring me more."

The waiter sighs and mutters, "Fine," before disappearing.

I suck in a courageous breath and sidle up to the table.

Nico grabs the last remaining breadstick from the basket and rips a piece off with his teeth. "What do you want?"

"You were right," I rush to tell him while I still have the words. "I thought you were him. I tried to make you him. But you weren't. You were never like him."

I swallow hard and close my eyes, letting the truth expand inside of me until it takes up all the space. Until there's no more room left for the lies. "You were never Jackson. *I* was."

# 7:02 P.M.

# FORT STEVENS STATE PARK, OR

## INVENTORY: STILL (0)

At the very northern tip of Oregon, where the Columbia River meets the Pacific Ocean, there's a beach hidden away from the rest of the world. On a clear day you can see the state of Washington. On a clear evening, like tonight, you can see the most spectacular sunset.

That's where Nico and I sit. In the sand. Watching the darkened surf struggle to reach our toes, inching closer with each inflow and outflow of the tide.

I suddenly feel like we're back where we started in Fort Bragg, sitting in front of the vast Pacific Ocean, hoping it will save us. Hoping it has at least one drop of forgiveness left for us.

For the past five minutes, since I showed Nico the text messages I read on his phone, we've been sitting in silence. At first, I thought he would be mad at me for reading them. But he clearly wasn't. He almost looked relieved.

"She's sick," he says, finally breaking the silence.

Two words. Two syllables. Eight letters.

That's all it takes to tilt the world.

"She . . ." He falters, kicking at a pebble in the sand. And another. And another. Until there are no rocks left. "She doesn't know what she's doing when she does it. She can't stop. She . . . it's a sickness. It . . ." Nico's voice breaks.

He turns away, but I still see it. The moisture pooling in his eyes. The hard line of his jaw as he tries to hold it back.

"Is that what happened to your laptop?" I ask gently.

He nods and rubs his nose with the back of his hand. "She sold it."

"On Craigslist?"

"No, she prefers pawnshops. They're quicker." His breathing comes out in ragged bursts. Like tiny explosions. "She's an . . . an . . ." It's like he can't say it. Can't put the label on it. Can't get it to stick.

But I'm good with labels.

Maybe even too good.

"An addict?"

He closes his eyes, letting the word sink in, wash over him. I understand, in that moment, that it's the right one. "The night of the comet . . ." Nico opens his eyes, but his gaze stays trained on the ocean. "When I didn't show up. It was because I had to go all the way out to Middleton to pick her up. I got a call from the Twin Peaks Casino. They said if I didn't come get her, they'd call the police. She gets belligerent when she loses. She tries to negotiate. Tries to sell things she doesn't even have. And then when that doesn't work, she starts stealing."

I suck in a breath. "The money. In the glove box."

He nods like he can follow my line of reasoning all the way to the end. "It's a stash I keep hidden. I trade up on Craigslist to earn money and replace the stuff she sells. She's sold practically everything. Our TV. Our microwave. All of our dishes. From the inside, our house looks like it's been robbed. And in a way, it has. She thinks if she can just get one more dollar, she can win it all back." He pauses to let out a shaky breath. "She never wins it back."

My head is spinning. The explanation is so simple. It makes so much sense. And yet, out of all the possible scenarios that ran through my head that night and every night since, none of them was this.

None of them was a scenario in which Nico is innocent.

That's because all of them were scenarios in which Nico was Jackson.

"What about your dad?" I ask. "Why doesn't he do anything to try to stop it?"

Nico snorts. "My dad has completely checked out. He won't even acknowledge she has a problem. He travels so much for work, he's never home. And, to be honest, I think he prefers it that way. He can stay in denial if he's not around to see it. He stopped going to pick her up years ago. That became my job."

"Have you ever, I don't know, confronted her about it?"

"Yes. Plenty of times. It's why we left Reno. She claimed it was all the city's fault. Too much temptation. She said that if we just moved far enough away from the big casinos, she wouldn't be tempted anymore." He lets out a dark laugh. "And I was stupid enough to believe that." He shakes his head. "I guess I *wanted* to believe her. I always want to believe her."

"I know," I tell him in a fragile voice. "Trust me, I know what it's like to want to believe."

Nico pulls his knees up to his chest and buries his face in them. "I'm sorry. I tried to tell you. I just . . . I've been keeping her secret for so long, it's become second nature. Lie to the neighbors. Lie to my mom's parents. Lie to the police. Lie to protect her. I don't even know I'm doing it sometimes. The lies come out easier than the truths. Trust me, I *wanted* to tell you. I really did, you just . . ."

He doesn't finish that thought. But it doesn't matter. Because I can finish it for him.

"I didn't give you the chance."

The words echo around me like they're bouncing off the air. I glance up, and I swear I can still see that comet streaking across the sky. It's followed me all the way to Oregon. It seems like whenever I look up, I will always see it. For the rest of my life. Not as a beautiful, celestial object soaring gracefully through space. But as a ghost haunting me. A constant reminder of everything I didn't hear that night. Everything I couldn't hear.

Everything I threw away.

Everything I lost.

And now "I'm sorry" is all I can say.

So I do.

Nico smiles. "Me too."

A moment later, he pushes himself to his feet and

brushes the sand from the back of his jeans. I assume he's ready to go back to the car, but he just stands there, staring at the ocean.

Then, before I can process what's happening, he's pulling his shirt over his head. He's kicking off his shoes and peeling off his jeans. I watch in total disbelief as he strips right down to his boxers and starts running.

Running, running, running.

Straight into the ocean.

A wave rises up to greet him, and he dives under it, disappearing beneath the dark, foamy surf for what feels like too long. I stand, panic coursing through me.

*What is he doing?*

*Should I call for help?*

*Should I dive in after him?*

But then, a second later, his head appears above the water. It bobs there for a moment before Nico flips onto his back and floats, as though he's perfectly ready and willing to let the ocean take him straight to the other side of the world.

The panic slips away, and all that's left is a sad smile.

I think he's been wanting to do this since we stopped at Glass Beach.

I sit back down in the sand and watch him. I wonder how cold that water is. I wonder if he even feels it. After everything he's told me tonight, my guess is he feels nothing but relief.

Keeping someone's secret is a lot of weight for a kid to carry around. Especially when it's your parent's secret. I know because I did it too. In fact, I'm still doing it. No one except Nico and June knows about the house foreclosure. No one knows just how deep our financial problems go. My mom doesn't even know I'm here. Doesn't know about the car. About the trades. About the money we almost had but lost.

Even after he's dead, I feel like I'm still keeping Jackson's secrets.

When Nico emerges from the ocean a few minutes later, the world looks different. But most important, *he* looks different. It's as though all of his sharp edges have been smoothed down. Everything that I once thought was dangerous about him—that I once thought I had to protect my heart from—has been worn away. Polished clean. Transformed by the ever-forgiving ocean. Until he's just another piece of sea glass washing up on the shore.

A treasure made with time.

Sometimes we throw things away and we never get them back. But sometimes, when we're really lucky, they come back to us.

# TUESDAY

*There's a man who's lost his sanity,*
*He's waiting for the sky to sing*
*He shouts into the void, "I tried to warn ya!"*
*But I'd still do anything, anything,*
*anything for California*

—"Anything for California," from the album
*Anarchy in a Cup* by Fear Epidemic
Written by Nolan Cook
Released July 19, 1998

# 2:05 P.M.

# PORTLAND, OR

INVENTORY: 1968 FIREBIRD CONVERTIBLE (1),
CASH ($181.25), SEA GLASS (1 PIECE),
LOST-KEY BUTTERFLY SCULPTURE (1),
USELESS PHOTOGRAPH (1)

"Are you sure you want to do this?" Nico asks as we pull
up to the entrance of Hank's Classic Garage in downtown
Portland.

I nod and take a breath. "Yes. I'm sure."

Nico parks the car and I unbuckle my seat belt, but I
don't make a move for the door. Not yet. For a moment, I
just sit there, staring at the interior of the Firebird. Trying
to take a mental snapshot of this journey so that I can store
it away in a scrapbook in my mind and never forget it.

Hank Callahan was another one of the people who
e-mailed me about the Firebird back when I first posted
it on Craigslist. I called him earlier this morning and told
him the whole situation: it's not a 400, but I'm still interested in selling it if he's still interested in buying it.

He was.

He even told me he could match Tom Lancaster's offer of three thousand dollars. It's not going to save the house, but at least it's something.

I sigh, grab my backpack, and unzip the large pocket. "I guess we should clean out the car."

"Okay," Nico says, sounding uncertain. But he still helps. He steps out, tips the seat forward, and begins rummaging around the back.

I search the front—the glove box, the center console, and the floor. There's not much. Some candy bar wrappers, a few water bottles, and a plastic bag that still has the empty box from the Sea-Bands Nico bought me. And of course, Kunjee, my butterfly statue. I place her carefully inside my backpack and crumple up the rest, stuffing it into the plastic bag.

I zip up my backpack and am about to get out of the car when my gaze lands on the radio. Or more specifically, on the tape player that Jackson installed. The cassette tape that I started listening to at the drive-in is still sticking out of the slot from when I hastily ejected it last night.

"I think that's everything." Nico leans in to the open driver's-side door to speak to me. "I'm just going to check the . . ." His voice trails off when he notices me just staring vacantly at the tape player.

Suddenly I can't help thinking about Jackson's voice on that recording. Why was this tape in his car when he died? Why was it important to him?

"Are you okay?" Nico sits back down behind the wheel,

following my gaze to the tape player. "Should I . . . um . . . like, give you a moment alone or something?"

I shake my head and grab on to his hand. "No. Don't go. I need you here for what I'm about to do."

Nico looks confused, and just the slightest bit terrified. "What *are* you about to do?"

Instead of answering his question, I take a deep breath, reach toward the stereo, and push the black cassette tape back into the slot.

This tape was the last thing Jackson ever listened to in his precious Firebird. It clearly meant something to him. It clearly had value. Even if it feels worthless to me, I owe it to Jackson—to his car—to hear it all the way through. To find out why he kept it.

The cassette clicks, and the recording resumes, picking up in the middle of the conversation that I stopped abruptly at the drive-in. I jab at the rewind button and back it up a few seconds so I can remember what was said.

When I hit play, the crudely recorded song that Nolan Cook was singing is just coming to an end.

"Well, that royally blew," Adam French, the band's drummer, says spitefully.

"Thanks, Adam. Way to be constructive. How about when you start contributing lyrics, you get to have a say?"

"If I recall, my face is still on the album covers, and my name is still on the copyright."

"Well, you know what they say. Change a word, get a credit."

"You know what, Nolan? Why don't you go fu—"

"Guys! Guys! Calm down. You're getting worked up over nothing."

I freeze again at the sound of Jackson's voice, the reaction almost as gut-wrenching as the first time I heard this. I must be squeezing Nico's hand because he looks over at me and asks, "Who is that?"

I swallow. "That's my dad."

Suddenly, he understands what this is all about. Why we're sitting in this car outside of Hank's Classic Garage listening to an old cassette tape.

"It's not nothing," Adam French fires back. "It's the whole future of the band, and if Nolan wants to ruin it with a bunch of whiny garbage on the third album, then I don't want to be a part of it."

"Shut up, French." This is a new voice. I assume it must belong to one of the other two members of the band. Slate Miller, the bass player, or Chris McCaden, the backup guitar player.

"No, you shut up," Adam shoots back. "Cook and his enormous ego are going to take us all down in flames."

"That's enough!" someone yells, and it takes me a moment to realize that it's Jackson again. The sound startles me. I've never heard Jackson yell at anyone. Even when my mother would be screaming at him to get his act together, grow up, get a job, pay some bills like a responsible adult, he would never raise his voice back to her. He might have had the maturity of a child, but he had the patience of a saint. "If you keep this up, there won't *be* a third album."

The group falls silent, apart from a low muttering sound, which I assume is Adam French grumbling.

"I'm so sick of hearing you guys argue," Jackson goes on, his voice somewhat calmer now, but his frustration is still foreign. "Don't you realize how much this band means to people? How much your music means to people?"

A familiar knot forms in my stomach, and I feel the urge to reach out and eject the tape again. I don't need to hear more of Jackson Collins professing his love for this stupid band. But I force myself to keep listening.

"You guys are the luckiest people I know," Jackson goes on. "You get to live your dream every single day. With nothing tying you down or holding you back. And yet all you do is sit on this tour bus and rag on each other like a bunch of spoiled kids. Grow up!"

I snort aloud at that. Jackson giving people advice on how to *grow up*? That's laughable.

"I'll grow up when Cook here learns how to write some decent lyrics."

"Hey! Cook's lyrics have made you a lot of money," Jackson fires back.

I blink in disbelief at the stereo. Did Jackson just tell off Adam French, the drummer of Fear Epidemic? He's sounding a lot more like their manager right now than their roadie.

"That was years ago," Adam reminds the group. "If you could hear the garbage he's coming up with now, you'd sell your stock, Collins."

There's a rustling sound, followed by a bang. Someone

is getting up—and not gracefully. "That's it!" Nolan Cook bellows. "I'm not going to just sit here and listen to you insult me. Unless any of *you* losers have some better lyrics, you can all just shove it."

There's a long beat in which no one speaks and all I can hear on the recording is the sound of Nolan Cook clearly trying to move to some other room on the bus. I picture him clambering over legs and instruments, bumping into stuff. Is he drunk? Or is the tour bus just that cramped?

"Wait," someone says, and once again, it takes me a moment to identify the voice as Jackson's. He doesn't sound angry anymore. He's done a complete 180-degree turn. Now, he sounds almost afraid. "I might have something."

Stunned silence fills the tour bus. Even the whoosh of the passing traffic seems to have died down.

"I didn't know you wrote, Jack," Nolan Cooks says.

"I . . ." Jackson hesitates. "I don't normally. I just . . . it's something that's been weighing on me. So, a few hotels ago, back in Salt Lake City, I grabbed a pen and started writing down some lyrics."

My throat goes dry.

*Salt Lake City.*

That was one of the last cities Jackson called from on the road. After I'd stopped answering the phone.

"Well, let's see them," Nolan says.

There's a soft rustling of paper, followed by a long silence. "I don't know if it's any good," Jackson says. "I just—"

"No," Nolan interrupts him. "It's good. It's really good. Are these lyrics about her?"

Jackson doesn't respond right away. My breathing grows shallow. Then, a moment later, in a quiet, tentative voice he says, "Yeah."

Nico turns and looks at me. Like he just knows. Like he was there that day in that tour bus. Like he read whatever was written on that paper.

*About her.*

*Her.*

The word was said so casually. So knowingly. Like they'd had countless conversations about this elusive *her.*

"Let me see that." It's Adam again. There's another rustling of paper as he evidently grabs the song lyrics from Nolan. Then a few seconds later, he says, "Damn, Jack. You've been holding out on us! These are good."

Jackson lets out an embarrassed chuckle, and I marvel at how much he sounds like a little boy. "Thanks."

"Are you sure you want to give us these lyrics?" Nolan asks.

"Yeah," Jackson says immediately. "I mean, definitely. If you think you can use them, use them."

"Oh, believe me, we can use them," Adam says. "We *need* them."

"Hold up," Nolan interjects. "Jack, think about this. If we use these lyrics—if we record this song for the album—these words will be heard by millions. Are you sure you want that?"

This time, there's a pause before Jackson speaks. "I'm sure. I don't care if millions of people hear it. The only person I care about hearing it is her. I need her to know, and this is the only way I can think to tell her."

A chill runs over me, causing me to tremble. I jab my hand against all the stereo buttons at once until the tape finally stops playing.

"Do you think . . . ?" Nico begins to ask, but I hastily shake my head before he can even finish the thought.

"No. No way."

I can't bring myself to believe it. There's no possible way Jackson is talking about me. It must be about some other *her*. Some random groupie he managed to charm on the road. Another bleached-blond Marylou in a tight leather skirt.

"But what if—" Nico starts again.

"I would have known if Jackson had written a song about me," I say with certainty. But then, a soft voice in the back of my mind crashes right through that certainty.

*Not if it was never recorded.*

I shiver again. Fear Epidemic broke up before they could record their third album. Whatever lyrics Jackson wrote on that paper were never set to music. They were never given voice. Never saw the light of day.

Unless . . .

My gaze drifts back to the stereo again. The tape is still inside. Just waiting for me to find the courage to listen.

Just waiting for me to ask the question.

Just waiting for me to push play.

After Jackson left the second time, there were no phone calls from exotic places. There was no bragging about all the exciting things he was doing on tour with his favorite band. That band was long gone, and Jackson seemed anchorless without them.

No, when Jackson left that second time, he left without a trace. For a while, we actually did wonder if he was dead.

Then my mom got a bill for another credit card in her name, maxed out with charges from hotels, bars, restaurants, and auto-supply shops.

And that was the final straw.

It took the private investigator my mother hired an entire month to track Jackson down just to serve him the divorce papers.

Two days later, we heard the Firebird zooming down the driveway once again.

That's when he came back for the second time.

With the nerve to ask Mom what this "nonsense" was all about.

"Divorce, Janie? Isn't that a bit extreme?"

My mom showed him the box where she kept all of the unpaid bills.

Jackson smiled his same disarming smile. "Janie, c'mon." The way he said my mom's name set my teeth on edge. "We can work this out. I'll stay. I'll get a job in town. I'll help you get this all settled. I'll fix everything. There's no need for a divorce."

I wanted to believe that was true. That there was no need for them to break up now that he was home. But I also knew how distressed my mother had become over the past few months. Over the past few years, really. How could we ever be sure he would stay this time?

The sensation that streamed through me as I stood by and watched my mother yell and my father defend was so powerful, so debilitating, I could barely breathe.

As Jackson said those words, "C'mon, Janie, give me another chance," I felt like a giant gash in the earth was spreading right beneath my feet, and I had to choose a side.

*Please, say yes, Mom.*

*Please, say no, Mom.*

*Please, let him stay.*

*Please, tell him to go.*

And I knew whichever side I picked, I would have to leap. And I would have to stay. It was now or never. There was no going back. There was no time. The crack was too wide. The chasm was too deep.

"Jackson," Mom began, and I heard the brokenness in her voice. I heard the sounds of walls crumbling. Her heart caving yet again. Her last ounce of forgiveness bubbling up.

And I leaped.

"No," I told him. The authority in my voice was too old for a thirteen-year-old. Too resolved. Which, I guess, made sense. I didn't feel *thirteen* in that moment. I felt infinite. "You can't stay, Dad."

The questions that had been bubbling up in my mind since the first day he walked out on us started to pop one by one, like pins to a room full of balloons.

*Is he ever coming back?*

Pop.

*Why did he really leave?*

Pop.

*Did he ever care about either of us?*

Pop.

Mom blinked, as though coming out of a trance. A trance she'd been stuck in for the past sixteen years. She glanced hesitantly between me and Jackson, like she, too, was feeling the chasm open beneath her.

Then she walked over to me and put her arm around my shoulders.

"No," she repeated. "Ali is right. I think it's best that you leave."

That was the moment that unified us for good. Those words solidified the adhesive that would keep us locked together for the next six years.

That was the day we made a silent pact. To close that chapter of our lives. To stop wondering. To stop searching. To stop hoping for magical explanations that would fix everything.

After that day, there were no more questions asked about Jackson Collins.

I push play.

The tape clicks.

I hold my breath.

Then clicks again.

Silence.

"What happened?" I ask, looking desperately from the stereo to Nico.

Nico flashes me a pained expression but doesn't respond.

I lunge for the controls again, hitting fast-forward, then play, then fast-forward, then play.

More silence.

My breathing grows shallow. My vision blurs. I feel that familiar rage building inside of me. It's a rage that has only ever come from Jackson. From letting him in only to have him disappoint me again. And again. And again.

"I think that's the end of the recording," Nico finally says.

"No!" I shout at the cassette player. "No! You can't do that! You can't come this close to telling me the truth and then take it away!"

Fast-forward.

Play.

Fast-forward.

Play.

Nothing but silence.

I dared to ask one more question.

But Jackson didn't answer.

"NO!" I cry again. "It doesn't end this way. You don't get to do that. You don't get to tell *Nolan Cook* and not me. You don't get to just die with a secret like that!"

Fast-forward.

Play.

Fast-forward.

Play.

Silence.

*Click.*

The tape ends.

# 2:29 P.M.

## PORTLAND, OR

### INVENTORY: 1968 FIREBIRD CONVERTIBLE (1), CASH ($181.25), SEA GLASS (1 PIECE), LOST-KEY BUTTERFLY SCULPTURE (1), USELESS PHOTOGRAPH (1)

I sit in the cramped office of Hank's Classic Garage, listening to the whir of the printer as it spits out the last page of the sales contract. Nico is outside finishing cleaning out the Firebird.

Hank grabs the stack of papers from the printer tray, gives them a tap, and sets them down in front of me with a pen. I sigh and start to flip through the contract. Most of the language is gibberish to me, but the gist is clear.

I am giving up my father's car. His prized possession. His pride and joy. He cared more about this car and that band than he ever did for me and my mom.

This is an easy decision.

And yet, when I get to the last page and see my name printed underneath the signature line—my full legal name—my hand starts to shake. I grip the pen tighter.

*Do it, Ali*, I urge myself. *This is what you wanted. You wanted to get rid of it. You wanted to throw it away. Of all the things to throw away, this should be the most obvious choice.*

I press the nib against the page, feeling how heavy the pen is in my hand. Like it's made of lead.

I stare at the name right above the signature line.

California Collins.

The name my father gave me. Because of a stupid song by a stupid band.

*Anything for California.*

Tears start to well up in my eyes. What a load of crap. Jackson wouldn't have done anything for me. He did nothing for me. Except leave me a fake car that's barely worth enough to pay off just *one* of the credit cards he maxed out in my mother's name.

But those words from the tape keep replaying in my mind.

*"I need her to know, and this is the only way I can think to tell her."*

What did he want me to know? What did he need to tell me so badly that he could only write in an unrecorded song that will never be heard by anyone? Including me.

"Are you okay?" Hank asks, startling me. I blink back the tears and look up at him.

I clear my throat. "Yes. I'm fine."

He smiles, as though he understands exactly what I'm feeling. As though he, too, was abandoned by a father who cared more about a car than a child. "It can be tough to say good-bye to things we love," he says.

I chuckle. "That's the funny part. I always hated that car."

"I wasn't talking about the car."

I let out a shudder of a breath. "Oh. Right."

"I'll give you a minute," he says, and then pushes his chair back and steps out of the office, leaving me alone with the contract.

I stare down at it again. Why does it feel like I'm selling so much more than just a car? Why does it feel like when I sign my name on this line, I'll be letting him down? He let me down countless times!

I pull the piece of sea glass out of my pocket and turn it around in my hand, remembering the words the man on the beach said to me.

*"The ocean forgives."*

But I can't.

I just . . . *can't.*

I take a steeling breath and press the tip of the pen into the paper again. "Maybe someday I can forgive you," I say to the page in front of me. "But for now, I just have to say good-bye to you."

Then, slowly, I scribble out a *C*, an *A*, an *L*, an *I*, an *F*.

But that's as far as I get, because just then, Nico bursts into the office screaming, "No penamen! No penamen!"

I jump. My hand slips; the *O* of "California" becomes a jagged line halfway up the page. "Jeez, Nico! What are you doing? Don't scare me like that."

"No penamen!"

My faces scrunches up. "What?"

"No *penamen*," he repeats with more emphasis, as if that's supposed to help.

"What are you talking about?"

Nico rolls his eyes. "We just watched it *last* night. 'No penamen!'"

I smile as I recognize the quote from the end of *The Goonies*. It's the scene where Rosalita, the Spanish-speaking housekeeper, is trying to stop Mikey's father from signing the paperwork to sell his house. Except she doesn't speak any English, and the Goonie named Mouth has to translate.

I finish the quote. "'No pen. No write. No sign!'"

Nico beams. "No penamen!"

I glance down at my messed-up half-signature. "What are you talking about? Why shouldn't I sign it?"

Nico steps farther into the office, and it's only now that I notice he's hiding something behind his back.

I scoff. "Are you going to tell me you found a bag full of jewels that's going to save all of Astoria from evil land developers? Just like in the movie?"

"Um, no," Nico says.

I laugh. "Then what are you doing?"

Nico steps forward, still hiding the mysterious object behind his back. "I don't think you should sell the car."

I roll my eyes. "This again? Are we going on another trade-up adventure? Because I think I've had enough Craigslist for one lifetime."

He holds up his hand. "Let me finish. I don't think you should sell the car . . . yet."

"Yet?"

"At least not until you have all the answers you need."

I give him a quizzical look.

"About Jackson," he clarifies.

I sigh, trying to keep myself from getting worked up.

"Just hear me out," Nico pleads. "I've been thinking about what Jackson said on that tape. What if there *is* some lost song he wrote about you? What if there was something he wanted to tell you?"

"Then he should have told me when he was alive," I argue. "He had plenty of chances."

Nico offers me a forlorn smile. "It's not always that easy, and I think you know that."

I sigh and slump in the chair.

Because I do that.

We *both* know how hard it is, sometimes, to tell the truth.

"If there's something out there about your father that you don't know, don't you think it's at least worth trying to figure out what it is? I'd just hate for you to sell this car and then later regret it."

"Are you saying you magically have all the answers about my dead father?"

"No," Nico says, before revealing what he's been holding behind his back. He sets it down on the desk, and I see that it's the photograph of Jackson and Nolan Cook, posing like rock stars in front of the Fear Epidemic tour bus.

The one I found in the trunk of the car. Then, from the back pocket of his jeans, Nico pulls out the white envelope that the photograph came in. "But he might."

He points to the return address scribbled in the top left corner, and, for first time, I read what it says.

*Nolan Cook*
*4250 NW 159th St.*
*Tacoma, WA 98406*

# 3:25 P.M.

# INTERSTATE 5 FREEWAY

## INVENTORY: 1968 FIREBIRD CONVERTIBLE (1), CASH ($181.25), SEA GLASS (1 PIECE), LOST-KEY BUTTERFLY SCULPTURE (1), PHOTO OF JACKSON COLLINS AND NOLAN COOK (1)

"This is it," Nico says as we follow the traffic onto the bridge that will take us across the Columbia River. "There's no turning back now. Are you ready to enter enemy territory?"

I chuckle and rest my hand atop Nico's on the stick shift. "I'm ready."

Halfway across the bridge we pass a sign that says LEAVING OREGON, and a few seconds later, we sail under a second sign that reads ENTERING WASHINGTON.

And just like that, I've left the safety of the rest of the world and entered his domain. The state where Fear Epidemic was born and Jackson died.

It's time to face the loud, angry music.

Two and a half hours later, we pull up in front of a

modest two-story rustic house at the end of a tree-lined cul-de-sac in Tacoma, and Nico kills the engine of the Firebird.

I always imagined the lead singer of Fear Epidemic living in a giant mansion overlooking the ocean or something. This house is nice, but it's not rock-star nice. Maybe they weren't as popular as Jackson made them out to be. That certainly wouldn't surprise me.

We sit inside the Firebird for a long time without speaking. It's a different kind of silence now. It's not the shadowy pit that has followed us around since we left Russellville. There's something almost comforting about the quiet between us. It's become a constant along a road of unknowns.

Finally, Nico turns to me from the driver's seat and cocks an eyebrow. "Are you ready for this?"

I keep my gaze trained on the house. "What if he doesn't even live here anymore? Or wants nothing to do with me?"

Nico shrugs. "I guess we won't know until we knock."

"I guess," I say, but I still don't move.

Nico places a warm hand on mine. "You can do this."

I take a deep breath and open the door. Nico jumps out of the driver's side and runs around the front of the car to walk next to me. As though he's afraid I might collapse and he wants to be right there if I do.

It's not a bad idea. I very well might collapse.

I've spent my entire life hating this band. Blaming them for Jackson's absence in my life. And here I am ready to walk into their lair like a sheep walking into the lion's den.

With my heart in my throat, I climb the steps of the front porch and ring the bell. A moment later, a middle-aged man opens the door. He looks nothing like the rock star I saw in all of those pictures. This man doesn't have wild, untamed black locks. His salt-and-pepper hair is cut short and neatly combed. This man doesn't have dark eyeliner rimming his lids. He wears square spectacles instead. And he's not dressed in a sleeveless white T-shirt with a tangle of silver chains around his neck. He's dressed smartly in dark jeans and a button-down navy-blue shirt. Like he's going to brunch.

At first, I'm convinced I'm too late. The lead singer of Fear Epidemic doesn't live here anymore. This house belongs to someone else.

But then I look a little closer. Behind the glasses. Past the gray hair and leathery skin. And that's when I see it. That's when I see *him*.

The man who took my father away from me.

The man with whom I was in constant competition for Jackson's affection.

Nolan Cook.

But before I can say a single word, his hand goes to his mouth, and he takes a small step back from the door. "Oh my God." He squints at me through the lenses of his glasses. "California?"

I cringe at the sound of my own name spoken by the very voice that first sang it to Jackson.

"You recognize me?" I ask.

Nolan blinks again, as though making sure I'm real. "Yeah . . . of course. I . . . I mean, Jackson only showed me your photo a thousand times." He lets out a small stutter of a laugh.

*Is he nervous?*

He runs his hands through his short hair, causing a few strands to stick up. It makes him look just the slightest bit more like the Nolan Cook I remember from the pictures. "I can't believe it's really you."

"Nice to meet you," I say timidly. I'm not sure what the proper protocol is here. Do I shake his hand? Ask if I can come in? I've never met an actual celebrity before. Even though he's never been renowned in my mind, in Jackson's mind this man was a god. A legend. And despite my longtime hatred for anything to do with Fear Epidemic, a little of that star power seems to rub off on me.

I extend my hand toward him at the very same moment that he pulls me into a hug. Like I'm his own long-lost daughter, and not the daughter of one of his random roadies.

I wrap my arms clumsily around his back and give it a double pat.

"It's just so great to finally meet you," he says. "Although I feel like I already know you." He pulls away. "And who's your friend?"

"This is Nico," I say, and Nico gives Nolan a little wave, clearly feeling just as awkward as I do.

"Well, come in, come in." Nolan opens the door wide, and we step into a vast great room with a gorgeous rustic décor. There's a giant stone-covered fireplace on the back wall and a log beam running across the tall vaulted ceilings.

"Beautiful house," Nico says.

"Thanks," replies Nolan, sounding somewhat sheepish. "Royalty checks aren't what they used to be, but I get by." He starts to fidget with the hem of his shirt.

*Definitely nervous.*

But what on earth does *he* have to be nervous about?

"Um," Nolan begins, waving his hands around as though he doesn't know where to put them. "Why don't you sit down. Do you guys want anything to drink? Coffee? Water? Soda? Whiskey?" He stops himself. "Wait, how old are you two?"

"Eighteen," we both reply at once.

"Soda," Nolan decides, and walks into the kitchen to get the drinks.

Nico and I sink down into the brown leather couch, and it's only then, after we're seated, that I notice the wall to the left of the fireplace is decorated with four black frames. Each of them holds a gold-coated record. I immediately stand back up and wander over to the wall, reading the plaque on each frame.

"NEARLY A SAINT" – SINGLE.

"SLEEP" – SINGLE.

"DONE" – SINGLE.

"ANYTHING FOR CALIFORNIA" – SINGLE.

"We had four singles go gold," Nolan says, reemerging from the kitchen with three cans—two sodas and a beer. He hands the sodas to us and pops open the beer for himself. "One of them was the song Jackson named you after."

"Right." I take a sip of my soda. The taste is too sweet in my mouth, and I have to force myself to swallow it.

"You'll notice there are no singles from *Salvage Lot* up there," Nolan says with a bitter laugh. He takes a long pull from his beer. "Yeah, that was what I think you kids today call an 'epic fail.'"

Nico guffaws, and I chuckle politely.

"The whole tour was a disaster from the start," Nolan goes on, taking a seat on one of the red armchairs. I sit back down next to Nico on the couch. He immediately grabs my hand and gives it a squeeze, reminding me that he's right here. Ready to catch me if anything goes wrong.

"Jackson," I begin, but quickly correct myself: "My *dad* seemed to think it was the best experience of his life."

Nolan laughs at this and takes another sip of beer. "That's Jackson for you. He made everything fun. The rest of us fought the whole time, but Jackson, he was always ready with a joke or a good story. He could always be counted on to break up the tension and keep us on track."

I think about the recording I found in the cassette player of the car. How Jackson was trying so hard to keep the guys from fighting. Clearly it didn't work because they broke up anyway.

"He was one of the best roadies we ever had," Nolan goes on. "In fact, he was more than a roadie. At least to me. He was a friend."

I nod politely, because I don't know what to say to that.

*I'm glad he was good at something?*

*Too bad he was better at being a roadie than a dad?*

"How is he, by the way?" Nolan asks. "I haven't heard from him in a few months."

And that's when I feel all the blood drain from my face.

Oh my God. He doesn't know. How can he not know? How good of a friend could Jackson have been to him if he doesn't even know that he's dead?

Nico gives my hand another squeeze, and I look desperately over at him. He raises his eyebrows, asking, *Do you want me to do it?*

I shake my head. *No, it has to be me.*

"He's . . . ," I begin, feeling my voice catch. Although I have no idea why. I had no problem telling Nico he was dead. Why are *these* words getting stuck in my throat? They're the exact same words.

Maybe because it's not actually the words themselves that matter.

It's the audience.

It's the speaker.

And I'm definitely a different person now than I was five days ago.

I take a giant gulp of my soda and swallow hard. "He died."

Nolan's whole body seems to cave in on itself. But for some reason he doesn't look surprised. Did he, too, see it coming? Just like Mom and I did? Did he, too, understood that Jackson Collins was never going to last?

"I'm sorry," he finally says. "He was a great guy."

I feel the familiar reaction bubbling up inside of me. The heat. The frustration. The angry words.

*A great guy? Really? Because that's not the person I remember. That's not the Jackson I grew up with. I grew up with a man who constantly disappointed us. Who was never there for us. You might have gotten to hang out with the good Jackson, the fun Jackson, the best-roadie-ever Jackson. Meanwhile, we got stuck with the other one.*

But I don't say any of that. Because I'm not here to yell and fight and blame. I've been doing that my whole life, and I'm done. Jackson will never be the man I wanted him to be. He will never be the father that I felt I deserved. I get that. I've accepted it.

Now I just want to know *why*.

I take a deep breath, reach into the pocket of my hoodie, and pull out the cassette tape. I place it on the coffee table between us.

Nolan seems to recognize it right away. His eyes light up like he's seeing an old friend across a crowded room. "Whoa. Is that . . . ?" He answers his own question when he picks up the tape and reads the label. "It is. Oh my God. Where did you get this?"

"Jackson had it when he died. He left it in the tape player of his car."

Nolan nods slowly, remembering something. "Right. I forgot I gave this to him after the band broke up."

"Why?"

Nolan shrugs and turns the tape around in his hand. "He really wanted it, and we had no use for it. The third album was doomed from the start. We couldn't write a good song to save our lives, and we all knew it. We were

**437** →

grasping at straws at that point, trying to resurrect something that should have stayed dead and buried."

"Do you—" I begin haltingly, trying to build up the courage to ask what I came here to ask. "Do you remember what was on this tape?"

Nolan clearly hears the break in my voice because he flashes me a curious look before returning his gaze to the cassette. "Not really. No. I assume it's a recording of me and Adam going at each other like drunks brawling in a bar."

Despite myself, I chuckle at that. "Yeah, there's some of that on there."

Nolan snorts like it's still a sore spot. "He was always jealous of the attention I got as the lead singer."

"But there was something else on there too. Something important. Or maybe important. I don't know. I can't tell. It was cut off." I feel myself start to ramble. I press my lips together.

Nolan lifts his eyebrows. "What?"

I falter, wondering if coming here was a huge mistake. What if he has no idea what I'm talking about? What if he doesn't remember the song Jackson wrote?

I feel a gentle nudge on my leg, and I look over at Nico. He's nodding encouragingly. "It's okay," he whispers, as though he can feel the courage slipping out of me.

I take another deep breath. "A song. That Jackson wrote."

For a long, painful moment, Nolan's expression is completely blank. And in that moment, I convince myself that we came all this way for nothing. There are no answers to be found about Jackson Collins. There are only more questions. *Always* more questions. Like a maze that never ends. Just when you think you've found your way out, you turn into another dead end. Another disappointment.

*SNAP!*

I blink and look at Nolan. He's snapping his fingers rapidly, like he's trying to jog his memory.

Then, with one final click, it comes to him.

"'While She Sleeps.'"

"What?" I ask.

"That was the name of the song he wrote. We were going to put it on the third album." He scoffs. "It would have been the only decent thing on that album."

I'm suddenly speechless. I don't think I ever fully believed that we'd get to this point. That he'd actually remember. I think somewhere deep down inside, I prayed he wouldn't.

But now here we are. On the precipice. On the edge of that same gaping chasm where I stood six years ago as my parents' marriage ended and I had to choose which side I would stay on. Somehow I've returned to that same terrifying ledge. That same terrifying choice.

To forgive Jackson.

Or to forget him.

"Do you remember," I begin, my voice shaking, "what the song was about?"

"Yeah." Nolan grows very quiet. "Jackson wrote it about the night you almost died."

I shake my head, chuckling nervously. "You must be mistaken. I didn't almost die."

Nolan blows out a heavy breath. "Jackson told me about it on the tour. We were having drinks after the show one night, and it all just came pouring out. He told me about how he almost got you killed."

"What?" I ask, flabbergasted. "The song must be about someone else, then. That never happened to me."

"You never knew," Nolan says with such confidence, it makes me shudder. "It happened right before your ninth birthday. You were supposed to go to—"

"Tomato and Vine," I say numbly.

"That's it," Nolan says. "Jackson was drunk, but he took you in the car anyway. He blacked out behind the wheel, and when he came to, the car was no longer on the road. He couldn't even remember what had happened."

A chill travels up my spine as the missing pieces from that night begin to rain down on me.

The empty park.

The crumbling swing set.

The strange man who came to pick us up.

Jackson's vacant smile.

*"Change of plans! We're going to the park! Tomato and Vine is closed."*

"He . . . ," I start to say, but I can't bring myself to finish.

Thankfully Nolan finishes for me. "He never forgave himself for that. For putting you in that kind of danger. He said for a while he couldn't even bring himself to look at you. It was too painful."

"So he left," I conclude.

Nolan nods. "He loved being on the road with us. But I think more than anything, he just felt like it was better that way. Safer. That night really weighed on his mind. All the time. I remember him calling me once, after the band had broken up. He had gone back home to you because he said he wanted to try to be a father again. But when he called, he was a total wreck. Drunk and rambling from a bar somewhere. He told me he just couldn't do it. He was too terrified he'd make another mistake."

Suddenly, I feel like the room is spinning. The world is blurring. The familiar shapes and colors don't make sense anymore. Everything is all jumbled up. Blue is red and red is green and black and white smear together to form the murkiest shade of gray.

*"Do you remember your ninth birthday?"*

*"I think about that night all the time."*

*"About how badly I screwed up. About what a mess I was."*

That's what he said to me when I was twelve years old. It was the day he taught me how to shift gears in his Firebird and then took me to the Frosty Frog for ice cream. Right before he left for the second time. He was trying to apologize. I just didn't know what he was apologizing for. I had it all wrong.

*"I just wanted you to know I will never do that to you again. I promise."*

I thought he was promising not to leave.

But really, he was promising me that he *would* leave. If that's what it took to protect me.

From him.

"Are you okay?" Nico asks, and it's only then that I realize I'm crying. For how long, I can't be sure.

I sniffle and wipe the tears with the back of my hand. "I don't know."

"I'm sorry to be the one to tell you," Nolan says. "I think Jackson really wanted you to know. He just never had the courage to tell you himself. That's why he wrote the song. The best ones usually come from the darkest places."

I let out a quiet sob. I feel helpless and lost. I thought coming here would make me feel *better*, but now I'm more confused than ever.

"Do you remember *any* of the words?" I ask Nolan. Because I don't know what else to ask for. I don't know what to hope for anymore. I don't know what my life looks like when I leave this house.

Nolan flashes me a pitying look, and I feel my heart sink yet again.

He stands up and reaches out his hand for me to take.

"I can do even better," he says. "I still have the lyrics."

The entire basement of Nolan Cook's house has been converted into an impressive music studio, filled with guitars, drum kits, keyboards, a fully enclosed glass vocal booth, and a professional mixing board.

The search takes almost an hour, and by the end, Nolan has torn apart the whole room. But, miraculously, he finds it.

He holds up a single sheet of cream-colored paper, monogrammed with the logo for the Radisson Hotel in Salt Lake City. The edges are creased and bent, but I recognize the handwriting that fills both sides of the page.

It's the same handwriting that was carelessly scribbled on two separate Post-it Notes stuck to the fridge.

*I'm sorry. I have to do this.*

The same handwriting that appeared on a large yellow envelope that showed up at my front door six days ago, along with a set of car keys.

*For California Collins.*

Three life-changing messages.

One messenger.

And now, a fourth. A final message.

One that I'm certain is about to change my life again.

Nolan hands me the piece of paper, but I don't dare look at it. In my mind, I run through all the possible outcomes of this moment. All the possible people I will become when it's over.

> **The lead singer of a semi-famous, washed-up, post-grunge band hands you the key to unlocking your whole relationship with your father.**
> **Do you feel:**
> **A** *More sad?*
> **B** *More angry?*
> **C** *Less angry?*

And that last option, that's the one that scares me.

For the past nine years, my anger toward Jackson is all I've had. It's what has kept me connected to him. It's the glue that's held me together. As long as I felt anger toward my father, I could hold on to some semblance of sanity.

But what happens if I have to let that go?

What will I be left with then?

I glance over at Nico, who's watching me with that intense blue-eyed gaze of his. And that's when I realize what the anger could *never* do for me.

It could never allow me to trust.

It could never allow me to love.

At least not fully. At least not with everything I am. Because the anger always laid claim on a small piece of me. It always had one hand on the wheel, steering me away from people. Away from possible heartache. Away from Nico.

I will never have a second chance with Jackson. I will never be able to have the relationship I wanted with him.

But I *do* have a second chance with Nico.

I have a chance to be the person I want to be.

I blink away the tears and stare down at the piece of paper in my hand.

Without a word, just a silent understanding, Nolan and Nico bow out of the room, and I'm left alone.

With Jackson.

## "While She Sleeps"

Tires squeal,
Brakes fail.
I fall off the edge
While she sleeps.

Lives flash,
Glass cracks.
I destroy what's left
While she sleeps.

I hope she never wakes to see
The man that I've turned out to be.
The demons that I fight
Are better fought at night.
And I'm a better man by far
When she can't see the scars.

Doors slam
At three a.m.
I try to forget
While she sleeps.

Night descends,
Shadows bend.
I shake hands with death
While she sleeps.

*I hope she never wakes to see*
*The man that I've turned out to be.*
*The demons that I fight*
*Are better fought at night.*
*And I'm a better man by far*
*When she can't see the scars.*


*So the last time that I leave,*
*I'll do it while she sleeps.*

By the time Nolan Cook walks us back to the foyer and opens the front door, the sun is already dipping below the horizon, turning the sky into a breathtaking, iridescent shade of pink.

"Well," Nolan says, still sounding just as nervous as he did when we arrived. "It was nice to finally meet the famous California. I'm glad you stopped by."

I clutch the piece of paper with Jackson's scribbled lyrics to my chest. "I am too." I flash him a grin. "And it was nice to finally meet the famous Nolan Cook."

"Oh, wait," Nolan says, suddenly remembering something. He dashes back into the great room and returns a moment later holding the black cassette tape I found in Jackson's stereo. "You forgot this."

He starts to hand it to me, but then his eyes seem to catch on the handwritten label, and his gaze clouds over for a moment. "Actually, um"—he runs his hands through his hair—"do you mind if I keep this? I don't have a lot of mementos from that tour. I threw almost everything away after the band broke up. It wasn't the best time of my life, but it would still be nice to have something to remember it by, you know?"

I nod, because I do know.

I exactly know.

"No," I say, keeping my voice stern. "You can't have it."

Nico and Nolan both look up at me in surprise.

I crack a small smile and gesture to the paper still clutched to my chest. "But I *will* trade you for it."

Nolan guffaws. "Sounds like a good deal to me."

Ten minutes later, Nico and I sit in the Firebird, still parked outside of Nolan Cook's house, surrounded by the remnants of our trip.

I've spread them all out around me—on the dashboard, across the center console, even in my lap. And one by one, I let my gaze fall over every single item, starting from the very beginning.

The large yellow envelope delivered to my door, containing the title to a car that I never thought I would keep.

The amber-colored sea glass I found on the beach in Fort Bragg, proof that the ocean really does forgive.

The butterfly statue that Wes crafted out of found keys.

The photograph of Jackson posing with Nolan Cook outside the Fear Epidemic tour bus.

And finally, the lyrics to Jackson's song.

A shiver runs through me as I realize that somehow each of these things has led me to the next. If Pete hadn't delivered that yellow envelope to me, I never would have found my way back to Fort Bragg. If I hadn't picked up that piece of sea glass on the beach, I probably never would have been lured into Wes's shop by the sea glass wind chime in the window. If Wes hadn't given me that butterfly statue, I never would have rediscovered Jackson's cassette tape in the center console. And if I never listened to that tape, I never would have sought out the man in this photograph. And I never would have read Jackson's lyrics.

The final rewrite of my story.

*I'm sorry. I have to do this.*

In my mind those words were always tangled up with the band. With the man in this photograph.

*I have to do this.*

*I have to be with them.*

*I have to go where they are.*

*I have to do what I want to do.*

*Because I'm selfish and irresponsible and immature.*

But really, all of this time, those exact same words were tangled up in something else. Something I never understood until now.

Until this car, this road, this coast, this collection of lost things led me to it.

Like landmarks on a treasure map. A trail leading to some buried chest of jewels or a pirate ship full of gold.

Or maybe just something as simple and precious as the truth.

# WEDNESDAY

*I hope she never wakes to see*
*The man that I've turned out to be.*
*The demons that I fight*
*Are better fought at night.*
*And I'm a better man by far*
*When she can't see the scars.*


—"While She Sleeps,"
from the Untitled Third Album
by Fear Epidemic
Written by Jackson Collins
Never released

# 9:30 A.M.

## TACOMA, WA

### INVENTORY: ENOUGH

Nico parks the Firebird in front of the post office and kills the ignition. His eyes are bloodshot, and his cheek still shows the indentation from the Firebird's back seat, where we slept last night.

I reach into the glove box, pull out the white envelope that's been sitting at the bottom of my backpack for the past month, and run my fingertips over the words "University of California at Davis."

"I'm sorry," I told the nice woman at the admissions office on the phone earlier this morning, as I was begging for an extension for my financial aid award. "I had to work out a few family issues first. But I definitely still want to go."

I get out of the car, and Nico walks beside me to the mailbox. I hold the envelope with two hands, as though I'm afraid it might blow away.

"My mom will be okay," I say aloud, though I'm not sure who I'm talking to, exactly. Nico, the envelope, myself?

**451** →

It's Nico who responds. "She'll be okay."

I take a deep breath and finally slide the envelope into the slot. I wait for the panic, but it doesn't come. All that follows is the sweet exhilaration of possibility.

"So, what now?" Nico asks. He takes my hand, and we walk back to the parking lot.

I eye the Firebird, glinting in the sunlight. "I guess we have to go home. I need to finish packing up the house. The moving truck is coming at the end of the week. And graduation is on Saturday."

Nico stares off into the distance, and I can tell he's thinking about everything that's waiting for him back in Russellville. "Yes. Home would definitely be the responsible location."

"But," I say tauntingly, "we don't necessarily need to go *straight* home."

He cocks a single eyebrow. "Where did you have in mind?"

I smirk back at him. "Does it really matter?"

**Ali and Nico's <u>New</u> Rules of the Road:**

1.  Fungicide the rules.

Nico leans in close to me and brushes a strand of curly hair away from my ear. If he were any other boy, in any other story, he would whisper something sweet and romantic like, "I'd go anywhere with you." Or even "I'd do anything for you, California."

But he doesn't.

Because he's not.

So, instead he whispers, "I think Peanut M&M's are way better than plain."

The chills travel up my body, and before he can pull away from my ear, I turn and capture his mouth with mine. I wrap my arms around the back of his neck and press my body into him. It feels like a first kiss and a last kiss all wrapped into one.

It feels like a promise.

A promise he will keep.

We both will.

We walk over to the Firebird, and Nico tosses me the silver key ring. "How about we stay off the freeways for a while. Just until you get better at downshifting."

"Hey, I can downshift."

He scoffs. "Yeah, if you call downshifting 'causing your passenger to lose his breakfast.'"

"I was just trying to show you what this car can really do."

Nico crosses his arms over his chest. "Okay, hot stuff. Show me what this old clunker can do."

I point the silver key at him and in a sharp tone say, "Do *not* call my car an old clunker. This is a classic."

Then I run straight toward the car and leap over the driver's-side door, landing adeptly in the front seat.

Okay, *mostly* adeptly. My back foot does catch on the top of the door, and I sort of tumble into the gearshift while my face barely misses the steering wheel.

Nico guffaws from the curb. "You all right in there?"

"I'll have to work on that!" I call back.

Nico uses the door, lowering himself into the passenger seat. I press down on the brake and the clutch and turn the key in the ignition. The engine hums to life. "Now *that* is a beautiful sound."

I shift into reverse and ease my foot off the clutch until I feel the engine start to tremble a little. Then I press slowly down on the gas. The car inches backward.

"Nice!" Nico commends.

I shift into first, spinning the wheel around and slowly crawl out of the parking lot.

When we reach the street, I look left and then right.

"Which way?" I ask.

Nico leans back in the passenger seat and props his hands behind his head. "Driver's choice."

> **You've got nothing but open road ahead of you! Which way do you go?**
>
> **A**
>
> **B**
>
> **C**

I smile and ease off the clutch, letting the car roll forward. Then, at the last minute, I make a choice. I turn the wheel and we go.

To where? I have no idea.

But that's the thing about roads. Sometimes we choose them, and sometimes they choose us. Sometimes they bring us to unexpected destinations. Sometimes they lead us straight toward heartbreak. Sometimes we turn around, hoping to follow that same road back in time, only to find that it's gone. Swept away by the past. And we're left stranded.

But every once in a while, if we're really lucky, a road can lead us right to where we need to go.

Straight toward the things we lost.

# ACKNOWLEDGMENTS

First and foremost, the person who deserves the most gratitude for this book is Nicole Ellul, my brilliant brilliant editor, who worked with me through revision after revision and who fixed everything that was broken (and there was a lot). When you wrote those magical words, "I think this story is actually about Jackson," everything finally started to fall into place. You are a dream to work with. Thank you for your seemingly endless supply of patience and wisdom, and for continually saying, "WE GOT THIS!" (I think we finally did!) And a special shout out to Nicole's dad! Thanks for reading! ☺

Also, as always, thank you to my wonderful agent, Jim McCarthy, who never ceases to amaze me. Even with broken bones, you work your butt off for your clients and I know this client is eternally grateful!

Thank you to the truly remarkable team at Simon and Schuster, including (but certainly not limited to): Emily Hutton, Nicole Russo, Samantha Benson, Mara Anastas, Liesa Abrams, Jessica Smith, Jennifer Ung, Steve Scott, Chriscynethia Floyd, Jill Hacking, Elizabeth Mims, Rebecca Vitkus, Jodie Hockensmith, Russell Gordon, Sarah McCabe, Christina Pecorale, and Mary Nubla. Thank you for everything you to do for authors and books!

To my writing "tribe"—Jessica Khoury, Joanne Rendell, Jennifer Wolfe, Morgan Matson, Tamara Ireland Stone, BT Gottfred, Julie Buxbaum, Marie Lu, Emmy Laybourne, Jenn Johansson, Suzanne Young,

Alex Monir, Robin Benway, and Andrea Cremer. My life would be so lonely (and frustrating!) without all of your support, friendship, and writing wisdom. I miss you all!

Thank you to Len Vlahos for "lending me" some of your lyrics and to Tom VanNess at Farland Classic Restoration in Colorado for giving me a crash course on Firebirds and classic cars.

Thank you to Kristen Gilligan at Tattered Cover, Cathy Berner at Blue Willow, Julie Poling at Red Balloon, Emily Hall at Main Street Books, Maryelizabeth Yturralde at Mysterious Galaxy, and Courtney Saldana at the Ontario Public Library for being such amazing champions for my books. I'm so honored and lucky to know all of you!

*The Geography of Lost Things* is my fourteenth released novel. I can hardly believe it. And even after all this time, my amazing parents still read every single book before it's released. That's the mark of a true fan. Thank you for that. And of course, thank you to Charlie, for constantly saving me from getting lost (both figuratively and literally . . . we both know how I am with directions). I love you.

And finally, I would never ever get to do this amazing job without the support and love I get from my readers. Thank you to each and everyone of you who has ever turned the final page of one of my books and smiled. It's that very image that keeps me going, even when the road gets dark and windy and I feel like giving up. It's because of you, I'm able to keep driving until the end.